Julia Agnes Fraser

Shilrick, the Drummer

Or, Loyal and true. A romance of the Irish Rebellion of 1798. Vol. 2

Julia Agnes Fraser

Shilrick, the Drummer
Or, Loyal and true. A romance of the Irish Rebellion of 1798. Vol. 2

ISBN/EAN: 9783337065874

Printed in Europe, USA, Canada, Australia, Japan

Cover: Foto ©Andreas Hilbeck / pixelio.de

More available books at **www.hansebooks.com**

" Roll drums merrily, march away,
Soldier's glory lives in story!"

SHILRICK, THE DRUMMER

Or, LOYAL AND TRUE

A Romance of the Irish Rebellion of 1798

BY

JULIA AGNES FRASER

Author of " Dermot O'Donoghue; or, the Stranger from Belfast." " Patrick's Vow; or a Rival's Revenge." " Pat of Mullingar; or, an Irish Lothario." " Hubert's Pride." " A Slight Mistake." " Barrington's Busby; or, Weathering the Admiral." " Skeletons in the Cupboard; or, the Captain's Troubles." " Court Lovers; or, the Sentinel of the King's Guard." " The Star-Spangled Banner; or, the Far West." &c., &c., &c.

IN THREE VOLUMES—VOLUME II

REMINGTON AND COMPANY, LIMITED

LONDON :

15, KING STREET, COVENT GARDEN

AND SYDNEY

1894

All Rights Reserved

SHILRICK, THE DRUMMER;

OR, LOYAL AND TRUE.

CHAPTER I.

" The cauld blasts o' the Winter wind,
    That thirl'd thro' my heart
They're a' blawn by, I hae him safe,
    Till death will never pairt.
But what puts pairtin' in my mind ?
    It may be far awa';
The present moment is our ain,
    The neist we never saw,
For there's nae luck aboot the hoose,
    There's nae luck ava
There's little pleasure in the hoose,
    When our guidman's awa'."

OLD SCOTCH SONG.

For some time past, Mrs. Kinahan and her daughter Anty had been in the greatest anxiety regarding their charge, Estelle O'Neill.

Naturally delicate and fragile, Estelle had never appeared really well since the night on which she had been in such terror for the safety of Morven O'Neill, and when she had so bravely thrown herself in front of her husband and received the accidental wound from Captain Annesley's sword. This, combined with the wild, rough ride over the mountains, her horror at the peril in which O'Neill was placed, and having been drenched with rain, which poured down upon them in torrents before they could reach the shelter of the Rebels' Cave, all helped to hasten on the illness with which she had long been threatened. O'Neill could only approach within a certain distance of the cave on horseback : on his arrival at a particular spot there was always Owen Maguire or one of the other " Bhoys " waiting in readiness to take the horse by an unfrequented and circuitous route to an old stable belonging to a lonely farm, the tenant of which secretly favoured " *the cause*," and was the *nominal* owner of the beautiful, sure-footed animal, that was loving and faithful as any dog to O'Neill, and was valued and appreciated accordingly by his master.

After dismounting, O'Neill had to carry the unconscious form of Estelle some distance to the Rebels' Cave. On that night she was not even so fortunate as Eveleen Corrie, for there was no comfortable shanty, with its cheerful peat fire to shelter her, no kind attendant like poor Thalia Coghlan. It was impossible for O'Neill, at that late hour, and in her half-fainting condition, to take Estelle back to the " Shamrock," and they dare not incur the risk, so soon, of again leaving their place of concealment in the mountains ; therefore, he could but give her the poor shelter that his own private recess in the Rebels' Cave could afford, albeit, the innate gallantry of the men, rough as they appeared, soon showed itself, and, when the secret was revealed to them of Estelle's relationship to O'Neill, she might have had the coat of every man in the Rebel band to form a couch and covering for her, had she so desired. It was not until late the following day that Morven O'Neill dare venture forth to convey his beautiful young wife back to the "Shamrock," and the devoted care of Mrs. Kinahan, who had been in a state of the most terrible anxiety concerning the fate of O'Neill and Estelle, when the latter did not return at the hour she expected, and when the night passed without any tidings reaching her of either. Warm, indeed, was the welcome they received from the widow and her daughter, when they appeared before her the following afternoon.

From that day, however, Estelle's health seemed to decline; but it was wonderful and touching to see how she would hold out before O'Neill whenever he went to visit her. Her great love for him appeared to give her strength for the time that he was with her.

She had determined within her true, brave heart that he should never know nor imagine how ill she really was, his mind should not be disturbed, his heart made sorrowful, by the thought of her failing health.

Estelle also insisted on Mrs. Kinahan promising that she would not tell O'Neill of her illness, a promise which the widow was very reluctant to give, and still more reluctant to keep, as time went on and she could see no improvement in Estelle, who seemed indeed to be fading away before their eyes. Bravely she would keep up while O'Neill was present, but the instant he had left her she would droop once more, and groping her way to the nearest chair would often fall, half-fainting, into Anty's arms.

The doctor, for whom Mrs. Kinahan had at last insisted on sending, stated that heart disease, with a tendency to consumption, were the causes of Estelle's illness, which had been hastened and accelerated by the shock she had received on the night when she accompanied Morven O'Neill to keep his moonlight tryst with Eveleen Corrie on the dark shore of the haunted lake, with what result has already been told.

Estelle must be kept free from all care and anxiety, were the strict injunctions of the doctor; but this, unfortunately, was a prescription that Mrs. Kinahan knew only too well was impossible to carry out, for, when O'Neill was present, Estelle was full of pleasant excitement; but when he left, and all the time that he was absent from her, she was tormented, and her mind racked with fears for his safety, so that between her hope, anxiety, and constant dread that evil might befall him, she was worked up into a perfect fever, that would have proved trying, even to one in full health and strength.

Estelle was constantly watching for Morven—listening for his whistle, every nerve strained to hear the first tone of her loved one's voice, the first sound of his well-known footstep. At other times, too, she would eagerly watch for the coming of Owen Maguire, in the hope of hearing news of O'Neill, or that she might at least receive a loving letter or message from him.

"Heaven kape her!" exclaimed Mrs. Kinahan, fervently, one day to her daughter. "Sure, it does be makin' me heart ache lookin' at her. D'ye see her watchin' the path from the mountains all the blissid dhay, ontil it's too dhark for the thired eyes av her to see anny moor? Night an' dhay she's thinkin' an' dhraamin' av his honour, an, Anty *alannah*, sure I can't sthand it much longer, it's mesilf that *must* tell Misther O'Neill how ill her ladyship is, or whin she gets woorse, an', troth! I belave 'tis doin' that she is ivery dhay—sure he'll be blamin' us, an'," cried the widow, with a sob, as she buried her face in her apron, "*ochone! ochone!* 'twill be the sad blow to him, enthirely. Oh, Misther Morven! Misther Morven! the purty bhoy that I've nursed in me two arms, the bhoy that's been dear to me as if he'd been me own son, I belave it'll break his heart. Oh! Heaven kape this blow from him!"

"But mother," said Anty, "sure wasn't it the docthor himself said that wid care an' attintion Misthress O'Neill might get betther, and if we'd kape her calm an' quiet—"

"Calm an' quiet is it!" interrupted Mrs. Kinahan, "an' how can *we* give her that, whin the pace an' rest isn't in her own heart? But there, Anty *alannah*, 'tis wrong I am to be croakin' that way, for isn't it said there's 'the silver linin' to ivery cloud," an' maybes it'll shine out for *us* in good thime if we've the faith an' the hope. Go to her ladyship, Anty, it's long enough she's been her lone as it is."

Slowly, and with a heavy heart, Anty went her way to Estelle, whom she found, as usual, in her favourite room, seated in the large, old-fashioned easy-chair, near the window, anxiously gazing at the distant mountains, with a sad, dreamy expression upon her pale, but beautiful face. She was robed in a long, flowing garment of some soft, warm, white material, confined at the waist by a cord and tassels. Her long, golden hair was unbound, and fell like a veil about her shoulders. Wrapped around her was a magnificent fur mantle, which had been the wedding gift of the Italian priest, Father Antonelli, when the run-away pair left France.

To one who had seen Estelle, even a few months before, the change would have been startling. She looked, indeed, as Mrs. Kinahan had said, to be literally fading away. The delicate colour was constantly coming and going in her fair, ethereal face, her eyes appeared unnaturally large and brilliant, and there was a strange languor and weariness about every movement, which was easily discernible to those who had known her before, when she was full of life and vivacity.

When Anty Kinahan entered the room Estelle was leaning back among the crimson cushions of the chair, her hands clasped listlessly before her, her eyes still fixed upon the mountain path, though the dark shadows of evening were fast hiding it from her view.

"Anty!" she said, sadly, as the girl approached her, and stood gravely looking down upon her, as she thought seriously of her mother's words, "I do fear dat he will not come dis day now."

"Ah, no, me lady!" replied Anty, striving to speak carelessly, "sure didn't Owen say his honour *couldn't* come anny thime to-day?"

"Yes," murmured Estelle, sighing. "He *did* so say, Anty, still, I do always hope."

"It's somethin' mighty impoorthant was to be goin' on this same avenin'; d'ye see, me lady, there's some new Bhoys to thake the oath, an' there's to be a grand matin, for drill somewhere; that's what Owen was tellin us."

"Ah! I had forgotten. But oh, Anty!" said Estelle. "It is indeed long de days do seem when he comes not, and it is weary, weary waiting, and hoping, and longing."

"But sure whin his honour *does* come, isn't the joy all the greater, Misthress O'Neill darlin'!"

"Oh, it is happiness unspeakable!" answered Estelle, fervently. "It is as if de sight of his dear face did bring wid it de fresh life to me an' chase away de gloom an' de fear from my heart; de tones of his voice, his very footstep, all dese do sound like music to my ear. Indeed it does seem as if dere could be no sorrow, no trouble, when my Morven is nigh."

"Thrue for ye, ma'am!" said Anty, solemnly, thinking within her own heart that the same sentiments might apply to herself, so far as Owen Maguire was concerned. True love is true love all the world over, whether it be Prince or Peasant who is under its spell, and the words of the old

Scotch song might apply to all, without distinction of persons ;
what words could be more simple, and yet more full of real
earnest love than the following :

> " Sae sweet his voice, sae smooth his tongue
>   His breath's like caller air ;
> His very tread has music in't
>   As he comes up the stair.
> And will I see his face again ?
>   And will I hear him speak ?
> I'm downright dizzy wi' the joy,
>   In truth, I'm like tae greet.
> For there's nae luck aboot the hoose,
>   There nae luck ava,
> There's little pleasure in the hoose,
>   When our guidman's awa'.
>
> " Since Colin's weel, I'm weel content ;
>   I hae nae mair tae crave ;
> Could I but live to mak him blest,
>   I'm blest aboon the lave,
> And will I see his face again ?
>   And will I hear him speak ?
> I'm downright dizzy wi the thocht
>   In truth I'm like tae greet.
> For there's nae luck aboot the hoose,
>   There's nae luck ava,
> There's little pleasure in the hoose,
>   When our guidman's awa'."

" Ah, yes ! " said Estelle, after a few moments' silence, as
she looked up at Anty, who was still standing beside her,
and was struck by the seriousness in the girl's face and
voice. " You, too, do know what it is to have a dear one who
is absent and in danger."

" Yes, me lady," returned Anty, sighing, " sure an' I
do."

There was again silence for some minutes, while Estelle
continued to look out of the window and to watch the moon
slowly rising above the distant hills. Anty went over to
the old chest that stood in a corner of the room, and took
therefrom her wool· and knitting-needles, with which she
generally employed herself in the long evenings, but she
was not destined to work that night.

" Anty ! " said Estelle, at last. " Come here ! dere is much dat I would say to you, an' dere is no time like de present."

Anty looked at her apprehensively; she fancied that the sweet voice sounded weaker, but, perhaps, she thought, it was her mother's anxiety that had frightened her and caused her to imagine what might really not be the case ; however she hurried across the room to Estelle, and knelt down beside her.

"Sure 'tis like an angel she is, or some blissed saint! How could we hope to kape her here," murmured Anty to herself, in awe-struck tones, as she watched the beautiful face with its aureole of golden hair now looking more ethereal than ever, as a pale moonbeam fell upon it through the still uncurtained window.

"Ah! dat is well!" said Estelle, laying her hand kindly on Anty's shoulder, and speaking in a low, earnest voice. "I have been thinking much, and wid one *great* anxiety, dese few last days."

"Too much, me lady!" replied Anty, hastily, " axin' yer pardon, sure it's the docthor said—"

"He is a kind, clever man, Anty," interrupted Estelle, gently, " but he can do me no good.   Listen, my friend! for I have much to say to you dis night."

"Oh, Misthress O'Neill, darlin'!" cried Anty, "lave it ontil the mornin'; sure 'tis thired an' fair worn out ye are this night."

"No, my good Anty," returned Estelle, "I would put off no longer—we know not what to-morrow may have in store for any of us."

Again she paused as if even these few words had cost her some effort.

Anty watched her anxiously, and at last she continued, but her voice was weaker, and there was a sad tone of pathos in it, that touched the heart of the sympathetic listener.

"Anty, I do not tink dat it will be long—de time I have to watch, and wait, and hope.   I *know* dat it is as I say—I feel it.   De parting may come soon, and—ah! do not weep so, Anty—look up, dear!" she said, as she tenderly laid her hand upon the bowed head of her companion, who was now sobbing bitterly.   "You cannot hear what I have to say if you do weep so sadly, and, dear friend, I would leave one message wid you for my Morven.   I have said dat we know not what may happen—who can tell?   But see how I am placing one great trust in you, Anty."

"Oh! sure ye'll not be spakin' anny moor, now, Misthress O'Neill, dear!" said Anty, coaxingly.   "Sure, now ye're wake an' thired, an' that's puttin' all thim sorrowful notions into yer head this night."

"Ah! but I *must* speak now; dis trial may not come yet— we know not—all may yet be well, it is possible; and so it is dat I wish him to be told not one word while I do live ; but, Anty, when I am gone, I would have you and your good mother comfort him—my Morven—by de knowledge dat he did make me so truly happy. He could come to me but seldom —dat is true—but dere was in each meeting, even if de time were short, one lifetime of happiness. Anty ! Anty ! my heart it does ache to see your grief. Dear, if dis parting is de will of Heaven, it were better so—dat I should go before him. And it is dese last days I have had one deep impression—what you call a presentiment—dat he is in danger—dat dere is some trouble coming to him. Oh ! if aught befell my Morven I should pray dat I too might be taken, for I could not live widout him. And, Anty, when I hear how much pain and sorrow dere is in de world I can thank Heaven dat I have been so free from it. Dere are some who have de bitter grief of giving a wealth of love and meeting no return dis side of de grave—dere are others who find dat de hearts in which dey have trusted have failed in dere direst need—dey find dat for dem love and friendship have been but empty names. Dere are others—ah ! but it is dey who are de saddest of all—who have built up one grand idol in dere hearts, only to find it fall broken and crushed at dere feet, to feel, and to know dat de heart in which was centred all dere hopes, dere love, and trust, had been taken from dem and given to another. Oh, Anty, surely dat parting must be worse dan death. But none of dese troubles have been mine. I have been spared all such sorrow. A nobler, truer man dan my Morven does not live. I know dat I have won his love—I know dat I shall keep it as long as we shall both live."

"Thrue for ye, ma'am!" said Anty, earnestly. "Sure it's his honour that has the love an' rispict av all who know him, moor power to him!"

"And you will remember what I have said, my good Anty! You will give him my message when I am gone!"

"Oh, me lady!" cried Anty, sorrowfully, "don't be spakin' that way! Sure, it's the docthor said wid care an' attintion ye would get well, an' is there annythin' we *wouldn't* do for ye, for yer own dear sake as well as for his honour—Misther O'Neill."

"Ah! I know well dat you and your good mother have been to me and my Morven de truest of friends. And it *may* be as de doctor has said, Anty, we shall see," replied Estelle, unwilling to dispel the hopes of the affectionate girl, whose grief was so genuine.

"An' maybes there's brighter dhays comin' for us all!" said Anty, as she rose to her feet, intending to go for her mother, for she was full of anxiety concerning Estelle, her fragile appearance and her grave conversation caused her to fear the worst. "If only Misther O'Neill was safe, an' she had pace an' aise in her mind, sure, it would all be well, enthirely!" murmured Anty to herself.

Estelle now seemed fairly exhausted, and, as she lay back among the crimson cushions of her chair, the look of weariness in the dark eyes deepened, and there was a wistful, pathetic expression about the pale lips. Once more her gaze was bent upon the distant mountain path, the outline of which could now be faintly seen by the light of the moon. It is strange how the fair romantic moonbeams seem to fall so softly, so soothingly upon our hearts when we are happy and at peace, and still, like some uncanny syren who fascinates and yet repels, they mock us with their unearthly beauty, and glance coldly and pitilessly upon us when we are in sorrow and trouble.

Cold and desolate indeed, appeared the old familiar scene, on this night, to the sorrowful hearts of the two anxious, loving women who, with such yearning, longing eyes, looked out upon it from the window of the "Shamrock," knowing that, among the gathering mists and shadows of the grand purple mountains, were hidden those who were dearest to them on earth, and who lived in daily, hourly danger of discovery, which could only result in death, or life-long imprisonment, the latter being a fate far more dreaded than the former by those bold, free sons of Erin.

Truly no men could be more worthy of a woman's best and truest love than Morven O'Neill and his faithful follower and friend Owen Maguire. O'Neill with the heart and soul of the true patriot, who has nobly sacrificed all that a man holds most dear on earth for his country, and Owen who, with a feeling well nigh as noble and as praiseworthy in its way, has determined to follow the chequered fortunes of the young master he loves so well, and who has, in his close intercourse with the high-souled, unselfish nature of O'Neill, caught much of his enthusiasm and spirit of self-sacrifice and devotion to the "*great cause.*"

Well might Estelle O'Neill and Anty Kinahan value the hearts they had won—well might they rejoice in their love, for truly they had entrusted their life's happiness into the keeping of brave men who would not fail them, who would prove faithful alike through storm or sunshine.

Estelle and Anty remained silent for some minutes, each one seemingly absorbed in her own thoughts. At last, with a sudden, nervous movement, Estelle bent forward, and clasping Anty's hand in hers, she said, in a voice full of emotion :

"Anty ! De time may not be far distant when he, whom I do love, shall come by dat lonely mountain path, and shall find no Estelle to welcome him at de end of it ; but you will tell him all dat I have said, is it not so ? You will promise ? " she asked, earnestly.

"Oh, me lady !" sobbed Anty, "don't, don't be afther sayin' anny moor ! Sure it isn't woorse ye're falin' this night, that ye'd be spakin' that way ? "

"And tell him," continued Estelle, heedless of the interruption, "tell him dat de parting is not for ever—say to him—my own true Morven—dat de time may be short—it may be long—but beyond de valley of death, wid its dark shadows, dere is a bright, beautiful land, where we shall meet again, where dere will be no more parting, no sorrow nor care, where he will be safe, safe for evermore. Tell him dat he shall find his Estelle still watching, still waiting for him, at Heaven's golden gates."

CHAPTER II.

"Not too warm, nor yet too cold ;
  For, with but little pressing,
He will show a heart of gold,
  Past all Californian guessing.

Look ! All virtues in him found
  Pierce the outward surface glowing—
Truth, Love, Courage, Knowledge sound,
  And a few errors worth your knowing."

BARRY CORNWALL,

Neither Kerry O'Toole nor Silas Charleston were able to take much rest on that eventful night, after Captain Annesley and Father Bernard had been made prisoners by the " Bold Boys."

Kerry was too sorrowful—too full of remorse—for the thought that he had been the chief cause of the misfortune which had happened to his foster brother weighed heavily upon his mind, and what might be the consequences of Annesley's detention yet remained to be seen.

There was Shilrick, too. How would he fare on his return to barracks ? Kerry well knew the boy's nature—he would sacrifice his own life any day rather than betray another ; but this would be a severe test for him—would he stand that test ? How would he be able to reconcile his strict sense of honour and duty as a loyal soldier, with his horror against playing the part of informer? In truth, it would be a trial to his warm, true, and affectionate heart—a heart of gold, as Annesley had often called it, and as more than one among his comrades had proved it to be. Immediately on Shilrick's return to barracks, Kerry knew that he would be plied with questions on all sides. His officers would demand an explanation, his comrades, one and all, would, naturally, use every effort to extract information from him concerning his mysterious absence, and to discover if he knew aught of the strange disappearance of Captain Annesley.

How would the poor boy reply? How parry their questions, and how keep true to both parties?

All these thoughts passed through the distracted mind of Kerry, and kept him awake through the long weary hours of the night.

Silas Charleston was too anxious to rest. Having once determined and promised to do all in his power to assist in the escape of Captain Annesley, he was not a man to draw back, or to be deterred from his purpose, however great the dangers and difficulties might appear; wild and rough as his life had been, and often not too scrupulous his companions, yet there still remained within this man's heart the germs of true goodness and human kindness. Gratitude, too, and a sincere admiration for all that was best, bravest, and noblest in others, were strong points in the young American's character. To his enemies he was openly, unmistakably antagonistic, but there was no treachery in the nature of Silas Charleston, and fortunate indeed were those for whom he formed a friendship, for they would never find him wanting in the time of need. Thus it was, that ere the first faint streaks of rosy dawn had appeared in the sky, Kerry O'Toole and Silas Charleston were to be seen aimlessly wandering among the mountains, far from the Rebels' Cave, anxiously conversing together concerning the events that had occurred the evening before, striving to think of some means by which they might accomplish the escape of Captain Annesley and Father Bernard, but each time, when their plans had appeared feasible, some insurmountable difficulty had presented itself, so that after a consultation of some hours they were still undecided as ever as to what steps they must first take in the matter, and the chance of Annesley's rescue seemed to grow fainter and farther in the distance.

"Wa'al!" said Charleston, at last, "I calc'late that spry

young   foster brother of yours has got himself fixed this time, and how we air ever to get him out of the scrape I'm dashed if *I* can tell."

"Sorra wan *o' me* knows," was Kerry's disconsolate response.

"I hev promised to help," continued Charleston, "and I guess I'll keep my word, I'll do my best, Kerry O'Toole. I can't do more."

"An' I thank ye, Charleston, I know it's yersilf that'll hape yer word, but it'll not be aisy."

"I guess it won't," returned the American, quietly. "And my oath to the brotherhood prevents me doing all I might. I'd risk a deal if I were the only one to run that risk, but I cannot, and I will not endanger the lives of any of the rest of the band, and so in part my hands are tied. *You*, Kerry O'Toole," he continued, gravely, "you were free—only a few short hours ago—to act as you would. You might hev been free at this moment if you had taken my advice. But I calc'late its useless thinking of that now, you hev taken the oath—you must abide by the consequences."

"I know it, sure I know it." answered Kerry, despairingly.

"Wa'al ! It's a pity you didn't think of that before, but all you can do now is to be as much around as possible, keeping an eye on Magin, and seeing that he doesn't harm your foster brother before we can rescue him."

"That's thrue for ye !" said Kerry. "Sure it's himsilf that's just the mane blackguard that would do it if he had the chance—woorse luck to him. Och !" he cried, as pausing suddenly, he seized hold of Charleston's arm, and pulled him back a few paces, then hastily sweeping the snow aside with his shillelagh, he discovered that the earth and rocks beneath their feet were loose and broken.

"Have a care where ye're stheppin', Charleston ! Sure it isn't over-safe here, we're too near the edge av wan av thim mountain gorges."

"I guess we are," agreed the American, but instead of coming away from the dangerous spot indicated by Kerry, he seemed to be seized with a fit of curiosity, or that strange fascination which sometimes draws the unwary to the edge of a precipice, too often to their own destruction ; but Silas

Charleston was cautious, he approached slowly, and looked over into the abyss beneath, only, however to start back with a cry of horror, as seizing hold of Kerry's arm he pulled him away from the perilous spot.

"What's wrong ? " asked Kerry, in utter astonishment at the agitation displayed by the usually calm Silas Charleston.

"Kerry O'Toole," came the reply, in tones full of sympathy and genuine feeling. "There's something down thar—a sight 'tis well you should be prepared for. There's been an accident—that brave little soldier brother of yours —I guess he must have— "

The American could say no more, for Kerry hastily pushed him aside, and with a bound was at the edge of the abyss.

"Shilrick—oh, Shilrick !" he cried, despairingly, " *Oh, ma bouchalcen dhas*—my own darlin' brother !—lyin' cowld and still there, an' mesilf goin' about careless an' aisy, an' knowin' nothin' av it, at all, at all."

"Calm yourself, O'Toole !" said Charleston, kindly, laying his hand on the other's shoulder, "he *may* be only stunned by the fall ; we may be in time to save him yet."

"Oh, Charleston, ! don't be afther puttin' the hope into me heart—sure, how *could* he be livin' afther fallin' that height, an' lyin' all night in the bitther cowld, wid the snow round him."

"I guess he's sheltered down there," replied Charleston, hopefully, "and the boy has fallen into a perfect nest of thick, snow-covered bracken ; but how can we get him up here again?—that's the question."

"I'll go down afther him," said Kerry, promptly, and eagerly preparing to put his words into practice.

"Stay !" cried the American, quietly, "If you go down thar, how do you think you'd get up again ? I calc'late thar'd be *two* down at the bottom of that gorge then instead of one. We must first get a rope—it's the only way."

"Thrue for ye, there's wan belongin' to 'the Bhoys,' at the 'Shamrock.' It's kept there in case av accidents."

"Ay ! so there is. One of us must go and ask Mrs. Kinahan for that rope—shall *I* go, or will *you*, O'Toole ?"

"Sure, I couldn't lave the place an' Shilrick lyin' there all his lone; troth, I'll take it mighty kind if ye'll go, Charleston."

"Right, then,—I guess I'll go; but don't be rash while I'm away, remember we can do nothing without that rope. I shan't be long."

"Oh, Shilrick!" murmured Kerry, as he bent over the precipice, "sure 'tis yersilf that was all I had in the world. Heaven grant we haven't come too late."

Again and again he called to the little drummer, using every term of endearment, and entreating him to make some sign if he still lived and was conscious; but all in vain, there was no sound to gladden his anxious heart, the prostrate form, lying so far beneath him, remained still and quiet as though with the stillness of death.

Suddenly as Kerry stood hopelessly watching his brother, there flashed across his mind the thought of how disastrous would be the consequences if Thaddeus Magin should appear, before Charleston and himself had been able to take Shilrick to some place of concealment if he were still living. Kerry felt assured that the wily, vengeful Yankee would never allow the boy to go free, and he knew that his life would not be safe for a single day when in the power of Magin, whose own treachery made him fear that Shilrick might betray the Bold Boys into the hands of the military.

The same thoughts as those which had just caused Kerry so much anxiety, now disturbed the mind of Silas Charleston as he hurried along on his kindly errand to the "Shamrock." He soon, however, explained matters to Mrs. Kinahan and obtained from her a long, stout rope that belonged to the Rebels, and which was frequently used by them for various purposes.

The idea next struck him that more help might be required, and chancing to see Andy Rafferty in the kitchen of the inn, engaged in his usual employment of doing nothing and watching everyone else working, and knowing that he was a particular friend of the O'Tooles, Charleston, after binding him to secrecy, told him of the accident, and asked if he would accompany him to the spot, to assist Kerry, to which Andy readily agreed; for, though indolent and lazy to a degree, the man was good-hearted enough, and thoroughly trustworthy ; and besides, the little drummer was a favourite with all who knew him. Hastening back with all speed, Charleston, accompanied by Rafferty, arrived once more, in an incredibly short time, at the scene of poor Shilrick's accident.

"Now, O'Toole," said Charleston, as he gently pulled Kerry away from the brink of the precipice. "Don't go looking down thar till you air giddy. You must lie down on the ground, and keep firm hold of the end of this rope."

"Ah, no!" interrupted Kerry. "Sure it's not yersilf that'll thake the danger av goin' down there—I'm goin'—"

"No yer don't," returned Charleston, determinedly, "I guess I hev made up my mind to go down after that thar boy, an' I'll do it. I calc'late I owe him something for warning me one day in the 'Shamrock,' of the approach of that darned spying young cavalry officer and his men, he gave me time to keep up my character of the honest Kentucky farmer, come over to see the state of agricultur' in Ireland," and here Charleston flourished a whip he often carried, as being in keeping with the above rôle, which he usually essayed when mingling with the people, or going in the neighbourhood of the barracks. "So now, O'Toole I just step aside" he continued, "I guess it would he worse than useless *your* going down thar—your heart's too much in it—you'd let it run away with your head, that's what *you* always do."

"Charleston, sure I thank ye from me heart, but it's mesilf that must be goin' dhown afther Shilrick ;" repeated Kerry, obstinately, "sure he'll maybes notice my voice sooner if he's still livin' an' conscious."

"That's so ! but where's the use of his knowing any body's voice while he's down there ?" demanded the American. " You let me bring him up here and then yer can hold a long conversation if you like. Quick now ! there's no time to lose. You and Rafferty air both to lie down and lay hold of that thar rope—remember, that climbing ropes and poles is second natur' to me, I've had good training in carryin' heavy loads, too, with one hand, I calc'late our little soldier boy will be a feather-weight to me. Hold on fast for your lives," he cried, as hastily taking off his coat and hat, he grasped the other end of the rope, and going to the brink of the abyss, he slowly and gradually let himself down until he stood beside Shilrick.

For a moment he remained silently looking down upon the drummer, as if half afraid of the result of a closer examination ; his kind heart almost failed him, when he thought of Kerry's sorrow and despair if it were but a lifeless form he was able to bring to him; but living or dead the boy must not remain there, so stooping over him Charleston gently and tenderly lifted Shilrick in his arms ; even then he feared that they had come too late, for the silent little form never moved, the beautiful eyes with their heavily-fringed lids were closed as if in a last long sleep ; but when Charleston placed his hand over the heart he felt a slight pulsation, then, hastily unsheathing the drummer's sword, he placed the bright steel close to his lips, withdrawing it with an exclamation of delight, for the shining metal was quite dim.

"Ah ! then he is alive—he breathes still ! "

Once more taking Shilrick in his strong arms, the American prepared for his perilous ascent.

"O'Toole ! Rafferty ! " he cried, to the two men who were waiting above, in a state of breathless anxiety, for his reappearance. "Keep a firm hold ! I guess we air coming up now. Hold on for your lives. Best begin an' tighten the rope. Keep up your heart, O'Toole—an' pull hard, boys. Remember, there's double weight to haul up."

Carefully, and with a will, Kerry and Rafferty followed Charleston's injunctions, and in a few minutes the American, with his still unconscious burden, was safely landed beside them.

CHAPTER   III.

" There is an earnest longing
   In those who onward gaze,
Looking with weary patience,
   Towards the coming days.
There is a deeper longing,
   More sad, more strong, more keen ;
Those know it who look backward,
   And yearn for what has been."

ADELAIDE A. PROCTER.

There were many anxious hearts in Glencree Barracks, when another day had passed, another evening far advanced, and still no news had reached them either of Captain Annesley or Shilrick O'Toole.

In the drummers' room the boys' merry voices were hushed ; there was neither fun nor mischief going on there, each bright, boyish face wore a sorrowful, perplexed expression, and the sergeant-in-charge of the little band of drummers, fifers and buglers, who had been sent with the Battalion of Marines to Ireland, had but little to do to keep order among these youthful sons of Mars that night, for Shilrick had ever been the life of the party and a favourite with all, his Irish wit and humour and his light heart had kept his comrades always cheerful and happy ; harmless, boyish mirth and merriment had hitherto reigned supreme in the drummers' room.

One of the younger boys had been employed at the drum practice, on a wooden bench, (this being the means by which the drummers are tanght to play the instrument, thereby saving the otherwise inevitable destruction of drum-heads). It had been the wish of the boy's heart to learn to play the drum, but now he was listless and careless about it, he could not forget that it was the absence of his particular friend, Shilrick O'Toole, which had been the cause of another drummer being required, and the means of his gaining that which had been his earnest desire. The thoughts of the elder boy who was trying to instruct him, were sad as those of his pupil, so they made but sorry progress, and at last they had discontinued their practice and joined their comrades, who were seated in grave silence around the fire. The sergeant tried in vain to amuse the boys and to dispel the gloom that had fallen upon this sad and anxious group of youthful soldiers; he could not instil into the hearts of others the hope that was not in his own, and at length giving up his good-natured, though futile, attempts in despair, he, like his young companions, relapsed into sorrowful, thoughtful silence, while, from time to time, his eyes wandered to that corner of the room where stood the drum and bugle used by the absent one, and where on a wooden stool near these, Shilrick had placed, just before leaving barracks, the half-finished model of a boat, with his tools lying beside it, and a well-worn book, out of which the boy had been reading a stirring military story to his delighted comrades.

How unspeakably sad is the contemplation of such simple inanimate objects—even where there has only been the tie of passing friendship between ourselves, and the one to whom those relics belonged—when we are parted from that one, it may be for awhile, or it may be for ever. The memory of past days, of well-loved scenes and faces, the last occasion on which those mementoes had been used, the words then spoken, the hopes, perhaps never realized, all these return to us, making the most common-place relics appear sacred in our eyes ; thoughts of the past and the future mingle in our dreams by night and by day, saddening our hearts, while the intense longing for the sound of a voice we may never hear again, the yearning for a touch of the hand we may never more clasp, in love, or friendship, well-nigh overpowers us.

The sergeant was not overburdened with sentiment, still, thoughts like these would intrude even into *his* practical mind, and he had been both fond and proud of Shilrick O'Toole.

"Where could the little wanderer be ?   Was he living or
dead ?" wondered the sergeant as he sat gazing into the fire,
surrounded by the picturesque group of drummers and fifers
who might have been statues, for the silence they had maintained for the last hour.

By this time some of the younger boys were thoroughly
weary, and worn out with eager discussion concerning
Shilrick's disappearance, and the never ceasing questions
with which they had throughout the whole day been plying
the long-suffering sergeant, and under the soothing influence
of the warm fire, and the soft, grey twilight they had fallen
asleep, with their heads upon the shoulders of their older
comrades ; while one bright-eyed little fellow, an especial
friend of Shilrick, who had been employed stitching some
small pieces of canvas by the flickering firelight, sat at the
sergeant's feet, his head resting against his knee, from which
position he now and again glanced up wistfully at the
sergeant, as if to read his thoughts and gather hope from the
expression of his face, as he, for the third or fourth time, asked
if there was *any* chance that Shilrick would *ever* come back
to them, or care to have the sails he had been making with
such pride, for the model boat.

The little face was clouded with boyish disappointment,
for those sails had been done in secret, as a pleasing surprise
for his favourite comrade, the other boys being bound over
to strictest silence.   This, too, was the evening of Shilrick's
birthday, when it had been arranged that the said boat was to
be completed, duly launched, and christened by the name of
"Erin's Hope," and the drummers' room was to have been
the scene of unusual festivities.   But, alas ! the young hero
of the day had gone, none knew whither, and the sergeant
could give his eager questioner no hope, he could only shake
his head, despondingly ; it was a problem he could not solve.
Not for one moment, however, did he entertain the thought
that Shilrick had deserted, or joined the Rebel cause, and
knowing well the boy's loyalty and love of the service, he had
indignantly refuted such an idea when it had been mooted by
soldiers of the cavalry regiment, who, despite the commands
and wishes of Colonel Corrie, and other Marine officers, had
somehow become possessed of the knowledge of the mysteri-

ous disappearance of Captain Annesley and the drummer. Unfortunately, there was not one of the Battalion at Glencree Barracks, from the Colonel to the youngest drummer, who could give the slightest clue as to the whereabouts of Annesley, or Shilrick, nor could they even guess the reason of their sudden departure and continued absence. Eveleen Corrie was the only one to whom Annesley had made any mention of his intended expedition, and then he had only told her that it *might* be one of danger, but that he was not going out of Wicklow. He had given her no farther information, and when Eveleen repeated this conversation to Colonel Corrie, he felt more puzzled and anxious than before ; it certainly threw no light on the subject, but rather made matters appear more mysterious. Ever since that interview with Annesley, Eveleen had never ceased to blame herself for her coldness to him, and also for her refusal to bestow on her lover the confidence to which he most certainly had a right. Had she acted differently he would doubtless have in turn confided in her with regard to the present mystery, and the sorrow and trouble of the past two days might have been spared them ; but fate, combined with Annesley's pride and Eveleen's own wilfulness, had worked against the happiness of both, and the unfortunate entrance of the young cavalry officer on that occasion had prevented all chance of a reconciliation between the lovers. Regrets, however, are useless, we can never recall the past. How many thousands of men and women there are in the world who would give all they possess just to be able to live over again one hour of their lives, in which they had, by one fatal mistake, one stroke of folly, shattered their fairest hopes and prospects, and destroyed every chance of happiness they might have in the future, going down to their graves haunted by the cruelest, the bitterest of all sorrows—the thought and the knowledge of "*what might have been.*"

It was in vain that Lady Mabel O'Hara, who was never far away when her friends were in trouble, sought to comfort Eveleen ; she could not restore to her the happiness she had thrown away.

Poor Nap, too, seemed to share in the general depression

and gloom that cast its shadows over all in Glencree
Barracks ; his keen instinct told him that those he loved were
in trouble, he would not leave Eveleen's side for a moment,
and his eyes expressed more eloquently than any words
could do, his loving sympathy and faithful affection.

Early on the morning after the news of the disappearance
of Captain Annesley and the drummer had become generally
known, Eveleen, accompanied by Lady Mabel O'Hara had,
unknown to any one else, started on a voyage of discovery.
They intended to have proceeded along the lonely moorland
paths which skirted the mountains, and they had taken Nap
with them ; knowing how attached he was to both Annesley
and Shilrick they thought that his scent, like that of all
Skye terriers, being very keen, and his instinct and intelligence especially bright, he might possibly by his manœuvres,
show some sign of the late presence of either of his friends,
and perhaps guide the two fair and anxious explorers along
the road taken by them, and so betray their whereabouts.

At one time their efforts appeared about to be crowned
with success. When they arrived at the end of a narrow,
rugged path, leading up the mountain side, Nap came to a
halt, and after much sniffing and scraping, and most energetic wagging of his tail, he appeared anxious to proceed in
that direction, and the two girls, heedless of danger, were
eager to follow the lead of their faithful little guide.
Their faint hope of succeeding in their search was, however, too soon dispelled, and the expedition was aban-
doned in despair, for more snow had fallen during the
night, and now lay deep upon the ground, effectually
concealing the mountain path, and destroying all scent,
so that, at last, Nap once more paused, and again wagging
his tail, though much less vigorously than before, he looked
up into Eveleen's face with a mute, questioning appeal in his
pathetic brown eyes.

"It is no use going any farther, Eveleen," said Lady Mabel,
"we can do no good, and we shall only be giving more trouble, and causing more anxiety if we, too, are lost among the
mountains. Come, dear!" she added, gently, trying to draw
Eveleen away from the spot, "let us go home, there may even

now be good news awaiting us when we return to barracks."

"I fear not, Mabel," returned Eveleen, sadly, "There have been pickets of our men out all night, and this morning, too, but not a trace has been discovered of the missing ones. Still, I am afraid as you say, that *our* expedition is not likely to be more fortunate ; we cannot proceed farther in this direction, and oh, Mabel !" she cried, hopelessly, "I suppose there is nothing for it but to return home. Come, Nap! we have done our best, we can only wait now."

Catching up her little favourite in her arms, she buried her face in the long, shaggy hair, and wept sorrowfully, Nap looking up in silent wonder and sympathy when he felt the fast falling tears on his head.

If Eveleen and Lady Mabel had but known, poor little Nap had really found the very path by which Annesley and Shilrick had commenced their ascent up the mountain side, and had it not been for the snow-drifts, which from this point were very deep and covered the path, the faithful little creature would probably have tracked his two friends to the very entrance to the Rebels' Cave. Eveleen Corrie's mind might have been so far at ease, even had she known that Annesley and Shilrick were prisoners in the hands of the Rebels, as their comrades feared, for she would have felt sure that they would come to no harm, her cousin, Morven O'Neill, being chief of the band in that neighbourhood ; but she had suddenly remembered, with horror, the interrupted duel between her lover and O'Neill, on the night of her interview with the latter, and which they had agreed to continue at their next meeting. Both men, as Eveleen had good cause to know, were hot-headed, brave, and determined, and she was certain that each would remain firm to his purpose. Had they already met ? she wondered anxiously, and, if so, what had been the result ? But the drummer—where could *he* have gone ? The duel would not in any way account for *his* absence.

Only to Mrs. Corrie could Eveleen confide the terrible fear that was in her heart; for no one else knew of her secret meeting with O'Neill, and the scene of which she had been a witness.

The more she thought over matters, the more mysterious

and complicated grew the circumstances attending Annesley's disappearance.

On their way back to Glencree Barracks, Eveleen and Lady Mabel, to their great annoyance, encountered Lieutenant Rochfort, and they had to listen to various surmises and many suppositions that were anything but pleasing to Eveleen, together with significant remarks concerning their early walk, and the neighbourhood in which he had found them. Rochfort, however, was allowed to imagine what he pleased, and that gallant gentleman's imagination being of the most vivid description he soon formed his own opinions, and arranged in his mind a satisfactory romance in which he figured as the hero, and with which he intended to enliven a select few of his brother officers of the cavalry detachment. No doubt Eveleen Corrie had taken that early walk, and had chosen one of the roads leading to Bray, in the hope that she might meet *him;* thus ran the thoughts of the young cavalry officer, his vanity assuring him of the fact that while *he* was to the fore, safe and well, Eveleen could not possibly be in very great distress concerning the safety of Annesley or any other man. Nap resented the addition to their party quite as much as his mistress, and the continued hostility which was maintained between Eveleen's sagacious little four-footed friend and his hated enemy, Rochfort, did not tend to make the walk more agreeable; it was therefore with the greatest relief that both Eveleen Corrie and Lady Mabel O'Hara found themselves once more at home, safe within the precincts of Glencree Barracks.

But, alas! no good news awaited them on their return. Eveleen's patience was yet to be tried to its utmost limits ; she must still live in sorrow and remorse, to regret the irrevocable past, to fear for the uncertain future ; with the sad thoughts that have been in the hearts of thousands of brave, true women since the world began, when those they loved have been far away and in deadly peril, or trouble ; thoughts that have been so beautifully expressed in the words of Mrs. Browning :

> " And is this like love to stand,
> With no help in my hand,
> When, strong as death,
> I fain would watch about thee ? "

CHAPTER IV.

" Come send round the wine, and leave points of belief
  To simpletons, sages, and reasoning fools ;
This moment's a flower too fair and brief
  To be withered and stained with the dust of the schools.

Shall I ask the brave soldier who fights by my side
  In the cause of mankind, if our creeds agree ?
Shall I give up the friend I have valued and tried,
  If he kneel not before the same altar with me ? "

MOORE.

If anxiety and wonder filled the thoughts, and the hearts of Shilrick O'Toole's comrades in the drummers' room ; if sorrow and suspense held their sway within the Colonel's family circle and household, they also occupied, with equal force and persistence, the thoughts of one and all of Captain Annesley's brother officers, who were assembled around the mess-table on the second evening after his strange disappearance.

It chanced to be a public night at the Mess, when each of the officers, according to custom, had invited their military, naval, or civilian friends to dine with them.

Colonel Corrie was present with his friend, Major Ricardo, and there arrived two guests whom Captain Annesley had invited, but he was not there to receive them ; they appeared awkward and bewildered at first, but several other officers soon came forward, willing and ready to do their best to entertain them, and to offer hospitality in Annesley's name.

Although the minds of the Marine officers were, naturally enough, filled with thoughts of their missing comrade, they had, as yet, respected Colonel Corrie's wishes, and had refrained from any mention of Annesley's absence before the guests at the mess-table. Politics appeared chiefly to occupy the attention of all, the arguments being amicable enough for some time. Gradually, however, as the hours passed, and the wine was freely circulated, the voices grew louder and more determined, the opinions more hostile, until at last both Colonel Corrie and Major Ricardo looked anxiously at each other, wishing, if possible, to put an end to the altercations going on around them, yet half afraid of making matters worse by their interference.

It is needless to say that the young Lieutenants, Rochfort and Digby, both being present, lost no opportunity of differing from each other on every subject, and expressing those differences of opinion in terms at once plain and forcible.

Occasionally Drelincourt, one of the cavalry officers present, being Rochfort's friend, would try to put in a word to smooth matters, and to prevent his comrade going too far with Annesley's brother officer, in his mad jealousy of the absent Captain of Marines ; but Saunders generally contrived to set them going again, by some ill-timed remark, and would then sit silent, but smiling, enjoying the passage of arms between the two young officers, Saunders being one of those sort of people who like to stir the cauldron, and then move away to a safe distance, whence they can watch it bubbling and boiling over without fear of themselves being burned or injured thereby.

There was an Irish Marine officer of decided Orange tendencies, called Geoghegan, who, though very young, was by no means backward in trying to impress *his* ideas upon an elderly civilian guest, a most determined adherent of the opposite party. More than once had the young Scotch Lieutenant, McIvor, the adjutant of the Marines, gallantly come to the rescue, and prevented an open rupture.

The Englishmen present seemed to forget, in their excitement, that the Colonel, who was their host, was an

Irishman himself, and that anything they might say against his countrymen would scarcely be well received, however he as a loyal soldier might, in his own mind, condemn the means taken by them to gain their ends. As yet, he had taken no active part in the argument, but some of his officers, who knew him best, could see by the stern expression of their Colonel's face, that much that was being said was the reverse of pleasing to him, though gentlemanly feeling, and courtesy prevented him from contradicting his guests, or making matters unpleasant at his own mess-table.

Every point was discussed, in a sensible and disinterested spirit by some, and with unspeakable bitterness by others. All the rancour generally displayed in religious controversy, appeared in full force on this occasion, while the difference in politics, and nationality, of those assembled added to the heat of the discussion.

Severe censure was, by some, bestowed upon the famous Pitt for his action at the time, in first raising the expectations of the Roman Catholics throughout the country, and sending Lord Fitzwilliam to Ireland with such unlimited powers to act as *he* thought best, only to dispel all their hopes and cause the bitterest disappointment by his sudden recall, which was as unexpected as it proved disastrous ; for, as many alleged, and with truth, Fitzwilliam was a favourite with all, and had he remained at his post there might have been some chance of peace for Ireland ; but from the day of his recall the country prepared for insurrection. This, others asserted, was just what Pitt wanted, and in the carrying out of his own designs he neither thought nor cared for the bloodshed and terrible consequences which must inevitably follow, nor the hatred he thus gained for the English Government.

Lord Clare came in for a fair share of praise from some of the disputants, for the rapid and determined steps he had taken, inasmuch that, in three months, he had the nation in full military training for the Rebellion. The civilians present did not fail to remind their opponents that Lord Fitzgerald had warned the Government of the result of their policy, but his warning had passed unheeded, and Pitt had actually taken means to force the insurrection, at a time

when he thought, probably, that the country would be un-
prepared to meet the emergency.

The military guests naturally did their best to defend Pitt's
action, though some of them in their hearts felt that he had
really done much to sow the seeds of discord and disloyalty,
and to goad the Irish people into rebellion.

A stormy altercation ensued concerning the famous Henry
Grattan and all that he had done for his country, and the
manner in which he had been deceived by English states-
men, who, at the very time when the Parliament were
declaring that the right of Ireland to self-government was
at no time henceforward to be questioned, were actually
plotting to carry on the Act of Legislative Union, and every
effort of Grattan had been opposed and thwarted by English
ministers, who determinedly kept in view *their* project of the
Union.

Throughout this argument, however, there appeared to be
but one opinion regarding the patriotism and single-hearted
motives of Henry Grattan ; even his political opponents spoke
of him with sincere admiration. Next followed a discussion,
the reverse of amicable, as to the society of " *The United
Irishmen*," establised in 1791, which might, many considered,
have proved most satisfactory in its results, for at the first
organization the society had given every promise of being
both powerful and successful ; it was slowly but surely leading the Irish people to prosperity, by endeavouring earnestly
to crush out the spirit of religious animosity, which must
ever prove the ruin of any nation where it exists to such an
extent as it did in Ireland at that period.

On the arrival of Lord Fitzwilliam it had appeared, for a
short time, as if the Irish question would be settled, with
perfect freedom for all classes and creeds throughout Ireland ;
but this hope was not destined to be fulfilled, for the sudden
withdrawal of such a universal favourite as Lord Fitzwilliam,
and Pitt's bestowal of his appointment on Lord Camden, who
at once restored his friends, Cooke and Beresford, to their
former positions, placed the government of this most unhappy country again in the hands of those whose policy was
to suppress all popular liberties, and rouse up party antago-
nism, which had for a time been subdued, and this had been

the signal for the outbreak of the disastrous Rebellion of 1798, and caused the change in the Society of "*United Irishmen*," which from that date became a secret, instead of an open and peaceful organization, and later on displayed strong revolutionary tendencies.

These, and many other points, such as the Coercive Legislation, which had been carried through Parliament, session after session, the Orange persecutions in Armagh and other parts of Ireland, the suppression of the public Press (which was so ostensibly the voice of the people), the failure of Ponsonby's motion for reform, and last, but perhaps most important, the secession of Grattan and his faithful adherents from Parliament, all were argued with great heat on both sides, and in some cases, considerable animosity, the conduct of many of the celebrities, Roman Catholic and Protestant, who had formed the Society of "*United Irishmen*," duly coming in for their share of censure or praise, justly and unjustly, according as their special admirers, or adversaries might approve, or disapprove of their actions, until Colonel Corrie, on meeting a significant and anxious glance from Major Ricardo, at last felt himself necessitated to interfere, and to stem, if it were possible, the tide of angry feeling that threatened to terminate more seriously than was desirable.

"I think," he said, his clear, commanding voice being heard distinctly, and claiming the immediate attention of all, " I think this argument has been sufficiently prolonged ; it is not well to turn a friendly party into a political meeting. I have noticed, however," he continued, smiling, " that there is at least one point upon which all appear to agree, and that is in praise of the noble, guileless nature of Henry Grattan : a true patriot he is without doubt, *his* designs, *his* wishes have all been for the good of his country. Let me remind you, then, of his own words, when he said that he '*desired not a Catholic nor a Protestant settlement, but —An Irish Nation,*' and has he not upheld that the leaders of the Patriotic party should base Irish liberty upon the recognition of the *entire people?* Should not all agree then, with the declaration of the Irish Volunteers at Dungannon in '*holding the right of private judgment in matters of religion to be equally sacred in others as in ourselves?*' Most earnestly, then, I ask you

Irishmen now present—Are we not *one nation*, though our *creeds* may differ?   Let us never forget this fact, for it is such forgetfulness that has ever been the ruin of Ireland: this discord and enmity between people of one land, one race, that has given alien countries the chance of condemning us, with seeming justice, that has rendered it an easy task for hostile nations to rouse that ill-feeling and bitter animosity within the hearts of our people, that could only result, as it has now done, in civil warfare, and prove the death-knell of all prosperity and fame for Ireland. '*A house divided against itself cannot stand.*'   Oh, I pray you, my countrymen, to remember this—our only hope in Erin is in that union of hearts and hands in the common cause—the welfare of our beloved country.   I, as an Irishman, feel keenly any wrongs, real or fancied, from which our people may be suffering; my heart still clings to the hope of my boyhood, that brighter days may yet dawn for Ireland, that I may live to see the restoration of her former fame and glory.   I cannot close my eyes to the fatal manner in which our most unfortunate country has been misgoverned, but as long as I hold the King's commission, I am bound in all honour to keep silence with regard to the action of the English Government, under which I serve."

This speech was vociferously applauded by all present, and the intense excitement which had prevailed was somewhat calmed by Colonel Corrie's quiet, dignified demeanour, yet ready to break out again on the slightest provocation.   A few ill-timed, thoughtless remarks had in the first instance led to, and ended in, this fierce political and religious controversy.

The applause which had greeted the words of Colonel Corrie had scarcely died away ere an orderly hastily entered the mess-room, and placing in the Colonel's hands an official-looking document, he, in a low voice, gave him a message to the effect that someone desired to speak to him on a matter of the greatest importance, and that despatches awaited him in the office, the messenger refusing to give them into any other hands than his own.   With an apology to Major Ricado and the other guests present, the Colonel rose from the table, and left the mess-room, promising, however, a speedy return.

No sooner had Colonel Corrie disappeared than the unfortunate political questions which had before caused so much diversity of opinion, were again resumed, on some foolish remark of the young Irish officer, Geoghegan, addressed to a Roman Catholic landlord, one of the guests who was seated beside him.

At the other end of the table, Lieutenant Rochfort, taking immediate advantage of the absence of the Colonel, had commenced a conversation with Lieutenant Digby concerning the disappearance of Annesley.

"I think," he said, significantly, "that there is something *strangely mysterious* and suspicious about the whole affair, don't you know !"

"In what way?" demanded Digby, sharply.

"Well," returned Rochfort, sneeringly, "have you forgotten the fact that he is an Irishman,—and—may he not have taken it into his head to serve his own country under the colours of those famous *Patriots*, and have left the gallant Marines for ever, taking with him that wonderful drummer ? "

"Sir !" exclaimed Digby, haughtily, "excuse me for reminding you that you are speaking of my brother officer."

"Oh, I did not speak inadvertently," returned Rochfort, coolly, "and have no reason to retract my words. I am only expressing the thoughts of many others besides myself."

"Ah ! then kindly keep such expressions for others who may appreciate your confidence. Annesley is one of my dearest friends," replied Digby.

"Well, you need not be so indignant," laughed Rochfort, contemptuously. "You must know as well as I do, though you will not own it, that *all* the Irish are rebels at heart, all tarred with the same brush of disloyalty, and love of intrigue against our Government. Even that charming little friend of yours, Lady Mabel O'Hara—"

"I must request that you will be good enough to leave that lady's name out of your conversation," interrupted Digby, proudly.

"Ah ! *that's* the way the wind blows, is it ? " said Rochfort, smiling sarcastically, as he watched the other curiously.

" I hope ' *whichever way the wind blows,*' as you express it, that the officers of *our* corps may never be found wanting in courtesy, or acting otherwise than as gentlemen ; we are not in the habit of making ladies, or *any* women whom we *respect*, the subject of discussion at the mess-table, or in the barrack-room," was Digby's reply.

" Ah !" returned Rochfort, "you are scrupulous ; but, my dear fellow, let me give you a word of warning : see that *your friend*, Annesley, if he ever returns, which seems somewhat doubtful, does not snatch the prize from you. The last time I saw the Lady Mabel and the gallant Captain together, I do assure you that he seemed more of *the lover* than *the friend.*"

" It is false, and you know it ! " replied Digby, his face flushed with indignation. " You know, as well as I do, that Annesley has been the affianced husband, for some time, of our Colonel's daughter."

" He *was*," said Rochfort, with such insolent significance in his tones, that Digby felt sorely tempted to knock him down ; " at least, I heard some such story a short time ago ; but what if the lady has changed her mind ; what would you say then ? " he asked, tauntingly.

" Why, that it is no concern of *yours* or of *mine*," retorted Digby.

" Ellis ! " said a cavalry officer, who was seated next the Captain of Marines. " I heard once from one of your officers (Geoghegan, I think it was) that Captain Annesley had distinguished himself greatly in the service, but that he had at one time serious thoughts of resigning his commission ; and also a young Irish Lieutenant of your corps— called 'O'Neill'—a nephew of your Colonel, on account, so I was told, of their having received some shabby treatment at the hands of the Government ; what was the truth of it ? Do you mind telling me ? " he asked, politely, "or was the affair secret and confidential between the officers of your corps ? "

For a moment Ellis did not reply, he darted an angry look at the unconscious Geoghegan before he spoke, but on second thoughts he considered that it would be best policy to make no mystery of the occurrence, and so answered in a manner as easy and indifferent as he could assume, treating the question as a simple matter of ordinary conversation, yet withal he decided to be watchful, and to have a care over his words, for Captain Ellis was shrewd, somewhat suspicious, and ever on the alert, and he fancied that the question had not been asked without some intent, especially as he noticed that Rochfort's eyes were fixed upon him, and that he was listening eagerly to all that might be said.

"Yes!" replied Ellis, slowly and thoughtfully, "and O'Neill was as fine a fellow as ever entered our corps; a splendid officer, a kindly, pleasant comrade, and a true gentleman in every sense of the word. We all felt his loss, and grieved over his decision to leave the old corps. We used every effort to persuade him to remain with us, but when once O'Neill had determined upon any step, his will was unalterable. With Annesley, I am glad to say, we were more successful."

"Ah! probably Miss Corrie had some power *then* to influence his decision," said Rochfort, with his insolent smile. "But what was the grievance of these two officers?" he asked, "not but the fact of their being *Irish* makes it a *sine qua non* that they should have a grievance of some sort; but what was it in *this* case, Captain? I never exactly heard the *whole* story."

"Nor do I see how it could possibly interest *you* if you did," returned Ellis, coldly, and looking fixedly at his questioner across the mess-table. "It is an old story now, still, as the affair has been raked up again, I may as well explain matters. In our last campaign, Annesley and O'Neill had distinguished themselves in many ways, by their indomitable courage; there was not a sortie, but they volunteered for the duty, there was not a forlorn hope, not a danger to be undergone, but they were foremost in the midst of it; and on one occasion especially, they saved the lives of many wounded, by carrying them to a place of safety, while shot and shell were storming around them."

"I have heard something of this before," said Major Ricardo, turning to Captain Norton who was seated beside him. "Were they not both shamefully overlooked by the authorities after all their gallant deeds?"

" Yes, Major !" replied Norton.   "Though they had proved an honour to the British Army, though they had gained fresh laurels for our corps, yet they received not the slightest acknowledgment of those brilliant services."

" That is always the way—always the same old story," returned the Major.

" The Colonel who was with us," continued Ellis, " wrote an express report of both officers, and telling of the number of lives they had saved ; at the same time saying that they were deserving of any reward the service could bestow upon them."

" But I suppose it was of no use ? " queried Major Ricardo.

" Not the slightest," answered Ellis ; " the authorities replied to the Colonel, that they ' *highly commended*' the conduct of the young Marine officers in question, but at the same time they had '*gone out of their way*' in taking charge of the wounded, that not being in the '*regular course*' of their duties, etc.   You know the usual style of these communication, Major?"

" Indeed I do," answered Major Ricardo, laughing, "only too well."

" At the same time," continued Ellis, " the authorities wrote to Annesley and O'Neill, (who, not knowing that the Colonel had written about them at all, were somewhat astonished to receive letters from the said authorities) begging that in future they would desist from making applications for rewards through their Colonel.   This, and other important reasons, which need scarcely be mentioned at this late date, and to those who have no possible interest in the matter, caused O'Neill to send in his papers resigning his commission immediately, and although he was known to be such an exceptionally good officer, one of a type that are so much wanted in the army, yet the resignation was readily accepted."

" Possibly," suggested Rochfort, who was ever ready to detract from any praise bestowed upon Annesley, "the authorities might consider that Colonel Corrie's favourable report of those officers was naturally prejudiced, both being Irish, and one his *own nephew*, while the other was betrothed to his daughter."

" Pardon me," said Digby, "if I advise you to *think* before you speak, Rochfort ; Colonel Corrie was *not* with the Marines in *that* campaign at all, and had, therefore, nothing whatever to do with the report that was sent."

"And would have been the last man in the world to have used his influence to obtain rewards for those connected with him," added McIvor, the Scotch Adjutant, indignantly. "He never did it for himself, he has always kept in the background."

"Aye!" said Captain Collingwood, a naval officer, "I can fully endorse your words, McIvor, for your Colonel has been a messmate of mine, and we have always been friends."

"And I should think that there could scarcely be a more loyal officer in our Army or Navy than Captain Annesley, of the Marines," said a naval lieutenant. "I also knew O'Neill," he continued, "and can only say that he was liked and respected by officers and men when he was our shipmate."

"I think if anyone has a word to say against Captain Annesley, or Mr. O'Neill, he should withhold his opinion until he can express it in the presence of the gentlemen, and not run them down when they are absent," chimed in a clear, boyish voice.

The speaker was a young midshipman, who, having a sailor's love of fair-play, could no longer keep silent, especially as, being a guest of the Corries, he naturally favoured Annesley and O'Neill. As he spoke, he looked defiantly at those who had wished to cast a doubt upon the loyalty of the missing Captain, and, boy as he was, the Honourable Harry Nelson's remark was a rebuke to more than one of the older officers at the mess-table.

"Well said, Harry!" cried Digby; "a thousand thanks for your defence of my friends in their absence!"

"At the time O'Neill sent in his resignation," said Ellis, quietly proceeding with his account of the two officers, and taking no more notice of Rochfort than if he had never spoken, "Annesley would have followed suit, if we had not found out what he was doing in time and, as I have said, persuaded him to remain with us. But thus it is that our best and noblest men are treated. Bravery and merit are of no account unless they happen to

have some *special interest in influential quarters*, when
they are sure to enjoy the highest rewards of the service in no scant measure ; merit in *that case* being quite a
secondary consideration. This is why really good officers,
who have distinguished themselves in our corps, or, indeed,
in other branches of the service, but who have no friends
in power, seem actually objects of intense dislike to the
authorities. That they should go unrewarded is a standing
reproach to themselves, while yet they do not choose to bestow the good things of the service on any but their own
favourites or those of their special friends."

"You are right, Captain," agreed Major Ricardo. "You
have spoken only too truly."

"As I know by experience," said Captain Collingwood.

"I suppose," said McIvor, "that those who shirk active
service, and always contrive, by exchanges, or some other
means, to remain at home, filling good appointments, have
time to ingratiate themselves with the heads of departments,
by a course of unlimited toadyism ; while the real hard-
working officers, who are true to their duty, and faithful to
their country, are far away and forgotten. 'Out of sight,
out of mind,'" he added, bitterly, for McIvor, too, had some
experience of the injustice of those in power.

"Why don't you stand up for the *authorities* now,
Nelson ?" asked Rochfort, mischievously ; "they're absent,
you know." To this the young midshipman made no reply,
but looked over scornfully at Rochfort.

"If I remember rightly," commenced one of the civilian
guests, "O'Neill's father had something to do with the
revolutionary party in Ireland many years ago ; he was a
great politician, got into hot water with the Government, and
had to fly the country."

"Yes ! Died in exile," supplemented the officious
Geoghegan, triumphant in the opportunity of being able to
afford such important information.

"Ah !" exclaimed Rochfort, quickly, "and what became of
the son—the Colonel's nephew—when he left the Marines?"

"Excuse me !" replied McIvor, haughtily. "We are not
in the habit of making the private affairs of our Colonel's
family, the subject of discussion."

"Quite right—quite right!" remarked Major Ricardo. "Rochfort, you are too inquisitive;" he added, turning to the young lieutenant.

"It only struck me, sir," answered the incorrigible Rochfort, "that possibly this O'Neill and the missing Captain may have met again, and agreed to avenge their grievances by joining *the Patriots*."

"Sir, this is too much!" cried Digby, angrily, "that you should dare to accuse our brother officer of desertion and treason."

"He wouldn't *dare* to say it to their faces," said the midshipman, boldly.

"Now, now, gentlemen!" interrupted the Major, in tones which he intended to be conciliatory, "pray let us drop the subject. You hot-headed young men are growing too excited; this is the way quarrels are brought about and duels ensue, and all about nothing, after all. No doubt Captain Annesley will return, and the missing drummer also, and they will in due course explain their absence to the entire satisfaction of their Colonel and their comrades."

"Cannot some one give us a song?" asked McIver at last, in the hope of diverting the thoughts of the disputants into a more pleasing channel.

"Ah, yes! go ahead, Geoghegan," commanded Digby, peremptorily. "You're the fellow for singing—do tune up now!—something to put life into us."

Lieutenant Geoghegan, nothing loth, and considerably elated at being selected as entertainer to so large a company, accordingly did "tune up," and commenced immediately, without any demur, and, to the horror of all present, to sing some verses by Moore, to the tune of "*Boyne Water*."

"Well, of all the—" began the horrified Digby, but he paused suddenly at a signal from Captain Ellis, not, however, before he had contrived to bring down his foot with some force upon the toes of the unfortunate Geoghegan, who was not far from him, thereby causing that gallant young subaltern to utter an exclamation certainly not introduced into the song by the famous bard.

The feelings of the majority of those present may be

better imagined than described. The company was a mixed one, and numbered among the guests a Roman Catholic priest, an Episcopalian clergyman, and a Presbyterian minister.

From the moment that the first notes of the fatal *party tune* fell upon their ears, Captain Ellis and his brother officers could foresee the consequences of Geoghegan's unfortunate selection; but Ellis had hastened to prevent Digby from saying more at the first, in the faint hope that the guests would allow the matter to pass without remark.

Geoghegan was, meanwhile, quite unaware of the consternation that he was causing, and indeed he was priding himself, and figuratively speaking, clapping himself on the back, in self-congratulation at his own genius in having chosen a song so appropriate, as he thought, to the arguments which had preceded it, and to Colonel Corrie's speech; he knew not the sensation he was causing, or of the fierce flame that he was kindling in the hearts around him, a flame that would take the united efforts of all the English officers at the mess-table to extinguish, he therefore sang on in his innocence, the words and melody so fraught with political meaning and sad pathos:

> " As vanquished Erin wept beside
>   The Boyne's ill-fated river,
> She saw where discord in the tide,
>   Had dropped his loaded quiver.
> ' Lie hid ! ' she cried, ' ye venomed darts,
>   Where mortal eye may shun you;
> Lie hid—for oh ! the stain of hearts
>   That bled for me is on you.''
>
> " But vain her wish, her weeping vain—
>   As time too well hath taught her;
> Each year the fiend returns again,
>   And dives into that water:
> And brings triumphant, from beneath,
>   His shafts of desolation,
> And sends them winged with worse than death
>   Throughout her maddening nation.''
>
> " Alas ! for her who sits and mourns
>   Even now beside that river,—
> Unwearied still the fiend returns
>   And stored is still his quiver.
> ' When will this end ? ye Powers of Good ! '
>   She weeping asks for ever;
> But only hears, from out that flood,
>   The demon answer ' Never ! ' ''

Geoghegan's voice was very beautiful and sympathetic in tone; his song therefore had the more disastrous effect in touching the hearts of his hearers; it was only when he had concluded, and looked around for the applause which he had never before failed to receive, that he felt the ominous silence, and noticed the still more ominous frown on the faces of all present, and he began to think that *something* must be wrong.

He was about to ask an explanation from Digby, when the storm which had been slowly gathering, now broke, the fierce party-spirit was once more roused; the controversy was soon again at its height, the war of words became fast and furious. In truth, Geoghegan *had* given them a song to " put life into them," as Digby had requested, but not in the manner he had intended. It was some time before it dawned upon the former that he was to blame for this renewed outbreak, and then his regret was keen indeed, but his apologies, and explanations were unheeded and unheard, no notice being taken, even of his repeated offers to settle the dispute by singing " *Garryowen* " to please the opposite party; he was unceremoniously pulled down into his seat by Digby, and requested " to keep quiet, and not make more mischief than he had already done."

At last, Major Ricardo, thinking that it was necessary for him, being the senior officer present, to interfere, contrived to create a diversion among the disputants by rising hastily, and on pretence of the lateness of the hour and that it was time they returned to their own barracks, almost commanded his officers to accompany him, and so left the other guests no choice but to retire also, Captain Collingwood taking care that the spirited midshipman left the room with himself and the naval Lieutenant; and this brought to a close the only unpleasant evening that had ever been passed at the genial, hospitable mess of the Marines. Unfortunately the mischief did not end there; the quarrels on that occasion were afterwards made the cause of more than one fatal duel, and much ill-feeling had been roused between those who had hitherto, though they differed in religion and politics, been amicably and peaceably disposed towards each other.

Lieutenant Geoghegan, however, always maintained that all would have been well, had he only been allowed to sing " *Garryowen.*"

CHAPTER V.

" Rise from your dreams of the Future
  Of gaining some hard-fought field ;
Of storming some airy fortress,
  Or bidding some giant yield ;
Your Future has deeds of glory,
  Of honour (God grant it may !) ;
But your arm will never be stronger,
  Or the need so great as To-day."

ADELAIDE A. PROCTER.

Thanks to the tender care and attention of Mrs. Kinahan and her daughter Anty, Shilrick awoke the following morning after he had been found by Kerry and Silas Charleston, but little the worse for his accident, beyond a slight feeling of weakness, and a few bruises. He had fallen, as Charleston said, in the very midst of thick bunches of snow-covered bracken, while his head was pillowed on a couch of Nature's own forming, of softest emerald-green moss.

Here the poor boy had lain throughout the long weary hours of the night. When pursued by the Rebels he had thrown off his heavy military cloak, which had considerably impeded his proguss. so he had not even that to protect him from the chilly mountain air, but fortunately, he was sheltered by the rocks on all sides from the intense cold, and his fall had been broken by the thick furze bushes growing out of the mountain side, but his head had struck against a rock, and he was thus rendered unconscious for some time, from which unconsciousness he partially recovered, only, however, to fall into that dangerous state of stupor which would probably have proved fatal but for the timely arrival of his brother Kerry and the American. It was about mid-day when Shilrick roused himself from the deep sleep into which he had fallen, as he reclined upon the old wooden settle by the fire in the small parlour of the "Shamrock." On looking round him he discovered that he was not alone, the other occupants of the room being Kerry, Silas Charleston, and Andy Rafferty. "Kerry!" he called to his brother, who immediately put aside the pipe he had been smoking, and went up to him.

"Well, *ma bouchaleen*! Sure ye're awake agin!" said Kerry, kindly. "Are ye falin' betther?"

"Troth, I am, Kerry," answered Shilrick, "well an' hearty agin, but sure it's yersilf shouldn't have let me slape all this thime, it must be gettin' late, an' I'll have to be movin'—but Kerry!" said the boy, suddenly, "last night whin I was so ill, there was somewan bendin' over me, an' givin' me the hot dhrinks, an spakin', oh, so softly. She was dressed in white, Kerry—all in white, enthirely, an' wid her long goulden hair, fallin' around her, she looked all as wan as some beautiful angel come down from Heaven—who was it, Kerry, wisha?"

"Ochone!" murmured Kerry, sorrowfully, to himself. "Troth! that's where she'll be, I'm feared, before many weeks have passed, poor Misthress O'Neill! it's not long for this world she is!"

"Who was it?" repeated Shilrick, finding that his brother did not reply to his question. "Sure, it wasn't the purty French colleen, Misthress Kinahan used to be callin' her naace?"

"Sorra wan ilse, Shilrick!" replied Kerry, remembering suddenly that no outsiders knew that Estelle was the wife of O'Neill.

"Sure, Kerry, I'd like to spake to her, an' thank her for what she done for me last night."

"Maybes ye will before ye go, Shilrick, though I do be feared not, for Misthress—I mane the wan ye're spakin' av this minute—has been ill, an' 'tis hersilf that's none the betther av last night's work, but she *would* be in it," said Kerry.

"Troth! it's sorry I am if I done her harm," returned the boy, gently, "but I didn't know annythin' about it, at all, at all. Now, Kerry," he added, determinedly, "it's mesilf that must be sthartin'."

"Where to?" asked Charleston.

"Back to barracks," replied Shilrick.

"Why, I guess you airn't fit to stand yet, let alone to walk all that tarnation long road. We might as well have left you at the foot of the mountain gorge if you air goin' to try to commit suicide that way," said the American.

"Sure, Shilrick," remonstrated Kerry, "'tis Charleston that's right enough. Ye haven't the sthringth yet to go yer lone."

"Faith I have, Kerry, an' go I *must*," answered the boy, determinedly. "Enough thime has been lost as it is, it'll be avenin' before I rache barracks; they'll have been wondherin' there what's come av his honour, Captain Annesley, an' mesilf, an' maybes thinkin' we've desarted an' joined the Ribils, an' small blame to thim, for 'tis nigh three dhays since we left. There was to be fine doin's last night in the drummer's room," continued Shilrick, "by raison av its bein' my birthday. Sure *you* forgot it, Kerry," he added, reproachfully.

"Och, Shilrick! how could I think av that, or anny other thing that was plasin', an' yersilf so ill an' onsensible we thought ye'd niver live to see the mornin's light."

"Ah, well! sure it's right enough I am now, annyhow," returned the drummer. "I hope the bhoys would have their fun all the same at the barracks," he said, in his ready thought for others. "His honour, the Captain, gave thim money to kape it up in illigant sthyle; but troth, I hope," he added, suddenly, "that the sergeant would kape an eye on Parker and Smith, that they'd not be afther dhrawin' picthures an' figures on my dhrum-head, for it's the divil that's in thim two bhoys for playin' divarsions. But, *Kerry wisha!* where's me hat, an' me belt and swoord? I'm off now!"

Silas Charleston now rose from his seat and approached Shilrick.

Andy Rafferty remained seated, but though his whole mind seemed concentrated on the pipe which he was smoking, yet he was, for all that, listening with anxiety to the conversation that ensued. Too indolent to take any active part in it himself, he was content to leave all argument to Silas Charleston and Kerry O'Toole.

"Shilrick!" said the American, slowly and solemnly, as he withdrew the pipe from his mouth, and laid one hand kindly on the drummer's shoulder, "I guess we can trust you, if we let you go free. You will not betray 'the Boys'?"

"Oh, how can ye ax me such a quistion?" cried Shilrick, reproachfully. "'Tis a hard enough task ye're givin' me—that's thrue for ye—not in axin' me not to bethray the 'Bould Boys,' but—but sure there's me own Captain."

"I calc'late you can leave him to us," interrupted Charleston. "Here's his foster brother—an' here am I, an' we air both determined to rescue him, at any cost to ourselves. There's Andy Rafferty, too—I guess he'll not take any *active* steps, but there he is, ready to back us up as far as looking on an' keeping silence is concerned. An' now look you, young mister! You hev made a friend of Silas Charleston —wa'al! he'll not deceive you. You trust us to rescue Captain Annesley, meanwhile he's safe enough from any harm, for *our* Captain is *his* friend."

"*Ua Néill* will help us, Shilrick," added Kerry, "my fosther brother shall be free before many dhays have passed."

"You can say he's a prisoner, but you didn't see where he was taken," said Charleston; "you know where we are located, certainly, but if *you* don't tell the military, I guess no one else can find the way, or guide them to our cave."

"Sure, it's yersilves can thrust me, Misther Charleston," returned Shilrick earnestly. The American, meeting the glance of those truthful, honest 'eyes, felt satisfied that the trust would not be misplaced.

At a second request from the drummer, his brother Kerry reluctantly brought forward his hat, belt, and sword, and while Shilrick was buckling on the latter, Charleston and Kerry both continued to give him various instructions as to how he was to act in any emergency that might occur. Even Andy Rafferty was at last roused from his normal state of indolence, and, slowly rising from his seat, he joined the group, and now and then ventured to put in a word.

How often it is that we, in our blindness, plan and

rehearse, so to speak, all that we are to say, or to do, on some important occasion, to avert some catastrophe, to bring about some desired end, or, it may be, to escape some danger or difficulty, only to find that our exertions have been useless, and that much anxious thought has been wasted. Probably, we may have passed many a sad and sleepless night, and been harassed by day, almost beyond the power of endurance, with fears for that which, after all, has never occurred, while, in our planning to avert one evil, we may have neglected to shield ourselves from another. " It is the unexpected that happens," is an old and a true saying, we can never be certain of, or fully prepared for, anything that may occur in this world.

Thus it was that while these three men, in their worldly wisdom, were warning the drummer, and using every effort to instil into his mind their lesson of how he was to speak, and to act on his arrival at barracks, they knew not of the greater trial and the danger that awaited them all, through the treachery of one man, nor of the sorrow that was so soon to fall upon poor Shilrick, clouding all his young life, robbing him for ever of the free, happy thoughts of boyhood.

None of the occupants of the room had noticed that during their eager conversation, the door had been opened softly, and that Estelle O'Neill, followed by Anty Kinahan, had entered, and that they were now standing just within the doorway.

On hearing Kerry's last words of advice to his brother, and seeing that Shilrick was now fairly equipped and about to set out on his return to barracks, Estelle came forward hastily and stood before the astonished group, looking, in her long white robe, and with the veil of golden hair falling over her shoulders, as Shilrick had said, like some spirit from the other world.

"Ah !" she exclaimed, her face pallid with fear, her eyes full of despair—" I did hear all—it is dat de window of de room where I was resting is open, an' I do come myself, now to pray you dat you will not let him go. Oh ! say dat you will not," she cried, as she turned from one man to the other, " you do know well dat in dis boy's hands rests de life of your Captain O'Neill.   However willing it is dat *he*,—dis child, may be, de officers of his corps will not dat he shall keep dis secret, and for yourselves, my good men, if it is dat you do help dis Captain of de soldiers to escape, den he also will be able, if he does so dispose, to betray all your band into de hands of de military."

Kerry had started forward, an indignant reply on his lips, but Silas Charleston laid his hand on his arm to restrain him, and then turned to Estelle.

"Madame," said the American, politely, but firmly, "the boy must go free, and more, we must detain him no longer; at any moment that arch-fiend, Magin, may appear, and I could not answer for the drummer's safety if found here. And remember, it was Captain Annesley who saved our Captain O'Neill's life—I guess he saved mine too. In return, all that *I* can do for him shall be done. I calc'late you may rest assured," he continued. laying his hand on Shilrick's shoulder, "that this boy will not betray us. I could stake my life on his good faith, an' is not his own brother one of our band now? Here are three of us before you at this moment, madame, *our* lives are all in his hands, yet *we* trust him."

"Troth, ma'am," said Shilrick, in some scorn for the doubt he still saw written so plainly on Estelle's face, "'tis the lives av *all* the band av 'Bould Bhoys' have been in my hands since the first dhay the Marines set foot in Wicklow an' mesilf wid thim. Sure I know ivery cave an' hidin' place in the mountains, an' in the Divil's Glen, too, where they somethimes do be hidin' thimselves. I know all the habits an' many av the sacrits av the band. It's mesilf that could have guided the souldiers to the Ribil's Cave ; or the spot where they hould their parade, jist as aisy as I could guide yersilf to the barracks this minute, if 'twas plasin' to me ; but I haven't done it yet—why would I do it now ? "

"An' sure, what call is it ye'd have to be thinkin' so ill av my brother, ma'am, that, ye'd be afther misthrustin' him that way ? " demanded Kerry, indignantly.

"Och ! niver mind, Kerry, sure it's herself didn't mane anny harm, at all, at all," said Shilrick. "I am sorry if 'tis anxious ye are about it," he added, gently, as he again turned to Estelle, "for 'tis mighty kind ye were to mesilf last night, ma'am, and sure I thank ye for it ; but—but troth, it's hard to be misthrusted, and whin its mesilf that

could have had the gould in *galore*.   I could have helped
me brother whin he was in bittherly poverty.   I could have
made ould Granny Coghlan's life aisier an' moor plaisin' for
her while she lived—may the Heavens be her bed this
dhay !   I could have got advancement in me corps if I'd
been the wan to bethray the Ribil Chafe and all his ' Bould
Bhoys ' into the hands of the milithairey. Faith I could have
got most annythin' I'd have liked to ax for, an' oh ! " he continued, earnestly, " Heaven knows the ambition that's in
me heart, the hope an' the wish that I could win fame an'
glory, but it must be *wid honour*, an' so that I'd be a credit
to me corps ; not by manes av treachery so cruel an' cowardly
that ivery thrue souldier would despise me, an' me comrades
scorn to spake to me, at all, at all. But there—let me pass ! "
cried the boy, suddenly, "sure I've sthayed long enough."

Estelle O'Neill was still standing determinedly between
Shilrick and the door ; she made no movement to let him
pass, and, to get out of the room, he must have put her
aside, but this his innate gallantry prevented him from
doing, and while he stood proudly before her, she made
another attempt to detain him.

Holding out her clasped hands beseechingly to him, she
cried in terror and despair :

"Do not go !—oh, do not go !   Ah ! hear me, I pray you—
it is not for myself I do plead.   It is for de one who is
dearer to me dan life—it is for my husband ; he will be in
danger.   You are young, but you are a good, brave boy.
Oh, surely, it is dat you will pity me when I do tell you dat
I am *Captain O'Neill's wife !* "

Anty Kinahan had drawn nearer to Estelle, and was
watching her anxiously, fearing the serious effect this unwonted excitement might have upon her.

"Me lady ! " said Shilrick, sorrowfully, "sure 'tis me
heart that's sad for yersilf enthirely, for his honour, *Ua
Néill*, *is* in dhanger, but not through anny harm *I'd* be
doin' him—niver, *niver* though *me*. Sure, wasn't it himsilf
that saved me wanst—the last fight we were in togither—
it was afther a sortie our men had made.   I'd somehow got
separated from the others, an' lay wounded an' surrounded
by the enemy ; but 'twas Misther O'Neill rushed into the

very midst av thim, an', fightin' his way through thim, he carried me to a place of safety. Don't ye think thin, me lady," asked the boy, proudly, "that it's mesilf would rayther die this minute than bethray *him?* That the best av blissins may be wid him this dhay an' for iver, is *my* prayer, for all the good he done to me, an' moor than mesilf."

For a few moments Estelle looked earnestly and searchingly at Shilrick ; then, approaching him, she laid her hands on his shoulders.

"Yes, I *do* feel dat I can trust you," she said at last. "Go, den, brave boy, and, oh, may Heaven guide you !"

"An' save thim that's in dhanger this dhay !" added the boy, fervently crossing himself, as he went towards the door, fearful of farther delay ; but looking back at the strange group gathered together, he seemed suddenly to realise his trying position, he felt as one leaving the last friend he had, the last haven of refuge from the coming storm. Once more he spoke, in a low, sobbing voice, as he stretched out his arms to his brother :

"Good-bye, Kerry, darlin' ! Ah ! sure 'tis maybe *farewell;* but don't to be throublin' about mesilf, I'll manage right enough," he added, as his elder brother, hastening towards him, wound his arms protectingly around the brave little form.

"Troth ! ye shan't go, at all, at all," cried Kerry. "*Och, ma bouchaleen!* 'tis yersilf that's not sthrong enough yet to hould out agin all this throuble. Sthay here another dhay, annyhow," he entreated.

"I can't, Kerry," replied Shilrick, firmly, "let me go, dear ! Sure, I'll do me best for all. Good-bye, and Heaven save all here."

Disengaging himself from Kerry's arms, Shilrick hurriedly left the room, murmuring sadly to himself as he went on his way :

"Oh ! why is it that Fate does be playin' this way wid mesilf ? How will I *iver* be able to kape thrue to thim all, enthirely ? "

Little did those, whom Shilrick left behind him in the "Shamrock," dream of the danger, the misery, and sorrow

this poor innocent boy was to endure, of the fierce furnace
of trial and despair in which his truth and honour would be
tested, or of the fearful scene of horror in which they would
next meet him.

The excitement had been too much for Estelle ; she had
hastened, with the others, to the outer door of the hostelry,
but on returning to the room she fainted in Anty's arms, after
they had watched the little red-coated figure disappear in
the distance, along the lonely road.

Shilrick would soon be in barracks, once more among his
friends and comrades, yet in his heart he would still feel alone
—the coming trouble none could share—he could ask neither
help nor counsel, he knew that he must stand alone—that
brave boy, so young in years, yet so steadfast, so tender and
true.

CHAPTER VI.

" Heat not a furnace for your foe so hot
That it may singe yourself : we may outrun
By violent swiftness, that which we run at,
And lose all by over running."

SHAKESPEARE.

The next morning Captain Ellis was seated at the table in his barrack-room, with a curious-looking letter before him ; it was much soiled and crumpled, and appeared as though it had passed through many, and none too particular, hands, ere it had reached its destination. Captain Ellis had read and re-read the uninviting epistle, and seemed still pondering as to the steps he should take with regard to the information it contained. His brows were contracted in deep thought, and there was a stern, grieved expression on his face, as he sat with his head resting on his hands, his eyes still bent upon the open letter which was causing him so much trouble.

"What *shall* I do ?" he exclaimed to himself for the third, or fourth time, as, with an impatient gesture, he swept back the hair from his forehead.

"Poor boy—poor little lad !" he added, with a gentleness that would have surprised many who knew Captain Ellis only as the strict officer, and the firm, although just, disciplinarian.

His reverie was at last disturbed by a knock at the door of his room.

"Come in !" he cried, somewhat testily, being annoyed at the interruption at such a time, when his mind was so harassed. He hastily covered the letter before him, however, and prepared to receive the intruder with as good a grace as possible, being much relieved on finding that his visitors were his friends, Digby, and young Geoghegan, who had so unfortunately distinguished himself at mess the previous evening.

"Ellis !" said Digby, after the usual salutations of the morning had passed between the three friends, "we have just heard that the drummer, Shilrick O'Toole, turned up again last night after we had retired to our rooms. Is this true ?"

"Yes, Digby !" replied Ellis. "But I have stranger news—that Annesley is a prisoner in the hands of the Rebels."

"Impossible !" cried Digby.

"I am sorry to say that it is only too true !" returned the other.

"How did you hear this, Captain?" asked Geoghegan, eagerly.

"From Colonel Corrie. He saw Shilrick last night, but finding that the boy looked worn out and ill, and that he had evidently had some difficulty in reaching the barracks at all, he refrained from tormenting him with questions. Early this morning, however, the drummer was at the Colonel's quarters, anxiously asking to speak to him. It appears that he gave the important information that Annesley had been wandering over the mountains on the afternoon of the day on which he left barracks, and that he had fallen in with that notorious party of the Rebels, known as 'The Bold Boys of Wicklow,' who made him prisoner."

"But how came Annesley there at all ?" asked Digby, wonderingly.

"Ah! that, for some reason best known to himself, Shilrick O'Toole will not tell," replied Ellis, thoughtfully. "I cannot understand it all, yet."

"And where has the boy been all this time ?" demanded Geoghegan, suspiciously.

"He was with Annesley, and was also made prisoner, but contrived to escape."

"Ah! a strange tale," observed Geoghegan. "We must remember the boy is a Roman Catholic and—"

"Geoghegan," struck in Digby, impatiently, "for goodness sake do not begin upon that subject again just now. Let me

beg of you to remember the experience of last night, and
'*Boyne Water*'."

"Well ! anyhow, Shilrick managed to save himself," returned Geoghegan, obstinately.

"Yes !" said Ellis, quietly, "but the boy was most un-
unwilling to leave Annesley, and it was only at his express
desire that he did so."

"*He* says so, of course," remarked the young Orangeman,
doubtfully.

"The Colonel told me that he had questioned and cross-
questioned him on every point," continued Ellis, "but it was of
no avail, the more he asked, the harder and more determined
the boy's face seemed to grow ; he was perfectly respectful,
but firm as a rock."

"But, Ellis !" said Digby, wonderingly, "what on earth
could have caused Annesley to start off to the mountains in
such a manner, and without saying a word to any of us ?
He must have known there would be danger, and though his
bravery is an indisputable fact, yet this was an act of fool-
hardiness and bravado in which I should have imagined he
would have been the last man to indulge, and especially at
such a time, too, when every available officer in our corps is
required to be in readiness for active service."

"And how came the drummer to be with Annesley, Captain ?" asked Geoghegan.

"That we have not yet been able to find out," replied Ellis ;
" and indeed, beyond the mere fact that Shilrick O'Toole has
returned, bringing with him the information that Annesley
is a prisoner in the hands of the Rebels, I know no more than
yourselves. The whole affair is most unaccountable to me."

"What does the Colonel propose doing now?" asked
Digby.

"He intends to send a strong party of our men to the
mountains this afternoon in search of Annesley, and as it is
my turn for that duty, I am to have the command. You,
Digby, I believe, are also to be one of the party," replied
Ellis.

"I am glad of that," said Digby.

"I expect, however," continued Ellis, "that we shall not
start until nightfall now."

"Why this delay, when Annesley is in danger ? " asked Digby, sharply.

"Surely, it would be better to have daylight for the expedition," observed Geoghegan.

"The Colonel must see *this* first," said Ellis, as he slowly and with some hesitation drew forth, from beneath the papers where he had concealed it, the unwelcome letter which had caused him so much annoyance and anxious thought. "I received it about an hour ago from that wretched, sneaking fellow, Stalker, the patrol. He told me that it had been thrust into his hand by some ragged boy, whom he did not know at all, and who scampered off immediately on handing him the letter, with strict injunctions that it was on no account to be given *first* to '*the Irish Colonel,*' but to *the English Officer, the Chief Captain of the Marines at Glencree*, by which I suppose he meant the *senior* captain, and, therefore, I being that individual, during the absence of Annesley, accordingly opened the letter, and I can assure you that when I had read it, I felt that I would rather be the junior subaltern in the battalion than have to act upon the contents of that most diabolical, treacherous letter. But there, Digby and Geoghegan, you can read it for yourselves," added Ellis, as he handed the missive to them.

All was silent in the room, not a word was spoken by either of the three friends, while Digby, with Geoghegan looking over his shoulder, slowly perused the letter that was to prove so disastrous in its consequences to many, but the faces of the young officers now bent over the paper, expressed, only too plainly, the indignation, scorn and horror at the base treachery and cruelty of the writer, as with some difficulty they managed to decipher the very illegible scrawl, and read the following :

"MISTER,

"I guess it has been the wish of the militairey for a long time to get a hold of *Michael Cluny*, the Captain of the 'Bold Boys,' and I calc'late it's the wish of all who are loyal and want to put down the disturbances in Ireland, that this man, calling himself *Cluny*, should be fixed ; he being in conspiracy with Holt, Emmet, and those thar other insurgents. Now, stranger, if it's yer will to bring yer men up about eight o'clock this night, to a place in the mountains called 'The Rebels' Rest,' a small party of the 'Bold Boys' will be on the move, under the command of the very man yer want, *Michael Cluny*. I guess they air intendin' to remove their prisoners to some other locality, so if yer pay attention to my advice, and air around with yer men the time I hev told yer, wa'al, I calc'late yer will fix *Cluny*, an', at the same time, rescue yer officer, an the old priest into the bargain. Don't mind the other Boys, they air helpless enough when their leader is out of the road ; but I reckon yer will hev to be precious slick an' careful, or *Michael Cluny* will slip through yer fingers, for though young, he is an uncommon spry man ; an' it would be a caution to know all the dodges *he* is up to.

"An' now about that thar reward, mister, offered by the Government. I guess *I* am not too proud, nor particklar, to take money honestly and squarely earned, so when yer hev secured yer prisoner safe, I shall come forward an' yer can then hand over the reward promised in those thar posters for the apprehension of *Michael Cluny*, to *me*. I hev sent this notice to you, stranger, for if yer Colonel had read it first I calc'late it's tarnation likely *you* would never hev heard of it, nor yer other officers nayther, considerin' he is Irish, and I guess it's a case of six of one and half-dozen of the other—they air all alike, born traitors. It's my misfortun' to belong to the 'Bold Boys' myself, but I guess it's long since *I* disapproved of them. I should never hev joined them at all, but did so in ignorance, bein' over persuaded by their daring young Captain, an' one called Silas Charleston, an American. I reckon *I'm* weary begging and entreating the Boys to chuck up all this darned nonsense of patriotism—as they call it—and return to their homes, but they won't. I could not leave them after taking the oath, my life would hev been in danger, but *now* I calc'late I'll hev the protection of the militairey, seeing that I hev proved my loyalty and horror of treason, an' being the one to lead to the capture of *Michael Cluny* an' all his Rebil band I'll be entitled to a free pardon as well as the rewards promised. There will be no difficulty about yer men findin' their way to the '*Rebels' Rest* ;' the drummer, Shilrick O'Toole, *knows it well.* I guess yer could not hev a better guide, but as he might deceive yer, having friends among the Rebel band, and secretly favouring them, I calc'late yer had best get that young farmer, Sheymus Malloy, to go with yer men, as well as the boy, he is a tenant of Lord Powerscourt, an' holds with the militairey, he knows all the roads to the mountains. I may conclude this letter by remarking that yer had best keep an eye on that starched-up young Captain of yours, called Annersley ; he, like the drummer, favours the Rebellion in secret, and is a sworn friend and ally of the traitor, *Michael Cluny.* He is with the band now of his own free will, heving come to the mountains with the drummer. So now I hev given fair warning of the treachery in the very midst of yer corps, I reckon, stranger, that it will be considered how I hev worked to keep down the Rebellion, always persuadin' an prayin' of the Boys not to join the cause. I guess I shall hev to give my name now, as I mean to claim the just reward for my valuable services to the British Government, but it must be kept *a strict secret*, or I should not be safe for a day or a hour. Havin' no more to say at present,

"I remain, yours to command,

"THADDEUS MAGIN."

There was a stern expression on the faces of Digby and Geoghegan (who had been reading over his shoulder) as the former slowly and silently returned the Yankee's most villainous letter to his anxious comrade, Captain Ellis.

" Well ! what do you think of it, Digby ? " asked that officer.

" That this man, Thaddeus Magin, is a consummate scoundrel," was Digby's reply.

" A mean, treacherous blackguard !" added Geoghegan, emphatically.

" Exactly *my* opinion!" said Ellis.

" Do you think that the information of such a man is to be relied on ? " queried Digby, doubtfully.

" Certainly!" replied Ellis, " it is evident that he is a most avaricious man, as well as a traitor, and wants the reward."

"And for this he would turn *informer*," said Geoghegan ; all the true Irishman's innate horror of such an action immediately showing itself in words and look, despite his steady loyalty as an officer.

"For the sake of this reward he would ruthlessly sell the lives and liberty of those men, whom I have no doubt *he* has been the chief means of leading on to their own destruction," said Digby, sorrowfully, "and the poor fellows whom this man is so anxious to betray are probably at this moment placing the most implicit faith in his honour. Oh ! how thoroughly I despise a traitor to any cause," he added, contemptuously.

"What is your opinion of the scoundrel's warning concerning Annesley and Shilrick O'Toole ?" asked Geoghegan.

"That the information is the greatest falsehood ever fabricated ! " was the reply ; "but I must take this letter to the Colonel at once, and receive his orders as to when we are to start on this expedition to the mountains," said Ellis, rising reluctantly.

"Stay, Ellis ! " cried Digby, hurriedly, "you surely will not act on such information, and from a source so very untrustworthy as this villain Magin ? "

"Not act on it ? Why, my dear fellow, what else can I do ? " asked Ellis. "You cannot but see, as I do, that this man is anxious for the promised rewards offered for the apprehension of the Rebel Chief, *Michael Cluny,* and any of his band; he has no cause, therefore, to deceive us as to their whereabouts."

"Why not treat the letter with the scorn it deserves, and leave it unanswered and unnoticed ? " said young Geoghegan, hotly.

"I dare not do so, Geoghegan," replied Ellis, seriously. "I dare not pass over such information. Both you and Digby must know the consequences if it were found out afterwards that I had done so; besides, it would be against my principles ; I understand my duty as an English officer, and were it ever so hard, ever so painful, I would not shirk

it. I fear that there is no other course left to me than to take
this letter to the Colonel."

"But, what will he think of the complimentary clause in it
concerning himself?" queried Geoghegan, smiling.

"He will treat it with the contempt it merits," replied
Ellis.

"Oh, Ellis!" said Digby, earnestly, "let me beg of you to
think again before you act in this matter. There is something in such deliberate treachery that is so utterly opposed
to every true and honourable feeling in the heart, and to the
love of fair-play that is second nature to every true British
soldier."

"What, Digby!" exclaimed Ellis, gravely; "are *you* going
to turn in favour of these rascally Rebels now ? I think there
must surely be something in the very air of this country that
is conducive to intrigue and rebellion."

"Sir!" cried Geoghegan, angrily, his face flushed and his
hand clenched, as he stood looking defiantly at Ellis. "Sure
is it making us *all* out Rebels you'd be?" he demanded,
his native brogue asserting itself in the excitement of the
moment.

"No, no," said Digby, in conciliatory tones, "keep cool,
Geoghegan, and do not be trailing those coat tails of yours,
which you always have in readiness, for there is no one to
tread on them at present."

Then laying his hand on Geoghegan's arm to restrain
him from farther speech, knowing, that in the heat of
his temper, the young Irishman might possibly say to his
senior officer that which he might afterwards regret, Digby
turned with some dignity and again addressed Captain Ellis.
"I have to thank you, Ellis, for the compliment you pay
me in accusing me of favouring the Rebels. Far be it from
me to do so, and there can be no one who would more
willingly meet these 'Bold Boys,' and fight it out with them
in a proper, straightforward, soldierly manner; but not in
this way," he added, shuddering. "Oh, not in this way, to
entrap brave men by such a stealthy, cold-blooded stratagem."

"I agree with you in one way, Digby," replied Ellis,
"and I am sincerely sorry that I ever received this contemptible missive. Many of these Rebels are men of the

most daring courage, who are sacrificing their lives for (as they imagine) the good of their country ; and I have heard so much of the exploits of this brave young *Cluny*, that I do not feel at all proud of being the one selected to assist in such a treacherous plan for his capture. However, I *must* do my duty, and we were sent here to put down the Rebellion ; besides, we are forgetting that Annesley is a prisoner in their hands and he must be rescued without delay, so I fear there is no help for it, Digby, I shall have to tell the Colonel of this letter, and I must also arrange for Shilrick O'Toole to accompany us as guide."

"Poor boy!" said Digby, compassionately. "Why should the villain have implicated *him*, and cause him to take such an active part in the betrayal of his own countrymen ? I expect this Thaddeus Magin, in his greed and evident hatred against the Rebel Chief, *Michael Cluny*, will over-reach himself, and find that he, too, is caught in the trap that he has laid for others ; it is often thus with such cold-blooded traitors."

"Can't you get Shilrick O'Toole off this duty, Ellis ?" asked Geoghegan, "it will be deuced hard on *him*."

"The poor lad will be in the deepest distress when he is ordered to go to the mountains with the men," said Digby.

"Yet what can we do ?" asked Ellis ; "there is no one else whom we could thoroughly trust, and probably there is not a peasant in all Wicklow who knows every wild mountain pass better than Shilrick O'Toole. We *must* have a guide. What *can* we do? Ah !" he added, suddenly, as lifting Magin's letter from the table, he hastily re-read it, "I had forgotten, this man mentions a farmer called Sheymus Malloy. Do you know him, Geoghegan !"

"Yes, I know him well," was the reply. "But, though he is loyal and true, you might as well expect to obtain information as to the whereabouts or the movements of the Rebels from a stone wall as hope to find a guide and an *informer* in the person of Sheymus Malloy."

"Nevertheless, we must make the attempt," returned Ellis, "if *he* will not help us, I am afraid there is nothing for· it but to employ the drummer. He is on duty somewhere to-day, but, if we can find no other guide, he must be re-lieved. We are bound to take notice of this letter, and to hasten to the rescue of Annesley. Geoghegan, you know where this man Malloy is to be found; will you and Digby accompany me to his farm, and add your persuasions to mine?"

"Not for twenty years' pay," answered Geoghegan, ener-getically, "and that is saying a great deal, considering the manner in which my *English* creditors have been tormenting me, and my father being at present a landed proprietor with no income. Worse luck to the same creditors; sure they ought to feel honoured by having the custom of an officer in his Majesty's service, and a Geoghegan of Ballycrankie into the bargain. No, Captain," he added, seriously, "I don't mind showing you the road to Sheymus Malloy's farm, but for no consideration in the wide world would I make such a request to him. There is no harm in *trying*, but I can tell you beforehand, that you are going on a fruitless errand."

"Well!" said Ellis, sighing, "you Irish are, certainly, a people difficult to understand; such a strange mixture of loyalty and treason, of right and wrong. But there, we must lose no more time. I shall first take this letter to the Colonel and receive his orders, afterwards, you and I, Digby, will go to Malloy's farm. I know it would be Annesley's wish that we should, if possible, get his little favourite off this disagreeable duty."

"I think I know the way to Ballymacreagh Farm, so we need not trouble Geoghegan," said Digby, coldly; for he thought that, being a countryman of his own, Sheymus Malloy might have been more easily influenced by the young Irish officer, than by either Ellis or himself, and that he might possibly look with less suspicion upon any request made by Geoghegan.

By this time, Ellis having buckled on his sword, and being fully equipped, the three officers left the room and repaired to the Colonel's office.

Little did they think how full of import would be this expedition to the mountains; or of the sorrow and despair that would, ere the rising of another dawn, fall upon so many in whom they were deeply interested. Bad as they knew Thaddeus Magin must be, from the letter he had written and which they had just read ; cruel, avaricious, and unscrupulous as it had appeared to them, yet they dreamed not of the deadly cunning and treachery in this man's nature that had caused him to suggest the choice of Shilrick O'Toole, or Sheymus Malloy, as guide ; he knew well, that when either the drummer, or the young farmer appeared upon the scene with the soldiers, the Rebels would naturally conclude that *they* had betrayed the band, and that he would thus avert all suspicions from himself.

With infinite care and diabolical cunning, he had plotted, and planned, until it appeared to him that the coveted reward was almost within his grasp, his savage revenge almost accomplished.

He recked nought of the death and desolation that must follow, of the proud hearts languishing for years in imprisonment, of the bitter tears and sighs of those mourning for the dear ones, whose loved voices they would never hear again, whose smiles would never more gladden their hearts in this world.

In truth, Fortune for a time seemed to favour the schemes of the traitor Magin—Fate played into his hands, and he saw not the shadowy forms of Justice and Vengeance hovering near him ; he heard not the footsteps of Nemesis, as silently, but swiftly, she followed in his track.

CHAPTER VII.

"What Fates impose, that men must needs abide,
It boots not to resist both wind and tide."

SHAKESPEARE.

Colonel Corrie was no less annoyed at the contents of Thaddeus Magin's letter, than were the young officers of his corps, who had just read it, but after much serious thought, he could only come to the same conclusion as Captain Ellis.

Unless they could, by any means, induce Sheymus Malloy to act as guide to the party of Marines, on their expedition to the mountains that evening, there would be no other course left open to him than to give orders for the immediate relief of Shilrick O'Toole, who was on duty at an old tower, then used as a guard-room, and forming one of the most important out-posts at some distance from Glencree Barracks. The Colonel felt instinctively that the order for the drummer to guide the men to the "Rebels' Rest" would meet with opposition, and he thought, with horror, of the consequences that must follow any such opposition, more especially during the time of warfare, and when it would be regarded as treason. He therefore urged Captain Ellis to use every effort to persuade Sheymus Malloy to accede to their request, but it was with a heavy heart he did so, for he, like Lieutenant Geoghegan, had but little hope that the determined young farmer (loyal though he was known to be), would agree to aid, in any way, in the capture of the young Rebel Chief and his band of "Bold Boys."

Inwardly burning with indignation that the villain, Magin,

had chosen to select the men of his corps to perform such an unpleasant duty, the Colonel yet knew that he dare not allow the letter to pass unnoticed, as by so doing he would be, in a measure, aiding and abetting in the concealment of the Rebel band ; he also felt the greatest anxiety concerning the fate of Captain Annesley, and it was certain that there must be no delay in sending the Marines to his rescue. It was well that the Yankee had given the information as to when, and where they might find the missing officer, for Shilrick O'Toole had not been able, even had he been willing, to tell where the Rebels had taken Annesley and Father Bernard, nor even in what direction they had gone after he had escaped ; and, on farther consideration, Colonel Corrie thought that things might not be so bad after all, for the drummer was so devoted to his Captain, that he would probably be anxious to assist in his rescue, and the more readily overcome his scruples with regard to turning "*informer*"—as the boy would no doubt call it—and guiding the party of Marines to the "Rebels' Rest."

Nevertheless, the Colonel thought it well to be prepared for all emergencies, and so was anxious for Ellis to make the attempt to secure the services of Sheymus Malloy.

"You can but try, Ellis," he said at last, after a long and serious consultation, "but I fear you will not succeed. Upon my honour," he added, indignantly, " I would give much to have a hold this minute of the scoundrel who wrote that letter. Would there be any fate too bad for such a contemptible blackguard ? It makes my blood boil, when I think that we shall not only have to hand over the reward to him, but also to allow him to go free with the price in his treacherous hands of the lives of these brave men, for brave they are, though they be Rebels. Ay ! and from all we hear, their young leader, *Michael Cluny*, is as noble-hearted a patriot as ever set foot on Irish soil, or took up arms for old Erin's sake, one of the *real genuine* sort, he is giving his life for his country. But I am detaining you, Ellis. There is no time to lose, we have but a few hours before the men must start for the mountains. Go then, and God speed you on your errand ! Poor little Shilrick ! if you are not successful, it will indeed be a hard trial for him—duty against inclination. You are looking gravely at me, Ellis," added the Colonel, smiling. "You are, maybe, thinking that the words of the immortal bard might apply to myself—

> 'Which is the side that I must go withal?
> I am with both.'

But, indeed, I feel the deepest sympathy for our poor little drummer, knowing, as I do, the fierce battle he will have to fight in his brave, true heart, between his duty, his affection for Annesley, and the deep-rooted prejudices of his race. I pity him—from my heart I pity him. There, Ellis! I have said enough—more than enough. You said, I think, that Digby was going with you to assist in persuading Sheymus Malloy. Do your best, then—you two young fellows. Sure, I need not appeal to your feelings, and I need scarcely give you any directions as to the manner of executing so difficult and delicate a mission. I know that you will both act in this —as in every other case—like officers and gentlemen."

With these words, Colonel Corrie rose from his seat, and, after gathering up a few papers which lay scattered on the table before him, and giving some commands to an orderly, who was standing at the door, he left the office, followed by Captain Ellis, who, on returning to his own quarters, found his friend, Lieutenant Digby, waiting for him, and together, without loss of time, they proceeded on their errand to Sheymus Malloy's farm.

They had just arrived at the entrance-gate leading to Ballymacreagh Farm, when they saw approaching, from an opposite direction, a tall, stalwart young man in farmer's attire, carrying a gun over his shoulder, and some long eagle's feathers in his hand.

"Why, here is Malloy, himself!" exclaimed Digby. "How fortunate that we have found him at home."

"The top av the mornin' to yer honours," said Sheymus, politely raising his soft felt *caubeen* as he approached the two officers.

"Good morning, Malloy!" returned Digby, who, on the strength of having met the young farmer before, when in the company of Annesley, thought he should take the initiative and, as it were, "open fire."

"You have been shooting, I see," remarked Ellis, entirely at a loss how to commence proceedings, especially when he met the gaze of the frank, honest-looking eyes, and noted the firm, resolute expression on the face before him. "We shall not easily shake the determination of such a man as this," was his inward comment.

"Troth then, yer honour! 'twas wid the intintion av shootin' I went out, but sorra thing have *I* sane this same mornin,' at all, at all, barrin' a big aigle," replied Sheymus.

"I see you have some of the wing feathers; they are beautiful specimens, too, splendidly marked," observed Ellis.

"Thrue for ye, sir," agreed Sheymus, spreading them out more prominently for the inspection of the officers, "sure, I've niver sane finer."

"They are for your sweetheart, I suppose, Malloy?" said Digby, smiling. "Is it not the custom in this country to reserve such offerings especially for love gifts?"

"It is, sir," answered Sheymus, with a shy laugh, "an' troth it isn't mesilf that would be conthradictin' yer honour, when it's for that same purpose I'm kapin' these illigant feathers."

"This is not advancing the business we have in hand," said Ellis aside to Digby.

"No, Ellis, I have been wondering when, and how, you intended to commence," was the reply, spoken in the same low tones.

"Better go in for it at once," murmured Ellis, at the same time wishing himself miles away from Sheymus Malloy's farm, or that he had followed Geoghegan's example, and not come at all.

"Malloy!" he began at last, in desperation, "I, that is, we—came over here to-day expressly to see you and to ask—that is to—"

Here the Captain came to a dead pause, he gazed earnestly, first at the sky above him, then at the ground beneath his feet, but from neither could he gain the desired inspiration; he appeared to take an especial interest in two cows which were browsing quietly in an adjacent field; but they proved of no assistance to him; for once in his life the shrewd, clever, eminently practical officer was in a dilemma.

Lieutenant Digby, however, seeing how matters stood, gallantly came to the rescue.

"We had some news for you—some important business to talk over, don't you know," he said, turning to the farmer.

"Oh!" replied Sheymus Malloy, looking the surprise he felt. "Sure, then 'tis in yondher yer honours will be afther comin'; bad luck to me manners that I'd be lettin' ye sthand out here in the bitther cowld all this thime an' not axin yez inside me dures before. Ye're kindly welcome!" he added, as he preceded Ellis and Digby up the path leading to the house and ushered them in with a courtly grace that would have done honour to a nobleman; proffering his hospitality in that sincere, generous, whole-hearted manner which is a peculiar characteristic of the Irish and Scotch people, whether they be rich or poor, dwellers in a lordly castle, or a humble shanty, there is ever the same warm, kindly welcome for "the stranger within their gates." Sheymus Malloy did not attempt to satisfy his curiosity regarding the unexpected visit of the two officers, until he had seen both his guests seated at the table with steaming *cruiskeens* of *poteen*, and a piled-up platter of cakes before each of them, of which he had insisted on their partaking, and which they did not like to refuse, lest they might give offence to their young host.

At last, however, having fulfilled all the duties of hospitality, Sheymus took up his position on one side of the wide hearth, on which burnt a large peat fire, and leaning against the high, old fashioned, carved mantel-board, he turned to Digby, whom he thought seemed most disposed to be communicative, and to act as spokesman, and addressed him.

"Sure, sir, ye said this minute that 'twas impoorthant business ye had wid mesilf—what can I do for yer honours?" he asked, courteously.

"I think, Malloy, that you know an Irish officer belonging to our corps, called Captain Annesley?" inquired Digby.

"Ye mane Kerry O'Toole's fosther brother, sir? Troth, I know him as well as mesilf," was the reply, "sure its fine divarshions the three av us would be afther havin' many a thime whin we were all bits av gossoons togither."

"I suppose you have not yet heard the news that he has

been made prisoner by the Rebels?" asked Ellis, now summoning up courage to follow Digby's lead.

"Sure an' I have, yer honour!" answered Sheymus, quietly, "'tis ill news thravels fast; it was tould me at dhaybreak this mornin'!"

"By whom?" demanded Ellis, sharply.

"I ax pardon, sir," returned Sheymus, " but I'd raythur not answer that quistion."

"Ah!" exclaimed Ellis, significantly.

"You would be sorry to hear the news, I am sure, Malloy," struck in Digby, afraid from the tone in which Ellis spoke of the turn affairs might take.

"Troth an' I was, yer honour," returned Sheymus.

"He must be rescued at once," said Ellis.

"Thrue for ye, sir!"

"But how? That is the question."

"Faith then, 'tis yer honour that's right enough there. *That's* the quistion; an' begorrah! it just bothers mesilf enthirely to answer that same," replied Sheymus, looking cautiously at Captain Ellis.

"A party of our men are ordered to proceed to the mountains, to-night," said Digby.

"And we shall require a guide," added Ellis.

Something in the expression of the officer's face as he spoke, and the tone of anxiety in his voice, led Sheymus Malloy to suspect the cause of his visit, and those were times when, a man's suspicions once roused, he was immediately put upon his guard and was therefore careful of every word he uttered.

There was that also in the quiet demeanour, the calm voice, and even in the easy, graceful attitude of the young farmer that, in his present mood, proved most exasperating to Captain Ellis.

"Sure, yes!" replied Malloy, slowly, and looking fixedly at the officer. "There's niver a lie in it, but yer honours *will* be nadin' a guide. It's not over safe aven for thim that's been accusthomed to be wandherin' over the mountains afther nightfall; an' there's some purty bhogs, an' hollows, an' precipices that would bother sthrangers enthirely, an' sure there's parts that would swallow up an army av souldiers that didn't know their way."

"Nevertheless, we have orders to go," said Ellis. "*So go we must.*"

"Do *you* know of any one who would go with us as guide?" asked Digby.

"Any one who did so would be well paid for it," said Ellis.

In an instant Digby felt the serious mistake his brother officer had made, and feared that his words might prove fatal to their cause, but he knew that for him to interfere would only make matters worse ; the words had been spoken, they could not be re-called, and all he could do was to wait, and listen anxiously for Malloy's reply. It came at last ; in a tone of haughty sarcasm the young farmer spoke, but more to himself than as if he were addressing Captain Ellis.

"Sure 'tis the *English* gintlemen that like to be spoortin' their money in the eyes av thim that's not so well off as thimsilves. No ! " he added, looking straight at Ellis. "The sorra wan do *I* know who *would* go, yer honour, moor praise to thim, enthirely."

"We understood that *you* would be able and willing to help us," said Ellis.

"*Able* enough, sir ; but not *willin'*," replied Malloy. "'Tis proud I'd be if I could sarve yer honours in *anny other* way, but not to do what ye're axin' me now."

"Ah! I have been mistaken in you," said Ellis, sternly, "I considered that the fact of your being *a loyal subject* would have caused you *at once* to comply with our request, and to consent *yourself* to accompany us to the mountains as guide."

"Is it *me*, yer honour ! " exclaimed the farmer, indignantly, and with heightened colour.

"Yes, why not ? " asked the Captain, wonderingly.

"You must not be offended with my friend," Digby hastened to explain. "You said that you would be proud to serve us, and from the fact of your being Lord Powerscourt's tenant, we naturally imagined that you would be as desirous as ourselves to use every effort to quell this Rebellion, which cannot prove otherwise than the ruin of your country."

"I did not intend to offer *you* money, Malloy, if that is what you are so indignant about," said Ellis. "I heard that you were loyal and true, but I see that I have been misinformed ; we are in a perfect nest of traitors here," he added, rising hastily.

"Thim's hard words to use, sir!" returned Malloy, with flashing eyes, and threatening voice.

"Possibly!" replied Ellis, coolly. "Yet what else can I say, when you persist in refusing such small aid as we now ask of you?"

"An' *is* it *small* aid ye're axin av me, sir?" demanded the young farmer, proudly. "Troth thin, it couldn't well be moor. 'Tis maybes from no grand quality like yer honour that I come, but it's from a good ould yeoman sthock, for all that ; an' we've thried to kape the honour bright in our hearts, through many ginerations, an' begorrah," he added, passionately, "this is the first thime that anny wan has daured to doubt that same honour, at all, at all."

"I have neither the time, nor the inclination to inquire into the genealogy or the traditions of your family, Malloy," returned Ellis, impatiently. "No doubt they were most worthy people ; and I have not in any way questioned *your* honour."

"Then why ax *me*, sir, to be turnin' *informer*, an' to guide a party av your souldiers to the mountains?" demanded Malloy, passionately. "Sure it's the poor Bhoys that are hunted hard enough as it is, by the human blood-hounds that's afther thim from morn till night, widout mesilf helpin' to dhrive thim from the only home an' shilter they have now."

"Pardon me!" said Ellis, "I did not think that Lord Powerscourt favoured the Rebels, and I have always con- sidered, from what I have heard, that his tenants, one and all, shared his lordship's loyal opinions. I find, however, that we have been egregiously mistaken, therefore I must apolo- gize for this visit. I might have known what to expect," he added, contemptuously. "Loyalty is evidently a plant that can never flourish on Irish soil."

"Oh, come away, Ellis!" whispered Digby, anxiously, laying his hand on the Captain's arm and attempting to draw him towards the door.

"Wan moment, yer honour!" cried Malloy, indignantly, "Lord Powerscourt does *not favour* the Ribils, nor the risin'

in our counthry, 'tis himself thinks that 'the Bhoys' are wrong
enthirely in what they're doin'. But jist ax him if he'd approve
av anny av *his* paple turnin' *informers*. Och, begorrah !
maybes it's his lordship that wouldn't have him that done
it, shown out av his dures an' aff av his land purty quick,
annyhow."

"Oh, indeed ! " returned Ellis, sarcastically, taking no
notice of Digby's energetic signals and evident anxiety to
end the discussion. "Then I suppose that is the reason
why my Lord Powerscourt and his family have been allowed
to reside here unmolested through the very worst of the
Rebellion ; while others had to fly the country in terror for
their lives ! "

"No, yer honour," replied Malloy, with dignity. " 'Tis
yersilf that's wrong there enthirely. The sacrit av his lordship's safety here, is that he loves an' thrusts his paple, an'
in return they love an' thrust him, moor power to his honour,
an' long may the dhark throuble an' sorrow be kept from *his*
home."

"I am very sorry if we have offended you, Malloy," said
Digby, courteously, "but, believe me, it was quite unin-
tentional."

For a moment the farmer stood looking admiringly at the
bright, honest face of the young officer—"the peacemaker,"
as Digby was often called by his comrades—then, with a
smile he said, kindly :

"Sure, *you* have not offended me, sir, tis yer heart that's
too good for that, an' I sane the thrue gintleman in ivery
word ye'd be spakin'."

"You see our English ways are so *very* different from
yours, that we scarcely understand each other," said Ellis,
coldly. "Come, Digby," he added, "we are only wasting
time and words here."

"*Our* ways different from *yours*, is it ? " exclaimed Malloy,
contemptuously. "Troth, I'm glad to hear it, sir ; if the
bhoys in the counthry where you come from would be the
mane blackguards enough to do what ye've axed av mesilf
this dhay."

"You see our opinions upon *that* point, and with regard to
duty, differ widely, Malloy, so we had better drop the sub-

ject," returned Ellis. "As I have said, we are only losing time. I must go at once and arrange for the drummer, Shilrick O'Toole, to be relieved from guard to-night, for he will have to be our guide."

Malloy started, and glanced anxiously at Captain Ellis. "Och, sure yer honour wouldn't be afther forcin' the poor little gossoon to go wid ye ? " he asked, earnestly. "Oh ! don't ax *him*, 'twill nigh break his heart if he's ordhered to do this."

"I have no alternative now," said Ellis, coldly.

"He'll refuse—sure, I know he will," continued Malloy.

"My good man ! you do not know what you are talking about," returned the officer, impatiently. "He *dare not* make any objection ; he is quite aware of the consequences of a soldier disobeying orders, more especially at such a time as this."

"Shilrick O'Toole is no coward, yer honour, an' I know that the bhoy would rayther suffer death than bethray his own counthrymen," replied the farmer, determinedly.

"You are right, Malloy," said Digby, sorrowfully, "Shilrick is a brave little lad, full of real pluck and determination. I only wish we could have saved him from this trial. Captain Annesley, too, is deeply attached to him, and he will be grieved that any trouble should have come to the boy while he was absent."

"A soldier must do his duty, however disagreeable it may be," said Ellis. "Others have had to do so before young O'Toole. We must leave you now, Malloy, but first allow me to express my regret if you have felt hurt at anything I have said ; I did not intend my words to be personal, I was speaking in a general sense. You should not be so ready to take offence."

"Och, niver mind, sir ! sure may the good luck be wid yer honours, an' may the thime come whin ye larn to know our counthrymen betther."

After a courteous leave-taking on both sides, and many thanks from the officers for the kindly hospitality they had received from the young farmer, Ellis and Digby returned to barracks to inform Colonel Corrie of the unsuccessful issue of their interview with Malloy.

CHAPTER VIII.

" Thou see'st we are not all alone unhappy,
This wide and universal theatre
Presents more woeful pageants than the scene
Wherein we play in."

SHAKESPEARE.

Although Captain Ellis and Lieutenant Digby had been
unable to shift their burden of anxiety on to the shoulders
of Sheymus Malloy, yet much of the weight of trouble had
fallen upon the young farmer's heart.

For long after the officers had left him he sat buried in
thought, while he smoked his *dhudeen* by the side of the large
peat fire, his eyes fixed with a far, unseeing gaze upon the
bright embers. Over and over again he pondered in his
mind how he should act for the best, and if he could, by any
means, warn the " Bold Boys " of their danger, without being
himself suspected by the military. For his own safety
he cared nothing ; it was the thought of Lord Powerscourt
alone that caused him to hesitate. Sheymus· Malloy would
rather have incurred any danger himself, than have the
thought on his conscience that so many of his brave countrymen were in deadly peril, and that he had not put forth one
effort to save them ; but he also felt that he must be cautious,
for he, being Lord Powerscourt's principal, and most trusted
tenant, any act of treason on his part might cause the suspicion of the English Government to fall upon the landlord to
whom he was much attached. For generations past the
tenantry of the Powerscourt family had proved themselves
loyal subjects and now the slightest deviation from this rule

would most probably attract the notice of the military and naturally give rise to the supposition that his lordship was secretly favouring the Rebellion.

Having been born and bred on the Powerscourt estate, Sheymus Malloy's principles and opinions were decidedly *against* the insurgents, but, on the other hand, hearing of their danger, and the manner in which they were to be entrapped, without a chance of defending themselves, his sympathies were, Irish-like, immediately enlisted on the side of his patriotic countrymen, who had evidently been so basely betrayed; their peril appealed to his manhood, and he resolved to warn them, if it were possible to do so without endangering the lives and the liberty of others.

Then he thought sadly of the coming trial for the poor little drummer, who was so much liked by all who knew him, and after much anxious consideration, the kindly young farmer decided that he might help him out of his difficulty, so far, if he could only contrive to get a warning conveyed to the Rebels, then, even should Shilrick O'Toole be forced to go as guide to the mountains, he might do so without betraying his countrymen; as the "Bold Boys" would, in that case, have time and opportunity to secure their own safety.

At last Sheymus, having determined on, and arranged his course of action, rose hastily, threw aside his *dhudeen* and, again taking up his gun and the eagle's feathers, left the farm-house and proceeded in the direction of Thalia Coghlan's shanty, hoping to see her on his way to the "Shamrock," where he made certain that he should meet some of the Rebel band, by whom he could send his warning; but, if not, he had decided on continuing his way up the mountains on pretence of shooting wild fowl, his gun being sufficient proof of his purpose.

Sheymus had not gone far on his road before he met Thalia Coghlan. At first, she did not appear to notice his approach, her step was slow and wearied, the hood of her red cloak had fallen back over her shoulders, displaying to the gaze of her devoted lover a face that was perfectly colourless, and on which there were deep lines of care and sorrow, eyes that were full of unutterable despair; all these traces of grief caused the greatest pain to Sheymus Malloy, for he felt

that *he* could not remove them ; strive as he would he could
not bring back the light of happiness to those eyes, nor the
bright, radiant smile that used, like a sunbeam, to gladden the
hearts of those who loved Thalia Coghlan in the days that
were gone.

It was with many a pang of sorrow and impatience that
Sheymus asked of himself, again and again, was it to be always thus ?   Was he for ever to pour out the great wealth
of his love and meet no return this side of the grave ?
Would Thalia, in the years to come—despite his earnest
pleading and yearning affection—still persist in clinging to
the memory of a man who, to say the least, had mistrusted
her upon the first breath of suspicion, and even treated her,
as Sheymus thought, with harshness and contempt when
the girl's faithful love for him had been so apparent, that
even his rival could read it in every look, word, and action.
Was his deep, unselfish affection to be wasted ?   All these
queries, from time to time, passed through the mind of the
warm-hearted young farmer, but the future alone could answer them.

There was no kind friend to bid him take heart—to be of
good courage, to entreat him not to allow the disappointments, and the crosses that he must so surely meet in his path
through this weary world, to mar his true, honourable life.

Longfellow, one of the most heart-stirring, hope-inspiring
poets of *our* day, has said, and said truly—

> " Affection never was wasted,
> If it enrich not the heart of another, its waters returning
> Back to their springs, like the rain, shall fill them full of refreshment;
> That which the fountain sends forth returns again to the fountain."

When Sheymus met Thalia Coghlan, she was on her way
to a shanty at some distance from her own home, and in-
habited by a family called Murphy.   She was there frequently, and, indeed, spent every moment of her leisure in
assisting the poor, over-wrought mother in her care of eight
very refractory children, and a husband who was dying of
decline, and required constant attention.

At the time of Granny Coghlan's death, and all through

Thalia's long illness that followed, when she lay for weeks hovering between life and death, Mrs. Murphy, despite all her own heavy burden of care and trouble, had proved a ministering angel to the friendless girl, and, although poor in this world's goods, she was immeasurably rich in that most beautiful trait of character, which is nearly always to be found among the Irish poor, who will share their last crust, or the last " pratee," with their still poorer neighbours.

It is true that Mrs. Murphy had some secret help from Malloy. Without that she could not have provided the many little luxuries, and even necessaries, required for her young invalid, but, of all she had, she gave ungrudgingly, neither hoping for, nor expecting, any return, knowing well that Thalia, on her recovery, would, owing to her enforced idleness for so long, be in a state of destitution.

The poor girl had since felt that she could not do enough to show her gratitude for the kindness that had been bestowed upon her when she was left, alone and desolate, in sickness and sorrow; while all blamed, and none seemed to trust her save the Murphys and Sheymus Malloy. She had been indefatigable in her attempts to earn money for the family who had ever been her great trial, but were as dear to her as though they had been of her own flesh and blood.

Unfortunately the flower season was over, but no opportunity did Thalia lose of earning an honest penny by other means, however hard the work offered might chance to be.

Even now, as she was approaching Sheymus, her thoughts were intent upon some scheme by which she might help the mother, and add to the funds of the family, which were then at a very low ebb.

Yet, as she thought of their heavy trials, there stole into her own sad heart the feeling that—with all their poverty, which at times reached to the very verge of starvation, in spite of their struggles to pay a harsh English land agent who was constantly raising the rent on them, until it amounted to far more than the value of the piece of ground, and the miserable mud cabin they held on lease—they were happier than her, for *she* had neither friends nor kindred. The remembrance came to her at that moment, of some words of Mrs. Murphy, spoken a few days before, in reply to Lady Mabel

O'Hara, who had been paying a kindly visit, and had expressed her warmest sympathy for the poor, weary mother in her anxieties and many cares, some of "the childer" having been especially mischievous, and her husband requiring all the attention she could give him.

"Sure, me lady," Mrs. Murphy had said, "an' they do be stirrin' an' frolicsome some dhays, an' up to all thim soort av divarsions, enthirely, moor by thoken, it often happens that way whin my poor bhoy is wakest an' wants the most care; but, d'ye see, childer must be childer, we can't be puttin' the sinse into thim bafore nathure intinded. Glory be to God! they kape brave an' hearty, an' that's all we can look to, me lady; an', troth, *I* wouldn't exchange all me throubles for the greatest wealth ye could hape on me, if I'd to give up me poor ailin' bhoy yondher, or *wan* av thim swate, innocint childer that's so dear to me heart."

It was then that Thalia had felt most keenly her own lonely life. In truth, she could not say that she was quite friendless, as long as Mrs. Murphy and her family lived, not to speak of the faithful and devoted Sheymus Malloy; but to the former she was bound by no ties of blood or kindred, and in the years to come the children would grow up and go out into the world, probably forgetting her, much as they loved and clung to her now; while, as far as the young farmer was concerned, she had repeatedly refused to give him her love, and she knew that he would not for ever be content with mere friendship.

Yet there were times when the dreary future would, like a vista, stretch itself before her weary eyes, and she would see, as in a dream, the long, sad years when she would be left alone, without friends or kindred, without *one* heart to call her own, without even a *home* worthy of the sacred name. Then it was that the thought would come to her— was she wise thus to reject the shelter of a good man's heart and home, a love so generously offered to her? Oh! not *wise*, perhaps, but she could not so wrong him as to take all and give nought in return. And this was the subject of Thalia's deep reverie, when she suddenly raised her eyes and discovered Sheymus Malloy himself standing before her.

Owing to Kerry O'Toole's secret having been kept so well,

Thalia was still under the impression that her lover had been drowned on the night of the quarrel, which had proved so fatal to her life's peace and happiness ; but Sheymus Malloy had refrained, hitherto, from reminding her, or from claiming the fulfilment of her promise to him ; he had hoped, and earnestly striven, to win her love before again urging her to become his wife. At last, however, he had grown weary of waiting, and hoping against hope, his patience had been often most severely tried, yet he seemed no nearer to the attainment of his heart's desire ; he had, therefore, determined that very morning once more to try his fate and, if possible, to win Thalia's willing consent to accept his offer.

"Sheymus !" she cried, in a low, startled voice, for there was something in the expression of his face, and a look of quiet determination in the eyes that met hers, which caused her to regard him anxiously, and to wait in some trepidation for his words of greeting.

"Why, Thalia ! light av me life !—is it yersilf, darlin' ? Sure, an' ye tould me it's at home ye'd be all the mornin', an' 'tis mesilf was on the road to see ye this minute," said Sheymus, in an aggrieved tone.

"So I did be thinkin' av sthayin' at home, for I had the work to do ; but an hour ago wan av the childer came wid a missage from Misthress Murphy, sayin' she'd be mighty glad if I could go over an' hilp her, as there was a hape of work to get through, an' no wan to do it, barrin' mesilf at all, at all, so 'tis on me way there I am now."

"An' what call has Misthress Murphy, or anny other wan, to be afther sendin' for yersilf that way ?" asked Sheymus, indignantly. "Sure what would she have done if ye hadn't been near, at all ?   Troth, its hard enough wrought ye are annyhow, widout workin' yer life out for others, an' that's what ye're doin' now, Thalia *mavourneen.*"

"Ah, Sheymus !" replied Thalia, earnestly. "Sure, there's no wan, in all the wide world, that has so much right to be axin' for *my* help as Misthress Murphy. When I was left alone an' in throuble, an' near dyin', didn't she tend me, an' watch over me night an' dhay ? Poor as they were, didn't ivery wan av the family share wid me all they had, spendin' their thime, an' the money they could ill spare, on

the lonely, desolate colleen in her poverty an' sorrow ?   Oh,
Sheymus ! is there *annything* I could do that would repay
thim for all they done for me ? "

Sheymus did not tell Thalia, as he might have done, how
it was *his* generosity that enabled the Murphys to do so
much for·her ; it is true their hearts were willing enough,
and each member of the family was ready to use every
effort, to make any sacrifice for her ; they would have done
all they could had there been no Sheymus Malloy to help
them, but without the assistance of the young farmer it
would not have been in their power to provide all that was
absolutely required for her during her long and serious illness.   Of this, however, Thalia neither knew nor guessed,
for Sheymus had bound the whole of the Murphy family
over to secrecy.

" But sure, darlin', it's yersilf that's just worn out enthirely,
ye thake naythur rest nor pleasure," remonstrated Sheymus.

" *Rest* ! *pleasure* !" repeated the girl, bitterly.   " Ah,
where would *I* iver find thim *now* ?   Sure it isn't much heart
I same to have for work or anny other thing, but I couldn't be
idle, there'd be no rest for me in that, for though me two
hands might be still, yet me mind would be busy wid the
dhays that are gone, an' if I'd sit down an be thinkin' av me
sorrow an' loss, sure I belave 'twould dhrive me mad
enthirely."

Here the poor girl fairly broke down, and burying her
face in her hands she wept bitterly, while Sheymus remained silently watching her for some moments, unwilling
to speak until she was calmer, but listening in deep distress
to the despairing sobs which from time to time shook her
slight frame.

" Ah, Thalia, Thalia, *acuishla machree* !" he at last
murmured, softly. " If I could only hilp to make the sorrow
lighter for ye to bear, darlin', 'tis happy I'd be."

" Oh, Sheymus ! sure there's no wan can do that ! " she
replied, mournfully, raising her tear-stained face to the kindly
one bending over her, so full of pity and tenderness ; " no
wan in this world, for the dead can niver be brought to life
agin.   Oh ! " she cried, mournfully, " if I could only see
himsilf wanst moor that I could tell him all he axed me the

night we parted, that I might let him know how thrue I was to him."

"Maybes he does know it, darlin'," said Sheymus, kindly, "'tis said by some, that those who are gone from us know what's goin' on among thim they'd loved here below. Can't ye thry an' thake comfort from that thought, *mavourneen*, for sure what's the use av wearin' yer heart out graavin' for the past, an' what can't be althered."

"That's thrue for ye, Sheymus, but it's the bitther remorse will be wid me all me life that I wouldn't aise Kerry's mind by tellin' him what he axed that night," said the poor girl, sadly; as, drawing the hood of her cloak over her head, she prepared to continue on her way.

"I must lave ye now, Sheymus; Misthress Murphy will be waitin' for me."

"Sthay wan moment, Thalia," said Sheymus, holding out the eagle's feathers to her, "look what I've got for ye, d'ye see how I've kept ye in me mind, though 'tis nadeless to say so, for sure 'tis yersilf knows well there's not a moment in the dhay that ye're not in it."

"No! no, I can't thake thim, Sheymus," cried Thalia, gently putting his offering aside. "'Tis the aigle's feathers that's a swateheart's gift, an' sure *I* can *niver* be *your* swateheart."

"What is it ye mane, Thalia," asked Sheymus, anxiously. "Didn't ye give me yer word that night on the ould bridge, that aven if *I thried to save* Kerry O'Toole, ye'd be me own wife, an' thry to give me the love I've wanted an' axed for so long ago from yersilf?"

"Sheymus! sure ye have the kind heart an' will listhen to what I'd be sayin' now," pleaded Thalia. "I thought maybes ye'd forgotten—I hoped that ye wouldn't remind me av me promise. Oh! how I've been hopin' ye'd niver spake av that night agin. Ye know well that I'd thry to kape me word to yersilf; but ye can niver know how hard that trial would be—sure it would wear me out wid sorrow —an break me heart enthirely."

"Those are hard words to be spakin' to mesilf, Thalia!" interrupted Sheymus, sternly.

Thalia did not reply at once, and Sheymus stood leaning

on his gun, regarding her silently, with determination written
upon every line of his expressive countenance. On glancing
at him the girl knew that he would not yield, that he would
remain firm as a rock to his purpose, yet, in her despair, she
made one more attempt; with a voice trembling with emotion,
and her hands laid pleadingly on his, she spoke :

"Sheymus, ye said just now that ye'd be happy enthirely
if there was annythin' ye could do for me.   Ah, sure there *is*
somethin' ye can do now—this minute—if 'tis yer *will* to
do it."

"What is it ye want av me, Thalia *cora-machree ?*" he
asked, gently.

" To relase me from the promise, I made to yersilf, an'
sure, 'tis me prayers an' best blissing, that'll be wid ye ontil
the last dhay av me life.   Oh, Sheymus ! " she cried, entreatingly, "ye *will* do as I ax?   'Twas a mad promise
enthirely—I scarce knew what I was sayin', at the thime."

" Mad or no, ye gave it yersilf, Thalia, av yer own free
will," he returned, gravely.   " An' troth, 'tis hard on mesilf
that ye'd want to be withdrawin' it now, whin ye should
rayther be thinkin' av kapin' it.   Sure I don't see the good
that this puttin' off the dhay is to do either to yersilf, or me
or the bhoy that's gone."

"Oh, Sheymus ! ye wouldn't be afther forcin' me to kape
by what I said that night."

" I think that a promise is a promise, Thalia, an' I tell ye
that ye gave yours widout bein' axed for it."

" Och, *wirra, wirra* I " cried the girl, hopelessly.   " It was
all to save Kerry's life !—an' to kape him from that awful
crime, that I done it."

" I'd have thried me best to do that widout anny promise
from yersilf, Thalia.   D'ye think so ill av me, as that I'd
sthand quietly by an' see another bhoy dhrowned an' not lift
a hand to help him ?   Listen, avourneen ! Sure, if Kerry
had been saved I belave I *might* have given ye back yer
promise—but I can't say for certain —an' if it were in me
power to bring that wild, hot-headed bhoy back to life it's
moor than likely I'd do it for *your* sake, *colleen machree,* just
to see the smile on yer lips an' the light av happiness in yer
eyes wanst moor ; but sure ye know I can't do this, an'

where would be the good to anny av us if I were to relase ye from yer promise this minute ? Kerry is gone now—rest his sowl ! but sure I did all I could for yersilf an' him ; is it ,so *very much* for me to ax in return, that ye should kape the promise ye made me ? Why would ye grudge me *that* happiness, Thalia ? ye've said ye were lonesome, an' poor, and friendless. Ah, *mavourneen !* why is it ye'd be castin' from ye the home an' the heart that's been waitin' for ye so long ? Is it my faithful love that makes the bargain so hard, Thalia ? " asked Sheymus, sorrowfully, as he placed his arm protectingly around her and drew her nearer to him, looking down upon her with eyes full of yearning tenderness. " Is my love such a heavy burden to bear, darlin' ? "

" 'Tis a heavy burden to mesilf, Sheymus, for I know that the dhay will niver come whin I can return it," replied Thalia. " But there, sure ye've said enough now, enthirely. Ah, no, no ! " she continued, hastily, as she gently, but firmly withdrew herself from his embrace, " I'll kape me word. I can force mesilf to be honourable an' thrue, an' to fulfil me promise ; but I can niver *make* the *love* come into me heart, but sure I'll be yer wife now—as soon as it's plasin' to ye—the sooner 'tis over, the betther," she cried, in her desperation. " 'Tis all as wan what becomes av me now."

" Oh, Thalia, Thalia ! Is it such a very hard fate to be my wife ? " demanded Sheymus, passionately.

" 'Tis a hard fate to mesilf to be the wife av annywan but Kerry O'Toole," she replied, " but now go !—go, Sheymus ! for fear I change me mind."

" Shall I call on his riverince to-night, an ax him to spake the words for us, *mavourneen ?* "

" Yes, yes ! " returned the girl, wearily. " Do annythin' that's plasin' to yersilf. If the sacrifice has to be made, it's little use houldin' back anny longer."

" Oh, Thalia ! this is poor payment for all my love ! " said Sheymus, sadly.

For a moment she stood looking at him, as if undecided whether to reply or not ; then the ring of pathos in his voice, and the sad expression of his face, as he was about to turn from her, seemed to touch her heart and, going up to him, she clasped his hand in hers, this unwonted caress on her part causing the young farmer's face to flush with hope and pleasure.

"Sheymus !" she said, softly, "maybes I've been spakin' harder words to yersilf than I should have spoken, for sure 'tis nothin' but good ye've iver done mesilf. Oh ! sure it's the bitther sorrow that's makin' me grow cowld an' hard-hearted enthirely. Heaven help me ! I fale as I'd niver moor know happiness, or pace in this world ; but ye'll forgive me, Sheymus, when I'd same ungrateful to yersilf, sure I know all the good that's in yer heart, an' ye'll always have me respect an likin' as a dear, thrue friend—but—but *I can't* give the love that's buried for iver in *his* grave."

"'Tis *your* friendship will be dear as life, to mesilf, darlin'," returned Sheymus, tenderly, "an' I'll use ivery power that's widin' me to bring back the light av hope an' happiness to yer heart."

"Sure I can thrust to ye, Sheymus, an' I thank ye for all yer love an' kindness to mesilf," said Thalia, gently. "Now I must lave ye ; no—don't come wid me, I'd rayther be me lone just now," she added, as with a deep, mournful sigh she turned and left him.

"Heaven bless an' kape ye now an' iver, jewel av me heart !" said the young farmer, fervently, as he stood watching his love until a turn in the winding road hid her from his sight.

"Ochone !" murmured Thalia, regretfully, as she wended her way towards the Murphys' shanty. "How I wish that I could care for him as he deserves, sure it isn't so ofthen that such thrue, honest love is to be won in this cowld world av sorrow an' throuble, that I should be throwin' it away from me an' losin' the best an' thruest friend I could iver have. An' to think av all the colleens that would have valued the devotion av such a bhoy as Sheymus Malloy, an' given their hearts' best love to him. Poor Sheymus ! why would he be so set on mesilf, an' I nothin' but friendship to give in return. Oh, I hope I've acted for the best this dhay, for him, an' for mesilf. Heaven forgive me if I've done wrong, an' help me to do me duty in the life that's before me now !"

When Thalia had fairly disappeared from his view,

Sheymu.s Malloy proceeded to the "Shamrock." On his arrival there, the first person he encountered was Thaddeus Magin. Five minutes later the Yankee would have left the hostelry ; but Sheymus just found him in time. He was in the act of removing his feet from their usual elegant and exalted position on the mantelshelf, and, at the same time, knocking the ashes out of his pipe, preparatory to taking his departure to the mountains.

Sheymus rejoiced that he had been, as he thought, so fortunate as to come across the very person of all others to whom he could safely intrust his warning to the Rebels.

Athough the honest farmer both disliked and mistrusted Magin, yet he thought, in this instance, that no one could possibly be more interested in securing the safety of the Rebel band than the second in command of the "Bold Boys."

Alas ! how often does Fate play into the hands of evil doers, how often has some trivial act, some trifling word, a moment's hesitation, or a hasty decision, altered the whole course of a life, or threatened to disturb the tranquility of a nation !

Had Thalia Coghlan only accepted the escort of Sheymus Malloy, had she not dismissed him so soon, Magin would have left the inn before Sheymus reached it, and thus would the fate of many who have figured in these pages have been very different to that which afterwards befel them.

Eagerly the wily Yankee listened to the warning of Malloy, and found, somewhat to his dismay, that he would be compelled to devise some counterplot, or all his schemes, which had been laid with such infinite care and cunning, would fall to the ground. Gradually he contrived to extract all the information he wanted from the young farmer, who, innocent of the harm he was doing, told him of his interview with the two officers, his own refusal to act as guide to the mountains, and his decided opinion that Shilrick O'Toole would never consent to accompany the soldiers in such a capacity.

That either Sheymus Malloy or the drummer would be likely to refuse to act as guide had never entered into Magin's calculations. He knew them both to be loyal, and he was also aware that they would be well rewarded if, by their means, the daring young Rebel Chief, *Michael Cluny*, and his "Bold Boys," were betrayed into the hands of the English Government; and he could not imagine, for a moment, that *any* man would let slip such a chance of gain to himself, let the cost to others be ever so great. He knew that the soldiers would never find the "Rebels' Rest" without a guide, and he therefore saw the necessity of preparing, without delay, for the turn affairs might take, and set to work in his busy brain to concoct a plan—that could scarcely be surpassed in its subtle cruelty—by which he might induce the poor little drummer to act as a *willing* guide to the soldiers on the expedition which proved so disastrous.

The conversation between Thaddeus Magin and Malloy lasted but a few minutes, yet in that short time mischief was unwittingly done, that was destined to bring death and desolation into many a home.

CHAPTER IX.

" Tender as a woman, manliness and meekness,
    In him were so allied,
That they, who judged him by his strength or weakness,
    Saw but a single side."

J. G. WHITTIER.

A few hours later, when the shadows of twilight were slowly closing in around the scene—a rough, dark, and very solitary-looking road at some distance from Glencree Barracks —the sky was of a dull leaden grey, with here and there a slight break in the clouds, yet scarce sufficient to give promise that the threatened storm would keep off for another night, for the snow was even then falling slowly but steadily, and lay quite an inch deep on the rugged road which led to the mountains, and continued its winding way round, among the snow-capped hills in the far distance.   The white feathery flakes fell softly on the forms of two pedestrians, who shivered under the influence of the intense cold, and drew their warm cloaks—with which they had both provided themselves— more closely around them.

It was too dark for their features to be recognised by any casual passer whom they might chance to encounter on their way, but the voices, as they spoke in low, earnest tones, were those of Eveleen Corrie and Thalia Coghlan.

At last they reached their destination, it had taken them longer than they had calculated, for they had not thought of the roughness of the road, and, moreover, they were nearly blinded by the snow which drifted into their faces.

The spot was always inexpressibly lonely and dreary, and especially so on such a night.

The old house—or rather castle—was partly in ruins, having on one side a clump of tall, leafless trees, and on the other a rugged wall, in which were many gaps, while the heaps of fallen stones and small boulders, which were scattered about, together with the groups of tangled bushes and shrubs, and a few sweet, old-fashioned flowers, that bravely reared their heads, year after year, amid storm and sunshine, formed a chaos of wild confusion, and were all that remained of what had once been a fair, sweet, old-time garden. Decay and time, with relentless progress had been at work with all. A side gable of the castle, being all that was now habitable, had latterly been used as a guard-house, being at a convenient distance between the mountains and Glencree Barracks and having a window that overlooked one of the principal mountain passes ; and, although the view was distant, yet the space between was clear and open, and any large parties of the Rebels who might have ventured to choose the pass as their route to or from the hills would have been easily discerned by the ever-watchful guard.

The long, neglected trails of ivy, with which the ruins were covered, were rising and falling with every breeze, blown hither and thither, tapping against the mouldering wall, and making a ghostly noise, as of the touch of invisible hands. The sough of the cold winter wind as it moaned and shrieked among the ruins, seemed like the voice of an unquiet spirit, and a prophecy of the tragedy that was to come, the shadow of which appeared to have fallen upon the two girls approaching the old castle, as upon the sentinel, steadily marching to and fro, who felt his duty on that night unusually dreary and monotonous. It had even penetrated into the guard-room itself, investing the stout-hearted Marines with an unwonted gravity ; neither the song, the jest, nor the merry laugh were to be heard *that* night, a state of affairs never before known when Shilrick O'Toole was the drummer on guard.

"Oh, Thalia, dear girl !" said Eveleen, softly, to her companion as they approached the guard-room door. "How *can* I thank you enough for consenting to come with me this evening ?   I feel that I can trust you, Thalia ; you know that it is my cousin who is the leader of these Rebels, but all of your family have been devoted to the Corries for generations past, and you have known Morven O'Neill from his boyhood."

"Oh, me lady ! who is it ye'd be thrustin', if not the child av the ould race that's been the followers av yer family through many a year av sthorm an sunshine ? " returned the girl, earnestly.

"I dared not send to my cousin to meet me, after the danger he was in at our last interview," continued Eveleen. " But, if we could only see the drummer, Shilrick O'Toole, he can tell us where these ' Bold Boys ' are hiding, and I shall then be able to find my cousin, Morven O'Neill."

" Sure it's mesilf that's afraid Shilrick will not tell us, Miss Eveleen," said Thalia, doubtfully.

"Then, if *he* does not, I know of no one who can help us, and oh, Thalia," cried Eveleen, "we shall neither have it in our power to persuade my cousin to release Captain Annesley, nor to warn him of his own danger, and that a party of our soldiers received orders to proceed to the mountains to-night."

" I've been thinkin' what we could do if Shilrick doesn't tell us, Miss Eveleen.   Sure there's Anty Kinahan, I belave, knows where ' the Bhoys ' are ; 'tis herself an her mother that supplies thim wid food, an' anny other thing they'd be wantin' ; an' Misthress Kinahan, she'd give her life for Misther O'Neill, anny dhay, bein' his honour's ould nurse, an' so if she knows it's to warn *him* we're afther, she'll help us ready enough."

"We will lose no time in going to her then, Thalia, if Shilrick refuses," replied Eveleen.   "I wish he would come out now."

" 'Twill be a long road for ye to thravel this night, Miss Eveleen, darlin', an' it's bitther cowld an' snowin', too ; but sure I know well 'tis yer heart that's in it, an' so ye'll niver heed anny trouble or danger that may come to yersilf on the way."

They had by this time approached nearer to the Marine sentry, who paused on his march, and stared at them in some surprise, for their footsteps had been light and noise-

less, and he had not heard them until they were close to
him.

"Who goes there ?" he called, repeating the usual challenge.

" A friend !" replied Eveleen.

" The parole !" demanded the sentry. For a moment
Eveleen was as though struck dumb in her consternation ;
she had forgotten that it would be required of her, in passing
any of the outposts, that she should be able to give the
parole ; while she paused irresolute some one within the
guard-room opened the door and a flood of light fell upon
the sentinel, when she immediately recognized the young
Marine soldier as a special favourite of Colonel Corrie's,
and one to whom she was well known. " Ah, it is you,
Pike !" she cried, eagerly.

" Miss Corrie !" exclaimed the Marine, in astonishment.

" Yes, Pike ! but hush !" she cried, softly, "I do not wish
it to be known that I am here. Shilrick O'Toole is the
drummer on guard at this post to-night, is he not ? "

" He is, miss."

" I want most particularly to see him ; could he come out
to speak to me ? " asked Eveleen.

" Well, Miss Corrie," answered Pike, reflecting, "it be
agin the rules of the sarvice, but p'raps, if he haxeses permission, he may be allowed for to speak for a minit seein'
as 'ow you've named that the bisness is particklar ; the
sergeant we got here to-night ain't no way bumptious or
dis'greable like some on 'em is.   I'll just step hover to the
door an' hask."

" One moment, Pike !" said Eveleen, detaining him. " Do
not mention that *I* am here to *anyone* ; but try to send
Shilrick O'Toole to me, if you can."

" Very good, miss," answered Pike, respectfully.   " This
'ere's a queer move," he murmured to himself, as he went
towards the guard-room door, "whathever is in the wind
now, I wonder, an' who be the hother young woman ?—her
maid, most like.   Well ! this 'ere that I'm a-doin' of is agin
all horders an' reg'lations, they ain't give the parole
neither, that's certain, yet here I be haidin' an' habettin'—
but there !" he concluded, hurriedly, " she's the Colonel's
daughter.   I'll take the risk."

When the sentry left them, Thalia turned to Eveleen, saying, sorrowfully, " Sure I'll go beyant an' wait for ye, Miss Eveleen, dear ; it's Shilrick would be angry, enthirely, if he sane *mesilf* here, an' then maybes he wouldn't tell yez annythin'. I'll be close at hand if ye want me."

" Well, Thalia, perhaps you may be right," replied Eveleen, as Thalia left her and disappeared among the ruins.

The first person Pike encountered when he reached the guard-room door was the sergeant, before mentioned as not being " bumptious or dis'greable."

" Well, Pike, what's up ? " asked the sergeant, anxiously.

" Nothin' particklar ain't up, sergeant, as I knows on," answered the sentry, hesitatingly, " honly—leastways—there's a young—" *lady*, he was about to say, but quickly substituted *woman*, as giving him a better chance of hiding Eveleen Corrie's identity. " There's a young woman as wants to speak a word with Shilrick O'Toole—*very particklar*, she says."

" Oh ! the women always says that when they want to speak to the men, and take 'em off of their dooty," said the sergeant, scornfully. " Dont 'ee give heed to un, my lad ; an' certain if this one don't do Shilrick no more good than that hartful creatur' did that wild brother of his'n, why then he won't be much made up by seein' of her, I reckon."

As Pike had his own views and opinions of the female sex in general, which scarcely coincided with those of the gallant sergeant, he wisely held his peace upon that subject, and simply repeated his request that Shilrick might be allowed to come outside for a few minutes.

" Well ! " replied the sergeant. " He may go out for a short spell, *I've* nothin' to say again it, happen it'll do the lad good, help to put life into un, and cheer un up a bit, he's low enough now. You must tell the young woman he can't go beyond call."

" Very good, sergeant ! " returned Pike, well pleased with the success of his mission, and congratulating himself upon the fact of the sergeant's indifference to the fair sex, which prevented his taking the trouble even to cast a passing glance outside, before he returned into the room and went up to the drummer, kindly laying his hand upon the boy's shoulder as he sat with his arms outstretched over the wooden table, and his head resting on them, his face concealed from everyone.

The attitude was one of such utter despondency, and one so uncharacteristic of the merry, light-hearted little soldier-boy, as to cause much surprise to his comrades, and won for him their rough, but kindly and sincere sympathy.

The poor boy knew that even if he escaped the bitter trial of being called upon to act as guide to the men of his corps that night, yet it would not prevent the Marines from being sent in search of the Rebels, it was even possible that they might meet, and that the encounter would be one of danger, to those who were dear to him, as well as to his comrades, Shilrick knew well. Again and again he reproached himself with being the cause of all, for it was the fact of Annesley and himself having fallen into the hands of the " Bold Boys," that had led to the present misfortune.

Such was the boy's state of mind when he felt the sergeant's hand upon his shoulder, and heard the cheery voice addressing him.

" Ah ! sure, have they come for me ? " he cried, starting to his feet. " I knew it. I knew I hadn't seen the ind av the throuble yet."

" There, dont'ee grieve that way, my lad, dont'ee now ! " said the sergeant, kindly, his strong Cornish accent and tone always coming to the fore when he was earnest or excited. " It's no manner of use brooding over trouble till it comes, time enough then ; it's just going through it twice, else," he continued. " It's only a young woman outside wants to speak to'ee, happen it may be for good, or she may bring trouble with her, I can't answer for *that* ; they most do, what *I've* seen of 'em ; but, mayhap, the lass has brought'ee good news, my lad, you'm best go to her now, or it'll be too near on the time for the officer's rounds," he added, with an encouraging slap on the boy's shoulder. " Do'ee go now, co, and cheer up, dont'ee be down-hearted, *that* don't make matters better, happen what may."

" Sure, I thank ye, sergeant, it's yersilf has always the kind word for us all," said the boy, as striving to appear more cheerful, he lifted his pale, wearied face, and looked up at the good-natured sergeant, but the effort was a futile one, for the earnest, eloquent eyes were sad and heavy with a long, sleepless night of sorrow and pain, and the mobile lips refused to form themselves into even the ghost of a smile.

"Faith it isn't much in the way av good news that's likely to come to mesilf," continued the drummer, as listlesly and slowly he walked towards the door, passing his arm over his eyes, as though to clear away the mist of trouble and anxiety which clouded them, and hung like a pall over his heart and spirits. "But I'll hear what the colleen has to say. Who can she be, I wondher? Ah!" he exclaimed, suddenly, in a lower tone. "Sure, I'd forgotten enthirely, maybes 'tis Anty Kinahan, an' sure it's herself *might* have news from the mountains; annyhow I'll see," he concluded, hastening his steps, and hurrying from the room.

"The lad's not fit to be sent to dooty yet," murmured the sergeant, somewhat resentfully to the corporal on guard, as he watched Shilrick's departure; for the drummer was a favourite of his. "He's that weak, poor little chap, though his spirits be brave enough; the will's there, but the strength isn't." The honest sergeant little thought that Colonel Corrie had purposely given orders that Shilrick should resume his duties at once, and take his turn on guard, in the hope that, by so doing, and the drummer being on other, and especial duty for the day, at some distance from barracks, he might possibly escape being sent as guide with the party of Marines, particularly if Captain Ellis, and his friend Digby, proved successful in finding someone else willing to undertake the unpleasant office.

As Shilrick passed Pike, the sentry silently pointed to the spot where Eveleen Corrie stood waiting for him, partly concealed beneath the shadow of the ivy-covered wall.

Immediately on the appearance of the drummer, Eveleen, who had been anxiously watching the door of the guard-room, went quickly forward to meet him. She had grown impatient even at the short delay, for the time was passing, it was late, and she had much to do, a task of danger and difficulty to perform before nightfall, and, in addition to this, there was the fear that some one might pass on the road, or come out of the guard-room, who would possibly recognize her, in which case the consequences might prove serious, and her position most embarrassing. As Eveleen approached nearer to Shilrick, she addressed him, speaking earnestly and rapidly, but in tones scarcely above a whisper, while she glanced anxiously around her, lest there should be anyone within earshot, "Ah, Shilrick ! I am indeed glad that you have come—I want to speak to you."

"Who is it, at all, at all ? " questioned the boy, doubtfully, and in considerable disappointment that it was not Anty Kinahan, as he had hoped.

"Sure, I don't know ye ! " he added, as he peered curiously at the face and form of his companion, but for a few moments he did not recognize her, for his eyes were dazzled, having just come from the lighted room into the dusky gloaming.

"It is I, Eveleen Corrie—why, Shilrick !—don't you know me ? " she asked, in surprise.

The drummer started back with an exclamation of astonishment. "Miss Corrie, is it ?—Och ! to think now I'd be such an *omadhaun* as not to know yer ladyship."

"I have something very particular to say to you," said Eveleen.

"Yes, me lady ? an' is it for long ye'd be afther wantin' mesilf ? "

"Only for a few minutes."

"Then sure I can sthay for that thime, annyhow."

"My reason for seeking you here is soon told," said Eveleen, " Shilrick I want your help ! "

"*My* help, is it, Miss Corrie ! Sure thin, 'tis willin' an' ready I'll be to sarve yez, but what could *I* be doin', at all, at all ? " asked the boy, eagerly.

"You *know*, and *can tell me* where the Rebels, called the ' Bold Boys of Wicklow ' are to be found," said Eveleen.

"*I*, me lady ? " exclaimed Shilrick, starting. "Sure, who could have tould ye that now, an' how is it I'd be know- in' annythin' about the ' Bhoys ' ? " queried the drummer, innocently.

"You *do* know, Shilrick ! " returned Eveleen, quietly but firmly.

"Ar' is it hearin' news about thim yer ladyship would be afther ? "

"Shilrick ! " remonstrated Eveleen, earnestly. "It is no use your wasting both my time and your own. I *must* know where these Rebels are to be found ; you *can* tell me if you *will.* I beg of you not to withhold information that may be of such importance to us all."

"Is it where the Ribils are, ye're axin', Miss Corrie ? Troth ! an' 'tis that same would be mighty difficult to tell, so it would. 'The Bhoys' is always movin' about, an' small blame to thim, when they're hunted the way they are, that they'd thry to kape their hidin' place sacrit," returned the boy, looking searchingly at Eveleen, to discover her motive for thus questioning him.

"Where *is* their hiding-place ? " asked Eveleen.

"How can I tell ye that, Miss Corrie ? " asked Shilrick, cautiously. "An' sure, me lady, what is it the likes of yer-silf would be wantin' wid the 'Bould Bhoys ? ' Belave me, 'tis safer at home ye'd be, enthirely ; 'the Bhoys' are not over-burdhened wid much manners to thim they'd be matin' on the road—sure I ax yer pardon for spakin' me mind so plain, me lady," he added, civilly.

"Shilrick ! why will you be so obstinate ? " cried Eveleen, impatiently. "Why did you give the information that Captain Annesley and Father Bernard were prisoners in the hands of the Rebels, when you were so determined not to tell where they are ? You were with them, so you must know. Oh ! what on earth were you all doing wandering about the mountains at that hour ? "

For a moment the drummer stood silently regarding Eveleen, until at last a bright smile crept into his face ; it was but momentary, however, and he turned aside so that the Colonel's daughter should not see it. Amid all his troubles, and serious thoughts, had come to him, suddenly, the pleasant certainty that—"his honour the Captain's swateheart," was still true to him and anxious on *his* account ; for the boy had taken an especial interest in the love affair of his Captain, and felt considerable sorrow to see the coldness which had of late sprung up between these proud lovers ; but when he again spoke to Eveleen, his face wore its former expression of gravity.

" Sure, me lady, what I done was all accordin' to his honour the Captain's own ordhers. I gave information bekase *he* tould me to do it. That's all I was to do, enthirely. 'Tis himself would be the last to wish me to bethray the poor Bhoys."

" ' *Poor Bhoys* ! ' do you call them ? " exclaimed Eveleen. " Shilrick you must be mad to speak so of these Rebels, and Captain Annesley at this moment a prisoner in their hands. You know well that *he* would never wish to defend anyone engaged in this Rebellion. Oh, tell me, I entreat of you ! What *can* I say to convince you of the consequence it is to myself and others that I should see the leader of these ' Bold Boys', and if possible persuade him to release Captain Annesley ? "

" Can she have discovered *who* the laader av the band is ?" thought Shilrick, anxiously.

" Sure, Miss Corrie, maybes 'tis his honour wouldn't care to be riscued by a lady," he said.

" Oh ! this evasion—this secresy is maddening to me," returned Eveleen, sorrowfully. " I see that I am only wasting time here, and need expect no help from *you*, Shilrick."

" Och, now me lady ! sure it's wrong ye are enthirely ; 'tis annythin' I'd be afther doin' to help ye—so I would."

" Anything but what I ask !" replied Eveleen, bitterly.

" What *can* I do, Miss Corrie ? "

" Tell me where the Rebels are to be found."

" Sure 'tis among the mountains they'll be, this minute, me lady, an' niver a lie in it."

" Enough !—I see you will not even help to rescue Captain Annesley, who has ever been your best, your truest friend. You always professed the greatest attachment for him," said Eveleen, indignantly.

" And I'd give me life for him anny dhay," returned the boy, earnestly.

"Then why hold back now, when I tell you that the chance has ccme for you to show your gratitude and affection for him."

" Troth I'd like to mate fair an' open the bhoy, that would daur be sayin' either av thim falins isn't in me heart for the Captain, moor power to him," cried the drummer, passionately. "An', Miss Corrie—hear me now—for his sake I'd do annythin' to sarve ye this minute; sure, if 'twas in me power, wouldn't I thake up the pace av ground yer standin' on, an' set it down right forninst the Ribil Chafe himself, to save ye the throuble av lookin' for him, if—if I could do it widout harmin' others. Oh, me lady!" he continued, sorrowfully, "sure if ye only knew *all*, 'tis yersilf that would fale the dape sorrow in yer heart if I gave information about ' the Bhoys.' I can't tell yez annythin' moor just now, but when the Captain comes bhack to barracks, sure it's himself that'll explain all to ye enthirely, an' maybes ye'll not be afther thinkin' quite so ill av me thin."

With a deep, sorrowful sigh, Shilrick turned from Eveleen, murmuring to himself, "Poor lady!—if she only knew about Misther O'Neill."

"Ah, Shilrick, do not leave me yet!" pleaded Eveleen, despairingly. "Nearly all the peasantry around know where the Rebels are hiding, and all day I have been trying to find one who would tell me, but they all refused to do so."

"'Tis proud I am to hear it," returned the drummer, triumphantly.

"Proud to hear it, Shilrick. *You a soldier?*"

"Troth an' I am, me lady, an' may ould Ireland niver have cause to be ashamed av her sons; for that's what she'd be, an' sorra lie in it, if they'd thurn *informers*."

"Well, Shilrick! you were almost my last chance, you know that *I* should never betray these men. I only wish to see and to speak to their leader, and if possible, to influence him to release Captain Annesley, as I have before explained to you."

"That's thrue for ye, Miss Corrie; but I hould the sacrit av these men, an' sure, 'tis their very lives are in my hands. They've thrusted me, an' I'll not bethray that thrust," said Shilrick, manfully. "Me lady! will it not contint ye, will ye not belave in me, whin I tell ye that his honour, the Captain, is safe, an' that it isn't long ye'll have to wait before ye set yer two eyes on him agin? Or, see now! if yer ladyship would like to write annythin', sure I'd conthrive to send it where ye want, whativer dhanger might be in it—if ye'd write a bit av a letther to the Ribil Chafe himself, maybes he'd do what ye ax. I'll go inside, an' I'll get a pace av paper, an' I'll bring out the drum, sure ye can write on the head av it, troth, it makes an iligant writin' thable!" continued the boy, eagerly. "I'll fetch it this minute, so I will."

"Stay, Shilrick!" said Eveleen, determinedly, as she laid her hand on the boy's arm to detain him, "I want more than this. I *must* know where the leader of these Rebels is to be found, I must see him *myself*."

"Then I'm sorry, me lady," he replied, firmly but respectfully, "there's nothin' moor that *I* can do for ye, at all, at all."

Again the drummer turned from her, and had taken a few steps towards the guard-room door; but Eveleen, after a moment's hesitation, followed him, and drawing a handsome ring from her finger, she held it before his eyes Even in the faint gleam of light that fell upon it from the half-open door, the jewel glittered and flashed like sparks of fire.

"See, my boy!" said Eveleen, eagerly, "it is of great value, perhaps more than you can ever imagine. I know that you have ever been ambitious and anxious for learning and education; the money you would receive for this little jewel would be a considerable help to you. Or, you have doubtless poor friends; if you prefer to do so you can give it to them. There!" she added, again holding out the ring to him. - "It is yours, and you shall have more gold still, if you will only do as I ask you."

The last words had scarcely crossed Eveleen's lips when she would have given worlds to recall them, for the boy turned, and, with a quick, impetuous movement, swept aside her hand, so causing the ring to fall to the ground, where it lay unheeded by either, then he looked at her with an intent gaze, in which so much pride, pain, and scorn where mingled, that it was long ere Eveleen could forget it, as she afterwards told Lady Mabel, in relating to her the incidents of that fatal night.

"Oh, Miss Corrie!" returned Shilrick, in a voice trembling with emotion, "sure is it insultin' mesilf, ye'd be? Ah! then, what is it I've iver done that ye'd be afther thinkin' so ill av me—that ye'd hould in yer heart—for wan moment, the thought that *gould* would buy *my* good faith; or that

Shilrick O'Toole—poor, though he is, an' only a drummer—would sell his *honour* for that glitterin' bauble, an' that he'd do for that, what he wouldn't do widout it ?   Oh ! niver, niver ! not if the same ring was worth thousands upon thousands, an' mesilf stharvin' for want. Ah, me lady ! don't be axin' me anny moor," he added, bitterly, " or—or, maybes I might be forgettin' that I'm spakin' to me Colonel's daughter."

" Then I may go, Shilrick," said Eveleen, sadly, " but remember—you have sent me from you in sorrow and despair, and never again need you fear that ' your Colonel's daughter ' will stoop to ask another favour of you."

" Sure, 'tis angry ye are now wid mesilf, Miss Corrie, but the crass av sorrow an' throuble is weighin' heavy on yer heart this night—that Heaven may remove it will be my prayer.   Maybes the thime will come whin ye'll judge me fairer ; but, annyhow, I can't help wishin' that it may be long before yer ladyship can persuade *anny* Irishman to *inform.*"

" My coming to you now, at such an hour, and in such a place, was a last resource, as you may imagine," said Eveleen, coldly. " I was foolish to have supposed that you would help me—foolish to feel such bitter disappointment at the failure of my last hope. I can only say now that I am sorry if I have offended you—it was certainly not intentional."

" Och, niver mind, Miss Corrie ! " cried the boy, quickly, " niver heed ; sure what's wanst been said, can't be unsaid. Thake back the ring agin, me lady," he continued, as he stooped to pick it up, and politely returned it to Eveleen. " Thake it, now, an' whiniver yer two eyes rest on it, ye'll remimber that there's wan poor, faithful bhoy in the ould corps that would go through fire an' wather—through anny thrial or dhanger to sarve yersilf—but not *that*; oh ! niver *that,* for a thrue souldier would rather die than sell his heart, or his honour, for all this world could give him."

Many a time, in the days of peril and of grief that followed, Eveleen recalled the earnest words of the little drummer, and knew then that they had not been mere idle words, to be forgotten as soon as spoken, but that they had come straight from the very heart and soul of the lad whose every thought seemed so noble, so brave and true.

"Shilrick !" she said, gently, "I cannot but respect your firmness and truth to a principle, which, I know, is inherent in the heart of every Irishman, against *informing*, but," she added, sorrowfully, "you must remember that in *this* instance, your good faith is my great misfortune."

During this interview, Pike, the sentry, had been marching to and fro in front of the guard-room door, watching Eveleen and Shilrick, with a countenance full of the most intense curiosity, but not passing near enough to hear the subject of their conversation. Thalia Coghlan, who had also been watching them anxiously from round the corner of the old wall, noticed that Eveleen was about to leave Shilrick, and thinking, from the dejected tones of the voices which had penetrated to her ivy-covered retreat, that Eveleen Corrie had failed in her mission, the girl made a sudden resolution, on the impulse of the moment, and summoning up all her courage to face the indignant little soldier brother of her lost and dearly-loved Kerry, she hastily came forth from her place of concealment and approached Shilrick.

The drummer gave a start of surprise on finding that Thalia Coghlan was beside him, and then stood still and cold as a statute before her, regarding her silently and angrily.

"Shilrick !" she cried, with a ring of earnest entreaty in her sweet, gentle voice, "Shilrick, oh! don't be lookin' at me that way—sure I didn't mane to let ye iver see mesilf agin, but I couldn't help it this thime—indade thin I couldn't, Shilrick dear. I *must* spake, for Miss Corrie's sake."

"So this is you agin is it ? " exclaimed the boy, passionately. "An' ye're wid Miss Corrie ; begorrah thin, 'tis her ladyship would have done betther to have chosen wan that was moor to be thrusted for company. Why don't ye go to *Sheymus Malloy?* " he continued, contemptuously. " Why don't ye ax *him* to thake ye to the ' Bould Bhoys ? ' Sure it's himself knows well enough where they're to be found, maybes *he'll* tell yez, as he worships the very ground ye sthand on, an' small blame to him, when ye left the purtiest bhoy that iver set foot on Irish soil for his sake."

"Oh, Shilrick !" returned Thalia, sadly, "don't be spakin'

av that now. Miss Corrie dear," she added, turning to
Eveleen, "sure ye'll tell him all, ye can thrust him enthirely;
he'll maybes hilp us, when he knows we don't want to
harm 'the Bhoys,' an' that it's for their own good we're sakin'
thim."

"Is it the thruth ye're spakin' this minute, Thalia Coghlan,
can I belave ye ?"

"Indeed you can, Shilrick, and I must once more add my
entreaties to hers, that you will help us," said Eveleen.

"Was there anny other raison for yer wantin' to find ' the
Bhoys,' Miss Corrie, besides relasin' his honour, Captain
Annesley ?" asked Shilrick, looking searchingly at her as he
spoke.

"Yes !" returned Eveleen, hesitating slightly, " I wish to
give the young Rebel Chief warning that a strong party of
soldiers will be sent to the mountains to-night."

"Och, musha !" cried the boy, in a startled voice. "Then
ye know who the Rebel Chief is, me lady ?"

"Yes," replied Eveleen. "Alas! I know only too well ;
he is my own cousin, Morven O'Neill ; he was in the old
corps once."

"An' 'tis well I remimber his honour bein' wid us thin.
May Heaven kape him from all harm this night is the prayer
av me heart. Does his honour, the Colonel, know that his
nephew is wid the Ribils, me lady ? For 'tis Captain
Annesley was anxious, enthirely, that he shouldn't hear av
it."

"No, Shilrick ! I am thankful to say that my father knows
nothing of this, our worst trouble."

"If ye had only thrusted me at first, Miss Corrie, an' tould
me that ye knew about Misther O'Neill, I'd have helped ye
at wanst, for sure ye'd niver bethray yer own cousin," said
Shilrick ; then turning to Thalia, he asked her :

"D'ye know where the ' Ribils' Rest ' is, Thalia
Coghlan ?"

"Sure, an' I do !" she replied.

"Could ye show Miss Corrie the way to it ?"

"I'm feared I couldn't find it, not whin it's so dhark an"
the snow fallin' fast forbye."

"Well !" returned Shilrick, bitterly, "sure ye must ax

Sheymus Malloy, *that* will be plasin' work for yersilf annyhow. Ye must go to Ballymacreagh Farm first, an if ye don't
find him there, it's like enough he'll be at Misthress Kinahan's;
if not, why thin there's Anty Kinahan, she knows ivery foot
av the road, an I belave it'll not snow much moor this night,
the sky is lookin' clarer now."

"And do you think that the Rebels are certain to be at
the place you have mentioned?" asked Eveleen, anxiously.

"I belave so," replied Shilrick. "They mate there for
dhrill ivery night—'tis a mighty secure place, an' onless
the souldiers were tould, they'd never find 'the Bhoys.'
But lose no thime if ye're goin' to give warnin', Miss Corrie,
for sure it's our men will be sthartin' in a few hours, an'
bedad, though 'tis loyal an' thrue I am, I can't find it in me
heart to wish them success. 'Tis wondherin' I've been all
dhay what I could do to help the poor Bhoys in the mountains, but bein' on guard I'd no power."

"We will try to help them, Shilrick," said Eveleen,
earnestly. "Perhaps Anty Kinahan, or Sheymus Malloy
can show us some short way to the 'Rebels' Rest.' Come,
Thalia."

"Wan moment, Miss Corrie!" said Shilrick. "I'd beg
av ye to kape nothin' back from Sheymus Malloy, nor Anty
Kinahan, sure there's neither av thim would harm 'the Bhoys';
an' if they don't know what ye're afther, they'll give no information, they'll not go to work blindfold, an' yersilf bein'
our Colonel's daughter, will make them the moor cautious."

"Many thanks for your warning, Shilrick. I understand,
perfectly. And now good-night! May you always prove
as loyal to your friends, and as faithful to every cause, as
you have been this evening."

"The top av the avenin' to yer ladyship, an' good luck be
wid ye," returned the drummer.

A curt good-night was all that passed between Shilrick
and Thalia, and the boy was once more alone. For some
minutes he stood watching the two brave-hearted girls, until
they disappeared from his sight

The attempt of Eveleen Corrie and Thalia Coghlan to
secure the assistance of Sheymus Malloy was unsuccessful
at the outset, for when they arrived at his farm they were

told, by a boy who had been left in charge, that " the masther hadn't 'crassed the dures since the mornin' ; " and as no farther information could be extracted from him (he having become suspicious at being so cross-questioned), Eveleen and Thalia started on their way to Mrs. Kinahan's hostelry. The road was long and dreary, the night dark, cold and stormy, but the grief, and trouble within each heart was so deep, that all the discomforts and the gloomy impressions of their strange expedition were alike unfelt and unheeded. Little did either think that they would soon—within a few short hours—be in the midst of the darkest of tragedies and most heart-rending sorrow.

CHAPTER X.

" Oh ! star of strength I see thee stand
  And smile upon my pain ;
Thou beckonest with thy mailed hand,
  And I am strong again,

The star of the unconquered will
  He rises in my breast,
Serene, and resolute, and still,
  And calm and self-possessed."

LONGFELLOW.

For some time after Eveleen and Thalia had left him, Shilrick still lingered outside the guard-room ; possibly he did not care to face the fire of questions with which he knew he would be greeted by his comrades, until he had considered, in his own mind, how far he could satisfy their natural curiosity without betraying the confidence which had been placed in him.

The cool evening air fell like refreshing dew upon his brain, fevered as it was with anxious thought and apprehension for the safety of those who were dearest to him, and the fear which, for the last two days, had been ever present with him, that he should be called upon to betray his countrymen, or to renounce his loyalty.

Three times had the sentry, Pike, paused on his march, and hoping to be first on the field with the news Shilrick might have to tell, put forward a leader in the most insinuating of tones :

" Queer move that, eh ? "

But it was useless, he received no answer from the sad-hearted boy, whose thoughts were far away. Indeed, Shilrick seemed to hear nothing, to see nothing, unless it might have been the pale star above him, on which his glorious, but tear-laden eyes were fixed with such a yearning, wistful expression, as he murmured anxiously to himself :

"Sure, 'tis a power av thime would have been saved if Miss Corrie had only thrusted me at first ; but the souldiers know nothin' av the 'Ribils' Rest,' an' sure they'll niver find it widout a guide. *Och, wirra, wirra!* I hope Misther O'Neill will niver be thaken, 'twould be woorse than death to him. Oh, why is it he left us all an' thurned Ribil, 'tis himself was loved by all his paple, an' sorra officer in the sarvice was a greater favourite than himself. Oh, *Ua Néill! Ua Néill!* 'twas always the kind word ye had for us all. May Heaven's blissin' be wid yersilf an' yer faithful followers this night."

"O'Toole!" cried Pike, suddenly, stepping out of his line of march, and going as close as possible to Shilrick, "There be a officer a-comin' this way, do'ee look out now ! I think as it's that there Captain Ellis."

The sharp, quick accents of the sentry, fairly roused Shilrick from his reverie, and Pike, seeing that he had succeeded in warning his young comrade, returned to his post, stepping out with an extra amount of energy, for Captain Ellis was known to be a strict disciplinarian. Shilrick, too, was returning to the guard-room with all speed, and had actually reached the door, when his progress was arrested by his hearing Captain Ellis calling to him in tones that were decidedly peremptory.

"Shilrick ! Come here ! I wish to speak to you."

"Yes, sir !" said the drummer, returning to Captain Ellis, saluting him, and then standing attention, waiting with the greatest anxiety for the questions that might be put to him.

"What were you doing out here just now, my lad ?" asked Ellis.

"*I*—sure I wasn't doin' annythin' at all, sir."

"That is nonsense, you must have had some motive for being out here alone. Had you leave from the sergeant on guard ?"

"Yes, sir !"

"For whom were you watching, when I first saw you ? "

" No one, yer honour."

With a gesture of impatience, Captain Ellis turned from him, and called to Pike, who was passing near them at the moment.

" Sentry ! what was this boy doing out here, before I came up to him ? "

The sentry hesitated, and glanced helplessly at Shilrick.

" Well ! I am waiting for your answer," said Ellis.

" He wasn't doing nothing, sir, as I could see—I can't say as I was noticing 'im particklar, sir."

" And what are *you* here for, if not to do your duty as sentinel, and to take notice of *all* that is going on ? " demanded the irate officer.

" Well, sir!" returned Pike, still hesitating and again looking appealingly at Shilrick, " since you mentions it, I must hown as I do remember noticing he once when I was a-passing of him."

" Ah ! what was he doing ? "

" Nothing particklar, sir, as *I* could see, he were only a-looking up at the stars, it's a trick the little chap has, sir, I often seen him do it."

" There—that is enough, you can go," said Ellis, sternly.

Pike marched off with great alacrity, delighted to have got so well out of a difficult dilemma, and more than repaid for his caution and reticence regarding Shilrick's two fair visitors, by the grateful look which the boy bestowed upon him.

Captain Ellis had no romance in his own nature, he was indeed one of the most practical, matter-of-fact men, and the idea that this little drummer, this very youthful son of Mars, would be likely to leave his cheerful comrades and the warm guard-room fire, on a dreary, cold winter night, simply for the purpose of star-gazing, was certainly more than this gallant officer could bring himself to believe ; but he saw that farther questioning would be a mere waste of words, and only land him in the ignominious position of one who has failed and been defeated—in plain words, hoodwinked—by a private soldier in his own corps.

His temper, too, never of the best, was decidedly at

its worst on this evening. All through the day he had been meeting with a series of little crosses and worries; and trifling as such crosses may be, they yet tend to make up and increase the sum of human trials, discomforts, and disappointments which we must all suffer, more or less, in our journey through life.

Now, as a culminating trial, Captain Ellis had this sad and disagreeable duty to perform; it was to him as the last straw, so that, grieved as he felt for the trouble that was to fall upon the little lad, now standing before him, yet his tones appeared harsh and stern to poor Shilrick, whose heart was so full of sorrow and fear for those who were dear to him, and in such peril.

As soon as Pike, the sentry, was out of hearing, Captain Ellis again addressed the boy.

"Shilrick O'Toole! you are wanted immediately; you are to go with the party of Marines to the mountains. We have received information that will lead to the discovery of the band of Rebels, known as the 'Bold Boys of Wicklow,' and we shall require a guide to a certain spot they call the 'Rebels' Rest.'"

"The Ribils' Rest!" exclaimed the drummer, starting. "Oh! who *could* have tould yer honour about *that* place? Oh, sure, *I* can't go wid ye, sir; I can't be yer guide *there*."

"This is nonsense!" replied Captain Ellis, sternly. "There is not a man or boy in all Wicklow who knows every mountain pass as you do; you *must* come—and *at once;* I have given orders for another drummer to take your place here."

"Oh, sir! if ye could only find some other bhoy!" pleaded Shilrick. "Sure, *I can't* be the wan to betray thim all."

"And how dare you stand and tell your officer that you will not do as you are ordered?" demanded Ellis, indignantly.

"Sir! I know me duty well, but for no man livin' would I do this!"

"Then you positively refuse to go?"

"I do, sir!" returned the drummer, firmly.

" You know the consequences of a soldier disobeying orders ? "

" Yes, sir."

" And in addition to that fault, you are at this moment trying to shield and protect these Rebels ; you will be tried by court-martial, and you know what the result will be," continued the officer.

" I know, sir," said Shilrick, sorrowfully ; " but, sure, I've given me word, an' it wouldn't be honourable to break it, an' bethray thim that thrusted me, enthirely."

" Then you are prepared to abide by the consequences of your folly and obstinacy ? "

" Yes, sir," replied the boy, slowly. " A thrue souldier would rayther mate death than dishonour."

" He is a noble-hearted little fellow," murmured Ellis to himself. " Would that this unpleasant duty could have been averted."

Then, determined to make one more effort to induce the drummer to obey orders, he laid his hand on his shoulder, and said, kindly :

"Shilrick, my lad ! You have ever been a favourite with us all ; for your own sake, for the sake of my friend, Captain Annesley—who has taken so much interest in your welfare —I give you one more chance. Will you go ? "

" No, sir !" came the gentle, but firm and unhesitating, reply.

" Then I can say no more," returned Captain Ellis, regretfully. " You must remain here for the present, until I can make this known to the Colonel, and receive farther orders from him. I only regret now, that *I*—your officer—thus stooped to try and persuade you, even to *plead* with you. Remember ! whatever comes of this—and you may prepare for the worst—I have done all I could, but it has been of no avail."

How little we know of the inmost thoughts and feelings, even of those with whom we daily come in contact, or who are nearest and dearest to us. Had any of his comrades been able to read aright the heart of Captain Ellis, to look into its depths, at that moment, they would truly have been surprised, and probably grieved, that they had so misjudged his real nature. He was known as a stern, strict officer; he had even gained for himself the name of "*Martinet*"; he won the esteem and respect of his men, because he was known to be a just man, and there was in his nature nothing of the tyrant or the bully, yet he had never gained their affection, or even liking, for he was shrewd and quick to discover faults that others might possibly pass unnoticed, but which he, with his zeal, and anxiety to maintain the strictest order and discipline of the service, never overlooked. Yet, under all his pride, his stern manner and outward reserve, there beat a heart that could be touched by real sorrow, and a genuine, if silent, sympathy for the suffering of others; and in one moment —a single glance—a softening of the voice— had betrayed this to the sensitive heart of the little drummer.

"Captain! oh, Captain darlin'!" he cried, his voice trembling with emotion, "sure don't be afther sayin' it's for no good. Our faith isn't the same, sir, but maybes it's me prayers an' blissins for yersilf will be heard, for all that. There's a beautiful world beyant, where Heaven grant we may mate," continued the boy, reverently, as he pointed to the sky, his luminous eyes fixed earnestly upon the pale star which still shone down upon them and seemed, like a solitary sentinel, to be keeping watch o'er the earth, the one spark of life and light, in all that wide expanse of leaden grey, and snow-laden clouds.

"'Tis Father Bernard that's always tellin' us about it, sir. His riverince said there's not a kind word, or action, iver spoken or done in this world, that's forgotten up *there;* an' sure what yer honour done for mesilf this night will be remimbered on ye for good, sir."

"Ah, Shilrick!" said the officer, in tones well nigh as unsteady as the boy's, "you know that soldiers have many disagreeable duties to perform. I own that yours is hard, terribly hard, my brave little lad—and mine to-night is sad enough, Heaven knows! do not make it worse for me. Once more I plead with you; oh, my boy! you will be forced to yield at last—why not do so ere you are arrested, not only for disobedience of orders, but for treason, and you know the consequences—the punishment for either of these crimes at such a time."

While Captain Ellis spoke, Shilrick stood silently before him, but his eyes were bent upon the ground, so that the officer could not judge from the drummer's countenance of the impression of his words, he could only see the nervous movement of the tightly-clasped hands and the tremour that passed over the slight, boyish frame.

At last, Shilrick once more raised his head and looked at Captain Ellis, who started back in horror at the change in the young face, for the poor boy was looking haggard and pale as death, his eyes were preternaturally large, and with an expression of hopeless despair in their depths that was sad to see; his lips were so tightly compressed between his teeth that the blood flowed from them, while the tears, which he could no longer restrain, coursed each other down his cheeks.

"Don't ax me anny moor, sir!" pleaded Shilrick, when he could speak. "Don't! oh, don't!" he continued, stretching out his hands, as if to ward off some object that was oppressing him. "Sure I know the consequence—'tis *death* —but oh, yer honour, why would I care?—as well mate it wan way as another, an' if all I loved were gone, sure I'd be axin' an' prayin' for it, as I would for a blissin'. I *can't* obey yer ordhers, sir, indade I can't!" he cried, as, burying his face in his hands, the boy sobbed as if his heart were broken.

With a sorrowful, compassionate glance at the forlorn little figure, Captain Ellis turned and hurried from the spot, murmuring to himself, "Poor little lad! There is, indeed, one of Nature's gentlemen; his heart true as steel, his honour dearer to him than life; and—oh, horror!—it is *I* who have to go to the Colonel and report his refusal to obey orders."

"*Och, wirra, wirra!*" sobbed Shilrick, as he saw the Captain depart, and felt that he was left alone to fight the fierce battle raging in his brave, boyish heart, between his love, his honour, and his duty.

"What will I do, at all, at all?" he cried. "Oh, Kerry, Kerry! sure if ye hadn't joined the Ribils, his honour, Captain Annesley, wouldn't have gone to the mountains, an' all this would niver have happened. Oh! why did I iver ax the Captain to go there wid me? Sure, I've not a friend to advise me, no wan to thurn to now. There's the Colonel—his honour is mighty kind—but he always goes agin anny wan that he thinks would be shirkin' his duty, an' small blame to him, for he niver done that himself. Captain Ellis will be forced to tell him what I've done, an' thin I'll be arristed, an'—— Ah !" he cried, wildly, "they're comin' now ! I hear thim ! Oh, Heaven help me to be brave !—to kape thrue to me word to thim that thrusted me—come what may ! "

Shilrick's nervous terror had caused him to mistake the measured tread of the sentry for the approach of the guard that he expected every moment would be sent to arrest him. It was, however, only Pike, who, as soon as Captain Ellis had disappeared, again went forward to Shilrick, and, seeing his grief, he tried to offer his sympathy and advice, which was genuine and kindly, if somewhat rough ; but, finding that his words of comfort were of no avail, the good-natured sentry once more resumed his march, contenting himself with the occasional admonition to his young comrade, as he passed him :

"Cheer up, little chap ! There now, dont'ee fret, it'll all come right in the end, I reckon."

Neither Pike nor Shilrick had observed the figure of a young girl emerge from the shadow of the wall, where she had been standing for some time, anxiously watching for an opportunity to approach the drummer, when Pike's back was turned, and the boy quite alone. At last the chance came to her, and Shilrick was startled by a voice close to him, calling him by name ; he raised his head, and to his utter astonishment found that it was Anty Kinahan who stood beside him, and was speaking to him rapidly, and in low tones.

"Shilrick , " she said, "sure 'tis everywhere I've been searching for yersilf, enthirely. Then they tould me ye were on guard here—see ! thake this quickly, an' hide it," she added, giving him a letter, after having looked around cautiously to make sure that they were alone.

" But, Anty," remonstrated Shilrick, finding she was about to leave him, and being anxious to gain some information, " sure sthay wan moment, I *must* spake wid ye."

"I can't sthop, an' 'tis no use axin me anny quistions,

sure I know nothin', at all, at all. 'Twas that Yankee Bhoy,
Thaddeus Magin, gave me the letther for yersilf this afthernoon ; but I couldn't bring it bafore—mother wanted me at
home—I must go now. Don't be afther houldin' moor cor-
respondence than ye can help with Magin, Shilrick, *ma
bouchaleen.* Heaven forgive me if I'd be misjudgin' a fellow
craythur, but I belave 'tis a mane thraitor an' a mighty great
blackguard at heart he is enthirely. Whist ! " she
whispered, starting suddenly, and listening, " I belave I
hear some wan comin'. The top av the avenin' to ye, Shilrick ; it's mesilf that hopes the news in the letther will be
plasin' to ye."

"There isn't much in the way av news that can be plasin'
to mesilf now," replied the drummer, " an' me heart mis-
doubts annythin' good comin' from that thafe o' the world,
Magin, but I thank ye for bringin' the letther all the same,
an' good night to ye, Anty agrah ! "

Before Shilrick had done speaking, Anty had disappeared.
He looked round for her, but not a vestige could he see,
even of her retreating figure. It was as if the girl had van-
ished into the earth, so silent and rapid had been her movements. Finding that he was again alone, and that Anty's
must have been a false alarm, he hastily opened the letter,
and, drawing nearer to the guard-room door, so that the
light from within might fall upon it, he slowly read the contents, which were as follows :

"Shilrick O'Toole.—In case you air ordered to guide
the darned militairey up the mountains after us, I guess
you air safe to bring them around to the 'Rebels' Rest' ;
the Boys will be far enough away by the time the military
can arrive, in the exact opposite direction. I calc'late we
mean to make some tracks from here as fast as convenient—
so be sure to come where I hev told yer an' keep the
soldiers about that thar spot on any pretence yer can think
of—yer officer, that starched-up young Captain, an' the old
priest are quite safe. At the 'Rebels' Rest,' I guess yer'll
meet a boy who can tell yer where to find them, so yer'll
be able to go to the rescue, if yer hev a notion that way,
but mind—that young O'Neill must never know that *I* hev
helped to set these prisoners free, or I calc'late he'd be

tarnation angry. Yer brother, Kerry O'Toole, not bein' able to write himself, axed me to do it for him, so as to ease yer mind, and let yer know yer could bring the soldiers up here with safety, and act the guide quite spry and pleasant, knowin' yer'll never find *us*. And this is why yer receive this here notification, from yer obligin' friend and well wisher,

" LIEUTENANT THADDEUS MAGIN,

" Second in command of the 'Bold Boys of Wicklow.'"

Seeing Pike again approaching, Shilrick hastily concealed the letter in the breast of his coat.

" 'Tis from that blackguard Magin, sure enough," said Shilrick, contemptuously, " *my friend*, indade ! Troth I niver could abide the sight av him, at all, at all. But I must thry an like him better now, for sure 'tis the good he's done mesilf *this thime*, annyhow, but someways I *can't* fale grateful to him—I don't know why, but there's a falin' widin me heart this minute that sames to spoil me off likin' him, and kapes houldin' me back from thrustin' him ; but sure he says *Kerry* axed him to write this letter, so it *must* be all right, enthirely. An'," he continued, joyfully, " sure I can go now wid our men to the mountains. Oh, blissed hour ! I can go. Captain Annesley and Father Bernard will be set free, an' 'the Bhoys' safe afther all. But oh, *Ua Néill! Ua Néill!*" he continued, sorrowfully, " aven if *Kerry* hadn't joined the ' Bould Bhoys,' sure it's yersilf that was wan av our officers, an' for *your* sake, as well as for the honour av the *ould* corps, I'd niver have bethrayed yersilf or the Bhoys that are thrue to ye, not though the silence was to cost me my life. Now I must see the sergeant at wanst, an' ax his lave to go afther Captain Ellis, it isn't long *I'll* be overthakin' him. But will his honour look over mesilf refusin' to obey his ordhers ? " added the boy, anxiously, " sure I'm feared not—he can't if he's tould the Colonel, or annywan else—but I'll thry."

Alas ! there was no one to warn Shilrick to have a care how he put too much faith in Magin's letter ; in his own heart he had doubted the man, but there was nothing to strengthen that doubt, and the mere mention of Kerry's name—the brother in whom the drummer had so much faith—had been enough, if not altogether, to remove his mistrust of Magin's purpose, at least to make him think that, in this instance, all was well.

There was no guardian angel to warn those brave hearts in their mountain stronghold of their deadly peril, or to prepare the true, loving-hearted women, to whom they were so dear, for the tragedy in which the cruel, diabolical treachery of Thaddeus Magin was so soon to involve them all.

CHAPTER XI.

" Oh ! the jumbles we make with our heads and our hands,
In this world that nobody understands ;
But with work and hope, and the right to call
Upon Him who sees it, and knows it all.''

It was in a strange scene, and amid strange company that Captain Annesley and Father Bernard found themselves, when compelled to accept the hospitality of the young Rebel Chief and his followers.

Still—rough as the majority of these Rebels were—they would probably have been much worse, but for their gallant young leader; the nobility and refinement of Morven O'Neill's own nature made itself felt, even among those wild, lawless men, and, in a measure, influenced them in their conduct ; and this influence would have been still more effectual had it not been for the constant presence of Thaddeus Magin, for there were many brave hearts and true among O'Neill's " Bold Boys," many in whom there existed the beautiful and genuine spirit of the *real* Patriot.

The cave, in which that band of Rebels known as the " Bold Boys of Wicklow " were now assembled, was long, and of considerable dimensions ; the hour was about six o'clock in the evening, but, being the winter season, darkness had set in long before, and, in any case, the cave was always lighted by artificial means, the lanterns hung around upon the rocky walls giving forth but a feeble and very uncertain glimmer. Even in the daytime, when the sun was at its brightest, the small slits, or apertures, in the rocks far overhead were only sufficient to afford air and ventilation to this strange apartment, or an outlet for the smoke,

when the occupants ventured to light a fire, which was only
on rare occasions, and always after darkness had closed in
around the scene, so that the smoke might not be visible
from the outside.   There were two secret entrances to the
cave, but these were always kept carefully closed, and concealed from the outside, while within, crimson curtains of
rough, heavy Irish frieze hung before them, giving an appearance of warmth and comfort.

Here and there, at irregular intervals, some of them ·a
considerable height from the ground, and sunk deep into the
rocky walls, were curious niches of Nature's own making,
and the projecting rocks forming the ground of these cavities,
had been so far levelled down to smooth, flat ledges, on
which were placed rough, wooden tables, stools, or any
other articles that would answer the same purpose ; for these
small apartments, and, indeed, the whole cave, had been supplied with an incongruous and heterogeneous collection of
furniture, by members of the Rebel band, who had, from
time to time, contrived secretly to smuggle various trifles of
necessity or comfort, into their stronghold, and thus causing
their young leader many anxious misgivings as to whether
the said articles had been lawfully obtained—whether they
had been begged, borrowed, or stolen.

The rugged, but picturesque, recesses described above,
were reached by means of rough steps hewn out of
the rocks, and they were generally occupied, for they
served as a retreat for special friends among the " Bold
Boys," who wished either to engage in confidential converse,
to indulge in card-playing, or to continue a dispute commenced in the cave below, from which they had been
banished by O'Neill, it being his usual custom to act thns at
the very outset of a brawl between two or three members of
his band, so as to separate them at once from the others, for
they were, for the most part, desperate characters with whom
he had to deal, and in a few moments the whole body of
wild, hot-headed men would be in a ferment, for on such
occasions all would immediately take sides and join in the
mélée, even though many of them might not have the most
remote idea of the cause for which they were fighting, or the
justice of the side they favoured, and the consequences of

such dissensions among his followers, O'Neill knew well would prove disastrous, if not fatal to the "*great cause*" which they had bound themselves to uphold.

The cave was very damp, and water was generally to be seen trickling down the rocks, in the crevices of which tufts of moss and other plants of a like nature seemed to flourish, and to a certain extent retain their verdure despite the want of fresh air and light.

On this particular night it was intensely cold, the sleet and snow found its way slowly but steadily through the apertures in the roof of the cave, while the water, which was usually streaming down the rugged walls, was now frozen, and hung in icicles, of the most wonderful and fantastic description, from the roof and the projecting rocks, forming a delicate tracery around the various niches before-mentioned, glittering even in the subdued, uncertain light of the lanterns, like myriads of diamonds, and with a soft, yet scintillating glow, giving forth all the varied and beautiful hues of the opal.

In one part of the cave was a rough, wide hearth, on which burnt a large peat fire, and around this were placed a few wooden chairs and stools, interspersed with couches, formed of bundles of heather and dried bracken. Over some of these were thrown rugs, made of the skins of hares and foxes sewn together, which gave them the appearance of comfort and luxuriousness.

Down the centre of the cave extended a long rustic table, evidently put together by inexperienced hands, on which stood drinking cups of the most primitive designs and patterns, and the remains of the supper of which the " Bold Boys " had been partaking, previous to holding themselves in readiness for orders to march to the spot where they were to meet at midnight, with other bands of insurgents, for the purpose of drill, reconnoitring, and afterwards being inspected by one of the chief leaders of the Rebel Forces in that part of Ireland.

Many of the " Bold Boys " were still seated at the table ; some had only just arrived, bringing with them the latest news from the outer world ; others, having finished their supper, had retired to the recesses above ; a few were still absent, but were expected to appear at any moment.

On one side of the hearth were seated Captain Annesley and Father Bernard, and opposite to them, on the end of one of the heather couches, sat Morven O'Neill, who seemed buried in thought, while from time to time he cast anxious glances at the young Marine officer and the priest, and from them to some of his band, seated at the long table. More especially was his attention fixed upon a group consisting of Thaddeus Magin, with Myles Lenigan and Shiel Casey on either side of him, and several others near hand, to whom the Yankee was holding forth in his usual dictatorial, insolent manner, and yet evidently rivetting their admiring attention, as he alternately made long speeches, and applied himself to the "liquor," of which he was always careful there should be a large jug at his side, before he "fixed himself" at the table.

At some distance from this group, of which Magin was the leading spirit, Kerry O'Toole and Owen Maguire were seated together, and apparently engaged in eager conference, but they spoke in tones so low as to be inaudible to anyone else in the cave, although, from their constant and furtive glances in the direction of Magin, it was evident that their conversation concerned him in particular; and so thought the American, Silas Charleston, who was ensconsed in one of the niches just above Magin and his *confreres*. Silas was *saying* nothing, he had indeed been silent for the best part of the day, but he was—as he himself would have expressed it—"*thinking* a deal," and now he was stooping forward the better to hear the conversation in the cave below, not a word of which escaped his keen ears, nor did his clear, searching eyes miss a single action or movement of importance on the part of those whom he was anxiously watching; and at times he smiled grimly and significantly between the whiffs of smoke from his pipe—at some remark he had overheard.

Occasionally, however, Charleston's attention became somewhat divided, as he stole glances—partly of contempt, partly of amusement—at the figure of Andy Rafferty, who was seated opposite to him, at the other side of the recess, reclining against the wall, in an attitude of indolent ease and repose, being fast asleep, with a calm, placid smile upon his features, and with the *dhudeen*, he had been lazily smoking, still between his lips.

" A real case of 'Rome burning and Nero fiddling,' I guess," said Charleston, to himself, smiling, "and I calc'late there'll be some tarnation hot work to-night yet ; there's a storm brewing, that's certain," he continued, as he good-naturedly stretched out his feet to the full extent of the recess, to prevent the catastrophe of Andy Rafferty falling over the brink, on to the heads of those beneath, and then returned to his former occupation of "keeping an eye " on Thaddeus Magin.

The central group around the hearth had been silent for some time, each one being engrossed with his own thoughts.

Morven O'Neill was full of anxiety concerning the fate of Annesley and Father Bernard ; he had not been idle, during the few days of their detention, in the way of planning, in his own mind, some means for the escape of his two friends ; he had indeed, that very day, made arrangements with certain trustworthy members of his band for their release, but there still remained the fear that by some mischance the attempt might fail, and he well knew that they would in that case be in a much worse position than before. It was necessary for him, therefore, to be careful, and he had decided—until he was more certain of the result of his scheme, and could see his way more clearly to success—that he would not mention the matter to either Annesley or Father Bernard. The priest, who had so generously volunteered to share the imprisonment of Annesley, was now much troubled with the thought of the poor, and the dying among his parishioners who would miss him, and wonder at his absence, particularly those fever-stricken ones in the distant and desolate cabins, whom he was on his way to visit when he chanced to encounter Annesley and Shilrick O'Toole, and who had been almost entirely dependent upon him for their spiritual comfort as well as for the means of livelihood ; and after all, thought the kindly old man, his presence in the Rebels' cave had been useless so far as Annesley was concerned. He had imagined that he might have been able to influence his old pupil and favourite, O'Neill, to release the young Marine officer at once ; but this the former could not do in direct opposition to the rest of his band.

It is true, however, that in a measure the presence of Father Bernard had some power, so far as the Irish Roman Catholics among the "Bold Boys " were concerned, in protecting Annesley from insult, and inducing the roughest of these Rebels to treat him with a certain amount of deference and civility ; but still the good old priest tormented himself with the thought that, for once at least, he had missed the path of duty, and grieved for those sick and ailing ones, who would be doubtless, even at that moment, bewailing his absence.

Captain Annesley's mind had been busy throughout the day, thinking over the news which his foster brother, Kerry O'Toole, had that morning contrived secretly to impart to him, concerning Shilrick's accident, his detention at Mrs. Kinahan's hostelry, and his subsequent departure for Glencree Barracks.

Had the poor boy arrived safely ; and what had been his reception at headquarters ? How would he account for his lengthy absence, and the strange disappearance of his Captain ? These, and similar questions, had been troubling Annesley all the day. He felt certain that, at all costs to himself, Shilrick would remain firm in his determination, and true to the promises he had made to his brother Kerry and Silas Charleston not to betray the " Bold Boys." He knew also that the drummer would, as far as possible, obey the orders that he himself had given him on the evening when he escaped from the Rebels.

That the poor boy would be hardly tried, Annesley was only too well aware ; he would have to pass through an ordeal from which many a brave, strong man might quail. Yet, when the young officer thought of the scene in the " Shamrock," between Shilrick and Estelle, which both Kerry and Silas Charleston had so graphically described to him, he could only hope and trust that the courage which had upheld the brave little soldier lad so far, would uphold him still, and that the noble, faithful heart would, like true gold that is tried by fire, only come forth purer and brighter from the crucible of sorrow and trouble into which it had been cast.

From these anxious thoughts Annesley's mind had wandered once more to Eveleen Corrie, and his parting with her. Again and again he went over the scene of their parting, and sadly wondered what might have been, had Lieutenant Rochfort not entered at that most inopportune moment.

Now all chance of their future reconciliation seemed to him hopeless, when he remembered that the last he saw of Eveleen was, as she stood in the centre of the room—apparently calm and untroubled, despite all that he had told her—holding out her hand to Rochfort with, as he (Annesley) thought, the sweetest of smiles, and that the last words he had heard on her lips were a pleasant greeting to the young cavalry officer, while she had allowed him—her old lover—to pass out of her presence with a few cold words, and a careless curtsey, such as she might have accorded to a mere acquaintance, while he bowed himself out of the room, with a gloomy cloud of wounded pride and grief upon his brow.

And Eveleen—was she happy with Rochfort, whom, in Annesley's presence, she had welcomed with such apparent pleasure? Ah, no! for her sad thoughts had followed the man for whose love she was breaking her heart, and who had now left her, going out alone, without one hopeful, cheering word from her—alone into the dark shadow-land of doubt and suspicion.

This cheerful train of thought, so diligently pursued by Annesley, naturally, in due course, recalled to his mind the time when he felt that he had good cause to consider that Morven O'Neill was his rival ; and in memory he was again enacting the events of that unfortunate meeting on the shore of the haunted lake, which had proved so fatal to his life's peace and happiness.

That Eveleen Corrie and the Rebel Chief were lovers he felt certain, how otherwise would O'Neill have so daringly risked his life or liberty, or the Colonel's daughter her fair fame, as to meet in such a manner, after nightfall, and so near the precincts of the barracks, with the chance that at any moment a picket of Marines, or the cavalry regiment, might come upon them. Yet—argued Annesley, in his own mind, having now thoroughly worked himself up to a pitch of unmitigated misery and despair—yet Eveleen still seemed to encourage Rochfort. Could it be, he wondered, that Eveleen was playing fast and loose with both these men ? Yet no— for, as he looked long and earnestly over at Morven O'Neill, he could not imagine that any woman who had once possessed the love of such a man, would, for a moment, think of transferring her affections to the young cavalry officer, who, though good-looking and attractive enough, and with a certain smart, military bearing, was, as Annesley and many even of his own brother officers thought at the time, empty-headed, shallow-hearted, and vain and egotistical to an inordinate degree.

But the young Rebel Chief ! Ah ! *he* in truth was a formidable rival for any man, and so felt Annesley, watching him jealously, as he sat in a careless, graceful attitude on the opposite side of the rough hearth, with the fitful gleam of the fire falling upon his face.

O'Neill did not wear his hair powdered, but the long silken locks of a dusky-brown shade were gathered into a queu after the fashion of the time, and swept back from a face that was perfect in its beauty, whether irradiated by the fire of enthusiasm, under the power of emotion, or in calm repose—a face not merely handsome in a physical sense, but good, noble and steadfast, with the purity of heart and soul shining in those glorious eyes, so wonderfully like his cousin Eveleen's as to be most disturbing to Captain Annesley's peace of mind, besides which, every now and again some tone of Morven's voice, some graceful trick of manner brought back the memory of his lost love, and saddened still more the heart of the young Marine officer.

Often as Morven's glance met that of Annesley, the former wondered at the stern, searching expression on the face of his old comrade, or at the wistful, yearning look that would at other times show itself in his dark, watchful eyes.

Occasionally Annesley would rouse himself from his gloomy reverie, and useless regrets for past words and actions, which he could not recall, and try to take comfort in the thought that O'Neill and Eveleen Corrie—according to the generally-accepted rule in such matters—·bore too great a resemblance to each other, both in personal appearance and temperament, ever to stand in the relationship of lovers; it was more natural that their feelings should assume the tone of brotherly and sisterly affection.

But the demon of jealousy, having once entered into the heart—whether it be of a man or woman—is not easily exorcised, and every careless word, every little action, even the most trivial incidents of the past few months connected with his intercourse with Eveleen, now rose up in grand array in the mind of Captain Annesley, and proved countless weapons of self-torture to his proud, but faithfully-loving nature.

His thoughts seldom ceased to dwell with bitter sorrow and suspicion upon the fact of Eveleen's refusal to trust in him, her determined concealment of the identity of O'Neill with that of the young Rebel Chief, whom she met secretly, and her obstinate resolution to maintain silence as to the reason of her strange conduct on the night of that clandestine meeting.

Had Eveleen only confided in him, much pain and sorrow might have been spared.

Thus we, in our blindness and self-reliance so often do, or leave undone, that which may alter the whole course of our lives, marring the future that might have held such bright possibilities for us, causing sorrow and despair where all might have been restful peace and happiness, wilfully shutting out the sunshine from our hearts, and refusing to let one ray penetrate the dark shadows which we have so persistently conjured up for ourselves.

Kerry O'Toole, was also, on this evening, one of the most miserable of men ; during the past few days he had been a prey to remorse, for by his own act of folly, in thus joining the insurgents, to try and drown his sorrow for the loss of a girl who —had she been as false as Kerry believed her—would not have been worth an honest man's thought, he had placed his brave little brother in a position of the greatest peril, for, like Annesley, he knew that the drummer would never betray the " Bold Boys," and yet, if he refused to do so, he must nevitably, according to the rules of the service, be tried by court-martial as a traitor, and one who was shielding the Rebels.

And now, here, too, was his foster brother, a prisoner in the hands of the insurgents, and although he (Kerry) had been doing his best to plan the officer's rescue, he could not, as yet, tell how this plan might succeed. Had it not been for him, Shilrick would have been spared the terrible ordeal that was now before him, and Captain Annesley would probably have been safe in barracks at that moment.

So the cloud of unavailing regrets, and self-reproach rested on the brow of more than one of those assembled in the Rebels' cave that fatal night. Many had made mistakes in their lives that could never be remedied this side of the grave, others, who had still time and opportunity left to them, were grieving that they could as yet see no way out of the labyrinth of dangers, difficulties, and blunders with which an adverse fate, or their own folly, had surrounded them, for their sad, weary eyes were too dim with sorrow to see, across that stormy ocean of trouble and pain, the fair land of hope and promise that lay beyond.

CHAPTER XII.

" Well had he learned to curb the crowd,
By arts that veil, and oft preserve the proud :
His was the lofty part, the distant mien,
That seems to shun the sight, and awes, if seen ;
The solemn aspect, and the high-born eye,
That checks low mirth, but lacks not courtesy."

Scott.

Some months before this time, the "Bold Boys" had all been supplied with the Rebel uniform, which has already been described in a previous chapter ; but, at that hour, and within the precincts of their own stronghold they usually presented a somewhat fantastic appearance, being arrayed in a sort of demi-toilet, which—if not particularly elegant, or in strict accordance with military regulations—was certainly, in many cases at least, most picturesque. The dark languishing eyes of the Spaniard, or the glittering orbs of the Italian, might still be seen peeping furtively from beneath the broad-brimmed hat, or sombrero, the fair locks of the German adorned with blue or red cap, the crafty physiognomy of the Greek, surmounted by the tasselled fez ; while the bright-coloured shirts and gay barcelonas of the Irish and American Rebels lent an appearance of warmth, and a variety of colour to the strange scene. On one point, however, all were alike, each man had his arms—a musket and pistols beside him, all being loaded and ready for immediate use, in the event of a surprise or sudden attack from without. Many of the men had been drinking heavily, and were now giving vent to their high spirits by singing one of the wildest of old Irish songs, namely, the far-famed " Garryowen."

The words appear to have in them but little sense or reason, and the rhyme does not, at times, run over-smoothly, but the air is very spirited, and the singers contrived to instil an amount of significant expression into the song, the real meaning of which was perfectly understood by, at least, the Irish portion of the assemblage, who joined lustily in the chorus, their voices coming from all parts of the cave, with wonderful effect.

The Irish and Scotch peasantry possess, as a rule, fine voices and keen ears for music, and they sing with a deep feeling or with a certain cheerful, merry ring in their tones that renders their vocalization more pleasing than is usually the case with that of untrained singers ; and thus the strains of " Garryowen," as they rose and fell in agreeable and effective rhythm, did not jar so unfavourably as might have been expected upon the senses of the silent and more culti-vated members of the audience then present.

Towards the end, however, the voices grew louder and more excited, and the time less carefully measured.

For the benefit of the reader who may not know the words, I now give some of the verses, as published in a book of old Irish songs—

> " We are the boys that take delight in
> Smashing the Limerick lamps when lighting
> Thro' the streets like sporters fighting,
> And tearing all before us.

> CHORUS.—Instead of spa, we'll drink brown ale,
> And pay the reck'ning on the nail,
> No man for debt shall go to jail,
> From Garryowen in glory !

> Oh ! we'll break windows, we'll break doors,
> The watch knock down by threes and fours,
> Then let the doctors work their cures,
> And timber up our bruises.

> CHORUS.—Instead of spa, we'll drink brown ale,
> And pay the reck'ning on the nail,
> No man for debt shall go to jail,
> From Garryowen in glory !

We'll beat the bailiffs out of fun,
We'll make the mayor and sheriffs run ;
We are the boys no man dares dun,
If he regards a whole skin.

CHORUS.—Instead of spa, we'll drink brown ale,
And pay the reck'ning on the nail,
No man for debt shall go to jail,
From Garryowen in glory !

Our hearts so stout have got no fame,
For soon 'tis known from whence we came ;
Wher'er we go they dread the name
Of Garryowen in glory.

CHORUS.—Instead of spa, we'll drink brown ale,
And pay the reck'ning on the nail,
No man for debt shall go to jail
From Garryowen in glory !

In those days the song of " Garryowen " was said to bear some strong political, as well as religious significance, like that of " Boyne Water ;" the latter being the war cry, so to speak, of the opposite party, and, even to this day, these two tunes, so widely different in style and sentiment, when played or sung in certain parts of Ireland, or on especial occasions, are frequently productive of the most disastrous results, the feelings of the people being roused to fury, or enthusiasm, and their hearts seemingly stirred to their very depths on hearing the first gay, daring notes of " Garryowen," or the tones of exquisite pathos that characterize " Boyne Water."

" The Boys are in good spirits to-night !" said Morven O'Neill, addressing Captain Annesley, when the Rebels had concluded their song.

" So it seems !" replied that young officer, dryly. " Yet *this* is scarcely the style of mess table, or the company in which I should have expected to find the fastidious Morven O'Neill."

Father Bernard looked up suddenly on hearing Annesley's words, glanced long and sorrowfully at O'Neill, and then, sighing, he turned from them both and buried his face in his hands, remaining thus for some time, evidently in deep and anxious thought, and hearing at first nothing of the conversation between the two young men beside him, beyond a passing word now and again which might chance to reach his ears.

It was some moments ere Morven spoke, in reply to Annesley's scornful remark, and, when he did so, there was considerable *hauteur* in his manner and voice.

" It is not from choice that I am here now, you know that well enough, Annesley ; but I should scarcely think of weighing my own personal comfort, and decided predilection for more refined company, against the welfare of Erin. Could anything equal the exquisite happiness to me of being of service to my own beloved, sorely-tried country ; and the hope of one day knowing that I have played, even the most humble part, in her rescue from that sorrow and bondage, which it makes my very heart's blood boil to see so many of my countrymen tacitly enduring, and even finding excuses for her tyrants, and their acts of coercion and cruelty. Ay ! and forgetting the injustice and the wrongs of centuries past. Oh, Annesley ! how I grieve to think that I cannot make you, and such men as you—brave, honourable, true-hearted men —feel as I feel. Oh, the pity of it ! that I cannot make you see these things in the same light that I see them. As far as my present comrades are concerned, poor and outlawed though they may be, yet I honour and respect them, for the noble and patriotic sentiments which have led them to join the '*great cause*' to fight for the rights and the liberty of Ireland."

" *Noble ! Patriotic sentiments !*—what—these men here to-night ! " exclaimed Annesley, as he looked around upon the motley assemblage in the cave, and for the life of him could not repress a smile of amusement.

" O'Neill ! " he said, wonderingly, " is it possible that your enthusiasm can carry *you*—a man of sense and intellect—so far as to believe in the integrity, or '*the patriotic sentiments*' —as you call them—of these men ? "

Annesley's words, and most of all, the incredulous smile which accompanied them, were perfectly exasperating to O'Neill, but he used every effort to conceal his indignation, his temper and feelings being always kept well under the control of an iron will.

"Enough of this, Annesley!" he answered, impatiently. "Let us not speak more of a subject upon which we can never agree. It is growing late, I must soon leave you, and I have yet much to say to you. Life is uncertain at the best," he continued, gravely, "and in these times mine is a precarious one, we know not what an hour may bring forth. There is something of importance which I must take this opportunity of telling you, before I leave the cave to-night, for there is a feeling in my heart, I cannot tell you why or wherefore, but it seems like a dim presentiment to me—that such an opportunity may never come again. You know now," he added, bending forward, and lowering his voice, "you know who was the companion of my cousin, Eveleen Corrie, on the night you encountered us at—"

"Yes, I know *now*," interrupted Annesley, coldly.

"I have been thankful ever since," continued Morven, "that it was *you*, instead of any of the other fellows belonging to the old corps, who came upon us, as I know you will keep the secret for my cousin's sake."

"Oh, certainly! You may rely on my discretion," replied Annesley, haughtily.

"I think," resumed Morven, "that in justice to Eveleen, I should tell you her reasons for coming to meet me. You will understand that I could not go so near the barracks in the daylight, so that I was forced to choose that untimely hour for our interview. I wanted to see my cousin; I had written some time previously to her, and, at my earnest request, she consented to meet me on the spot where you found us together. We made but little, however, of this meeting, for your appearance, followed by that of the soldiers, put a speedy end to our interview."

"Allow me to offer my most sincere regrets for the interruption," returned Annesley, sarcastically.

O'Neill glanced hurriedly at his friend, and seemed surprised at his strange manner of receiving the information he was giving him. After a moment's pause, however, he continued:

"And now for my reasons for so earnestly desiring that interview with my cousin, I must first tell you, Annesley, that I am married."

"Married! *You married!* and *to her!*" cried Annesley, in his distress and excitement starting to his feet and confronting Morven almost fiercely. "Oh, Eveleen! Eveleen!" he murmured to himself. "How *could* you deceive me thus?"

Again O'Neill looked bewildered and astonished at his companion.

"Yes, Annesley!" he said, quietly. "It was a secret marriage."

"Why secret?" demanded the other, shortly, having with an effort regained his self-possession and again seated himself opposite to Morven.

"Because my wife's friends would not have consented to our marriage, had they known of it," answered O'Neill.

"No, I should suppose not," retorted the young officer, bitterly.

"My bride is in Ireland now, Annesley, as you know, she is living in this very place," continued Morven.

"I think you need scarcely inform *me* of *that* fact, O'Neill," said the other, grimly. "But pardon me! Is there any absolute necessity that we should discuss her at all?"

"Assuredly there is!" replied Morven, "for I may never see Eveleen again, and, as I have said, mine is a life of danger, and our country is in such a state that we know not from day to day what may happen. Annesley!" he added, earnestly, "*you* are the only friend I have near me now; I know that I could safely trust life and honour in your hands. Will you promise that if aught befalls me, you will protect my wife?"

"*I* protect her?" exclaimed Annesley, sternly. "Ah, no, no! do not ask this of *me*, O'Neill. I shall never *willingly* see or speak to her again. Oh, Eveleen!" he muttered to himself, "miserable, false heart!"

"Not speak to her again!" cried Morven, in astonishment; "why, Annesley, what harm has my poor little wife ever done to *you?*"

"*That* I think we need not argue *here*, and I am certain that you are quite well aware of the relationship in which we stood to each other. You, O'Neill, have complimented me upon *my* honour, I regret that I cannot speak the same of *yours*, in this instance at least."

" Annesley ! " cried Morven, indignantly, rising to his feet.

" Wait ! " interrupted the other, holding up his hand peremptorily, " I have not done yet. You are no doubt quite prepared to offer countless excuses for *her*, and for your own conduct in this affair, but I do not wish to hear them. I was only about to say, that in my opinion, you should rather seek protection for your wife from her friends—her own father especially, and as she is still living under his roof, and possesses a loving and devoted mother, I do not fancy any harm is likely to befall her. In such an instance, and under the circumstances, I should imagine that any offers of protection from *me* would be considered as nothing less than gross impertinence."

" Annesley'" exclaimed Morven, drawing nearer to his friend, and regarding him with amazement, " have you taken leave of you senses, old comrade? or what idea, in the name of all that is wonderful, have you got into your head ? My wife's father and mother have both been dead for many years."

" O'Neill," cried Annesley, springing from his seat and clasping Morven's hands in his, " you have indeed lifted a load off my heart this night. Go on, go on ! " he continued, earnestly. " Tell me all ; I will most willingly promise to protect her, in short, I will do *anything* for her or for you."

" Upon my honour, Annesley, I do not understand what you mean, or of what you have been thinking," returned Morven, with some impatience. " Whom did you suppose I had married ? "

" Oh, never mind what I was thinking, or rather dreaming of, just now. You shall hear that again. Tell me all about your marriage, O'Neill."

" Well," commenced Morven, " to tell you the truth I met my love in France, and the marriage took place there. It was a clandestine affair altogether. My wife's guardian—who had been left with entire control over her—and his friends, having determined that I should not be a suitor for the hand of his ward, he was heard to threaten my life ; and on the night I eloped with Estelle, from the old French chateau, she was

to have been betrothed to a man old enough to be her grand-
father, and one of the worst characters to be found either
in, or out of Paris. We had a hard ride for it—my love
and I—but thanks to my faithful servant, Owen Maguire,
who managed to mislead those who were in pursuit, we got
off in safety, and were married that night by Father Antonelli, an old friend of my father. We left France immediately after, for Ireland. I had by that time received orders
from General Holt to proceed to Wicklow and take command
of these men whom you know by the name of 'The Bold
Boys of Wicklow.' I had also a pressing letter from Robert
Emmet, entreating me to return to old Ireland with all speed.
I accordingly returned at once, and answered both these
letters in person."

"But, O'Neill," asked Annesley, doubtfully, "who was
the beautiful girl—the little French *soubrette*—who was
wounded in trying to save you on the night of your meeting
with your cousin Eveleen ? "

"That was my bride, Annesley ; her name was Estelle de
Montmorenci, she is of a noble French family, and was heiress
to a very large fortune, which she forfeited on her marriage
with me, without the consent of her guardian ; preferring
however, to share the uncertain life, and fortune of the man
she loved, rather than remain in wealth and luxury, to meet
the miserable fate to which her guardian would have
consigned her, Estelle fled with me, and is now, as I have
explained, staying with Mrs. Kinahan at the 'Shamrock ;'
and that she might the better avoid observation, and pass as
Mrs. Kinahan's niece from France, she has worn the dress
of the French peasantry since she came here. But tell me,
Annesley, whom did you imagine she was, when you saw
her that night ? "

Seeing that his friend remained silent, and seemingly
puzzled how to reply, Morven repeated the question, with
considerable impatience and asperity in his tones.

" Well, since you *must* know, you must, I suppose," said
Annesley, half smiling, half angry. "I thought she might be
some love-sick little *soubrette* who had followed you over from
France, in the hope of sharing your very chequered fortunes.
Oh ! you need not glower at me so desperately, O'Neill.   I

own it was not like you to encourage any such romantic attachment, unless you could do so with honour, but still—what else *could* I think. I am afraid that your cousin may have formed the same opinion."

"True, the supposition was unfortunately probable enough, although I never thought of it before. But, Annesley, what do you think of Estelle—is she not fair and lovely as a poet's dream?" asked Morven, enthusiastically.

"Or a Rebel's, which is oftentimes much the same thing," thought Annesley. "Yes, O'Neill," he replied, kindly, "she is *very* beautiful, though I fear fragile and delicate; but you have not yet told me if your cousin knows of your marriage."

"Not yet. It was partly because I wished to introduce Estelle to her, and ask the protection of my friends for my wife, and partly from a longing to see once more the cousin, for whom I have ever had a brother's affection, that I asked Eveleen to meet me that night. Would that I had not done so, Annesley," added Morven, regretfully, "for I fear that it has disturbed the peace of mind both of Eveleen and yourself."

"If you had only trusted me *then*, O'Neill, all might have been well," said the other, reproachfully. "Oh, those wretched secrets!"

"I would have trusted you willingly, Annesley, but it was Eveleen's fear that you might consider it your duty to tell Colonel Corrie, and she did not wish my uncle to know that it was *I—his nephew*, who commanded this party, and was better known by the assumed name of *Michael Cluny*."

"It was a great mistake, O'Neill—but we must try and make the best of it now. I only wish I could but persuade you, even for your poor wife's sake, to leave this present life of yours. Oh, dear friend! think how evil companionship ruins a whole life, and spoils the finest character—the purest, the brightest honour remains not long untarnished under its fatal influence. You are in daily, hourly contact with these men, you cannot expect long to avoid the consequences of such intercourse."

"Morven!" said Father Bernard, sorrowfully, as he raised his head and looked over at O'Neill. "Let me also pray you to consider this—for I have heard your young friend's pleading. I tell you again, that this Rebellion will be a woful, miserable failure !"

In his earnestness, Father Bernard now rose from his seat, and approaching Morven, he laid his hands on his shoulders impressively. To the good old man, in his anxiety to influence O'Neill, the years that had passed seemed for the moment to have been but as a few months, and the enthusiastic young Patriot before him appeared still as the boy he had loved so well in the old days, and to whom he had so conscientiously striven to be a faithful tutor, filling his heart with high and noble aspirations, with pure and unselfish desires.

"Oh, my boy !" continued the priest, "when a country is obliged to call in foreign aid, when she is thankful to swell the ranks of her defenders with such men as you have here ; a collection of the rogues and vagabonds of other nations, whose worthless characters have made them outlaws from their own country. Men who only now join what they know to be a losing cause, for the sake of the little plunder they may chance to gather by the way. It is true that there are a few —but alas ! how *very* few in all your band who have joined it from a motive such as yours ? How many have enlisted in the Rebel forces unmoved by any passion, save that of love for their country, and desire for her freedom. In *you*, at least, Morven, I can recognise the true metal, the golden enthusiasm of the pure, single-hearted Patriot ; but I grieve sorely to see the purposes to which it is applied, the useless waste of time and energy ; to find even on some points that your sense of right and wrong is strangely perverted, and to think of the horrors of the civil war with which, if you could, you would devastate the land. You well know how the attempted invasion of the French failed utterly—how they have again retreated to their own land, and how most of the leaders of the Rebellion have fled to foreign shores, leaving you— and such as you—brave, but misguided, men—to struggle on alone with your scanty, half-disciplined, indifferently-armed bands, with the whole power of a kingdom against you. *They* themselves fly before the flames of the fire of rebellion which they have helped, encouraged, and even urged *you*, and such men as you, to raise, to your own utter ruin."

"I know it all, sir!" cried Morven, passionately. "I know how the false-hearted cowards have acted—basely, treacherously, and in a manner unworthy the name of men. But," he continued, his face aglow, his eyes blazing with the light of enthusiasm, "was it not so in the days of the Scottish Wallace, his noble co-patriot, Sir Simon Fraser, and the brave Douglas? Yet did *they* not rally their country around the standard of liberty, and win for her that glorious freedom which she has never again lost. Oh, Father! is it not a noble end that *we* have in view, the liberty of our own beloved land. It seems to me that the shedding of our very hearts' blood is far too poor a sacrifice for such a cause; and never shall *I* cease my labours for my country's sake until I close my eyes in death. I have given my life to the cause I maintain, and every man who joins us by any influence *I* may have used is a lasting joy to me, for have I not gained another sword, another heart for Erin in her trial; so that when the real crisis comes, our ranks will be filled with brave, enthusiastic men."

"That crisis will *never* come, O'Neill," said Annesley, once more joining in the discussion. "Oh!" he continued, earnestly, "am *I* not an Irishman as well as yourself. Think you not that I love my country, or that the true Celtic blood that we both claim, flows less warmly im *my* veins than in *yours?* Ah, no! I love every rock, hill, and tree, every sweet valley, rugged mountain, and lovely glen of our Green Isle; ay! and each blade of grass that springs from Irish soil is dear to my heart."

"Then why not leave the army, Annesley, and join us?" asked Morven, eagerly.

For a moment the young Marine officer stood gazing at the speaker in utter amazement; the sudden and cool suggestion almost appalled him, loyal soldier as he was, but at last his face relaxed, and the haughty expression gave place to a smile of amusement, as he replied.

"O'Neill, are you *mad*, to make such a suggestion to *me?* Do I look like a traitor, I wonder?" he asked, grimly.

"*A traitor*, Annesley! *you* a traitor?" exclaimed Morven, "why, what do you mean?"

"That I certainly should be one, and a most contemptible

one too, were I to act in the way you would wish. *You* have taken up one cause, O'Neill; I wear the King's uniform and belong to the side that disapproves of that cause. If you choose to continue in this banditti state of existence, in Heaven's name don't ask *me*—of all men in the world—to join you," retorted Annesley. "You know that I would give my life, willingly and cheerfully for my country," he added, earnestly. "But I will never take up arms for a cause which I consider to be wrong."

"And you would forget all the cruel wrongs and oppressions we have suffered from England?" demanded Morven, indignantly, "you would forget all the injustice meted out to us—the unfulfilled promises of those in power?"

"Not so, O'Neill!" replied Annesley, gravely, "but I would not avenge them on the innocent. The leaders of the present Government are doing all that lies in their power to counteract the evils, in the perpetration of which *they* had no part."

"Yes," returned Morven, contemptuously, "and under cover of benefits they lay down innumerable rules, and make many conditions, at once irritating and repugnant to the people. I tell you, Annesley, that before there is perfect peace in our country, the English nation *must find the key to our Irish hearts;* they must give us love for love before they can understand us, or win that trust which has been so often shaken by cruelty and indifference to the feelings of our people."

"Well!" replied Annesley, thoughtfully. "There is certainly much that is true in what you have now said, O'Neill, still, Irishman though I am, I cannot but say that there are faults on both sides in this instance. And, in addition to this, you must remember that any advances on the part of the present English Government were met with sullen hostilities on *our* side at the very outset."

"And small blame to 'our side,'" said O'Neill, "for their advances were such as no *true* men, who had the real interest of Ireland at heart, could meet, even half way. Were not disgraceful and tyrannical restrictions heaped upon us— upon our religion, our politics, ay, and even the most sacred of our home ties severed by laws made by strangers and aliens, who can claim neither religion, kindred, nor country in common with us. Erin's tears are not like those of a wayward child—they cannot be dried all at once by the sight of a new toy, or a few fair promises ; they come straight from the very hearts of a sorrowing and suffering people, and it would take years of love and kindness to wipe away those tears, and the haunting memory of the centuries of cruel wrongs which have caused them. But, Annesley, why should we argue farther on this subject ? *You* will not change your opinion, neither shall *I* change mine. I do not blame you, for as long as you hold the King's commission, honour bids you, both in word and action, to remain true to the colours under which you serve. I have cast from me for ever the chains of bondage in which England would fain hold us. I shall stand or fall with our noble leaders, who have so bravely unfurled the banner of liberty, feeling proud if I can take the smallest part in the struggle for the welfare and the freedom of our own beloved Ireland. Like our young bard, and mutual friend Tom Moore I would say—

> ' Far dearer the grave or the prison,
>   Illum'ed by one patriot name,
> Than the trophies of all who have risen
>   On Liberty's ruins to Fame.' "

CHAPTER   XIII.

" Remember the glories of Brien the brave,
  Though the days of the hero are o'er !
Though lost to Mononia and cold in the grave
  He returns to Kinkora no more.

That star of the field, which so often hath pour'd
  It's beam on the battle, is set ;
But enough of its glory remains on each sword,
  To lead us to victory yet."

MOORE.

For some time Thaddeus Magin had been watching the group by the hearth with considerable uneasiness, from his position near the table, upon which article of furniture his feet were elevated according to his usual custom. At last, he slowly rose from his seat, and withdrawing his pipe from between his lips, though still retaining it in his hand, he approached Morven O'Neill in a rough, swaggering manner, and with unsteady gait, his face wearing a dark, sinister expression as he addressed his young chief in tones of the rudest sarcasm, while he stole insolent glances out of the corners of his half-closed, baleful-looking eyes, at Father Bernard and Captain Annesley, furtively watching the effect of his words upon them all.

"Wa'al, now, Captain, I guess the time is going tolerable fast, an' I must say yer hev done yer duty uncommon slick as far as argefying is concerned, though I calc'late yer hedn't the most likely parties to try it on with ; yer might talk to the old rev'rend gentleman, an' that thar starched-up young officer for the next hundred years, an' I reckon they'd hold their own opinions to the end."

"Who called *you*, Thaddeus Magin?" asked Morven, haughtily, "I most certainly did not address you."

"*Lieutenant* Thaddeus Magin, if it's the same to you," corrected the Yankee, arrogantly. "I gave yer the title of Captain, I guess yer hev a right to give me mine. I tell yer the Boys ought to be on the move now."

"Well then, *Lieutenant* Thaddeus Magin, allow me to remark that I have not the slightest intention of placing myself under *your* orders," replied Morven, haughtily. "And moreover, I must request you to return to your seat, you see that I am engaged at present with my friends."

"Which friends air *our prisoners*, an' I calc'late any one of the Boys hev as good a right to speak to them as *you*, mister," said Magin. "But all right—all right, Captain O'Neill," he continued, as he slowly retired towards his seat, casting backward glances at Morven as he went, "I guess there isn't a Boy in the cave that hasn't had enough liquor as it is, if ye're much longer in startin' yer'll find it tarnation difficult to manage them."

As the Yankee resumed his seat, and his former elegant position, he murmured angrily to himself, "Dash it all! if he don't start soon I guess 'the Boys' will not reach the place at the proper time, an' the soldiers may go back to barracks thinkin' they've had false information. I *must* get him away at once."

Magin's warning to O'Neill had scarcely crossed his lips, when some of the men's voices were heard, raised in loud altercation, which showed that the Yankee had not been far wrong in his opinion with regard to the general condition of the occupants of the cave.

"*Vive la Republique*— dat is de one ting for us!" shouted the Frenchman, Felix Thiband.

"*Nein, nein!*" cried Heinrich Bruhm, a German, "it is not so—ve vill not have it so!"

"*Si— si*—it is the time that we go!" chimed in Guglielmo Focione, in his soft Italian accents. "Onward—*alla vittoria!*"

"That's so, strangers!" remarked Silas Charleston, from the recess where he was seated. "I guess we'll see the stars an' the stripes floating alongside of the green flag of old Ireland in less than no time ! "

The young American's tones were as usual cool and calm, and there was an expression of infinite amusement in his eyes, as he listened to the various disputes going on around him, while he leisurely continued to smoke. His comment, however, was not allowed to pass unnoticed, for Phelim O'Flanigan, who was always ready, either to join in an old quarrel, or to start a fresh one for himself, jumped up off his seat, shouting excitedly :

" Niver ! Sure it isn't anny sthars an' sthripes *we'll* have nare the grane flag av ould Ireland ! "

" Sit down, can't yer, an' don't be a fool ! " commanded Magin, from the opposite side of the table, for he was anxious to prevent a fight in the cave, knowing that it would cause a longer delay in their starting for the " Rebels' Rest." " Sit down, I tell yer ! " he roared again, but without the least effect upon Phelim O'Flanigan, whose pugilistic tendencies, once roused, were not easily subdued. He, therefore, in spite of Thaddeus Magin's scowls and signals, still remained standing, slowly and deliberately turning up his shirt sleeves, and loosening his neckerchief, looking defiantly around the cave as he did so.

" Sure, it's a King av our own an' the ould nobility back agin we're afther havin'," said Owen Maguire, excitedly.

" Ca' cannie !—ca' cannie, lad ! " remonstrated the Scotchman, Andrew Macnaughton, who had overheard Owen's words. " Dinna be makin' siccan a disturbance aboot naethin' ava. What's wrang wi ye the noo, laddie ? Ye needna fash yer thoom anent a King o' yer ain yet, mon, when ye ken unco weel it wad be ower muckle expense till ye all."

To this Owen had no time to reply, for, by the time Macnaughton had finished speaking, a fierce dispute had arisen in some other part of the cave, and men were jumping down from the niches, shouting, and waving their shillelaghs as they joined in the fight, which was the inevitable *finale* to such quarrels.

It was some time before O'Neill could make himself heard through the din of angry voices, but he gallantly went up to

the combatants and quietly pushing the men off him on every
side, contrived, by force of will, and strength of arm, to
make his way into the very midst of them, and thereby
separating them in such a manner that they were obliged to
pause for a moment, while Morven stood proud and erect,
his tall, slender form towering above those around him, his
hand upraised to enforce silence. "What do you mean by
this, Boys?" he demanded, "what is the matter now?"

Morven's question, however, was not destined to be very
quickly answered, as each man was alternately giving an account of his own especial grievance, and abusing the opposition party, while all were speaking at once.

"Well, Boys!" said Morven, at last, in despair, "I am
unable to hear amidst this disgraceful noise; I cannot tell
who is to blame, or what is the cause of discontent."

"Let thim fight it out, masther darlin'," urged Owen
Maguire, "sure, 'tis always moor satisfied the bhoys are whin
they've settled matthers in an honest, sthraightforward manner, enthirely."

Once more the angry chorus of voices was repeated, until
Morven caught a few words from one and another, and so
discovered that it was only an old subject of dispute which
had cropped up again, and had more than once disturbed the
peace of the cave.

"Silence!" he called, in a commanding tone, his peculiarly
musical and resonant voice penetrating into every corner of
the large cave. "Silence! every one of you, and to arms
at once! We have little time to waste, and I should have
thought that your minds would have been too much occupied
with more important subjects than to be indulging in petty
quarrels, and fights unworthy of a mob of street rioters."

"And certainly unworthy of *Erin's national defenders*,"
added Annesley, mischievously.

"*I* told yer what would happen, Captain, if yer didn't make
tracks when I advised yer," said Magin, looking over Morven's
shoulder, with a diabolical grin on his face. "I guess I always give yer good advice."

O'Neill looked round at the Yankee, but beyond a glance
of the most perfect contempt, took not the slightest notice
of his words.

"To arms, Boys!" the young Chief repeated, taking up his position in the centre of the cave.

This command was, however, under the circumstances, easier for Morven to give than for the Rebels to obey, owing to the free-and-easy style of demi-toilet, which has been described before, and in which the "Bold Boys" generally indulged whenever it was possible and admissible.

A rush was now made to all parts of the cave, from whence uniform coats and hats were brought forward and hastily donned—not, however, without considerable altercation as to their right ownership by some members of the gallant band—belts were buckled on, muskets shouldered, and, at last, all were ready.

Four of the men were always told off to carry the banners, and on this occasion those selected were Myles Lenigan, Phelim O'Flanigan, Tim Callaghan, and Andy Rafferty; the latter had to be roused up by Silas Charleston, and, while half-asleep, assisted on with his coat and hat, his banner being thrust into his hand, at the last moment, by the good-natured American.

Sheil Casey had been chosen as the one to carry the grand standard of the O'Neill, which was of green silk, with the crest, arms and supporters embroidered in gold, and the correct heraldic colours upon it, with the motto, "*Lamh Dhearg Eirin.*" Above all were the words, embroidered in gold, "*For Liberty.*" This standard was handsomely mounted on a light, sharp-pointed spear.

All the Rebels, in addition to their muskets, were armed with a pistol in their belts, and a small, light sword hanging at their sides.

Andrew Macnaughton chanced to be the last who was ready, for he had been watching the movements of Magin, the shrewd Scotchman having long since mistrusted the wily Yankee. On this day in particular there had appeared to Macnaughton much that was suspicious in the conduct of the other, and Magin seemed, by instinct, to feel that he was under the keen scrutiny of the Scotchman, and was, accordingly, disposed to resent it.

"Wa'al, old Scotchy, airn't yer ready yet?" he called, rudely, from the other end of the cave. "I guess if the

world had come to an end, you'd be the last to show
up."

"Maybe sae," answered Macnaughton, quietly, as he
busied himself buckling on his belt. "Maybe sae—'The
mair hurry, the less speed,' as the auld sayin' rins, an' it's
aye true eneuch I'm thinkin', but aebody maun be last, ye
ken, aebody maun be last."

"Why don't yer take example by *me*, eh ? " again shouted
Magin. "Don't yer see *I'm* always spry an' ready for *anything?* I calc'late there airn't a better lieutenant in the
whole of the British Army, let alone the Rebel forces, than
Thaddeus Magin."

"Aweel," replied the Scotchman, composedly, "it's gran'
tae hae siccan a guid opeenion o' yersel, ye ken ; an' better,
gin ye can gar ithers till think wi' ye," he added, pointedly.

To this Magin did not reply. He slunk away out of sight,
furious at the knowledge that he always got the worst of it in
an encounter with Macnaughton.

> " Oh that some frien' the gift wad gie us,
> Tae see oorsel's as ithers see us."

quoted the Scotchman, as if to himself, but really loud
enough for Magin to hear, and with a sly wink to Silas
Charleston who had been standing near, an amused witness
of all that had passed.

For many reasons Andrew Macnaughton had mistrusted and
suspected Magin ; he firmly believed that the Yankee intended
in some way or other to deal treacherously with the band,
and he also felt certain that he meant harm to the two
prisoners, whom Macnaughton really liked. Captain Annesley, he said, was " a braw young callant, an' had aye a ceevil
word for ilka ane, for a' the chiel was sae proudfu' lookin'."
He had also expressed his opinion that the priest was " a
guid, hairmless auld body, an' no that bad for a Papist," which
he considered was a wonderful concession for one to make who
belonged to the " auld Kirk o' Scotland," and was a staunch
Presbyterian, or rather, had been, in the days when he was
an innocent wee laddie, herding the sheep among the heather-
clad hills of bonnie Scotland, and later on, when he tended

the farm for his mother; but now, that good, loving mother was sleeping her last long sleep in the quiet little kirk-yard near their Highland home, and his father had lost his life, years ago, gallantly fighting in the Jacobite cause. Thus, their only son had left his lonely home and turned wanderer. In days gone by he had heard tales of how his forefathers had escaped in troublous times, and found a refuge in Ireland, where they had been cared for and hospitably treated, and it was therefore with a feeling of gratitude, as well as a desire for adventure, that caused this son of Scotia to go to the assistance of Erin in her trouble. Of *"the great cause,"* which he had so bravely sworn to uphold, Andrew Macnaughton knew but little, and cared less ; but he had left his home and become a wanderer, and having once cast in his lot with the " Bold Boys " he was determined to share their fortunes manfully, good, bad or indifferent as they might be ; and in *him*, at least, the Rebels had won a leal, true heart for their cause.

During the general confusion that followed O'Neill's orders, Kerry O'Toole contrived to approach close to Annesley, and they conversed together in low tones, for some minutes, unnoticed by the others—Owen Maguire went over to Morven, and stood beside him awaiting his commands.

Once more the men's voices were raised in angry altercation, but this time Magin, who was exasperated at the thought of farther delay, and probable failure of his plans, came to Morven's assistance, and the riot was soon quelled.

" You seem to have rather a noisy, troublesome company, my son ! " said Father Bernard.

" They are not always so, Father ; " replied Morven, " but they have been drinking heavily to-night, I fear, while I have been engaged talking to you and Annesley, and I believe that Magin has been trying to raise the spirit of discontent among the Boys—I doubt that man more and more every day," he added to himself, in an undertone.

At last the men, being all in position and ready to start, Magin called to Morven from the opposite end of the cave, " Now, Captain, I guess the Boys air all ready."

Magin was keeping well in the shadow, and as much as possible out of O'Neill's sight ; the latter, however, was

keenly observant at all times, and especially so with regard
to anything concerning the Yankee. On this occasion Morven was, on looking up suddenly in the direction where
Magin was standing, both startled and anxious to see that
he was not ready to accompany them, and that he still wore
his loose jacket, striped shirt, and large, high-crowned broad-
brimmed hat.

"Magin," cried Morven, sternly, "*you* are not ready!
Why have you not been preparing to go with us?"

"Bekase I reckon I'll remain behind to guard the prisoners," replied the Yankee, insolently.

"I have arranged for that already," said Morven, impatiently, but striving to suppress all outward sign of the
anxiety that Magin's present manœuvre was causing him, he
continued determinedly, "I have given my orders; Kerry
O'Toole and Owen Maguire remain as guards up to eight
o'clock, and then the other party of Boys from the western
side of the mountain will relieve them. *You* are not wanted
here at all."

During this brief dialogue Captain Annesley cast many an
anxious glance at Kerry, but the latter signalled for him to
remain silent, and with as much cool indifference as he could
assume, the young officer once more seated himself again beside the hearth, Father Bernard following his example, while
Kerry and Owen retired to a distant corner of the cave where
they remained conversing together.

Magin now came forward, and standing in a defiant position
before Morven, he spoke angrily: "I calc'late I don't move a
step from here; I shall fix myself in this cave until the relief
guard arrives, yer daren't tamper with *them*. *I* know yer
game, mister! Yer want these two prisoners to escape, so
yer hev left them with guards that yer think'll manage it all
slick an' square; Kerry O'Toole is that starched-up young
officer's foster brother, an' Owen Maguire is yer own faithful
sarvant. But I guess *I'm* equal to the occasion, an' airn't
such a darned fool as yer'd take me for. No, yer hev got
Thaddeus Magin to deal with this time, Captain O'Neill."

"Och, Misther Magin dear!" said Kerry, innocently, as
he now came forward, and joined the others. "Sure now it
isn't Owen Maguire an' mesilf that ye'd think would be afther

lettin' anny prisoners escape ?   Och, begorrah ! an' wouldn't it be bad luck to oursilves if we done that same ? " he added, with a well-assumed tone of injured innocence.

" That's thrue for ye, Kerry, me boy ! an' niver a lie in it," said Owen Maguire, also joining the group.   " An' to think that we've such a fine, iligant gintleman as yersilf helpin' us to win honour an' glory for ould Ireland, an' that we'd be afther spoilin' iverythin' by goin' agin yer wishes an' ordhers."

" Not likely ! " chimed in Kerry.   " An' Misther O'Neill himself always beggin' an' prayin' av us to pay attintion to all that *his honour* Misther Magin says, by raison that he's the best av laaders enthirely," added the young Irishman, with a side-long glance at Magin.

" Ah, I know yer both ! " returned the Yankee, cunningly. "I guess I can read you two boys tarnation plain, yer blarney airn't likely to catch *me* trippin'.   I hev made up my mind to remain here till the other boys come."

" Then 'tis glad we'll be av yer company, Misther Magin darlin'," said Kerry.   " Sure it would have been lonesome enough for Owen an' misilf whin all the bhoys were away."

" An troth, 'tis the plasin' company yer honour is," agreed Owen, insinuatingly, " for isn't it yersilf that has the larnin' an'—"

" Now look here, O'Toole and Maguire," interrupted Magin.   "I guess I want none of yer parlarverin', I don't believe one word that yer say, an' never did.   I know well enough that yer would both be most uncommon delighted if I said I'd go now, an' leave yer masters of the field ; but I calc'late I hev told yer before now that I'm no fool."

" The sorra lie in *that*, annyhow," retorted Kerry, his hot temper at last asserting itself, " for sure I've heard 'tis the *rogues* is most plintiful where *you* come from."

To this Magin vouchsafed no reply, but with a dark scowl on his face, retired to another part of the cave, and seating himself on the corner of the long table, he remained there until the departure of the " Bold Boys," his face wearing an expression of the most dogged determination.

Morven beckoned to Owen Maguire, who hastened over to him, and together they held an anxious consultation.

"I fear there is no chance for Captain Annesley and our good Father Bernard now, Owen," said Morven, hopelessly. "I can do nothing more for them."

"Och, niver heed, masther dear, sure it'll be all right enthirely," was the confident reply. "Jist ye be afther lavin' it to Kerry and mesilf—yer honour can thrust us."

"Yes, thank Heaven!" returned Morven, fervently, "I know that in you and O'Toole I have two faithful friends who will not fail me. But this was our only opportunity. You can do nothing when Magin is to be present."

"Troth thin, if we *haven't* the opportunity, we'll have to do widout it," said Owen; "but sure, sir, 'tis mesilf that's got out av woorse difficulties than the wan we're in now, an' we'll get out av this, too, plase goodness," added Owen, with an Irishman's lively power of surmounting—in imagination—obstacles that lay in the future.

"Misther O'Neill!" said Kerry, speaking hastily, and in a low tone, as, while passing Morven he made an almost imperceptible pause at his side, "we're prepared for this, don't be feared, at all, at all; sure I expicted the mane blackguard would be afther playin' some mane thrick, but it's aven we'll be wid him yet, so we will."

"You will use every effort to set Captain Annesley and Father Bernard free?" asked Morven, earnestly.

"His honour, the Captain, will be in barracks to-night, an' his riverince at the ould chapel in thime for early mornin' sarvice," whispered Kerry, cheerfully, as he passed on.

"An' niver a lie in it, masther darlin'," supplemented Owen.

"That is well. Now we must go," said Morven. "Are you ready, Boys?"

"Ivery sowl av us, Captain!"

"Ivery mother's son av us!"

"*Oui-oui, monsieur!*"

"*Si-si-alla vittoria!*"

"Ay, we're a' ready, Captain," said Macnaughton, dryly, "an' nane the better o' bein' kept waitin' sae lang, while oor gran' Lieutenant was claverin' aboot naethin'."

The above, and numerous other similar assurances and remarks reached O'Neill from all parts of the cave, some being in foreign languages, others in broken English, Erse, or with strong American accent and idiom.

"Good-bye, Father !" said Morven, as he once more stood beside the priest. "Forgive me if I seem to you to be straying from the right path, but, believe me, I am but following the dictates of my heart."

"Oh, my son !" answered Father Bernard, sorrowfully, "would that they led you to a truer sense of your duty. I must ever now reproach myself with the thought that I have failed in my early guidance of you ; it seems as if I, too, were to blame for your wasted life. But there, let me not distress you with my grief," he continued, kindly, taking Morven's hand in his, "good-bye, my boy, Heaven bless you, and grant that you may discover the fatal error in the choice you have made, ere it be too late."

"Annesley !" said Morven, earnestly, turning to the officer. "Let us part friends. Ours is a life of danger, we may never meet again ; we were old comrades once, and," he added, holding out his hands to Annesley, "for the sake of bygone days—"

"Farewell, O'Neill ! or shall we not rather say *au revoir* ?" returned the other, as he warmly pressed both Morven's hands in his ; "for I hope that we *may* meet again, but in better, happier times ; when we can renew these ties of affection and friendship that were so dear to us when we served together in the old corps."

"Farewell, Annesley, or *au revoir* if you will," said O'Neill sadly, and turning quickly away to hide his emotion he left his two faithful friends, and crossed over to the secret entrance to the cave, where Owen Maguire stood holding up the heavy crimson curtain.

"Come on, boys !" cried the young chief, as with one last, sorrowful, lingering look back at those he was leaving, he passed out of the cave, followed by all his band, with the exception of Magin, Kerry O'Toole, and Owen Maguire.

Was it farewell ?—Or were these two old comrades destined to meet again ?

Alas ! neither guessed how soon, or in what terrible circumstances they would next greet each other. Yet, as

Annesley's eyes met those of O'Neill, a chill fell upon their hearts, and spirits; both felt that prophetic instinct—that strange presentiment of coming sorrow and parting, which was—only too soon —to be realized.

CHAPTER XIV.

" Oh, could we from death but recover
Those hearts as they bounded before,
In the face of high Heaven to fight over
That combat for freedom once more."

MOORE.

As Morven O'Neill disappeared through the secret entrance, and the heavy folds of the crimson curtain again fell before it, Kerry O'Toole turned to Annesley, and spoke in low, eager tones.

" Misther Armoric !—sure ye'll thrust all to Owen Maguire an mesilf.   It isn't long ye'll be here now."

" And when we go, Kerry, you will come with us?" asked the officer, earnestly.

" *Armoric wisha !* isn't it enough we've been spakin' av that all this mornin'?   See !" he added, hurriedly, " Magin is lookin' ; don't be afther thakin' anny moor notice av mesilf, at all, at all."

Thaddeus Magin had now once more seated himself at the long table, taking care however to sit sideways, so that he faced Father Bernard and Annesley, his back being turned to Kerry O'Toole, who had also reseated himself at the table, Owen Maguire being almost directly opposite.

" Thake a dhrop moor av the 'craythur,' Liftinant Magin," said Kerry, coaxingly, and at the same time filling the large drinking cup which stood at the Yankee's side.

" Thank yer ! I guess I will ! " returned Magin, who after a long draught, stooped forward to address Annesley and Father Bernard.

"Wa'al now, strangers! airn't yer inclined to be a bit more sociable?" he demanded, with an insolent leer.

"Be silent, sir! If you have no respect for me, be so good as to have a little consideration for an officer in his Majesty's service, who is unaccustomed to such insolence as yours."

While Magin is engaged speaking to the others, Kerry again fills up the goblet, unseen by the former, and continues to do so at intervals throughout the conversation.

"Come now!" continued the Yankee, rudely, "that's not so bad, old gent, I guess I'm as good as him, and I calc'late I hev told yer before that I'm second in command of this 'ere noble battalion of gentlemen at arms," he added, as he quaffed deeply of the contents of the goblet beside him.

"We have not forgotten that fact, *Captain* or *Lieutenant* Magin, or whatever it may please you to call yourself," said Annesley, sarcastically, "but unfortunately in *this* instance military title is not synonymous with that of *gentleman.*"

"Eh! what d'yer mean," demanded Magin, suspiciously. "I reckon I'm Lieutenant *at present.* But I guess I don't intend to remain only Lieutenant much longer," he added, in a gruff, surly undertone.

By this time the liquor with which Kerry had been so diligently plying him was beginning to take the desired effect.

"It is the dire misfortune of the band to have such a man for one of its leaders—a man who would stand at nothing *to gain his own ends,*" returned Annesley, contemptuously.

"That's so, mister, an' I calc'late it's well for the 'Bold Boys' that they hev sich as *me* to uphold the credit of the band," said Magin, conceitedly, "for the young Captain O'Neill isn't equal to much, between his feelin's, his 'curtesies'—as he calls them—an' his everlastin' speechifyin' to the men, to teach them—as he says—'where to draw the line between justice an' revenge.' Confound him an' his gentlemanly ways—I say," added the man, fiercely.

"Well," replied Annesley, quietly, "I only wonder how he can bear with such company even for a single day."

"Do yer, mister?" retorted Magin, who by this time seemed to be growing utterly regardless of what he was saying, and had apparently forgotten the presence of Owen and Kerry:

" Do yer ? " he repeated, "wa'al! he *was* precious particklar when he first came here, dressed like a prince, wanted to fit up this 'ere cave like a palace, until his patriotism run riot an' got the upper hand of his notion of hevin' the place lookin' like a pictur'; an' then I guess he was for everything rough an' ready, an' darned uncomfortable, an' talked of sacrifices, an' voluntary hardships till I'm dashed if *I* ever heard his equal for speechifyin'. Why don't yer get him into Parliament, strangers, eh? I calc'late he'd take the starch out of the other members; before he'd been there a week, they'd be as limp as a barn door fowl after a thunder-storm," concluded Magin, again helping himself to a copious draught from his goblet, and feeling fully satisfied with himself and the way he had "spoken up" to the two strangers.

" I think," said Father Bernard, gravely, " that if you are second in command here, it would be decidedly more becoming on your part to speak with *some* respect of your superior, whatever may be your feelings of envy towards him."

" *My superior?*" shouted the Yankee. "I tell yer Thaddeus Magin never owns any man livin' as superior to himself. But there, let's hev done with *him*. I guess with all this argefyin' I hev been forgettin' the duties of hospitality," he continued, as, finding another goblet on the table near him, he filled it with an unsteady hand, and handed it to Annesley.

" Thar now, stranger! take a drop more of the refreshner, it's first-rate liquor; for you see through me bein' second in command, I guess I hev the best always. What! not take any?" he exclaimed, in astonishment, as Annesley turned away his head scornfully. "Wa'al, I guess the old gent will; the reverend gentlemen never refuse the goods the gods provide, as the sayin' is."

" Sir, this is unbearable," said Father Bernard, sternly, as he rose from his seat, and pushed aside the cup which was being so rudely offered to him.

" What! *you'll* take none neither, eh ? " cried Magin. " Wa'al!" he continued, again turning to Annesley, " I guess I'll give yer another chance, mister. That thar is the best liquor yer ever tasted in yer life," he added, holding the cup right in front of the outraged young officer, who with a quick, sudden movement dashed it out of his hand on to the ground.

"All right, mister!" continued the Yankee, "I guess yer can't say that I didn't do the thing hospitable, an' give yer the chance of having a high old time of it here: but not bein' of an' ill-natur'd turn of mind, I calc'late I'll do more, I'll make myself agreeable an' tell yer a piece of news."

"We do not desire to hear your conversation, sir!" said Annesley, haughtily.

"Now look here, young stranger!" returned Magin, "I guess you air a tarnation deal safer here than in Glencree Barracks, for 'the Boys' air goin' to blow every stone of them up to-morrow night, an' I calc'late thar'll be an extra conflagration in those quarters occupied by Colonel Corrie an' the officers—"

"*The Barracks*?" cried Annesley, rising excitedly—"speak man!—what mean you?"

On hearing Magin's words, Owen Maguire had also risen hastily, and shown great agitation, but Kerry had beckoned to him to keep silent, knowing that it was most important for them to hear all that the Yankee might say.

"I mean just what I say, mister," he continued. "Ah, I guess yer *may* start; it'll be a fine sight in the moonlight, yer'll see no more of Glencree Barracks, an' I'm dashed if I didn't plan the whole affair; young O'Neill knows nothin' of it yet, nor won't; he'd be sure to put his spoke in the wheel if he did, an' say *it wasn't gentlemanly*, or *honest*, or *courteous*, or some sich darned nonsense; I calc'late it *were* cleverly planned too."

"Villain! dastard! that you are," cried Father Bernard, indignantly, "to lead on the men to such deeds, knowing well that the blame will fall on a young man, whose enthusiasm and devotion to his country are causing him to follow a mistaken idea of patriotism."

"Why, certainly!—that's so," agreed Magin, coolly. "I guess you air about right thar, mister. But it's not long *he'll* be leader of this 'ere band; the young aristocrat airn't fit for it."

"Ah ! what do you mean by such words, sir ? " demanded Father Bernard.

"Wa'al ! now you air inclined to be a bit more sociable, I guess I don't mind tellin' yer," was the reply, as Magin drew his chair closer to the priest.   "*I* mean to be *leader* of this 'ere band, and that, too, before another week is over our heads ; an' there can't be two leaders yer know, mister."

"And pray, how do you intend to dispose of Captain O'Neill," asked Annesley, indignantly.

"Wa'al ! I calc'late there can't be much harm in tellin' yer *now*—" commenced Magin.   "I'm gettin' uncommon heavy," he muttered to himself, uneasily, brushing his arm across his eyes, "if the relief boys don't come soon I believe I shall be asleep."   With an effort, however, he managed to rouse himself, and drawing his chair nearer to Annesley, he continued aloud.

"You air not likely to get out of this place in a hurry, *neither* of yer.   Ah ! yer may draw back yer chair, an' hold up yer proud head if yer like, young mister.   I guess yer'll be brought down a bit yet ; pride always goes before a fall.   But you hev asked how I'm goin' to get rid of the Captain ? "

Magin here rose, and, approaching as near to Annesley as possible, he drew a pistol from his belt, and, with a grin of diabolical cunning, said, "*That's* how I dispose of those who stand in *my* path, stranger ! "

"Oh, scoundrel !   Miserable coward ! " cried Annesley, springing upon him and trying to seize the pistol.

Kerry and Owen had risen hastily from their seats, and were about to come forward, but, in the struggle, they heard the pistol go off before Annesley could secure it, and Kerry, seeing that their interference would be useless and only bring them under Magin's notice, again signalled to Owen to be silent, and drew him aside, so that they might—though themselves unseen—be witnesses of all that the Yankee did and said.

"An' now I guess I'll tell yer more," he continued, coolly looking at the pistol in his hand, and then replacing it in his belt.   "It airn't no use yer settin' up yer dander in that style, mister, yer'll never see young O'Neill again, but yer'll hear of his end ; which will be the only end all sich that give themselves the airs that he did, has any right to expect. A party of yer soldiers from Glencree Barracks will meet him this night at the spot in the mountains known as the 'Rebels' Rest,' an' I guess our spry young Captain will be a prisoner in the hands of the English troops before sun-rise to-morrow ; so he'll dratted soon be airin' some of his high-falutin' kinkles in Dublin Castle."

Kerry O'Toole had, at this moment, a hard task to keep Owen in the background, but he retained a firm hold on his arm, feeling that now, more than ever, it was necessary for them to hear Magin's plans, which, in his half-dazed, yet fierce condition, he was fast divulging ; and savagely rejoicing in the horror of his companions, and their inability to help their friends. Annesley was overcome with emotion, and forgetful of everything, save the fact of his friend's danger, he buried his face in his hands, as he exclaimed, sorrowfully :

"O'Neill ! O'Neill ! my friend—my dear old comrade ! "

"Oh, miserable wretch ! " said Father Bernard, indignantly, to Magin, " was your conscience not loaded enough with sin before, that you should commit this act ? Oh ! Morven, my poor boy ! "   •

Magin made no reply, but stood regarding the priest and the officer with a smile in which imbecility and savage exultation were strangely mingled ; he was delighted at the effect his words had produced upon his hearers.

"Father Bernard ! " cried Annesley, hastily, " there may yet be time to warn O'Neill. Quick ! Let us at least make the attempt."

No sooner had the words escaped his lips, however, when he felt how futile would be any effort on their part to escape; they did not even know the secret of how to open the door of the cave from the inside, and the Yankee still stood before them, defiant, fully armed, and not yet incapable of resistance.

If he, Annesley, called Kerry O'Toole and Owen Maguire to come to their assistance, while Magin was still conscious of all that was going on, then he knew that the lives of his foster brother, and O'Neill's faithful and much prized servant, would be forfeited, when it was known to the Rebels—

who were every moment expected to arrive—that they had connived at the escape of two prisoners, more especially when one was a captain of the Royal troops ; and this fact Magin would not be long in making known to them.

Annesley also knew, when too late, that he had inadvertently made a great mistake in giving vent to his feelings, and letting Magin know that he had thought escape possible ; for the Yankee was thus prepared to resist the attempt. The young officer, however, was a man of undaunted courage, and quick action ; with him, to think was to do, and a few minutes therefore decided him at least to make an effort for freedom. He remembered that he belonged to a gallant corps which had never been defeated, why then should *he* fail in the daring sortie he was about to attempt ? Resolutely seizing Father Bernard's arm he drew him towards the entrance to the cave, greatly to the old priest's astonishment. Then suddenly pushing Magin aside, and catching up a pistol which had been left by one of the Rebels, he reached the entrance, and, having lifted the crimson curtain, he stood at bay, holding in one hand the pistol, which he pointed at Magin, while, with the other, he eagerly sought the fastening of the door, an attempt which was rendered the more difficult, as having to face the Yankee. his back was to the entrance.

For a moment only, Magin was taken aback, Annesley's movements had been so rapid, but the former soon recovered himself, and hastily lifting his musket, he pointed it at Annesley's breast and prepared to fire ; but Kerry and Owen rushed forward, and the former, seizing Magin's arm, pushed it upward, the musket thus going off in the air, when Magin turned giddy, reeled, and fell to the ground at Annesley's feet.

"Ah ! what is this ?" cried Father Bernard, approaching the prostrate form of the Rebel. "It must be a fit, for the musket certainly did not wound him.'

"And this pistol I see is not loaded !" said Annesley. "I should have found that to my cost had it come to a fight between us."

"Sure, it's all right, yer riverince !" said Kerry, triumphantly. "'Tis mesilf an Owen had it all arranged betwane us enthirely. I kept on givin' him plinty av the dhrink widout his knowin' it, an' it's turned his head, for I had dhrugged it, d'ye see, sir. He'll be helpless enough for a shoort thime, an' may his rest be plasin' to him; but it won't last very long, so yer honours musn't be losin' a moment, if ye value yer lives and yer liberty. Oh, Armoric *wisha*!" he continued, earnestly, laying his hand on Annesley's arm, "rest not ontil ye're clear av these mountains. The other boys that were comin' to join our band will be here soon now. Maybes they're at the dure this minute, they're all sthrangers to yersilf, an' Magin will have warned thim to have a care ye don't escape. Heaven be praised that they've been so long, an' that I've been the manes av savin yersilf an' his riverince!"

"Kerry!" pleaded Father Bernard, anxiously, "tell me before we go, that you have not joined these lawless men beyond recall. Oh, my son! why did you leave your honourable calling, poor though you were—for such a life as *this*?"

"Come with us, Kerry!" urged Annesley. "You know that it was wandering in search of *you* that brought me here, and led your brother, Shilrick, into danger. Are all my persuasions, my prayers, to be in vain?"

"I can't lave 'the Bhoys' now, yer honour," returned Kerry, obstinately. "I've thaken the oath, sure I joined the band av me own free will, an' I'll sthay wid thim an' share their fortunes, whether for good or ill. An' in regard av the honest callin' his riverince was spakin' about, troth I don't know what call I had to do annythin'; I might as lief sat down aisy an' comfortable an' let 'the little folk' work they're way, for it's thimselves that's been playin' their pitsthroges on mesilf all me life, enthirely; nothin' iver goes right wid me, an' iverythin' I done for good always thurned out for woorse, and sorra bit av luck *I've* iver had, at all, at all."

"Nonsense, Kerry!" said Annesley, "come home with us now, and try again—you may have better luck this time."

"Ah, no, Misther Armoric! Sure I've thaken the oath, an' I wouldn't turn thraitor."

"But, Kerry, how shall you and Owen be able to account for our absence when the Rebels return ? "

"Och, niver mind Owen an' mesilf, Misther Armoric dear. Sure, the Bhoys will only think Magin had thaken a thrifle too much av the craythur. It isn't the *first* thime he done *that*, an' they'll suppose that yersilf an' his riverince has been able to overpower mesilf an' Owen. But there's no thime to waste," continued Kerry, anxiously. "D'ye know yer way, yer honour? The snow has been fallin' on the mountains, but 'tis over now, and the moon's bright enough to show the road marks clear and plain."

"I think we can find the road, Kerry. In any case, this is our only chance, but we must first try to overtake O'Neill, and warn him that he has been betrayed," said Annesley. "Poor fellow, he shall not be entrapped in such a treacherous manner !"

"No, Misther Armoric !" said Kerry, "don't ye be afther goin' near the 'Rebels' Rest,' for though Magin is here, some av the Bhoys that's wid Misther O'Neill isn't over-friendly to yersilf, bein' a souldier. Sure there's two av us goin' there. I'm not certain which road the Bhoys went, but Owen an' mesilf will ache thake a different path, an' wan av us will come up wid thim, in thime to warn thim. We'll save poor Misther Morven, niver fear. An' now don't be sthayin' anny longer here, *Armoric wisha* ; but sure ye've no arms— thake this wid ye," he added, as he handed Magin's musket to Annesley, together with a supply of power and shot.

"An' see, Captain Annesley !" cried Owen, appearing from the other end of the cave, with a sword and belt in his hand. "Here's yer honour's swoord—'twas Misther O'Neill tould me to give it to yersilf before ye left the cave, for sure it was his will ye shouldn't sthay another night here."

"Many thanks, Owen," said Annesley, as he buckled on his sword. "It was kind of your master to think of this, but he is ever generous and thoughtful for others. That sword has been my companion for many a day. I should have been grieved, indeed, to lose it."

Yet even as Annesley spoke, there came to his memory the night of Eveleen Corrie's meeting with O'Neill, when she had snatched that very sword from his hand, and cast it far away from them, an action he had condemned in bitter words at the time, and never since forgiven. Annesley knew now that Morven was married, but *Eveleen* did not know this. Did she still look upon him in the light of a lover? was the thought that again, even in that time of peril and anxiety, rose up in the mind of the young officer to trouble and perplex him.

"Now, Kerry, my son!" said Father Bernard, persuasively, "once more, will you not leave these Rebels, and come home with us?"

"I cannot, Father!" returned Kerry, sadly. "I shall niver see my ould home agin, wid my will."

"Ah, Kerry! you should not have come here at all," said Annesley, reproachfully.

"Sure, 'twas sorrow first brought me, an' now the wild life suits me well enough. But yer honours must promise that ye'll niver let anny wan know that I'm alive, at all, at all. The paple about the ould place think I was dhrownded; let thim think so still; 'tis only Shilrick knows to the conthrairey."

"But Thalia Coghlan, Kerry!" remonstrated Father Bernard, "sure the—"

"Spake not wan word av the colleen to me, yer riverince, if ye wouldn't dhrive me mad enthirely," cried Kerry, impatiently.

"Ah, Kerry! perhaps it may all have been a mistake—a misunderstanding between you," said Annesley, anxiously; desiring to persuade his foster brother to accept this argument, though it had brought no comfort to him in a similar case. "And even if it were not," continued the young officer, "should you feel such deep grief for a girl who could thus deceive you? Is it right that you should waste your whole life for the sake of one so utterly worthless?"

Kerry's dark eyes looked long and searchingly into those of his foster brother. He had heard from Shilrick that "things was going wrong enthirely" with his Captain and the Colonel's daughter, but he did not like to ask Annesley for the confidence which he seemed disposed to withhold, though, in days gone by, the foster brothers had no secrets from each other.

"Misther Armoric!—is there anny grief in all this world so great as that av seein' the idol ye've worshipped in yer heart lyin' broken an' in ruins at yer faat?" asked Kerry, with emotion.

"Heaven help me! I don't think there is," replied Annesley, sorrowfully, turning away to hide his own sadness.

Father Bernard looked from one to the other of the young men, so widely different in worldly rank and position—so like, so near akin in their sorrow.

"Annesley!" he said, kindly, laying his hand on the officer's shoulder, "have you, too, a trouble like Kerry's? I did not know it! Oh! let me implore of you both to waste not another day, nor hour in useless repining; the past we cannot recall, in the present, and the future alone is our hope. Rather strive to build up a holier faith, nobler ambition, and higher aspirations upon the ruins over which you have been so deeply grieving. Act so that your lives may be honest, true and upright, a lasting happiness to those who love you now, a glorious example to those who follow in your footsteps. Time will soothe your present sorrow, as it heals every wound, only, keep a firm hold of Faith and Hope."

"Ah, sir, I fear that is no easy task," returned Annesley.

"Sure I thank yer riverince for yer kind words," said Kerry, but in his own inmost heart he thought that good Father Bernard could scarcely sympathize with them in this present trouble, as probably "his riverince" had never known what it was to be in love, and to find the object of that love prove false. Perhaps much the same thoughts passed through Annesley's mind; but he, too, thanked the kind old priest.

"Now, Kerry, we must leave you; Captain Annesley is ready, I see, and anxious to start."

"Sure I naden't ax ye not to bethray us," said Kerry, "yer riverince wouldn't, I know; an' 'twould be an insult to a thrue souldier like my fosther brother to think for wan moment that he'd bethray thim that had befriended him."

"Your lives are safe in our hands, Kerry," returned Annesley.

" Then farewell, Father Bernard, and *Armoric machree,* an' my blissin's be wid ye ivery sthep av the way that ye go!"

" Thank you, and good-bye, Kerry," said Annesley, simply, as he clasped his foster brother's hands affectionately in his.

" Farewell, my son!" spoke the priest, solemnly, as Kerry knelt on one knee to receive his blessing. " Heaven protect you always, and guide you on your way this night!" Owen Maguire brought Annesley's cloak, and threw it over his shoulders, while Kerry went to the entrance of the cave, and, as he touched a secret spring, the door flew open, disclosing to view a long chain of snow-clad mountains upon which the moonbeams fell with a pale, glittering light.

Even Father Bernard and Captain Annesley, in the midst of all their care and trouble, paused often on their way to gaze with wonder and admiration at the scenes through which they were passing, so marvellously beautiful were they in their wild solitary grandeur, so ethereal-looking in the pure, snowy mantle in which each rock and mountain was enveloped.

For some minutes Kerry O'Toole and Owen Maguire stood at the entrance to the cave, their eyes strained to catch a last glimpse of the two figures now fast disappearing in the distance. " They're saved!—they're free!" cried Kerry, joyfully. " Good luck go wid thim. The night's fine an' the moon's clare now, an' sure it's thimsilves will find the road aisy enough."

" Troth, I hope they will!" returned Owen, doubtfully.

" Och! don't be afther croakin', Owen," said Kerry, " or 'tis the harm ye'll be bringin' on thim, an' faith, it's onaisy ye've made mesilf now, aven wid thim few words."

" Well, sure we've done all we can, annyhow," replied the other. " An' now we'll just thake a last look in at that blackguard Magin, an' thin we'll be sthartin'."

The two men re-entered the cave, where they found Thaddeus Magin, still wrapped in the heavy slumber of intoxication, but as they turned to leave him, he moved restlessly, and seemed to be muttering in his sleep, which fact caused Kerry considerable uneasiness.

"Sure I said that nothin' I done iver had the luck in it. I should have left the dhruggin' av Magin to yersilf, Owen, so I should. See! 'tis movin' he is now—bad 'cess to him— an' I belave the heaviness won't last long on him; he'll be afther us, yet. Och, slape on, ye thraitor!" he added, with a last contemptuous glance at the prostrate form of the Yankee. "An' now let us hurry afther poor Misther O'Neill, and warn him av his danger. Sure, 'twould be worse than death to him if he was made prisoner, an' 'tis a hard fight he'd have for it, annyhow, but, plase goodness, we'll be able to save his honour and the Bhoys from matin' wid the souldiers."

By this time Kerry O'Toole and Owen were once more outside the cave, and the former was doing his best to conceal the entrance, which was the usual custom of the Rebels when they left it for any length of time, when he was startled by a sound which seemed to freeze the very blood in his veins; the low, wailing cry appeared to proceed from some distant part of the mountains. Owen clutched Kerry's arm in a frenzy of horror, while both the men's faces were pale as death; again—and even a third time—the weird *ullagaun* rent the night air, while Kerry and Owen stood spell-bound, their eyes fixed with a terrified gaze upon a thin, grey, vapoury cloud, which seemed to float mid-way between earth and sky, bearing along with it the weird form of a woman. The long snow-white hair reaching to her feet, the pale, ethereal drapery, the long mantle, or scarf, clinging around her like a silken web, of most unearthly hue, were all re- vealed to the two horrified watchers. It was the form that had appeared before Annesley and Eveleen Corrie, and had so startled them, some time before, on the dark shore of the haunted lake.

With one last wailing cry of direst despair and sorrow, and with arms outstretched before her, this ghastly vision from the spirit-world seemed to fade gradually, and to melt away in a cloud of vapour.

"'Tis the Banshee! the Banshee of the O'Neills!" cried Owen Maguire.

"Oh, Heaven hould my masther in its kapin' this night! for there's death or dhark trouble comin' to him. Oh, masther darlin'! masther darlin'!" sobbed the faithful servant, as he fell on his knees, uttering prayer after prayer for the safety of the young master who was so dear to him. Then turning to Kerry, who had neither moved nor spoken, but still stood as if turned to stone, his face pallid, his dark eyes now preternaturally large and dazzling in their brilliancy—fixed upon the spot where the vision had disappeared. Owen shook him frantically, calling aloud to him, in his despair:

"Kerry! Kerry O'Toole! Don't ye hear me? Can't ye spake?"

"I sane it! sure, I sane it!" returned the other, slowly, and in an awe-struck whisper, "it glided along, ontil it stood —stood—wavin' its arms, an' givin' its last cry av warnin' right over 'The Ribils' Rest.'"

CHAPTER XV.

" Whither my heart has gone, there follows
    My hand, and not elsewhere,
For when the heart goes before, like a
    Lamp, and illumines the pathway,
Many things are made clear, that else lie
    Hidden in darkness."

LONGFELLOW.

On the same evening, but a few hours before the events recorded in the preceding chapter were taking place in the Rebels' Cave, the first soft grey shadows of the long December evening were gathering over the surrounding hills, lending an additional solemnity to their weird, silent grandeur, as two equestrians were making their way, with quick, steady pace along the crisp, frosty road which lay between the ancient Castle of the O'Haras, and Glencree Barracks.

The first of these equestrians was Lady Mabel O'Hara, who was mounted on a snow-white palfrey, with graceful arching neck, and flowing mane and tail.

In truth the beautiful animal seemed proud of his rider, and well he might, for fair indeed was his young mistress in her bright brunette beauty.

The keen, frosty air had added a deeper bloom to her cheeks, and lent a rare brilliancy to her clear, dark eyes. Lady Mabel was, moreover, attired in the most becoming of riding habits, of dark-green velvet, the lapels and cuffs of the jacket being handsomely embroidered with gold braid. This costume fitted perfectly, and suited well the graceful little form.

A cavalier hat of dark-green beaver, with a long feather

and a crimson aigrette, rested upon her dusky brown hair, a few short curls which had strayed from beneath the hat falling in tiny ringlets upon her forehead, while the remainder was carelessly gathered together, and confined with a crimson ribbon of the same deep hue as her aigrette. Long gauntlet gloves of tan-coloured leather, and a belt, in which a small, silver-mounted pistol was slung, completed her attire. This latter appendage was, however, only worn at the earnest solicitations of her friends, who were anxious on her account, knowing that she was so often, of necessity, out alone and unprotected, save for the occasional presence of the groom who accompanied her when she was riding; an aged and most faithful retainer of the O'Hara family, known by the name of Mick Rooney.

Lady Mabel was a fearless, and an accomplished horsewoman; she was, therefore, scarcely likely to come to grief on account of her daring equestrian exploits; but the times were troublous, and although no one to whom she was known would have harmed her by word or deed, yet Wicklow at that time was a hot-bed of rebellion and treason, and among the numerous bands of insurgents there were many strangers from distant parts of Ireland, as well as foreigners of very questionable repute, who neither knew nor felt any interest in the Earl's fair daughter.

Lady Mabel's mother had died some years before, and her father was constantly engrossed in political affairs, and very seldom at home, while his poverty, and his pride—of which he had an unlimited portion—prevented him from presenting his daughter at Court, or even in Dublin, or otherwise bringing her forward in a manner suitable to her rank and position. For the O'Haras were poor, miserably poor, for their station in life, and Lady Mabel was, in truth, "a penniless lass, wi' a lang pedigree," and, like her father, she was proud withal, inasmuch as that she felt no desire to take her place among her compeers in rank, unless she had the means to uphold the position to which she was justly entitled.

It is true that several ardent admirers—not wanting in wealth or title—who were political friends of her father, or whom she had met in her intercourse with the Corries, and the few friends she had among the county people in the neighbourhood of Wicklow, had actually found their way to the wilds of Castle O'Hara, and had even become suitors for the hand of its fair mistress ; but hitherto Lady Mabel had turned an indifferent ear to all their blandishments, and appeared to her friends to be perfectly heart-whole. Her beauty and her grace of manner might have made her a very queen in society, but she never seemed to desire this ; her sweet, contented disposition found happiness in the simple pleasures that occasionally fell to her lot, and in striving to make life easier for those either in her own rank, or among her poorer neighbours, who required comfort, help, or sympathy ; all of which they received ungrudgingly from Lady Mabel ; and she found her guerdon in the love and blessings of all with whom she came in contact.

Even now, on this cold December evening, she was bound on an errand of kindness. Having heard, in part, the news of Captain Annesley's detention by the Rebels, and knowing well the distress and anxiety it would cause her friend, Eveleen Corrie, she determined to go to her at once, and hear the real state of affairs, and at the same time offer her kindly, ever-ready aid and sympathy.

Lady Mabel was accompanied on this, as on other occasions, by her faithful attendant, old Mick Rooney. For more than two miles they had ridden without meeting a living creature, and the deep silence that reigned supreme, added a solemn, awe-inspiring beauty to the exquisite scenes through which they passed. Lady Mabel thought sadly, as her eyes wandered over the beautiful landscape on every side, how ill Nature, in her present mood—in her calm, untroubled repose—harmonized with the human hearts, so full of sorrow, anguish and pain, that dwelt within the very shadow of those majestic, everlasting hills. She was destined, however, to have no more leisure for such sorrowful, and solitary reflections, being awakened suddenly from her reverie by the sound of a quick, military step, and as she raised her head to see who was approaching, the sweet face beneath the broad-brimmed cavalier hat, was tinged with a deeper carmine, the eyes seemed to shine with a brighter light in their clear depths ; for despite the fast-gathering shades of the gloaming, Lady Mabel soon discovered that the pedestrian coming so quickly towards them was none other than the young Marine officer, Lieutenant Charles Digby.

Possibly, it *might* have been the chilly evening air, or the reflection of his red coat, which was partly showing beneath the military cloak, thrown carelessly over one shoulder, but, certain it was—whatever the cause—that his face might have competed fairly with that of Lady Mabel in its heightened colour, as she reined in her palfrey, and frankly held out her hand to him.

"Mr. Digby!" she exclaimed, gladly. "Who would have thought of meeting you here at such a time! Were you going to Castle O'Hara? I am glad I have not missed you. Tell me the latest news from Glencree Barracks. I am on my way there now, to see Eveleen Corrie."

"In answer to your first question, Lady Mabel," returned Digby, somewhat shyly, "I *was* going to Castle O'Hara; it is fortunate I have met you, for, at the very moment you came in sight, I had decided that I must return without giving myself the pleasure I had intended—I am afraid, from the fast falling darkness, that it is later than I thought, and I have to be in barracks in time to start with the party of our men on the important expedition to the mountains."

"Ah! then the news I have heard about Captain Annesley is correct—that he is a prisoner in the hands of the Rebels?" asked Lady Mabel, anxiously.

"I grieve to say that it is only too true," replied Digby. "But I am keeping you standing in the cold. I shall, if you will allow me, return with you," he continued, and turning, he walked beside her as they slowly wended their way towards Glencree Barracks, at the same time, giving her a full account of all that had befallen Annesley and Shilrick since they had so mysteriously disappeared, the distress of Colonel Corrie, and the unsuccessful attempt of Ellis and himself to gain the assistance of Sheymus Malloy; all this was poured into the ears of the most sympathetic of listeners.

"And now," enquired Lady Mabel, when she had heard all that Digby could tell her, "what is to be done?"

"A party of our men are under orders to start for the mountains to-night, in accordance with the information we have received from that Yankee villain, Thaddeus Magin."

"Ah! And—and will there be danger?" asked Lady Mabel, in anxious, hesitating tones, "for you—I mean for those who go to the mountains?"

"Would you care—would you?" questioned Digby, quickly, and in his earnestness he laid his hand caressingly on the neck of her horse, while he looked up at her with eager, loving eyes. "Yes!" he said, softly, "there *may* be danger—who can tell? In an encounter such as we expect to-night, some of us must suffer—we cannot all escape, and from what I have heard of this Rebel band, they will not surrender without a sharp fight for their lives and their liberty; aud—that is what caused me to come to you this evening — I felt that we might never meet again—and—"

"Oh, do not speak like that!" cried Lady Mabel, sharply, as in her intense feeling of anxiety, she let her hand rest for a moment on that of her companion, her voice trembling with emotion, her face pale as death with sudden pain, at the thought of what such a parting would mean for her—a parting which would have in it none of the softening sweetness of hope; for as yet Charles Digby had made no declaration of his feeling for her, while now the knowledge had come to her, in a moment, that this young soldier was dearer than life to her heart—that his love would be to her the most precious treasure the world could give.

But oh! how many good, true-hearted men, from a mistaken sense of honour, and because they consider that their means and their position are not sufficiently assured for them to make known their wishes, thus love the faithful and devoted women who are dearest to them, yet leave them in grief, suspense, and doubt, causing them, either to marry others in haste, out of pique, or in the false, fatal belief that they may thereby drown care, and forget their disappointment, only alas, to repent sadly at leisure, or else to live on in silent sorrow, and loneliness of heart, with the cruel, bitter humiliation of feeling that they had given the wealth of their affection unasked, and where it was wholly unappreciated; when a few loving words would have filled their lives with the sunshine of hope, and cheered their hearts through the years they might have to wait ere that hope could be realized.

Lady Mabel O'Hara might probably have added another to the long list of such victims of mistaken kindness and honour, but fortunately for the happiness of both her lover and herself, her earnest, expressive face betrayed her real feelings too unmistakably to her companion, as the young officer chanced at that moment to look up at her, with the lovelight shining in his own honest blue eyes, and he was emboldened to speak all that was in his heart.

" Lady Mabel, I could not start on this expedition without first seeing you. Ah, you do not think me presumptuous. *You*—who can number among your admirers some of the greatest in the land, I know well that many a coronet has been laid at your feet. Alas! how then can *I* dare to hope that amid the triumph of such conquests, the pleasure of knowing that you are so sought after, *you*, an *Earl's daughter*, would condescend to bestow one serious thought upon me, a poor subaltern with neither wealth nor title."

" Stay !" interrupted Lady Mabel, softly, and again her little hand rested on his. "There can be neither pleasure nor triumph to a true woman in giving pain and disappointment. It is true that coronets *have* been laid at my feet ; who may have told you this, I know not, but you have mentioned it, pray remember that I should never have done so—but those coronets did not satisfy *me*."

"Ah !" cried Digby, hastily withdrawing his hand. " You wanted more—a Duke, perhaps—maybe even a Prince ? " he added, bitterly. "Well! who can blame you, Lady Mabel. It is your duty to maintain the honour—the traditions of your house. You have the proper pride of race to keep up. I should be no fitting mate for you. I was mad to think of it for one moment !"

" Then I am afraid," said Lady Mabel, gravely, " that I am wofully inclined to forget that same duty—and sadly deficient in proper pride. Ah, me ! " she continued, sighing, "I hope that the wraiths of all the dead and gone O'Haras will not rise out of their graves to condemn such a degenerate daughter of their proud race ; for indeed *I* have quite made up my mind that my hand shall only be bestowed where my heart has gone before. Yet," she added, smiling, and with a gleam of mischief in her bright eyes, as she looked down upon her companion, " the one who wins those two inestimable treasures must have a crown to offer me."

" Ah !" returned Digby, coldly, as he withdrew himself further from her side, and continued, haughtily, " then it is, after all, just as I imagined—you are ambitious, Lady Mabel !"

" Yes!" she answered, earnestly, " you imagined rightly, Mr. Digby. The one whom *I* would choose must be able to crown me with the enduring love of an honourable, true-hearted gentleman ; he must bear with him always the stain-less shield of an unblemished life. To win such a heart is *my* ambition, for I should know that it would never fail me."

" Where will you find such a man, Lady Mabel ?" asked Digby, hopelessly, " where discover your ideal in this cold, practical world ?"

Lady Mabel did not reply at once ; during the silence between them, she was earnestly watching the downcast face of the young officer ; at last she spoke, in tones full of tenderness and affection.

" Perhaps I have found him already—only—you see he is so utterly wanting in vanity. So unconscious of his own merits, his many good qualities, that he never dreams that some woman, out of the depths of her own affection, may have read the thoughts of his innermost heart, and felt that were she a *Queen* the brightest jewel in all her crown would be *that man's love.*"

Some instinct caused Digby to raise his eyes at that moment, when they met those of his lady love, and in them —with the swiftness of a flash of lightning—was revealed to him her secret, and his own success. " Mabel !" he ex-claimed, eagerly, as with one firm hand clasped over hers, he seized the bridle of her horse with the other, caus-ing it to pause suddenly, a mode of treatment which that proud animal seemed at first inclined to resist, and it was only after much indignant tossing of the head, and pawing of the ground, that he was induced to stand steady, while Digby spoke.

"Mabel!" he continued, earnestly, "is it so, darling; will you try to love me a little?"

"I do not think that would be any use—*now*," replied Lady Mabel, gravely shaking her head. "Sure it would be a waste of time, you see," she added, a bright smile lighting up the charming face, "because—"

"Why?" asked the young officer, quickly, and with some anxiety in his voice.

"Because—I do so—already—a great deal too much for my own peace of mind, I am afraid—a great deal more than you deserve, Lieutenant Charles Digby, for it has only been by the merest chance that you had not gone and left me in sorrow and loneliness instead of happiness and hope."

"Darling, would you have cared so much?" he asked, tenderly.

Ere Lady Mabel could reply, the lovers were interrupted by the sound of the assembly bugle, at Glencree Barracks; clear, though distant, each note fell upon their startled senses.

"Ah!" cried Digby, in despair, "what *shall* I do? There is 'the assembly!' I have delayed too long, it will be impossible for me to reach the barracks before our men have started, and the consequences at such a time—to me—may be disastrous. Oh, confound it! that I should have forgotten how the time was flying, I have never before thus neglected my duty."

Never before in *her* life had Lady Mabel felt a moment's hesitation between right and wrong, never had she been so tempted. If she but remained silent, and allowed matters to take their course, then her lover might be saved from the danger of this expedition to the mountains, for it would be impossible for the swiftest pedestrian to reach Glencree Barracks before the Marines had started.

She might make it right for him afterwards with Colonel Corrie; his absence might be excused, or overlooked; but, —in thus sparing herself the anxiety for his safety—she would do it at the cost of her lover's honour. A nature such as Lady Mabel's, brave, strong and true, could not long hesitate.

In a moment, she had decided that the path of duty was the only path to be pursued by those who hope for future peace and happiness. Her face was very pale, but it wore a calm, determined expression, and her eyes shone with a pure, steadfast light, born of her good resolution.

"Charles!" she cried, earnestly, while her hand in which she had clasped Digby's was cold as ice, and trembling with the agitation she was so anxious, both for his sake and her own, to repress, "I feel that *I*, too, have been to blame—but oh, my darling!—believe me, *your honour* will always be safe with *me*. You are dearer than all the world to my heart, yet I bid you go. Thank Heaven, I can help you! I have Mick Rooney with me. You must take his horse; on foot you could never reach the barracks in time, but it may be possible for you to do so if well-mounted. We have not been riding quickly, Mick's horse is fresh yet, he will do it easily, if you give him the rein and ride across country."

"But you, Mabel!" remonstrated Digby. "I cannot leave you alone at this hour, and—"

"I do not intend to be left alone" interrupted Lady Mabel, quietly, "I am going with you. My brave Snow-flake and I can ride across country with the best of them," she added, as she gently caressed her white palfrey, that seemed fully to understand and to appreciate the praise and attention his mistress was bestowing upon him.

Lady Mabel called to Mick Rooney, who rode up quickly, in some wonderment as to why he was required. All was soon explained to him, however, and, dismounting quickly, he led his horse round to Lieutenant Digby, who was soon in the saddle, and ere a few moments had elapsed he and Lady Mabel had disappeared and were far out of Mick Rooney's sight. The old man paused awhile before continuing his journey on foot to Glencree Barracks, whither his young mistress had directed him to follow her. He gazed anxiously after the retreating figures until he could see them no longer; then sighing, and rubbing his eyes vigorously, he murmured :

"Troth, I wondher what *this* move is for, at all, at all? Not but I'm plased enough to have the change, for 'twas mighty cowld ridin' at that snail's pace, an' mesilf hadn't the love in me heart to kape out the shivers, like thim two young paple—good luck to thim !—'tis the illigant couple they are enthircly. But troth it's a divil av a crick I've got in me neck this minute, through kapin' me head turned first wan side, thin the other, an' sorra thing to look at on either but bare faldes, or bog-land ; an' if there *had* been, sure *I* couldn't kape me head foreninst the way we was ridin', or the young craythurs would have been thinkin' it's mesilf was afther spyin' on thim."

All this, with many wonderful additions, was afterwards duly reported to the housekeeper at Castle O'Hara, who taxed him with having " been afther somethin' that wouldn't bear the light av dhay," and blamed his suppcsed deviation from the right path as being the cause of an attack of " rheumatics " and the " crick in the neck," from which Mick afterwards suffered. The housekeeper and Mick had been " coortin " for the last forty years, but they never came the length of " axin' the praste to spake the words for thim ; " whose was the fault no one could exactly say, only it was whispered, in secret, in the servants' hall, that Biddy being prudent and cautious, had paused more than once when on the verge of " giving in," owing to a decided predilection on the part of Mick for " the laste dhrop in the woorld," though fortunately this predilection was only indulged in when his work for the day was over.

Mick Rooney was just about to follow Lady Mabel and Digby, when he was startled by the sound of cracking branches, and on looking round he discovered a man forcing his way through a hedge not far from where he was standing. Anxious to ascertain what the man's motive might be for thus breaking down the fences in such haste, instead of going a few yards farther where there was a gate, which was always open, Mick retired into the shadow of a tree near him, and watched with some interest the movements of the other man. As soon as Jeremiah Stalker, the English patrol—for he it was who had startled Mick—had contrived to squeeze himself through the hedge, he advanced in a slow, creeping manner so far along the road, then paused and looked anxiously around him, peering suspiciously with his small round eyes into the darkness. At last, seemingly

satisfied that there was no one near him, he rubbed his hands
gleefully, gave his hat an extra thump on the crown to set
it more firmly on his carrot-coloured locks, and muttered in
delighted tones :

" *There's* a fine catch for me—some'at myster'ous up 'ere
an' no mistake ! I couldn't come for'ard before, for I see
they was both on 'em harmed, even the young 'ooman, an' I
halways considers it best for to be on the safe side. Well,
well now ! if I ain't come in for a'most a fortoon *this* night,
my name ain't Jeremiah Stalker. That there young milingtary
gent was a hofficer of the King's troops, and the young
'ooman must have been a belongin' to they Rebels, the way
she was ridin'—an harmed, too, with her pistol. It's a pity
I couldn't ketch what was said, more'n she was agoin' to
' *save his honour*,' most like he'd a hoffered to turn Rebel to
please her. *I* never made such a fool of *myself* for no
'ooman, nor don't hintend. But lor ! I must make a note of
all this ; it'll make the grandest case hever was. I 'eard
some'at about Glencree Barracks—like enough the young
chap belongs there. I'll go in that direckshion. I may as
lief make that my beat to-night as any hother, an' it's the
safest."

" Troth, thin it's two insthead av wan there'll be on that
same bate this night, annyhow ! " cried Mick Rooney, as,
springing upon the astonished, terrified Stalker, he shook
him until the latter was out of breath. " Now," he continued,
" sure *that'll* tache ye to be afther papin' an' pryin' into what
doesn't concarn yersilf."

" I was a-goin' to Glencree Barracks," commenced Stalker,
with a most ineffectual attempt at bravado, for his knees were
trembling under him, and he was in mortal fear, for Mick
Rooney, though a much older man, was tall and powerful of
stature. " I 'ave as good a right for to go here, there, or
hanywhere, as you 'ave, an' I means to go ! " he concluded,
with another decisive blow on the crown of his hat, causing
it to reach the level of his eyebrows, or the pale yellow
streak that did duty for them.

" Bedad, *that's* thrue enough, me bhoy," returned Mick,
" for it's mesilf that's goin' to Glencree Barracks now—an'
by the piper that danced at his own wake, I mane to kape an
eye on yersilf, this night, annyhow."

CHAPTER XVI.

" Rebellion ! foul, dishonouring word,
  Whose wrongful blight so oft has stained
The holiest cause that tongue or sword
  Of mortal ever lost or gained—

How many a spirit born to bless,
  Has sunk beneath that withering name,
Whom but a day's—an hour's success,
  Had wafted to eternal fame."

MOORE.

For some hours Mrs. Corrie had been most anxiously waiting and watching for the return of Eveleen, who had started early in the day, in the vain hope that she might be able to procure a guide to the Rebels' Rest, or some part of the mountains where she might obtain an interview with her cousin, Morven O'Neill, and, if possible, persuade him to release Captain Annesley and Father Bernard, while, at the same time, she would warn him of his own danger. Mrs. Corrie had tried to read, she had made desperate attempts to give her attention to her tapestry work ; but it was all of no avail ; her mind wandered, there seemed neither sense nor meaning in what she was reading, and with her work she was equally unsuccessful ; many a confused, fantastic stitch was woven into her tapestry on that afternoon—which certainly never appeared in the copy of the classical subject upon which she was employed—until in sheer despair the distressed lady gave up both occupations, and endeavoured to find vent for her feelings in restlessly pacing to and fro, only varied by anxious watching at the window.

"Has Eveleen managed to procure an interview with
Morven, I wonder?" she was constantly repeating to herself.
"I fear not, or she would have returned before now. Where
can she be?   It was early morning when she left home, it
is almost dark now.   Oh! I hope that Eveleen would be
careful in appointing any spot for her cousin Morven to meet
her; every step he takes beyond his mountain stronghold is
fraught with danger; pickets of our men, as well as the
cavalry soldiers, are scattered all over the country.   Oh,
Morven! poor, hunted boy! I am no Rebel at heart, yet I
would pray night and day for his safety, and that of his
brave men, hoping that he may find out, ere it is too late,
that it is but a phantom he is following, a fatal mirage, the
fairy shores of which stretch mockingly before his longing
eyes, in all their verdant beauty, only to recede from him—
to lure him on to destruction, and then fade from his sight
for ever.   Yet such is the value of public favour, that even
now, if *success* were to crown his efforts, his followers
would all be heroes, and *he* would win the immortal fame
and glory of the Patriot."

Mrs. Corrie's anxiety for Eveleen's return was faithfully
shared by little Nap, who was at frequent intervals to
be seen racing up and down the stairs, when any distant
sound assailed his watchful ears, or going a regular round
of all the rooms in the house, in the vain hope that Eveleen
might have returned surreptitiously, and be hiding herself
from him; and on each occasion he made known to the
household in general, and even to outsiders, the fact of his
disappointment, by sitting at the foot of the staircase and
indulging in a long, mournful howl.   At last, however, in
despair, he sought consolation in the companionship of Mrs.
Corrie, and kept pace with her for some time as she walked
to and fro; moving whenever she moved, and pausing when
she paused, occasionally looking up into her face with
pathetic, speaking eyes, and whining piteously.   On one
occasion, when attracted to the window by some sound
outside, he discovered Shilrick in the distance, as he marched
past with the guard, to take his place near the men who
were then assembling for the mountain expedition.   The
sight of his favourite so near, and yet that he did not notice

him, was most exasperating to Nap, so, after one more
loud expression of his injured feelings, he retired to the
couch, on the end of which luxurious resting-place he
rolled into the tightest of balls, a position generally assumed
by Nap when he was tired of showing his indignation at
the state of affairs by other means. It was as if his anger
and disappointment could no further go, and he thus resigned
himself, and intended to show his utter indifference to all
the world.

"Still alone?" cried Colonel Corrie, as he suddenly entered the room, and was eagerly greeted by the delighted Nap.
"Why, where is Eveleen? Has *she* no anxiety about this
expedition to search for Annesley? Each time to-day when
I have been able to come in from parade for a few minutes,
I expected to find her ready to ply me with questions;
how strange that she should show such indifference. Where
is the child?" he asked.

"I—I don't know," replied Mrs. Corrie, confusedly, at the
same time in dreadful fear lest Nap should take it into his
head to make another of his excursions upstairs in search
of Eveleen, and by his renewed cries thus betray her
absence.

Had it not been for the darkness of the gloaming, and the
fact that Nap was at that moment claiming the attention of
the Colonel, by whom he was always much petted, Mrs.
Corrie's sudden pallor and agitation could scarcely have
escaped her husband's notice; as it was, however, he discovered nothing unusual in her manner.

"Ah!" he continued, "she is upstairs, I suppose, in her
own room. The anxious time she has had lately has no
doubt knocked her up; I am not surprised, but I thought
Eveleen was stouter-hearted. You had better send for her
now, however, and I will tell her the news, and explain all
that we have done for the rescue of Annesley."

"Yes," returned Mrs. Corrie, hesitating, and in great perplexity as to the excuse she should make for Eveleen's non-
appearance. "Oh!" she murmured to herself, "if he but
knew that she has not been home since the morning."

"There is one thing that has been a great trial to me to-
day," said the Colonel, thoughtfully, as he stood with his

arm resting on the old carved oak mantelshelf, and his eyes
gazing sadly into the bright embers of the large, wood fire
burning in the old-fashioned hearth.

Mrs. Corrie scarcely heard him : she was thinking of
Eveleen, hoping that she would surely never be so fool-
hardy, so daring as to venture up the mountains alone, in
search of her cousin; wondering if she had asked Thalia
Coghlan to accompany her, as she had once intended.

"It was a trying case of private feelings versus duty,"
continued the Colonel, still intent upon the recital of his own
story, "but you scarcely seem to be attending to what I am
saying, my dear," he added, at last struck with his wife's
silence, and most unusual want of sympathy.

"N—no—that is, I mean—yes.—About some trying case,
was it not ? " asked Mrs. Corrie. " Oh, if Eveleen were to
appear now, what should we do ? " she thought, in a fever
of anxiety. " Nap ! " she cried sharply, seeing that he was
proceeding towards the open door, with ears and tail erect
and renewed hope and spirits. "Come, Nap ! " she again
called, this time in a more insinuating tone, upon which Nap
returned, though reluctantly.

"Was there a court-martial then ? " she inquired, once
more turning to her husband.

" Court-martial, my dear !" exclaimed the amazed Colonel,
"how *could* there be one *yet* ? The offence was only committed
a few hours ago."

" Oh !—I thought you mentioned something about a trying
case and—"

" So I did ! " replied the Colonel, somewhat tartly, " and
I was about to tell you the whole circumstances. I am
sorry to say that Ellis—who is senior captain now, during
the absence of Annesley—reported the young drummer,
Shilrick O'Toole, to me this afternoon."

Once more Nap was about to start on a voyage of discovery, but was again recalled.

" Shilrick O'Toole ! " queried Mrs. Corrie, her interest at
last aroused. " Why did Captain Ellis report him ? I
thought he was always so steady, and bore such a good
character. Was it for anything serious ? What had he
been doing ? Eveleen *will* be distressed to hear this, the boy

was such a favourite of Armoric, and she was therefore interested in him."

"I know that," replied Colonel Corrie, "and it has been a greater trial to me than I can tell, to give orders for his arrest ; but he so persistently refused to obey the orders of Captain Ellis, that there was no other course left to me."

"What were the orders of Captain Ellis ?"

"That Shilrick should act as guide to his party, to the Rebels' Rest, in the mountains.   Poor boy! poor boy ! " continued the Colonel, sorrowfully, "he resolutely refused to be the one to betray his own countrymen.   I would have given half my fortune rather than that this had happened. He will be tried by court-martial, and I tremble to think of the sentence that may be pronounced against him ; disobedience of orders on active service, as you well know, is punishable with *death*, and the officers of other regiments who will attend that court-martial, will not be so lenient to our little favourite as we should be ; they will not even understand the motives of the boy, nor appreciate the noble thoughts that prompted his refusal."

"Oh ! why was that *Englishman*, Captain Ellis, so officious, and so ready to report the poor boy ? " cried Mrs. Corrie, indignantly.

"Nay," returned her husband, gently, "I believe, my dear, that it was with real regret he did so, but he is a good officer and at all times duty is foremost in his thoughts ; he told me he had tried very hard, and had even resorted to pleading, and coaxing, to persuade Shilrick to obey his orders, but all to no purpose; and as they had no other guide there was then no alternative left, either for me, or for Ellis ; it would have been out of the question for us to suffer, or to overlook, insubordination of any kind amongst the men. When Ellis returned with the guard to arrest Shilrick, the boy said he was ready to go with the party to the mountains, but of course it was then too late.   An officer could not be trifled with in that manner."

"So the men would have no guide after all," said Mrs. Corrie, evidently considerably relieved.   "Why then could they not have gone without one in the first instance ?   You might all have known what a trial it would be to the poor boy to be the means of betraying these Rebels ; born and brought up in Wicklow, as he was, it is probable he may have many friends, even relatives, among them."

"Ellis said it was necessary to arrest the drummer, and *force* him to go with the men, under a guard. I could not prevent him from giving these orders, when it was plainly his duty to do so. Ellis is strict, but just, and he is neither a tyrant nor a bully ; in this case he was obliged by the rules of the service to act as he did. Altogether it has been a most disagreeable affair ; and this hunting down of my own countrymen is painful in the extreme to me ; I should have endeavoured to procure an exchange before we left England, if I had not possessed such an innate horror of skulking out of any duty which came in my turn of service."

"If this wretched Rebellion were only at an end ! " said Mrs. Corrie, sadly.

"It cannot last very long now," returned the Colonel. "Indeed, I expect some important results from this night's expedition. We received information (worse luck to the villain who gave it) as to a certain spot where the Rebels were in the habit of meeting, 'called the Rebels' Rest ; and Ellis, I believe, has divided his men into several parties ; each party will go by a different route, and the Rebels will thus be surrounded ; nearly all chance of escape being cut off, on every hand, poor fellows !" he added, sadly.

During the latter part of the Colonel's speech, his wife stands gazing at him in silent horror ; but he continues, without noticing her agitation, "It is thought that it would be a great mercy for all the rest, if the young Chief of that daring band, the 'Bold Boys of Wicklow,' were taken prisoner. '*Michael Cluny*,' they call him ; he is bold and fearless, and one of the most devoted leaders of the Rebellion ; but—"

"*Michael Cluny!* Did you say *Michael Cluny ?* " cried Mrs. Corrie, desperately. "Stop ! oh, stop !—what *have* you done ? "

"Why, what is the matter, my dear ? " asked the Colonel, wonderingly. "Are you ill ? Let me call Eveleen !"

"No!—oh, no, no!" she almost wailed, in her despair. "Oh! tell me quickly—are all the men started yet? Tell me! tell me!"

"All have gone but one sergeant's party, on parade yet, and they will be starting immediately. But, my dear, why this terrible agitation?—what is the matter? I must certainly send for Eveleen," concluded the perplexed Colonel, again going towards the door.

"Oh! do *nothing* until you have prevented these men from starting! It may be a small party, but it will be one the less to hunt *him* down. Ah, I pray you lose not a moment!"

"But wherefore?"

Mrs. Corrie paused for a moment ere she replied; but, in her despair, she decided to tell her husband all, at the same time, thinking that it would have been well had matters been explained to him at the first, but the secret had been kept with a view to sparing him the sorrow and anxiety he must have felt had he known of his nephew's identity with *Michael Cluny;* and, like all such secrets, the keeping of it had brought nothing but trouble and deception to all who were concerned.

Having made up her mind, Mrs. Corrie went up to the Colonel, and laying her hand on his arm, she spoke in a voice trembling with anxiety :

"This young Rebel Chief, *Michael Cluny*, he—oh! why did we not tell you before!—he must not be taken. Oh, you *must* keep back the men!"

"What mean you?" demanded the astonished Colonel, sternly. "I do not understand. What can *you* possibly know of this notorious *Michael Cluny*? Stay, let me go for Eveleen, she may be able to explain, as you evidently cannot do so."

"No! no!" exclaimed Mrs. Corrie, wildly, "waste not a moment, the men will be gone ere you can prevent them. Listen!" she whispered, "the Rebel Chief is—is none other than your own dearly-loved nephew, *Morven O'Neill*."

Colonel Corrie started back, with a low cry of horror, and it was some moments ere he could reply. When at last he spoke, it was in tones so hopeless, so sorrowful, that Mrs. Corrie almost regretted having revealed the secret, which had, hitherto, been kept so well. The gallant old officer, like most brave men, possessed a warm, tender heart ; he had felt true sympathy for those of his countrymen whom he knew to be real *genuine* patriots—who were resigning every worldly advantage, and devoting their lives to their country. With all his firm sense of duty, and his well-known loyalty as a soldier, he had yet, in this instance, been almost tempted to find some excuse for overlooking the information he had received from Magin—some opportunity for delaying the departure of his men on the mountain expedition. He had, indeed, secretly hoped that they might be unsuccessful, and had even racked his brain with the thought of how he might possibly warn the brave men who would be thus entrapped without a chance of defending themselves.

How much more keen, then, was his grief when he heard that one who was so dear to him was actually the man, above all others, whose death, or capture, was most desired by the Government under which he served.

"Morven !" he cried, "my own nephew ! my brave boy, Morven ! Oh ! then Heaven help him, for there is scarcely a chance that he will escape the vigilance of the soldiers. The cavalry are out to-night, as well as our men. He will be taken—dead or alive—as sure as you are standing before me this minute."

" 'There *may* be some hope yet," said Mrs. Corrie, hesitating, "because Eveleen is out. I did not tell you before, as I did not wish you to know of our sad trouble, you have so much to think of. But she has been away all day, trying, if possible, to procure an interview with her cousin, Morven, to persuade him to release Captain Annesley and Father Bernard, and, at the same time, to warn him of his own danger. She thought to be able to find some one among the peasantry who would convey a message to him. Let us hope that she has been successful."

" Oh ! why was I not told of all this before ? " asked the Colonel, sorrowfully. " Yet what *could* I have done, that was compatible with my duty, my loyalty to my King ? Had I known it sooner, to what sad straits would not my heart have been reduced during all this trying time. And Eveleen— where is she now ? Has she seen Morven and warned him ?"

"Ah! stay not to think of that just now," cried Mrs. Corrie, anxiously, "only detain the rest of the men from starting ; there will be so many the less to hunt our poor boy from his mountain stronghold."

"I will see what can be done," replied her husband, "yet what *can* I do?—I dare not—may not, stop these men. Oh !" he cried, passionately, "my duty ! my loyalty ! my affection for that poor misguided boy ! how *can* I act betwixt them all. Ah, Morven !—Morven ! my only sister's child ; the lad whom I so cherished, in whose future I had so much pride ! has it all ended in this ? But I must go," he added, despairingly, "ay ! go, and try to think—to think if *anything* can be done to help, or to save him in this hour of danger. Oh ! Heaven grant he may not be taken—anything ! oh ! anything, but that ! A traitor's doom, for the bright, brave boy we all loved so well."

"Oh !" cried Mrs. Corrie, mournfully, "is there no guardian angel near to warn him of the shadow that is hovering over him ; of the cloud that is even now gliding onward, slowly and stealthily till it will hang o'er his bright young head, like a funeral pall— a cloud in whose dark, misty depths lurks the coming storm that must soon break so disastrously for him, and those who love him.—Oh, Eveleen ! Eveleen !— if you are not successful, Morven O'Neill will be lost to us for ever."

Colonel Corrie was about to leave the room, but ere he could reach the door, it was suddenly thrown open from without, and Lady Mabel O'Hara stood before that astonished officer and his wife.

Her habit hung limp and damp around her—for the sleet and snow had commenced to fall ere she had reached the barracks—and it was torn in several places by the branches of trees, and hedges which she, and her lover, had swept past in their rapid ride across country ; her long dark hair had escaped from the crimson ribbon which had confined it, and fell in wild confusion like a veil over her shoulders. Her face which had, such a short time before, been bright with hope and happiness, was now pale as death, and her eyes were dull and heavy. In truth she looked a forlorn little figure, and appeared in the last stage of exhaustion.

"Mabel!" exclaimed Mrs. Corrie, gladly. "Thank Heaven you have come! But my dear, what is the matter?"

"Child!" said the Colonel, "you always appear like an Angel of light when any one is in trouble or sorrow."

"Oh, Colonel!" cried Lady Mabel, "you must not call me by any such good name. Do not praise me—for, indeed, I feel down-right wicked. *He* was in time—but all the same, I know that during that dreadful ride I was half hoping in my heart that we might be too late. I even felt once—for a moment—that I *must* do something that would cause a delay, and *make* us too late—but—but duty conquered. I remembered *his honour* in time, and I brought him the shortest road I knew—brought him, it may be to his death, and my own bitter despair. Oh, my bright, bonnie Charlie!" she sobbed, "his mother's only treasure and pride, and my love!—my own true love!"

Thoroughly worn out with all she had gone through, the terrible strain, mental and physical, she swayed suddenly, and would have fallen, but for the timely aid of Mrs. Corrie, in whose kind, motherly arms she was clasped. For hours afterwards she lay mercifully unconscious of all trouble and care, when the sad, weary girl was lovingly tended by the Colonel's wife.

Poor Nap grew more hopeless, his cries more mournful, as hour after hour passed, and Eveleen was still absent; until, worn out with grief and suspense, he once more curled himself round among the sofa cushions, settling himself comfortably, but not to sleep—unless, indeed, he slept with one bright, keen-sighted little eye open—for he watched, with a calm steadiness of purpose, that would have done credit to the most patient of human beings, until his opportunity came to him.

In the general confusion of Lady Mabel's unexpected arrival, and the hasty departure of Colonel Corrie, Nap, finding himself unobserved, crept out of the room, and closely following the Colonel, passed out of the house, unseen by anyone. Great was the consternation when his absence was discovered; but no one knew when or whither he had gone.

The shadows of the gloaming deepened into the darkness

of night.   Night was followed by the cold, grey hour before dawn—the soft, rosy light of daybreak peeped in at the windows, yet, still neither Eveleen Corrie, nor her faithful little Nap, returned to the home where sad and anxious hearts waited for them in vain.

CHAPTER XVII.

"My sweet, my own loved Ireland !
Let foes say what they will,
The colours that of old ye wore,
'Tis ye are wearin' still ;
And never for their parchment laws
Cared ye a bare thawneen,
Sure, all your hills, this blessed hour,
Are proudly wearin' green.
The shamrock is a darlin' plant,
Like love, 'tis always new ;
It fades not with the summer,
But blooms the winter through ;
'Twill gem the sod that wraps my clay
When laws can't intervene,
Nor *Habeas Corpus* Acts suspend
My Wearin' o' the Green."

BARRY AYLMER.

Mrs. Kinahan's kitchen in the "Shamrock" was—as everyone who had enjoyed the privilege of being admitted within its sacred precincts could not but own—the very perfection of what the kitchen of an old-fashioned country hostelry should be, and, on this cold winter night, it appeared especially inviting, for all was warmth, peace, and comfort within, while without the sleet and snow were falling fast, and a keen, cold wind blew in wild, fitful gusts, chilling to the heart any unfortunate wayfarer who chanced to be out in such inclement weather. An old wooden settle was drawn up close to the wide hearth, in which burnt a blazing peat fire. The china, jugs, bowls, and dishes of marvellous patterns, the tin, copper, and brass cooking utensils that decorated the long dresser, and various shelves around the walls, all shone and glistened in the changing, flitting gleams of the firelight, doing full credit to Mrs. Kinahan and her daughter Anty, and amply repaying them for their industry of the early morning. At one corner of the large kitchen was a dark oak staircase, leading up to a long, narrow landing, or diminutive gallery, which extended along one side of the room, and terminated in a door that led to the apartments occupied by Estelle O'Neill. Before this door hung a heavy crimson curtain, to keep—as much as possible—all draught, or undue noise from penetrating to the room where Estelle usually sat, or rather reclined, for O'Neill's beautiful young bride was growing weaker every day. She was slowly, but surely, fading away before the very eyes of those who had loved her so well. There was no other light in the kitchen save that of the clear, bright fire, which had evidently had its due effect upon the widow Kinahan, who, 'tired out with a long day's hard work, and wearied with anxiety on Estelle's account, was now resting beside it, having fallen fast asleep, in an old arm-chair of wonderful dimensions.

Accustomed, however, to be roused at a moment's notice, she started, and suddenly sat up straight in her chair, all her faculties awake in an instant, as she heard the latch of the outer door lifted hastily, and some one enter.

The widow Kinahan was not one to be taken at a disadvantage, and her first thought was the arrangement of her cap and neckerchief, before she turned to greet the new comer.

"Sure, what in the world is kapin' that colleen Anty all this thime, an' hersilf knowin' I'd ivery heat av work to do me lone enthirely," she muttered to herself, and was somewhat nonplussed when, on turning to greet an expected guest, with a face wreathed in smiles, she found it was only her truant daughter, who had returned home after being absent for some hours.

"Sure, I've got back at last, mother darlin'!" said Anty, as she threw off her damp cloak, and went over to the fire.

"An' a purty long thime ye've been in doin' that same!" returned her mother, severely, as she resumed her seat, folding her hands and sitting up straight and stiff, like a stern judge, preparing to put her daughter through a regular course of cross-questioning. "Where is it ye went to, at all, at all, I'd like to be knowin', Anastasia ?" she commenced.

" I'd to thake a thrifle av a missage to the drummer, Shilrick O'Toole, an' 'twas long before I could find the bhoy, ontil wan av the souldiers tould me he was on guard at the ould house beyant, at the pass yondher," replied Anty, as she drew forward a low stool, and seated herself near the fire.

" Save us all ! " cried Mrs. Kinahan, indignantly. " An' is it such care they'd be afther thakin' av an ould ruin that isn't fit for annythin' barrin' the owls to live in, let alone human craythurs. Och, sure ! 'tis the love av gain that's the ruin av all that has it, enthirely. An' couldn't the grand English gintlemin in Parl'ment, an' the King av England lave aven *thim* ould bhricks an' morthar for Ireland an' the Irish ? 'Tis that same house was put up be wan av the *rale ould sthock*, an' troth, who is it that's a betther right to the remains nor thim who've lived on the same blissed soil for hunners av years ? "

Mrs. Kinahan here sat bolt-upright in her chair, and looked defiantly at Anty, as if *she* were especially to blame in the matter, and, as usual when the worthy widow's ire was aroused, the well-starched frills of her cap seemed to assume a peculiarly aggressive appearance. "Who is it that's a betther right to thim, I'd be for axin ? " she repeated, in a louder tone, for she imagined that her daughter had not been listening.

"Well, mother ! " said Anty, "sure it's the same ruin that's been sthandin' since iver *I* can remimber, an' no wan samed to have a notion av the bhricks an morthar, maybes they thought 'twould be thime enough to lift them whin they'd be wanted. But *that* isn't the raison why the souldiers is there *this* night, mother dear. They'd heard, somehow or other, d'ye see, that the 'Bould Bhoys' had been out afther provisions a few nights ago, an' that they always wint by that road. The Irish gintry, more power to thim, niver tuk anny notice av it, but 'twas the new English landlords that wasn't accustomed wid the Bhoys' ways, an' made a mighty great fuss bekase they'd be liftin' a cow here, an' a shaap there, or maybes a pig, if they could get hould av wan aisy."

"An' small blame to thim if they done it, whin they're nigh stharvin'," returned the widow, "an' I'd like to know who *should* have the best av the land if not an *O'Neill!* Good luck to our Misther Morven an' all his followers."

"Includin' me own thrue darlin' bhoy, Owen," murmured Anty, softly to herself.

"An' as for thim English," cried Mrs. Kinahan, angrily, "troth it's thim that would be thurnin' our blissed counthry upside down, they'd thurn all the Irish paple out av Ireland, an' be thryin' to make it a part av England, they'd be afther movin' our native mountains if they could, an' sittin' thim down in their own counthry which couldn't hould the candle to ould Erin in regard av hills an' mountains or anny-thin' that's illigant an' useful, at all, at all, an whin they'd no moor paple to evict, troth I belave they'd be thryin' it on the very wild birds, an' the innocint dumb craythurs that had found their livin' among thim hills an' valleys for hunners of years. They'd be thakin' from us our liberty, an' aven the blissed colour av our counthry—daurin us to wear only what they'd wish—but troth," she added, triumphantly, "the very faldes an' the threes is bravely wearin' grane this minute in spite av the English King an' his Coort an Parl'mint an' ivery wan av thim that's in it, an' they'll find that they can no more bend our Irish hearts to their will than they can force the green grass an' the laves to change colour at their biddin'."

Mrs. Kinahan here paused for sheer want of breath; and Anty sighed sadly, for the poor girl's heart and mind were often filled with the gravest anxiety for the safety of her lover; even in her happiest moments the sense of his danger was ever present with her, and, like most of her more peacefully-disposed countrywomen, she would fain have seen the constant warfare at an end. However, as she well knew, it was of no avail to argue with her mother upon political subjects, and she, therefore, quietly continued her account of all she had heard that day, of the movements of O'Neill and his "Bold Boys."

"They do be sayin', mother, that Misther Morven himself would be sittin' the back av his hand agin the bhoys sthalin' *annythin'*, aven though he'd be dyin' for want, so, d'ye see, they thake care not to tell his honour about what they're doin', at all, at all, an' sorra wan o' him knows but what the fine molleens and bonneens, and the illigant pigs and big bags av pratees they bring to the mountains are all' prisints enthirely sent by thim that favours '*the cause,*' an troth maybes it's the bhoys that haven't a dale av throuble pre-vintin' his honour from sendin' his thanks and best rispicts to thim he thought all the same providin' had come from."

"Sure, 'tis Misther Morven had always an' iver the warm, ginerous heart, an' was mighty 'grateful to thim that done him annythin'," said Mrs. Kinahan, complacently.

"That's thrue for ye, mother!" agreed Anty.

The girl hoped, that in thus telling her mother all the news she had heard, and by keeping her talking upon other subjects for a certain time, she might be able to interest and amuse her, so that the widow would forget to ask any more awkward questions about her daughter's tardy return home. In this instance, however, Anty had decidedly reckoned without her host, for Mrs. Kinahan had *not* forgotten ; on the contrary, her memory was particularly keen—her curiosity still keener ; and she returned to the charge with greater determination than before, and with the additional impetus of suspicion, for, in her own mind she made a shrewd guess as to who had communicated all the informa-tion she had just received from her daughter.

"And now, Anastasia," she commenced again, looking severely at the culprit, "maybes, if it's not displasin' to ye, it's yersilf that'll be afther namin' the wan ye heard all that from. An' moor by thoken I've wanted to ax ye what call ye had to be thakin' missages to Shilrick O'Toole ; sure, haven't yez enough work at home, widout sakin' it *outside ?*"

When Mrs. Kinahan addressed her daughter by her full baptismal name of Anastasia, the latter knew full well that a reprimand, and most probably, a long lecture would follow, and, on this occasion, she was especially anxious to avoid farther questioning, so she replied, innocently, and in as soothing tones as she could command :

"Sure, mother darlin', 'tis mesilf thought ye were always anxious to do annythin' to plase Misther O'Neill, an' wasn't it wan av his honour's own 'Bould Bhoys' that axed me to thake the letther an' the missage to Shilrick O'Toole ?"

"Owen Maguire! I'll go bail!" cried the widow, angrily.

"No, mother," said Anty, quietly, "it wasn't Owen at all. It was Thaddeus Magin, that Yankee bhoy."

"Faith thin it isn't much good that's in *him*, annyhow!" returned Mrs. Kinahan, contemptuously. "An' as for Owen Maguire, och musha! I do be wondherin' that ye'd be afther encouragin' the bhoy; sure haven't I tould yez agin an' agin to let him see ye don't care a *thrawneen* for him, an' that his company isn't plasin' to us!"

"But d'ye see, mother darlin'," returned Anty, slowly and hesitatingly, "that's not aisy whin—"

"Whin ye're over head an' ears in love wid him!" retorted Mrs. Kinahan, impatiently, "troth it's mesilf knows well, what ye'd be sayin', an' the words that's in yer heart, though ye wouldn't let thim crass yer lips."

To this remark Anty made no reply; she sat gazing dreamily at the fire, and thinking of the storm of words that would ensue should her mother chance to hear of the long, happy hours she had passed with her lover, Owen Maguire, that very afternoon.

"Och, wirra, wirra!" continued the widow, dolefully, "to think 'tis a colleen av me own would be so ongrateful as to go agin the match her mother—an' she a lone widdy—has set her heart on; an' to throw her love away on sich an idle, good-for-naught bhoy as Owen Maguire."

"Sure he *isn't* idle nor good-for-naught nayther, mother!" cried Anty, indignantly, as she rose from her seat, and with heightened colour and flashing eyes confronted Mrs. Kinahan, "an' I don't know what ye have agin Owen, he's faithful an' thrue to Misther O'Neill, an'—"

"An' hasn't a *cronagh-bawn* to bless himself wid," interrupted the irate woman. "Troth it's himself owns sorra thin' barrin' the coat that's on his bhack an' a *caubeen* that's so thinder ye daurn't touch it for fear the crown would be comin' out enthirely."

"Sure what do *I* care about the bhoy's coat, or his *caubeen* ayther, he has *my love* annyhow, an' faith *that's* what he'll *niver* lose," said Anty, bravely.

"Oh, yes! kape yer love for him, be all manes, an' may

ye prosper !" returned the widow, sarcastically, as she vigorously wiped her eyes with her apron. "An' sure don't be afther mindin' yer poor mother that's been sthrivin' an' workin' for yez all yer life, an' herself a lone widdy ; but in these dhays it isn't the gratitude we nade look for."

"But, mother, *a-vahr-dheelish* !" remonstrated Anty, coaxingly, as she put her arm affectionately round the indignant Mrs. Kinahan.

"Och, sure ! don't be afther thryin' to put the comedher on *mesilf*, Anastasia," said the angry woman, impatiently, pushing her daughter aside. "Troth, I know 'tis Owen Maguire has the purty face av his own—the woorse luck the dhay *your* two eyes fell on it—an' I can't gainsay but the bhoy has an innocent plasin' way wid him—maybes 'tis thim gifts that'll hilp to kape the pratees boilin' *that isn't in the pot*," she continued, with a glance of withering scorn at poor Anty. "Ochone ! woe is the dhay that yer own father's colleen—rest his sowl—would be throwin' away sich a chance. Sure 'tis Sheymus Molloy has the fine farm, an' the purtiest lot av cows an' pigs, forbye ducks an' fowls, in the counthry round, barrin' that the hens is wild an' will be afther sthraying away over the hills beyant—an' he's a fine bhoy himsilf an' has the illigant manners an' the good heart enthirely."

"Ah, mother ! hear that now, how ye'd be puttin' the bhoy himsilf an' his goodness last av all !" said Anty, smiling mischievously. "But faith, 'tis misthaken ye are enthirely in regard av Sheymus Malloy an mesilf, sure he doesn't want *me*, at all, at all ; his heart has been given this many a dhay to Thalia Coghlan."

"Thalia Coghlan, is it !" cried the widow, her wrath quickly turned into another channel, "ah, the designin' craythur ! An' didn't she decave her ould lover—poor Kerry O'Toole that was *omadhaun* enough to belave in her—jist that she might put the *furawn* on Sheymus Malloy."

"Maybes 'twas poor ould Granny Coghlan thought like yersilf, mother dear, that he'd be a mighty fine match for her grand-daughter," said Anty, slyly. "Poor Sheymus," she added, smiling, "how often the bhoy's given away widout his lave bein axed."

"Och, wirrasthrue! wirrasthrue!" sobbed Mrs. Kinahan, "to think I'd live to see the dhay that would find mesilf sheddin' salt thares this way—whin me own colleen would be houldin' hersilf in defiance, an' sittin' the back av her hand agin what I've sit me heart on enthirely."

These sentiments were accompanied by a vigorous rocking movement, a shaking of the head, and a series of the most heart-rending sobs between every two or three words, while Mrs. Kinahan stuffed the corners of her apron into each eye alternately with the strictest impartiality.

"Mother," remonstrated Anty, gently, "sure where's the use av yersilf, or me ayther, sittin' *our* hearts on a bhoy that doesn't be lookin' the same road I'm on, at all, at all? Ye wouldn't be havin' yer own daughter in love wid a bhoy that didn't care a thrawneen for her, barrin' in frindship. Ye wouldn't have her sthandin' by an' waitin', willin' an' ready to dhrop the curtsey to him an' say—'Sure I thank ye, Sheymus Malloy, for condescindin' to cast yer eyes on mesilf, now ye can't get annywan betther?' Not but the bhoy's eyes is well enough for the colleens that has a notion av him," added the girl, laughing, "but faith I'm not wan av thim."

Unfortunately, Anty's speech had the very opposite effect upon Mrs. Kinahan, to that intended. The widow was angry and excited, and between a pause in her sobbing, she only caught a few of the words, therefore, instead of soothing her mother, Anty found that she had only exasperated her the more, and again pushing her daughter aside, Mrs. Kinahan exclaimed, fiercely:

"Can't get annywan betther! An' troth, who *could* be betther than *yersilf*, I'd like to know?" she almost shrieked, "*yersilf—Mike Kinahan's daughter!* Let him daur say that to mesilf—him or anny other bhoy, an' troth, I'll——"

What she would have done in such a case, however, was never told, for, in her excitement, the old woman overbalanced herself and fell forward upon her hands. Anty hastened to her assistance, but was imperiously waved away.

"Och! don't come near me—I'm well, enthirely—not in the grave yet, as it's like enough I'm wanted to be, this minute."

"Mother darlin' ! " commenced Anty, soothingly, " sure——"

" Niver heed mesilf," interrupted Mrs. Kinahan, sarcastically. " Who am I that I'd be puttin' the crass on yer will ? Why, no wan at all, only yer poor, misforthunate ould mother. Ochone! 'tis the avil dhays we're livin' in now," she continued, slowly gathering herself up, in no way daunted by her accident, and still sitting on the floor, with her cap awry, and her neckerchief hanging suspended by one end over her shoulder. " But I'm not dead yet, nor dyin', and it isn't *your* sympathy I'd nade be lookin' for, Anastasia Kinahan ; an' I say agin, it's avil dhays whin thim we care most for would be denyin' us ivery thrifle we'd ax for—but sure *I've* always an' iver done *my* duty by yersilf—poor Mike's colleen !—may the Heavens be his bed this night !—an', plase goodness, I'll continue in the same, though I'd recaive no reward but the basest of ongrathitude."

With this noble resolution, the widow rose to her feet and confronted Anty, with an attempt at dignity that was most incongruous with her dishevelled appearance.   The merry girl's keen appreciation of the ludicrous, and Irish sense of humour was so great, that she could no longer restrain her amusement, and in spite of every effort to maintain a proper amount of gravity, she laughed until the tears streamed down her cheeks.

" Sure ye may laugh, an' wilcome, if it's plasin' to ye, Anastasia," remarked Mrs. Kinahan, scornfully, " but I've said—an' I'll say agin—that in *my* young dhays, things was diff'rint ; the colleens was contint, thin, to thake the bhoys that was chosen for thim by their parents, an' to be guided by thim that was oulder an' wiser than thimsilves, an' didn't be afther fallin' in love wid the wrong bhoys, enthirely, the owdacious way they do now."

Anty could have told, had she been so minded, how she had heard many a time, that her mother had certainly not been content to be so guided, and had indeed gone contrary to all advice and warning, when she married the handsome, but decidedly wild and careless, Mike Kinahan, the O'Neills' dashing young huntsman ; but the girl wisely refrained, and after all, as she thought, her mother was no different from others in her reminiscences of what she considered "the good ould thimes," for, as we grow older, we all look back with a certain lingering regret in our hearts to the days that are gone, when time has softened our past pain and trouble, until it appears to us as nothing when compared to present trials and sorrows, when the clouds have passed away, and revealed the silver lining beyond, in which our sad hearts were too unbelieving to trust—when a mist of tears hid from our eyes the light amid the darkness, for it is ofttimes in memory's garden that the sun shines brightest, and the flowers bloom the sweetest and the fairest. Now all Mike Kinahan's faults were forgotten, his good qualities alone remembered, by the wife and child to whom he had been true and loving, whatever might have been his other shortcomings.

Seeing that Anty had at last contrived to assume a more serious demeanour, Mrs. Kinahan again returned to the attack, and breathlessly poured forth a perfect volley of reproof, reproaches, advice, warnings, and entreaties, rendered more eloquent by tears and pathetic predictions ; and being fairly started upon her favourite subject it is probable that she might have gone on for an unlimited period, had she not been interrupted by the sound of a knock at the door. .Her first thoughts were her disordered attire, and she hurriedly commenced to replace her cap, apron, and neckerchief, in their proper positions, and to restore to her personal appearance somewhat of its usual comely tidiness, and dignity. This time she did not refuse her daughter's assistance, and when all had been arranged to her satisfaction, and the stranger having knocked a second time for admission—an occurrence hitherto unheard of at the hospitable and respectable hostelry of the " Shamrock," Anty was allowed to open the door, when, both to her surprise, and the secret delight of the widow Kinahan, there entered the very one who had been the chief cause of the recent discussion and altercation —the young farmer, Sheymus Malloy.

CHAPTER XVIII.

" My hairt is sair—I daurna tell—
 My hairt is sair for somebody ;
I could wake a winter nicht
 For the sake o' somebody,
 Oh-hon ! for somebody !
 Oh-hey ! for somebody !
I could range the world aroond,
 For the sake o' somebody."

BURNS.

" Save all here !" said Malloy, as he entered, after shaking off the snowflakes which still clung to his rough frieze coat. "The top av the avenin' to yez, Misthress Kinahan, ma'am ! "

" Save ye kindly, Sheymus ! ye're welcome !" returned the widow, her face now beaming with smiles, and giving no sign of the storm which had been raging but a few minutes before.

" Well, Anty, jewel ! 'tis yersilf that's well an' hearty, I hope," continued Malloy, kindly, and at the same time glancing curiously at the girl, for she had not bestowed upon him her usual friendly welcome, and was turning from him without speaking a word.

" An' I thank ye, Sheymus—I—sure I'm well, enthirely !" she replied, hesitatingly, for she had not so easily recovered her self-possession as her mother, and the very fact that the young man before her had actually been the cause of the previous discussion, naturally made her feel the more awkward in his presence.

"Thake a sate, Sheymus avick, an' I'll be afther bringin' ye some kitchen an' a dhrop of potheen, for it's the long road ye've come this cowld night, an' troth it's glad we are to see ye, both mesilf *an' Anty*," said Mrs. Kinahan, laying great stress upon the last words, as she moved about briskly, arranging and re-arranging various things in the kitchen, and casting, from time to time, anxious, side-long glances at her daughter, making energetic signals to her whenever she found an opportunity to do so unseen, by Sheymus. Finding, however, that Anty either could not, or would not, understand her meaning, and that the girl still remained silent, she thought it might be a good stroke of policy to leave her alone for a few minutes with the young farmer, knowing well that the genial, light-hearted Sheymus would not rest long without speaking.

"Don't sthir, Anty, me colleen !" she cried, hastily, seeing that her daughter was about to make her escape out of the kitchen, " sure it's Sheymus wouldn't like bein' left all his lone enthirely, an' 'tis plinty av work ye've done this dhay, annyhow, an' though I say it, that shouldn't, troth it's few mothers that's bliss'd wid a colleen like yersilf, *alannah*," added the wily widow, these last words being especially for the benefit of Sheymus.

"That's thrue for ye, ma'am," he replied, gallantly. •

When Mrs. Kinahan had disappeared, the young man crossed over to the side of the hearth where Anty was still standing, and laying his hands kindly on her shoulders, he looked down into her troubled face.

"Now, Anty, what's the matther, at all, at all ? Tell me about yer throuble. Where's the sunshine gone out av yer eyes, me colleen ? Is there annythin' wrong—annythin' about Owen Maguire? How is it all goin' on betwane yersilf an' him now, Anty ? "

"Just as bad as it can be, Sheymus," she replied, looking up gratefully at the sympathising face of her questioner. "Mother's thaken a dislike to him, d'ye see, bekase he's poor."

"That's a pity, Anty, for sure 'tis the good heart the bhoy has, an' he's thrue to yersilf, that I know well," said Sheymus, kindly. "Sure, ye can both thrust me—haven't I suffered mesilf, an' don't I know what it is to be denied what me heart is longin' for most in all the world."

Here the young farmer paused, and with a quick, impatient gesture, passed the sleeve of his coat over his eyes, while Anty looked on pityingly, understanding well what was in his mind. There was perfect confidence and friendship between these two. Such friendship and confidences between men and women, who are related to each other by no ties of kindred, seldom answer, but, in the case of Sheymus Malloy and Anty Kinahan there was a difference, for each knew of the unfortunate love affair of the other, and they were ever ready to express the sympathy they felt, for in neither instance was the course of true love running smoothly.

"See, now, Anty, me colleen," continued Sheymus. "'Tis mesilf an' Owen was great friends wanst, an' always will be, though it isn't ofthen we mate now, since he's joined 'the Bhoys' in the mountains; but if he'd be in anny throuble, I'd help him, if I could. An' yersilf, Anty, haven't I known ye all yer life. Thrust me, dear, an' tell me what it is that's makin' ye so sad this night?"

"Ah, sure, Sheymus! 'tis enough throuble ye have to bear yersilf," said Anty.

"That's no raison why I wouldn't be thryin' to make life brighter for others," returned Sheymus. "Tell me, Anty, would I be doin' anny good if I'd spake a word in favour av Owen to yer mother?"

"Sure I'm feared not, Sheymus," she answered, sorrowfully. "Ye see, whin wanst mother's thaken a notion agin annywan, it isn't aisy to thurn her. An' troth, why she'd be afther miscallin' Owen the way she does *I* can't think, at all, at all. There isn't another bhoy like my Owen in all the whole world, an' niver was in mother's thime naythur, for all she'd be thryin' to make me belave they were so much betther then, enthirely."

Anty was by this time in tears, with her pretty face buried in her hands.

"Oh, Anty! Anty!" said Sheymus, smiling, as he laid his hand kindly on the girl's shoulder, "sure if we could only make others think as we think, fale as we fale, an' see wid our eyes, what a mighty aisy, plasin' world it would be to live in! There, don't cry anny moor, *alannah!* Lave yer mother to me ; I'll see what I can do for yersilf an' Owen, before another night has passed away."

Little thought Sheymus Malloy of the sorrow and trouble that was to fall upon them all, ere morning dawned. He had made up his mind to have a serious conversation with the widow Kinahan ; he knew that he was a favourite of hers, but he had not been so blind as not to see, and to understand her tactics perfectly, he was well aware of the honour which that lady was so desirous of conferring upon him, and he also knew that Anty's feeling for him was that of friendship alone ; he had therefore determined at last to use his influence on behalf of Owen Maguire, and to explain to the mother how much her daughter's happiness depended upon her yielding to their wishes.

All the time that Sheymus had been talking to her, and offering his help in Owen's cause, Anty thought within her own mind how indignant her mother would be, could she hear the subject of their conversation, but, when at last Mrs. Kinahan decided that it would not look well for her to remain longer out of the kitchen, and therefore returned to that apartment with a beaming face, she was delighted with the sight that met her gaze, for she construed the kindly manner and attitude of the young farmer, and Anty's bright, trustful expression as she looked up at him, into a true love scene. This, however, did not trouble either Anty, or Sheymus, although both noticed with considerable amusement the evident satisfaction depicted on the widow's countenance, for each knew the feelings of the other, and felt secure in their compact of friendship.

Mrs. Kinahan also gathered additional comfort and pleasure from the fact that this was the second visit of the young farmer to her hostelry that day. His home was at some distance from the " Shamrock," the weather was anything but favourable and therefore she considered that her kitchen must have for him some special attraction, which attraction she decided in her own mind was her pretty colleen, Anastasia.

"Why, Anty !" she cried, as she came hurrying into the room once more, a steaming jug in one hand, and a plate piled up with newly-baked cakes in the other, both of which she placed on the table, "sure, is it yersilf that's been kapin' Sheymus sthandin' all this thime ? Thake a sate, me bhoy," she added, at the same time placing a chair near the table. " Troth, I've brought somethin' that'll put the life into yez ; sure, it's morthal cowld ; Heaven kape thim that's widout a roof over their heads this night ! "

" Thank ye, kindly, Misthress Kinahan," said Sheymus, as he seated himself at the table, and commenced to help himself to the fare that was spread before him, conversing the while with mother and daughter ! the former having taken up her old position in the large chair, where she sat stroking her apron and smiling complacently, giving from time to time a knowing nod or wink at Anty, which proved perfectly exasperating to the girl, who had again seated herself on the low stool near the fire.

"An' have yez anny news for us to-night, Sheymus ?" asked Mrs. Kinahan, at last, when several other subjects of conversation had been exhausted. "Sure, 'tis Anty and mesilf that likes to be hearin' all that's goin' on, enthirely."

A few moments elapsed before Malloy replied, then, leaning across the table, and regarding Mrs. Kinahan with such a steady gaze that not a look of hers could escape his notice, he answered, quietly :

" Nothing moor than ye know already, Misthress Kinahan, ma'am.   Sure it was a mighty great surprise to mesilf to hear that *Kerry O'Toole* was alive, an' well an' hearty, an' moor by thoken that he'd joined the Ribils ; 'twas Mike McCormack tould me about it this afthernoon," he added, " I was goin' to ax yersilf if it was thrue."

The widow had started at the mention of Kerry O'Toole's name, she had been, for once in her life, completely taken aback, for she had supposed that the secret concerning him was still safe in the keeping of herself, her daughter, and the members of O'Neill's band of " Bold Boys," the only exception being Mike McCormack, who had most unfortunately chanced to encounter Kerry, a few days before, in the " Shamrock ; " but he had promised faithfully to keep the secret ; how then had he come to reveal it to Malloy ? she wondered.   It was never long, however, before Mrs. Kinahan regained her self-possession, even in the most awkward of situations.

"Ax *mesilf* if it was thrue?" she exclaimed, innocently. "An' troth how is it *I* would be knowin' annythin' about Kerry O'Toole?—an' himsilf dhrownded, an'—"

"Come to life, agin'." interrupted Sheymus, with some impatience. "'Tis yersilf would know well enough, I'm thinkin'," he continued, decidedly, "sorra wan moor likely, seein' that 'twas here he used to come, an' it's in this very kitchen, McCormack sane him wid his own two eyes."

"His ghost, moor like," returned Mrs. Kinahan, "sure it's Mike McCormack does see mighty quare things afther he's had a dhrop av the craythur. Sure I wondher ye'd be heedin' him, Sheymus, wisha!"

"Ghosts don't ate bread an' chase, Mrs. Kinahan, ma'am!" replied Malloy, knowingly, "nor dhrink cruiskeens av whiskey nayther; an' faith, it's that same McCormack sane Kerry O'Toole doin' here just two nights past, an' whin the bhoy tould mesilf an Ryan this very afthernoon, sure, he nodded his head, an' closed wan eye, all as wan as to say that he knew a *dale moor* if it had been plasin' to himsilf to tell it."

"Sure, that must have been mighty aggravatin' to bhoys wid so much curiosity as yersilf an' Ryan!" retorted the widow, sharply.

"Niver a lie in it, ma'am!" said Sheymus, coolly," "so I dethermined to come on here at wanst, an' hear iverythin' from yersilf. Sure, I said to mesilf, says I: If there's annythin' worth knowin', at all, at all, it isn't Misthress Kinahan that would be afther kapin' it from her best friend, an' himself wantin' to hear all the news, enthirely, so I'll start at wanst an' ax her this minute, so I will. An' troth, here I am, sure enough, ma'am. Ye'll tell me all about it now?" he added, coaxingly.

Mrs. Kinahan was still indignant at the thought of Mc Cormack's betrayal of Kerry's secret; such breaches of confidence seldom occurred among the frequenters of her respectable hostelry; but at the same time she was considerably flattered and mollified at the young farmer's mode of questioning her upon the subject, and as she had no wish to offend him, she thought it wisest and most politic to confide to him all that she knew, seeing that so much of the secret had already been divulged.

"Sure 'twas no right McCormack had to tell annywan, at all ; he knew that Kerry O'Toole didn't want it to be known that he was alive and well, an' hadn't been dhrownded afther all ; but since ye've heard so much, Sheymus, avick, troth ye may all as wan hear moor."

"Thrue for ye, Misthress Kinahan," agreed Sheymus, "sure I'm all attintion."

The widow's mysterious revelations, however, were not to be made at *this* time, for at the outset she met with an unexpected interruption, and hastily started to her feet at the sound of a loud, sharp knock at the door.

"Who can that be at this hour? It isn't anny av 'the Bhoys,' for they don't throuble to knock. Anty! open the dure and see, *alannah*."

The girl hastened to do her mother's bidding, but ere she had time to reach the door, it was opened stealthily from without, and she started back in surprise at the sight of Eveleen Corrie, who was followed by Thalia Coghlan.

The latter seemed to shrink from meeting the widow and her daughter, as if she felt doubtful as to the welcome she might receive, and therefore kept well in the background, shyly hiding behind her companion in this wild, venture-some expedition.

"Are you and your mother alone, Anty ?" asked Eveleen Corrie, in low tones, as she paused for a moment on the threshold, and glanced cautiously round the room.

"Sure it's Miss Corrie, mother, dear !" exclaimed Anty, at last, getting the better of her astonishment at the unex-pected appearance of the Colonel's daughter at such an hour.

"Miss Eveleen Corrie is it !" cried Mrs. Kinahan, no less surprised than her daughter, as she eagerly hurried to the door to meet her favourite. "Come in, Miss Eveleen darlin'. Come in an' welcome ; sure there's sorra wan inside but Sheymus Malloy, a dacent bhoy enthirely."

The farmer, however, on hearing Eveleen's question, had risen from his seat, and now approached her respectfully.

"Sure, Miss Corrie, it isn't mesilf that'll be in the way, for I was goin' this minute, annyhow."

"Ah no, stay!" said Eveleen, quickly. "We have been to your farm, in search of you. I have much that is important to say to you to-night. Do not go—I will speak to you in a moment."

"Sure then I'll sthay, wid pleasure," replied Sheymus, courteously, as he retired to his former position near the hearth, and stood leaning against the mantel-shelf, waiting until Eveleen should again address him, feeling considerable curiosity to learn the cause of her evident anxiety.

"Miss Eveleen dear, sure is it anny throuble that brings ye here this night?" asked Mrs. Kinahan, anxiously. "Is there annythin' gone wrong at home; thake a sate, darlin'," she continued, drawing the old easy-chair nearer to the fire, and carefully arranging the cushions, "an' whin ye're rested, it's yersilf can tell us all about it enthirely! 'Tis, no small thrifle that would make his honour the Colonel be lettin' yez come all this way yer lone, at such a thime, on a cowld winter night, I'll go bail."

"You are right, Mrs. Kinahan; but he does not know I am here," replied Eveleen. "Oh! the misery of all this deception," she continued, sadly, "but we must, if it be possible, spare my father the sorrow of knowing that my cousin, the boy in whom he had so much pride—for whom he felt such warm affection—is the leader of these Rebels, known as the 'Bold Boys of Wicklow.' I can speak freely, here, for you all know this secret as well as I do: Captain Annesley and my cousin, Morven O'Neill, are both in great danger, they must be saved. I went first to Sheymus Malloy's farm to ask for his assistance, but not finding him I came on here, feeling sure that you would allow Anty to help me, for I know well how much attached you are to Mr. O'Neill."

"Attached is it?" exclaimed Mrs. Kinahan, her voice trembling with emotion, and her eyes filled with tears. "Och! sure an' wouldn't it be a wondher if I *hadn't* the warm love for the bhoy I've nursed in me own two arms, before he could walk, or spake wan word—oh! the pride in me heart, as I watched him, dhay afther dhay, year afther year, growin' up foreninst me very eyes, into the handsomest, bravest gintleman that iver set foot on Irish soil. Troth thin

if 'tis help for *him* ye want, Miss Eveleen jewel, it isn't twice
ye'll have to ax for it *here*, annyhow."

"An' in regard av mesilf, Miss Corrie," said Sheymus,
"faith 'tis ready an' willin' I'll be to do annythin' *I* can for ye,
me lady. Sure if ye wanted me to bring the Sugar Loaf
Mountain, an' lay it at yer faat, bedad I belave I'd thry
annyhow, an' if I couldn't—why thin—the woorse luck to
me ! "

"Many thanks, Sheymus ! " replied Eveleen, smiling at
the young man's eagerness.

"An' what can *I* do, me lady ? " asked Anty, equally anxious
to be of service to the Colonel's daughter.

Ere Eveleen could reply, however, they were all startled
by a sudden, and indignant exclamation from Mrs. Kinahan,
who had been the first to discover the presence of Thalia
Coghlan. The poor girl knowing that since her fatal
quarrel, and parting with her lover, Kerry O'Toole, and
the story of his tragic end had become known, she had been
coldly treated by most of her former friends, for Kerry had
always been a popular character, and many blamed Thalia
for all that had occurred. On this occasion, therefore, her
whole anxiety was to keep out of sight, and to escape
notice if possible, for she was well aware that Mrs. Kinahan
was one of those who had spoken most bitterly of her inconstancy to Kerry, and that she had moreover a grudge
against her on account of the attentions of Sheymus Malloy.
Seeing that she was not observed at first, when she followed
Eveleen into the room, she gladly retired out of sight, and
might still have remained unnoticed had not the widow
approached to shut the door behind which Thalia was partly
concealed.

Mrs. Kinahan's exclamation, however, attracted all the
occupants of the room to look in that direction.

"Save us all ! " she cried. "Is that yerself, Thalia
Coghlan that's sthandin' foreninst me this minute. Oh,
the false-hearted colleen ! An' may I be afther axin'
what brings ye here, at all, where yer poor decaived lover
was always the wilcome guest ? "

"Oh, mother darlin'," entreated Anty, gently, "don't be
spakin' so hard to her ; maybes 'twas for company to Miss

Corrie she came. There thin, Thalia Coghlan, don't be afther gravin' that way," she added, kindly, putting her arm around the poor girl, who was now weeping bitterly, and drawing her nearer to the fire. "Sure, ye're welcome, dear, mother doesn't mane half the hard words she's always spakin'. Ye're near dead wid the cowld, sthaying out there all this thime."

"Thank you, Anty; Thalia *did* come with me," said Eveleen, glancing reproachfully in Mrs. Kinahan's direction, "and her willingness to assist me to-night, at any danger, or inconvenience to herself, should, I think, alone be sufficient to win for her a warm welcome from your mother."

"Far be it from mesilf to thurn *annywan* from me dures, but 'tis nayther the likin' nor the respect that I can fale for the likes av *her*," answered the widow, sulkily. "Faith it's mightily plased I am she's no colleen av mine."

"Mrs. Kinahan !" said Sheymus, now coming boldly forward in defence of Thalia, "tis a misthake ye've all been makin' an' ye're accusin' the poor colleen wrongfully ; she niver was onthrue to Kerry O'Toole—she niver could be false to annywan, sure it isn't in her nathure, Heaven bless and comfort her !" added the young man, fervently, "for it's the sad life she's had for some thime now, an' moor shame to those who would be afther makin' her throubles harder for her to bear," he concluded, significantly.

"So she's come round yersilf finely, Sheymus Malloy !" cried Mrs. Kinahan, her face flushed, and her voice full of indignation, "she's found it mighty aisy to put the *furrawn* on ye, troth I'd niver have thought ye were such a *bocaun* as to be decaived that way !"

"Sure, I thank ye kindly for the complimint, Misthress Kinahan, ma'am," said Sheymus, quietly, "but in regard av Thalia Coghlan I tell ye that ye're wrong enthirely an'—"

"Its, *yersilf* that's wrong, Sheymus Malloy," retorted the widow, angrily, "I tell ye that she's as false as 'tis in the power av anny colleen to be. Ay !" she continued, turning to Thalia, who was still weeping, "ye may well sob an' cry, for 'tis yersilf knows that there's sorra lie in what I'm sayin' this minute."

"Oh, mother dear ! why would ye bother her that way,

an' her heart so full av sorrow ? " remonstrated Anty, reproachfully.

"An' doesn't she desarve it ? " cried Mrs. Kinahan.
" Wasn't it hersilf decaived wan av the thruest, an' best
av bhoys—an' sure wasn't Kerry O'Toole the favourite
av all the counthry round ?   But, ah Thalia Coghlan ! " she
added, relentlessly, "have yez niver heard the ould sayin'
that the gould that buys a heart burns the fingers.   Ay !
faith, an' the heart too—av thim that gets it ?   So it'll
burn *yours* whin ye thake Sheymus Malloy, the well-to-do
young farmer, afther forsakin' the bhoy that loved ye so thruly,
bekase he was poor.   Och, niver heed, but ye'll mate wid
yer just reward if ye *do* get that *omadhaun* yondher," she
added, contemptuously, as she pointed to Malloy, who stood
silently regarding her with a quiet, but significant smile on his
face.   " Ye'll find nayther luck nor happiness in yer bargain."

"Oh, will *no wan* sthop her ? " sobbed Thalia, despairingly.   " Has no wan anny pithy for me ?   Sure, I niver
harmed her, annyhow."

" Mrs. Kinahan ! " said Eveleen, gravely.   "It is high
time that I interfered to put an end to these bitter and unavailing recriminations against this poor girl ; I believe that
too many of those who *professed* to be her friends have
judged her wrongly ; and, indeed, who knows but that her
truth and constancy may yet be proved, to the shame of all
who have been her bitter accusers ; and now, from this time
forth, I shall use every effort to prove her innocence.   Ah !
surely there is enough sorrow and suffering in the world as
it is, why should we try to add one feather-weight to the
burden our neighbours have to bear.   Come, Thalia ! " she
added kindly, as she placed her arm around the shoulders
of the sorrowful, lonely girl, " keep up your heart, dear,
brighter days may yet be in store for you—for us all.
Remember the old, old saying, ' Dark is the hour before the
dawn.'   *I* have *always* believed in you, Thalia.   I believe
in you still, and you have a firm friend in that kind-hearted
boy, Sheymus Malloy.   But now," continued Eveleen,
anxiously, " forgive me if I remind you once more of the
cause of my visit here to-night—there is no time for idle
converse, we are losing precious moments."

"Thrue for ye, Miss Corrie!" said Sheymus, now coming forward and speaking eagerly, "sure I ax pardon, for it's mesilf that's been listenin' to all this wranglin', an' forgettin' what it is ye wanted av me this night. Sure, how is it I can help ye at all, me lady?"

In as few words as possible Eveleen explained all to Sheymus Malloy, as she had already done to Shilrick the drummer. The young farmer listened in respectful silence; but something in the expression of his face caused Eveleen to exclaim, suddenly:

"Ah! you are looking doubtful; do you not understand that I *must* find my cousin, Morven O'Neill, *at once*—that I *must* use every effort to persuade him to release Captain Annesley, and to warn him of his own danger. Have I not explained to you clearly? Several parties of the Marines— and I believe some of the cavalry regiment also—are to be sent to the mountains to-night, and oh! do you not see how Captain O'Neill and the 'Bold Boys' willl be entrapped and surrounded, without a chance of escape; for what power will his small party of men have against so many well-disciplined soldiers? I fear, too, that there must be a traitor in the Rebel camp, for—as I have told you—a letter was sent to my father, actually telling the very spot where the Marines would find the Rebels, and so take them at a disadvantage, and that is why I go now to warn my cousin, but without a guide I cannot find my way to the spot known as the 'Rebels' Rest.' Thalia Coghlan kindly consented to be my companion, and we hoped that the drummer, Shilrick O'Toole, would have come with us as guide; being on guard, however, he could not do so, but advised us to ask either you or Anty Kinahan, as you both knew the mountain passes so well, and could tell us the shortest and the safest road. Now, Sheymus Malloy, you know all—will you help me?"

"Miss Corrie," returned Sheymus, as going closer to her he spoke in a tone so low as to be inaudible to all save Eveleen herself, "1 will help you if I can—most of what you have just told me I knew before, and it's mesilf that's been all dhay thinkin' an' thurnin' over in me own mind what could be done, by raison, d'ye see, I'd like to prevint bloodshed, and kape *both* av thim from harm, so I would," he added, looking in some perplexity at Eveleen, " but the sorra wan o' me could find a way to do it, at all, at all."

" Both of them ? " asked Eveleen, curiously. " Why, what do you mean, Sheymus ? I do not quite understand."

" Sure, me lady, I mane the souldiers an' the ' Bould Bhoys,' good luck be wid thim both. To kape thim from matin', Miss Corrie, troth that's the plan I'd be afther."

" Exactly what *I* wish to do, Sheymus, and that is my reason for asking you to be my guide *now* to the ' Rebels' Rest.' Oh ! let us start at once, and lose no more time."

" Och, aisy now, Miss Corrie. Faith it's mesilf said I'd help yez sure enough, an' I'm ready an willin' to kape me word ; but I didn't mane to guide yer ladyship up thim mountains this night. The road is mighty rough an' dangerous, an' ye'd find no company for the likes av yersilf at the ind av it. Sure I'm goin' mesilf, me lady, an' if ye'll only thrust me wid yer message, troth the wan that is to recaive it'll hear it as faithful an' thrue as if ye'd been sthandin' foreninst him, an' spakin' the words wid yer own lips."

" Ah, no, Sheymus ! " replied Eveleen, " a thousand thanks for your kind offer ; I know well that I could trust you, but —I must see my cousin myself—I must indeed," she continued, entreatingly, " I care not what the risk or danger may be. Oh ! say that you will be my guide."

" Wan minute, Miss Corrie ! " said Sheymus, as he cautiously looked around, to make sure that no one else could hear him. " Whist ! be the whist now ! an' I'll tell yez somethin' I couldn't be namin' to anny other livin' craythur—see now !—for wanst in me life I've thurned thraitor. Ah ! ye're shrinkin' from me now, an' small blame to ye, for isn't his honour, the Colonel—moor power to him—a loyal souldier, an' yersilf, his own daughter ; but listen, 'tis for *Ua Néill's* sake I done it."

" Done what ? Oh ! what have you done, Sheymus ? " cried Eveleen, in terror for what she might hear next.

" Why thin," replied Malloy, " I heard about the letther that had been sent by some mane blackguard av an informer to the barracks—woorse luck to him—I heard about the souldiers bein' sent to the mountains, an' I—yes, *I*, who have

been thrue an' loyal all me life before this dhay, have now
thurned thraitor. Miss Corrie, 'tis yersilf may carry an aisy
heart an' mind wid ye, for," he added, in low, earnest tones,
" I've sent a warnin' to Misther O'Neill, by wan av his own
Bhoys. His honour has had that warnin' by this thime, an' is
safe enthirely, for, plase goodness, the souldiers an' the Ribils
will not mate this night annyhow."

" Oh, Sheymus Malloy! How can I *ever* thank you
enough for this ?" exclaimed Eveleen, gratefully. " What
can I say to—"

" Why then, nothin' at all, Miss Corrie !" he replied, "the
laste said the betther. I've been guided by me own heart in
this ; Heaven grant 'tis for the best."

" Oh, it must be, Sheymus ! it must be for the best, have
you not prevented much misery and bloodshed ?"

" Ay ! thrue enough, me lady ! but only for a shoort thime ;
the dhay may come whin this simple act av mine may prove
disthressful to my counthry. I've warned the Ribils ; but I
fale that I've only given thim thime to stringthen their
forces, an' to carry on the onaquil warfare that must lade to
their own desthruction ; but sure I was throubled, enthirely,
for it jist went agin me heart to let brave *Ua Néill* an' his
followers be thrapped that way ; so whin I found the
chance, I spoke the word av warnin'."

" And, Sheymus, are you certain that the one you warned
was a trustworthy messenger ?" asked Eveleen, anxiously.

"Sorra doubt av it, Miss Corrie !" returned Sheymus,
decidedly. " 'Twas to his own intherest to tell the other
Bhoys, he bein' second in command ; not that in a general
way I'd be afther puttin' anny faith in the likes av that
Yankee bhoy, Thaddeus Magin ; but—"

" Who—*who* did you say ?" cried Eveleen, as in her
terror she seized hold of Malloy's arm, and looked up at
him with eyes full of trouble and despair.

" Sure 'twas Thaddeus Magin that I named. I belave—
savin' yer ladyship's prisence—he's the biggest blackguard
that iver set his two faat on Irish soil ; but d'ye see, Miss
Corrie—"

" Thaddeus Magin ! Thaddeus Magin !!" wailed Eveleen,
hopelessly. " Oh, Sheymus !—if you had but known !

Your warning will never reach Captain O'Neill—for this man Magin is his bitterest enemy ; it was *he* who betrayed the ' Bold Boys '—*he* was the base traitor who sent that letter to the barracks."

CHAPTER XVIII.

" By the hope within us springing,
  Herald of to-morrow's strife ;
By that sun, whose light is bringing
  Chains or freedom, death or life—
Oh ! remember life can be
No charm for him who lives not free !
  Like the day-star in the wave,
  Sinks a hero in his grave,
  'Midst the dew-fall of a nation's tears."

MOORE.

For an instant the young farmer seemed to be struck speechless with horror ; for, with all his knowledge .of the villain Magin, this honest, leal-hearted man found such consummate deceit and treachery almost incredible ; but, at last, rousing himself with an effort, he exclaimed, hopelessly :

"Oh ! then Heaven help thim all ! 'tis lost they are, enthirely. Sorra word of warnin' will *Thaddeus Magin* give thim, there'll be nought to hinder ' the Bhoys ' an' the souldiers from matin' *this* night."

"Can nothing be done ? Oh, Sheymus ! think well !" said Eveleen, "we *must* try and save them yet."

" Troth, it's willin' an' ready I'll be to do that same, if 'tis in me power," returned the young man, fervently.

"Ah ! Who is that ? " cried Eveleen, suddenly, on hearing a loud and prolonged knocking at the door, which caused all the other occupants of the room to start from their seats, and stand looking in consternation at each other.

" Who *can* it be ? " continued Eveleen, anxiously ; " oh ! do not open the door yet, Mrs. Kinahan !"

"Sorra wan o' me, Miss Eveleen darlin'," returned the

widow, determinedly, " not ontil I find out who it is, annyhow. There's a thrifle av a hole in the dure, d'ye see, moor by thoken we niver had it minded, bekase it's mighty convanient to be afther seein' who's outside first, before we open it."

With these words Mrs. Kinahan proceeded to the door, and peered through the tiny opening she had just mentioned. As she turned from it her pale, terrified face struck fear into the hearts of those who were watching her so anxiously and silently.

" Sure, it's—it's the souldiers ! " she gasped at last. " What brings *thim* here this night ? Ochone ! what'll we do, at all, at all ?"

Again the loud knocking resounded through the house, and was this time accompanied by impatient voices demanding immediate admittance.

" Who—who is it that's there, at all ? " asked the widow, in as bold a tone of voice as she could command. " Distharbin' a dacent woman's house, an' hersilf a lone widdy, at this thime o' the avenin'—sure 'tis all in bed we are, an' fast aslape, ivery soul av us."

" That will not do, my good woman," a deep voice responded from outside, " we can hear the talking, and see the light under the door. Open in the King's name ! "

" Oh, it is the soldiers—the Marines too ; that was Sergeant Marks who spoke,"—exclaimed Eveleen, in despair. " They must not see me."

" Quick ! Miss Corrie," said Sheymus, " see yondher, the sthairs ! "

Eveleen was hastening towards them, her foot was on the first step, when she was frantically pulled back by Mrs. Kinahan.

" No !—no—no, Miss Eveleen darlin' ! " she cried, " not up there—sure there isn't thime—the—the dure's closed."

Even in the midst of all her terror and anxiety the widow was faithful to her trust, she thought of the consequences if Estelle O'Neill were suddenly roused, and frightened at the appearance of the soldiers, of whom she was in constant dread, as the enemies of her husband.

One look was sufficient for Mrs. Kinahan to communicate

her fears to Sheymus Malloy; and he quickly came to her aid. "Hide ondher the sthairs, Miss Corrie," he advised, hastily, "ye'll niver be seen there, sure it's the only chance."

In a moment Eveleen had availed herself of the concealment offered, and Sheymus Malloy returned to the table, and extinguished the light, thus leaving the kitchen in comparative darkness, save for the glimmer of the fire, which was now burning low on the hearth.

Again came the imperative demands for admission from without.

"Open, in the King's name!" once more commenced Sergeant Marks, this time shaking the door vigourously, for when Eveleen had first entered, and Mrs. Kinahan found that her errand was a secret one, she had, with a caution long since learnt from the constant sense of danger, and necessity for concealment to those who frequented her house, drawn the bolt of the door; had it not been so the soldiers would long since have effected an entrance; but in this instance he was not disposed, nor authorised, to use force, so, for the third time, the gallant sergeant determined to try the force of persuasion and command. "Come, come, my good woman! you surely wouldn't have the heart to keep us a-standing out here in the cold all night, and a comfortable fire inside? Don't everyone know there's not another house in all this 'ere country to come up to the widow Kinahan's for rest and refreshment—and a comely landlady into the bargain. Come! open in the King's name!" he repeated, impatiently, finding that, on this occasion, the widow was not so ready to listen to any blandishments on his part.

"Troth then, 'tis little his Majesty done for *us*," at last replied Mrs. Kinahan, severely, as she again applied her eye to the slit in the door, "little he done for us, barrin' upsittin' an' disthurbin' a quiet paceable counthry, an' sindin' his throops to bother a dacent, honest woman, an' her a lone widdy; forcin' their way into her house whin she's tould thim 'tis too late for company enthirely. Come in!—ye ill-mannered bhoys," she added, throwing open the door, standing aside to allow her unwelcome visitors to enter, and looking the very picture of injured innocence. " Sure it's to ould Ireland that the English nade to come to larn manners annyhow."

" Sorry to disturb you, missus," said the sergeant, politely, " but dooty is dooty, all the world over, as *you* will understand, ma'am, being a well reg'lated lady, as I may say, and having such a respectable house ; but you see we was bound, me and my men, to drop in here on our way, just for to ask a question or two, as it were. We shan't stay long, missus."

" Honly to hask a question or two, marm, that's hall," chimed in the voice of Jeremiah Stalker, the patrol, who had followed the sergeant into the room ; he having fallen in with the party of Marines had attached himself to them, much to the disgust of the sergeant and his men, who felt, one and all, the greatest contempt for him, and his mean, cowardly nature ; their dislike being fully shared by the hostess of the " Shamrock," and her guests.

"Troth ye may ax what quistions are plasin' to ye," returned the widow, tossing her head, proudly, " but maybes ye've heard the ould sayin' about thakin' the hoorse to the wather : the sorra word ye'll get for answer, barrin' what I'd choose to be spakin', and wanst for all I'll tell yez," she added, boldly, " if it's afther information agin annywan ye are, 'tis the wrong dure ye've come to enthirely, for my roof shall niver shilter *an informer.*"

" Now, missus," remonstrated the sergeant, good-naturedly, " you needn't be so hard on *us* ; it's not *that* sort of information we want—to tell truth, I believe that I should be agin such work myself. I hope that dooty may never fall to *my* lot. At present, ma'am, I only wanted to ask if any of our men have passed up this road before us to-night."

" Sorra wan that I know," replied Mrs. Kinahan, shortly.

" Then they must have gone the other way. We are all right then. One of our parties will be sure to meet with these rascally Rebels," said the sergeant.

Owing to the dim light in the room, fortunately, he did not notice the consternation of those around him. Stalker's pale, suspicious orbs, however, had been eagerly wandering from face to face, and noticed the sudden start with which the sergeant's words were heard by more than one present.

Approaching nearer to Mrs. Kinahan, and with head more on one side even than usual, he assumed, what he thought, a very insinuating tone and expression of countenance, but for which the widow thought she could have cheerfully boxed his ears, he remarked :

"I suppose now, as them Rebels don't go for to disturb you much, marm ? They'll be afear'd to come 'ere, for in course *you* wouldn't hencourage no sich charackters."

For a moment, Mrs. Kinahan stood looking at her questioner, as if she felt disposed to express her real opinion that not one, not even the roughest, wildest of those Rebels, bore such a hateful character as himself, but a look from Sheymus Malloy warned her of the necessity to dissemble before this man ; she therefore replied, with feigned indignation and surprise :

"Och, musha ! is it *mesilf* ye'd be avenin' to houldin' correspondince wid bhoys like *thim ?*"

"No, marm, certingly not, honly I did think as they might turn hup hoccasional ; but now you surely ain't a-going for to send *hus* away without the least drop of summat to keep hout the cold?" remarked Stalker, with a cunning leer ; he could see plainly that his presence, and that of the Marines, was at that time, most unwelcome, and evidently inconvenient to the hostess, and he therefore determined to linger, for at least as long as he could contrive to detain the soldiers, having no intention of facing the dangers of the dark, lonely road alone.

The feelings of Eveleen Corrie, and those who knew that every moment was of consequence, and that this delay might be fatal for the loved ones whom they wished to warn and to save, may be better imagined than described ; they dare not show the slightest anxiety to be rid of these unexpected visitors, nor dare they make any move to leave the inn at such a time, which would immediately have aroused a doubt and suspicion, at all events in the mind of the prying patrol, who would probably have followed and have kept an unwearied watch upon their movements.

After a brief hesitation, Mrs. Kinahan thought it advisable to produce the refreshment for which Stalker had asked her, and at once set about preparing it, talking all the time. "To think now I'd be afther forgetthin' to offer yez a thrifle av kitchin', or a dhrop av *potheen* this night; but d'ye see 'tis mesilf was flusthrated, enthirely, wid the honour av havin' two av the King's officers—moor power to his blissid Majesty—widin me two walls. Anty, jewel, ax the gintlemen that's waitin' outside to walk in, sure 'tis ill-mannered we've been not to think av thim before."

The party of Marines were only too ready to avail themselves of the widow's hospitality, but the woman's heart misgave her when she saw their number, and watched them trooping in, one after another, until the large kitchen was filled with the red-coated warriors, who, at the command of their sergeant, piled arms near the door, and quietly ranged themselves around the room.

Mrs. Kinahan imagined that they would all depart, after partaking of the refreshment she brought, but, to her horror, Sergeant Marks and Jeremiah Stalker, together with a young corporal, who had entered with the soldiers, coolly seated themselves at the table.

From herplace of concealment, Eveleen Corrie peeped around at the intruders, from time to time, her hands clasped tightly before her, her lips compressed firmly, lest in her anxiety some exclamation might escape them. For long after, the girl remembered that night of horror; the tension upon heart and nerves was fearful, the effort to keep silent, to remain inactive, while the precious moments were passing swiftly and relentlessly, yet she dare make no sign. Amidst all the anxiety, and the pre-occupation of those now assembled in Mrs. Kinahan's kitchen, they neither heard the faint sound of a door opening above them, at the head of the staircase, nor did they see the crimson curtain cautiously pulled aside, and a white, panic-stricken face peering down upon the scene, which was being enacted beneath, in the wildest terror and despair. Estelle O'Neill—for she was the unseen witness—had been fairly roused at last by the unusual sound of the tramping of the soldiers, her sleep having been considerably disturbed previously by the

excited voices which had ascended to her from the kitchen ;
now she stood leaning against the door for support, one hand
grasping the curtain, while the other was pressed closely to
her wildly-beating heart. A pale, *spirituel*-looking form, with
a face from which all life-like colour had fled, with eyes
dilated and burning with the fever light of intense excitement and horror. Her golden hair falling like a veil over her
shoulders, and her long white robe made her appear, in the
dim firelight, still more like some fair apparition from the
other world.

Poor, lovely Estelle O'Neill !—for the time she had been
forgotten—and now—ah ! in how sad a manner she was
destined to hear the news of Morven's danger, and to bear
the burden of fear and sorrow, which those who loved the
Rebel Chief's gentle bride so well, would fain have spared
her. Hitherto, Estelle had been carefully and faithfully
guarded from the storm, which was so soon to burst upon her
in all its fury.

During a lull in his process of eating and drinking, Stalker
suddenly discovered the silent figure seated by the side of
the hearth, and immediately recognised Thalia Coghlan.
Having indulged deeply in copious draughts of Mrs. Kinahan's
excellent *potheen*, he felt quite equal to the occasion, and
rising slowly from his seat, he approached Thalia.

The girl had been for some time gazing intently into the
fire, her thoughts evidently in dreamland, from which she
was most unpleasantly aroused by the sight of Jeremiah
Stalker, who now stood before her ; his bearing was insolent
in the extreme, with head on one side, and a smirk upon his
coarse features, which he imagined must give all observers
the impression of his great sharpness and cunning, he,
regardless of the look of utter contempt and dislike which
she bestowed upon him, thus addressed her :

"Ha ! so you be the young 'ooman as was halways a
givin' so much trouble, an' lurkin' about the roads with
that there hobstrep'rous drummer, and his vagabond of a
brother, that gipsy-lookin' young man of yourn as went and
drownded hisself, because you took up with another party."

"An' if ye want to know the *other party*, bedad then 'tis
himself that's sthandin' here foreninst ye this minute, ready

an' willin' to pay ye for yer insultin' spaches to his colleen!" cried the angry voice of Sheymus Malloy, as he hastened to Thalia Coghlan's side, and placed himself between the indignant girl and her tormentor, pushing aside the patrol with such force, and taking him so unexpectedly, that the irate emissary of the civil law fell back against the widow Kinahan, who was at that moment approaching the table with a *cruiskeen* of very hot punch in her hand, causing that lady also to lose her equilibrium, and to let the jug fall, the contents of which flowed in a steaming cascade down the neck, and over the uniform coat, of the corporal of Marines, who sprang to his feet with an exclamation more forcible than polite, and then stood gazing ruefully at the lost *potheen*, which he would so much rather had fallen to his share in another, if a less liberal, fashion. Mrs. Kinahan was politely assisted to her seat near the hearth, duly receiving the respectful sympathy of all the military gentlemen present, while she sat rocking herself, and shaking her head solemnly, lamenting once more the days that were gone, and the degeneracy of the times in which it had been her misfortune to spend the latter years of her life, though what this had to do with the foregoing accident it would have been difficult to have told.

Sergeant Marks, however, evidently considered that it behoved him, as the senior military representative present, to maintain the honour and chivalry of the British Army; he therefore made a point of commiserating the widow in her misfortunes, real and imaginary, and agreeing with her in every way, laudably endeavouring to smooth over matters as much as possible, while Anty was despatched on her errand for another supply of punch.

During this interesting conversation between the gallant sergeant and his hostess, it must not be supposed, for a moment, that Malloy and Jeremiah Stalker had remained silent, or that either of them had been influenced by the sergeant's frequent attempts to secure " peace with honour ;" on the contrary, their dispute was growing warmer—their voices louder every instant.

" I halways said, Mister Malloy," repeated Stalker, in his most aggressive tones, "as you was a suspicious party, for hall yer pertended loyalty, and a follerin' hup of Lord Powerscourt's ways; I believe as you 'ave a hinward 'ankerin' hafter them Rebels, hif the truth was told—so now—you know *my* sentlements on the subjeck!"

"Ah! an' maybes that's the raison ye come papin' an' pryin' around Ballymacreagh Farm, an' my faldes, whin ye think I'm not nigh; but, sure, I've heard ivery thime ye've been there—an' it's yer good luck ye may be after thankin' that *I* wasn't there mesilf—an' now *listhen*, Misther Jeremiah Stalker! I'd have ye to remimber, that if I iver catch that ugly face an' blinkin' eyes av yours, aven so much as lookin' over wan av my finces agin, by the piper that danced at his own wake, ye'll find I've forgotten me manners to a visitor, an' maybes it's yersilf that'll be afther consitherin' the wilcome isn't as plasin' as ye'd wish."

"Go on! go on! You ain't likely to be much longer before you betrays what side *you're* on, young man, then my watchin' won't be for nothink," retorted the patrol, defiantly. "It's my dooty for to keep a heye on hall charackters which I've a-had cause to suspeck, and dooty is a thing as I never neglecks, though I say it as shouldn't, and I ain't afraid of *you*, young man, nor *no one helse*, neither."

"Not whin ye have a sthrong guard av the Marines wid ye," laughed Sheymus, contemptuously. "But sure it'll not be *always* that way, me bhoy," he continued, significantly, and carelessly twirling his shillelagh. "We'll maybes mate agin at a moor convanient saison; manewhile it isn't mesilf that would be afther kapin' ye from yer duty— do it by all manes—only remimber the warnin' I've given ye, for it has been said that the shot fired by Sheymus Malloy niver misses its aim, and that his arm, at a fair, or a faction fight, is worth three others—it may be thrue, or it may not, but, if ye care to prove it, bedad thin! I'm ready an willin' to give ye the chance annyhow."

"Gentlemen! gentlemen!" remonstrated the sergeant, "don't waste no more time disputing matters to-night, talking till doomsday won't make neither of you think no different. And now, ma'am," he added, turning to Mrs. Kinahan "wouldn't it be more cheerful if we had a little extra light on the subject? The fire's a'most gone out."

" Sure an' we can't have moor light here ontil the mornin', misther sergeant, the lamp's gone out d'ye see, an' there isn't anny moor oil in the house " replied the widow, glibly. " Anty, *alannah !* sthir up the fire, an' make it burn brighter," she added, quickly, to stop farther questioning on the matter.

As may be imagined, Anty's efforts to " sthir up the fire," were not very vigorous ; indeed she rather contrived to lessen the light in the room, than to increase it.

" Ah well ! " said the sergeant, " it don't signify much, ma'am, as far as we're concerned, for now I come to think on it, I believe it's time for me and my men to be on the line of march again.   I expect the chief party of Marines have arrived at the ' Rebels' Rest,' as they call it, by now, for they had a sure guide with them."

" A   guide ? " cried Sheymus Malloy, in consternation. " A guide !—who could have been so base as to bethray ' the Bhoys ' that way.   Sure I mane," he added, hurriedly, anxious to hide all signs of his agitation from the sergeant—"sure I mane I was going to tell yez that I saw two av yer officers this afthernoon, an' its *mesilf* they axed to be their guide."

" And you refused, my lad.   I know that," returned the sergeant, kindly, " and no one couldn't blame you for it ; but they have got one now, the drummer, Shilrick O'Toole, is going with them."

" Shilrick O'Toole ! " exclaimed Thalia, in horror.   " Oh, how *could* he do it !   How could he do it ! "

Thalia might have said much that was unwise in her excitement, but for Sheymus Malloy, who gently pressed her back into the seat from which she had risen so hastily, and standing before her, with her hand clasped in his, he again turned to the sergeant.   " The officers tould me that Shilrick was on duty to-day—on guard somewhere—an couldn't go to the mountains."

" And *wouldn't* neither, if he'd been allowed to have *his* will in the matter ; but as no other guide was forthcoming they were obliged to relieve him from guard.   The lad positively refused to go, and Captain Ellis, much against his inclination, had to send a guard to arrest him. Leastways that was what I heard just before our party left barracks.   If the boy has gone after all, he will only have done so under compulsion. Officers and men were distressed enough about his refusal, knowing the consequences ; you see the lad is such a favourite with us all, and his grief was—well not pleasant to see, poor little chap !" said the sergeant, pity-ingly.

"I should a-thought as *you* was the last party for to hup-'old hofficers, or men a shirkin' of their dooty, sergeant," remarked the patrol, sneeringly, " and hall for the sake of a good-for-naught little Rebel, like that there himpident drummer, as is a born traitor, an' ain't got no respeck for law, nor nothink, so to speak."

The sergeant looked contemptuously at the speaker for a moment, then replied, quietly. " When the law is represented by such a party as *you*, I don't wonder at it—and in regard of your kind remarks about *me*, I may reply that I ain't in a position to uphold or disuphold the doings of my superior officers, but I know them to be brave, honourable gentlemen, who will always act with justice and kindness—the dooty went again' *their* hearts, as it would have gone again' *mine*, and I respect and honour them for the feeling."

" Well, it do seem queer as *you* should favour a lad as is a'most a Rebel—and you at this moment a-wearin' of the King's uniform—it is a suspicious case, of that there are no doubt," remarked the patrol, with one of his sly leers at the sergeant.

" Misther Stalker !" said the old soldier, looking steadily across the table at the other, " it is well for you that I *am* wearing the King's uniform, and in the position I hold at this moment. I'm here to keep discipline and order, not to make a riot—otherwise—well !—opportunities may occur again. You understand, eh, my friend ? And now in regard to your kind remarks about our little drummer, of whose life and character you are quite ignorant, I would tell you that in my home in England I've a little chap of my own, not so old as Shilrick, but I hope some day he may 'list, and follow in his father's footsteps, and, when the time of *his* trial and tempta-tion comes—as it does come to a'most all of us sooner or later in this world—some is tried one way, some another—when that time comes to *my* lad, Heaven grant he may act as noble as young O'Toole has acted, and I shall be proud of my son. Many of them rascally Rebels have been the drummer's friends from earliest childhood—leastways, so I've heard—and I don't believe there's an officer, or a man in all our corps who will not, in his inmost heart admire and honour the brave boy for his refusal to betray his own countrymen, even if his life pay the forfeit for disobedience of orders while on active service, eh, my lads?" he asked, turning to the Marines who were now standing around him.

"Ay, ay, sergeant!" replied the soldiers, heartily.

"There! put *that* in yer pipe and smoke it at yer laisure, Misther Jeremiah Stalker!" cried Sheymus Malloy, exultantly.

"Well, Mrs. Kinahan!" said the sergeant, rising from his seat, after having helped himself to what he intended for a *deoch-an-dhurris*, "the best of friends must part, ma'am, but here's to your good health, and thanks for your hospitality. You see, dooty is dooty, and we're bound for to drop in promiscuous, so to speak, at all houses of entertainment for man or beast, while the country's under martial law."

"Certingly, certingly," chimed in the patrol, "and if there ain't nothink wrong a-goin' on, no one needn't hobjeck," he concluded, looking fiercely around him.

"No—only I reckon folks don't always care to be troubled with prying strangers," said the sergeant with a contemptuous glance at Stalker. "Sorry we disturbed you, ma'am," he continued to Mrs. Kinahan, "you seemed to have a pleasant little party here before we came in. A family meeting, eh?"

"That's thrue for ye, sergeant, and niver a lie in it," replied the widow.

"Nothing for you to report here, Stalker; simple, quiet people—no plots—no conspiracies—nothing suspicious," said the sergeant, with a sarcastic smile at the patrol.

"I ain't so sure of that," retorted Stalker, "this young man Malloy ain't to ride the water on. I considers he's a suspicious character, and—"

"Och! sure it's yersilf that would be afther suspictin' aven an angel sthraight from Heaven, if wan came to pay ye a visit this minute," said Malloy.

"There's more in you than meets the heye, young man;

but I mean to keep a look hout on you hafter to-night," returned the patrol.

"Troth I hope the occupation will be plasin' to ye!" retorted the farmer.

"You be a longish way from 'ome now, Mister Malloy, and you ain't given no reason for bein' here yet, as far as *I* knows on."

"Long way, is it! Faith it's mighty little I'd be thinkin' av a walk like that; it's just a sthep for mesilf."

"Ah! Well, p'raps as the times is precar'ous, and all being hunder martial law, so to speak, as the sergeant was hobserving, you wouldn't take hoffence if so be as he was to hask what you came here for to-night?" said Stalker with a cunning leer.

"Is it mesilf thake offence? Och, sorra bit! He can ax —an' wilcome—but bedad he'll get no answer!"

"An' why should ye daur ax him such a quistion?" demanded Mrs. Kinahan, indignantly. "Sure, then, hasn't he the right to come an' go whin 'tis plasin' to himself? An' what's agin the bhoy payin' a visit to his swateheart, I'd be for axin'?"

"Oh! that's it, is it? I shouldn't a' thought it," said Stalker, incredulously, holding his head on one side, and with a sneering smile on his face.

"Troth an' it is, ye snakin', meddlin' ould spy; so ye naden't sthand there blinkin' yer eyes at mesilf that way, all as wan as an owl that's just waked up," cried the widow, forgetful of her usual caution, in the anger of the moment.

"Never mind him, ma'am," remonstrated the sergeant, soothingly. "*I* ain't going to ask the young gentleman no such questions. There's no law again' sweethearting that I know of, and I am glad to hear there's anything so peaceable going on in these here parts. Now, my lads!" he added to the soldiers, "we must be on the march—Mr. Stalker! you're coming with us to the mountains, ain't you?"

"Well!" replied the patrol, hesitating, "I'm afraid as I can't; 'twould be ill-convenient for me 'cause as 'ow I've a got particklar spots to keep a heye on, and particklar parties to look hafter, and I never neglecks my dooty. Howsomedever, I don't mind if I goes part of the way with you, in case of haccidents ; you won't be worse for 'avin' a hextra one in haddition to your number, and you can drop me at the nearest 'ouse we comes to, if so be as there are any more 'abitations between this and the mountains.''

The sergeant was well aware that there was not another dwelling within some miles, but seeing that the man was a most unwelcome guest in Mrs. Kinahan's kitchen, he good-naturedly urged the patrol to accompany him, and his picket of Marines, for which he received most grateful looks from the widow.

" And now, missus," said the gallant soldier, " we'll bid you all good-night, for we've a long way to go, I understand, and not over sure of the road neither, but we mean to hunt these Rebels down, we shan't leave the mountains to-night until we've found them, and brought home their daring young chief as prisoner ; but I hope we may meet in open, honest fight. I couldn't bear to be the one to catch such a brave man in the rat-trap that scoundrel of a Yankee fellow has set for him."

It was fortunate that, at this moment, the noise of the soldiers preparing for departure drowned Eveleen Corrie's exclamation of despair, and the creaking sound of the old railings at the stair-head, as Estelle O'Neill leant over the latter to see the speaker and to hear what was being said.

The soldiers having collected their arms, at the command of Sergeant Marks, now filed out of the inn, having first bid a hearty good-night to Mrs. Kinahan and her guests. " Good-night to _you_, ma'am ! and good-night, all here ! " said the sergeant, as he followed his men, the patrol bringing up the rear, not however before he had cast a last defiant and malignant look at the widow and Sheymus Malloy.

" The top av the avenin' to ye, sir ! " returned Mrs. Kinahan ; " an' worse luck to ye for huntin' dhown the poor bhoys in the mountains," she muttered fiercely, as they disappeared in the darkness.

CHAPTER XIX.

" Ye powers that smile on virtuous love
  O sweetly smile on somebody !
Frae ilka danger keep him free,
  And send me safe my somebody ! "

BURNS.

Sheymus Malloy stood at the door, watching the depart-
ing guests, his face grave, his kind heart full of sad and
anxious thoughts. " 'Tis a good sthrong parthy av souldiers
the sergeant has wid him, an' he said there were others on
the road before thim, an' moor to follow by different paths.
Oh, *Ua Néill ! Ua Néill !* " he murmured, sorrowfully, " sure,
I'm afraid it's a sad night, this'll be for yersilf an' all yer
faithful followers."

"What did you say, Sheymus ? " asked a gentle voice, and
on feeling a light touch on his arm he looked round quickly,
to find the Colonel's daughter at his side. " Oh ! do you
think there will be any danger for Captain O'Neill? Will
they find him, Sheymus ? Have they taken the right road to
the ' Rebels' Rest ?'"

" They *can* get there by that road, me lady."

"Oh, Morven ! Morven ! my cousin—he will be taken ! "

"There's a much shoorter way, Miss Corrie ; if I could
find it in the snow, sure I would get there first, afther all.
The souldiers know nothin' about the ' Ribils' Rest,' I belave
they'll niver get there, at all, at all, for 'tis a mighty difficult
place to get at, they'll niver find the road onless they knew
where to look for it. Sure now, don't be afther frettin',
me lady—kape yer mind aisy, there's not a craythur knows
av that same road but ' the Bhoys ' thimsilves, barrin' Anty
Kinahan an' mesilf, an' Shilrick O'Toole."

"Ah!" cried Eveleen, "but did you not hear the sergeant say that they had forced the boy to go under a guard?"

"I did, Miss Corrie, but that didn't throuble mesilf, d'ye see, bekase I know the drummer too well—I know that wan guard av souldiers might force him to go wid thim, but fifty guards couldn't make him spake agin his will, nor show thim the shoortest an' safest way up the mountains. It'll be aisy enough for the bhoy to forget iverythin' en- thirely, an' misthake the road by raison av the snow that's been fallin'," said the farmer, significantly. "Miss Corrie, I could thrust Shilrick O'Toole wid me life, *he'll* not bethray 'the Bhoys,' niver fear."

"Then, thank Heaven! there is no one else to guide the soldiers. If we go by the road you have mentioned, we may be in time yet. Come! oh, come! let us start at once!"

"Sure an' it's yersilf that'll be lettin' me go wid ye, me lady?" asked Anty, as she now came forward, eagerly, "ye'll not be the woorse av wan moor wid yer parthy, annyhow."

"An' what's the use of yersilf goin, Anty, *alannah?*" said Mrs. Kinahan, "haven't ye been philantherin' about the roads enough this dhay?"

"Mother! Oh, sure I *must* go!" pleaded Anty. "Ye wouldn't be afther previntin' me from goin' wid *Sheymus*, mother darlin'? Sheymus!" she said, in a low undertone, "there'll be dhanger for 'the Bhoys' this night; oh! let me go an' help to save Owen, mother'll heed what *you* say if ye ax her."

"Mrs. Kinahan!" said Sheymus, coaxingly, to the widow, "sure, ye'll let the colleen go wid *mesilf?* Ye can thrust her wid me."

"Och! thin if Anty has sich a notion of goin' wid *yersilf* an' Miss Eveleen, 'twould be little use to gainsay her; she's fondher av wandherin' about thim rough roads than I am, that's all *I'd* be saying," replied Mrs. Kinahan, evidently much gratified that Malloy should express a desire for her daughter's company. "But, Sheymus," she added, in a whisper, which was, however, perfectly audible to the other occupants of the room, "sure, it isn't yersilf that would be afther thakin' the likes av that colleen, Thalia Coghlan, wid ye?"

"'Tis wid Miss Corrie that Thalia came, an' if it's hersilf wishes to go—troth, then she *shall* go ! " returned the farmer, determinedly.

"Sheymus ! " remonstrated the widow, "think how it'll anger *him* to see the colleen agin', an' wid *yersilf*, too."

"Anger who ? " cried Thalia, starting forward, "who is it ye're spakin' about ? Oh, Sheymus ! what is it she manes, at all, at all ? "

" Maybes ye'd best tell her all now wid yer own lips, Misthress Kinahan, since ye've began—she's bound to hear now, soon enough, poor colleen," said Sheymus, indignantly.

" Thalia Coghlan ! " commenced the woman, by no means backward in carrying out the farmer's advice, " it's like enough ye'll be seein' somewan this night that ye niver thought to sit yer two eyes on agin in this world. An' whin ye mate him among the 'Bould Bhoys' in the mountains, an' his life not safe for a single dhay or hour, ye'd best kape in mind that 'twas yersilf done it all—yersilf that dhrove the poor, thrue-hearted bhoy to thurn Ribil."

"Oh, spake—tell me who it is ! " cried the poor girl, imploringly, yet, at the same time, fearing to hope too much from the widow's words.

" An' if he's killed or made prisoner," she continued, relentlessly, " ye may remimber 'tis at your dure all his misforthunes an' his death will lie."

" Sheymus ! " said Thalia, as she frantically clasped her hands round his arm, "*you* tell me, if *she* won't ; is—is it— Kerry ? Oh, spake the blissid words that'll tell me my own Kerry is livin' still."

" Yes, darlin', tis himsilf ! " replied the farmer, shortly ; and turning from her so that she might not read in his face what the admission had cost him.

"Oh, blissid hour ! I shall see him agin—wanst moor I'll be able to look upon the dear face that's been lost to me so long—hear the loved voice that's been silent to me all these sad, weary months. Oh, the joy av matin *him* agin ! " cried the girl, forgetting in her happiness and excitement the heavy blow her words would be to the man beside her. At last, however, she seemed to remember him ; but it was with a passionate, impatient gesture, and in tones of the bitterest reproach, that she addressed him :

"Sheymus Malloy !—did ye know this before ?   Is it yersilf that's done me this wrong—this cruel wrong ?   Have ye watched me, dhay afther dhay, bearin' such a weary burden av sorrow an' despair whin a few words from yersilf would have brought hope an' happiness to me breakin' heart. Oh !" she added, bitterly, " sure 'twas a manly dade to kape the news from me that Kerry was livin', an' all the thime I thrusted in ye, and thought 'twas yersilf was the wan thrue friend I had in all the world."

"I didn't know about Kerry mesilf ontil this mornin', Thalia," returned Sheymus, gently, but in a tone so sad that the girl looked up quickly, and meeting the gaze of the true, honest eyes, looking so tenderly and reproachfully down into hers, she was struck with remorse, for in that moment she felt in her inmost heart how she had wronged this true, generous man by her doubt and suspicion.

"Ah, forgive me, Sheymus !" she said, earnestly, " for the hard words I've spoken, sure 'tis yeisilf that has been the good friend to me, annyhow.   But sure, ye'll thake me to Kerry, now—at wanst," she added, eagerly, " an' I'll be able to explain iverythin', an' it'll be all right enthirely."

" Sthay, Thalia—aisy now," returned Malloy, "maybes it's yersilf that's forgotten that 'twas only yistherday ye tould me I might ax the praste to spake the words for us, an' so I done it, an' his riverince was ready an' willin' an' all his arrangements made before I left him last night."

"Oh, Sheymus !" cried Thalia, pleadingly, "sure 'twas different *thin*.   I didn't know Kerry was livin'."

"Whether the bhoy was livin', or whether he was dead, wasn't in the promise ye made me on the ould bridge the same night we thought he was dhrowned," replied Sheymus, quietly; but with a certain air of determination that boded ill for any chance Thalia might have of being able to induce him to change his purpose.

"Oh, *wirra! wirra!*" sobbed the girl, piteously, "was I *mad* whin I made such a bargain? Oh, Kerry! Kerry! *Shule, shule agrah.* Come back to me—oh, come back to me—my love! my love! "

"'Tis a bargain ye shouldn't have made, Thalia, if 'twas so hard to kape," said Malloy, coldly.

"But, Sheymus! sure ye'll thake me to him?" she implored, as she clung to his arm in despair. "Ye'll let me see him wanst moor—oh, sure it isn't hard-hearted ye are—it's not yersilf that would be refusin' me this! Only let me explain all to him, that he may know I was faithful an' thrue to himself, an' thin—thin sure I'll bid him farewell for iver, an' niver ax, or sake to see him agin. Afther that—I—oh, I don't care what happens, ye can bring me back, Sheymus, an'—an' thin—oh, *wirrasthrue! wirrasthrue!*" she wailed, mournfully, and, covering her eyes with her hands, sobbed as if her heart were broken.

Eveleen Corrie went up to her kindly and, placing her arm around the weeping girl, turned to the farmer, saying, reproachfully, "You surely cannot wish to hold her to her promise, Sheymus? Would you have an unwilling bride?"

"Sure, Sheymus, ye'll do what she axes ye?" said Anty, coaxingly.

What the farmer might have replied to these petitions was not heard, for at that moment the striking of the old clock startled Eveleen, and she exclaimed, anxiously:

"Oh! there is another hour gone. If Captain Annesley is to be rescued, and my cousin Morven saved, we are losing precious moments. Oh, come!"

"An' there's Kerry in dhanger as well!" cried Thalia. "Oh, Sheymus! sure, ye'll thry an' save the bhoy, an' I'll promise——"

Malloy here interrupted her, gently though firmly pushing her aside, and speaking proudly and sternly:

"Don't be afther makin' anny moor promises that ye don't want, or mane, to kape, Thalia Coghlan. Miss Corrie, I'm ready!"

"But, sure, ye'll persuade Kerry to lave the Ribils, Sheymus?" urged Thalia, entreatingly.

"I'll thry, *for your sake*, Thalia," replied Malloy, impatiently. "I thried to save him wanst before, I may as well thry agin, though this thime 'tis like enough I'll get sorra thin' ilse for me pains, barrin' a black eye, maybes woorse."

VOL. II.   Q

"Ah! sure *I* know 'tis yersilf will do yer best to save thim all, Sheymus," said Anty, "an'—an' ye'll not be afther forgettin' my Owen ? " she added, shyly.

"I'll not forgit him, Anty, never fear.   Begorrah ! thin I do wondher if it's mesilf was in the hands of the Ribils, how many colleens would think av comin' to rescue *me*.   Ochone ! 'tis this world's favours aren't over avinly divided.   Now, Miss Corrie, sure if it's plasin' to ye, we'll be sthartin' at wanst."

"I am quite ready, Sheymus," replied Eveleen.   "Goodnight, Mrs. Kinahan, and a thousand thanks for your warm welcome."

"Save ye kindly, Miss Eveleen darlin'," returned the widow.   "Sure 'tis anxious I'll be, enthirely, ontil I hear ye're safe home agin ; an' oh ! may the cloud av sorrow an' throuble soon be lifted from yer heart, Thalia ! " she added, turning kindly to the girl, and laying her hand on her shoulder.   "Sure, I'm sorry I spoke so sharply to ye, me colleen, for I see ye *did* love poor Kerry afther all, but ye'll forgive me, *alannah ?* "

"Sure an' I will, Misthress Kinahan dear, for 'twas the kind heart ye always had for Kerry, an' 'twas bekase ye thought I'd wronged him that ye spake thim hard words to mesilf."

"Ye'll thake care av thim all, Sheymus ? " said Mrs. Kinahan, anxiously.

"Troth an' I will.   Good-night to ye, ma'am, an' moor power to ye ! "

"Heaven protect ivery wan av ye, sure it's me prayers an' me blessins that'll be wid yez all, ivery foot av the way that ye go."

It was with the keenest anxiety that Mrs. Kinahan watched their departure, looking sorrowfully after them as they passed beyond her threshold out into the darkness of the night, bravely pressing onward, though uncertain of the fate that awaited them, or of the success of their difficult and perilous expedition.

The widow was still standing at her door and peering out through the mist, and the softly falling snow, striving to catch a last glimpse of her late guests, when she was startled by hearing the voice of Estelle O'Neill, and on looking round she saw the white-robed form of Morven's bride standing near her. In an instant the thought came to her :

How much of the previous conversation had Estelle heard ? How much had she seen ? Not for long, however, was she kept in suspense, the intense excitement so plainly depicted in Estelle's pale face, and eyes that were now dazzling in their brilliant, luminous light, her agitated manner, all told Mrs. Kinahan, only too surely, that she might fear the worst.

"Madame ! *you* here !" she gasped.

"Are—are dey all gone ?" asked Estelle, in low tremulous tones, as she looked wildly around her. "Oh ! how long it did seem to me, when I did count every moment until de time when dey should start."

"Save us all, ma'am !" cried Mrs. Kinahan, noticing for the first time that Estelle had thrown her long fur mantle over her shoulders, and was then drawing the hood over her head. "What is it yer ladyship is doin'—where is it ye're goin', at all, at all ?

"I do go to follow your good daughter, Anty, madame, and de people who have but now left you," replied Estelle, determinedly.

"Och, thin ! bad luck to me if I let ye do that same, Misthress O'Neill ma'am—an' why would ye do it, me lady ?"

"I have heard all—I know dat my husband he is in danger, dat is enough for me. I go to him now—on de instant—I will share de peril—I will live, or die wid him."

"Oh ! but think, yer ladyship—think well, first," pleaded Mrs. Kinahan, anxiously, " 'tis Misther O'Neill that has the proud thimper when he's crassed—an' small blame to his honour, for who's a betther right to his own way than *Ua Néill,* an' it's himself has the thrue blood an' brave spirit in him. Ochone ! what *would* his honour be sayin' to me, if I'd be lettin ye go up the mountains yer lone this night."

"I go not alone," said Estelle, impatiently. "I follow de oders, surely it is dat I have de better right to see him—to help to save him—my Morven—dan dey have ? I do command dat you do let me pass!" she added, imperatively, seeing that Mrs. Kinahan had determinedly placed herself in front of the door.

"Sure I daurn't let ye go, me lady, an' it's yersilf knows well that ye couldn't walk as far aven as the foot of the mountains, let alone climb thim, or go along thim rough roads, an' yersilf been so ill."

"Oh, let me pass quickly, or dey will be out of my sight. It would drive me mad to stay here quietly when my own Morven is in so great danger. Do you hear? It will drive me mad—quite—quite mad!" cried Estelle, wildly.

Mrs. Kinahan, looking at her anxiously, began to fear that what she had just heard of the danger of her husband, and the horror and suspense of the last hour had, owing to her weak state of health, really affected her reason, and accordingly the widow adopted a coaxing, soothing tone.

"See now, Misthress O'Neill ma'am, ye wouldn't have Misther Morven be afther blamin' mesilf for not having the care over yer ladyship. An' sure what could ye do, at all, at all, wanst ye *were* out? Thim that's gone up the mountains has the health an' sthringth to kape thim up through all that may happen this night; but for yersilf, oh, me lady, sure ye'd only be breakin' down on the road an' maybes kapin' bhack, or hindherin' thim that might be of rale use, in hilpin' to save his honour. An' troth it's makin' yersilf worse ye are, Misthress O'Neill ma'am, gettin' raised up an' excited this way, an' the nixt thime Misther Morven comes to see ye—which Heaven grant may be soon—sure he'll be sayin' *I* haven't kept the promise I made, to watch over an' care for the wan' that's dearest to him in all the world."

For a moment, Estelle stood gazing silently at the speaker, then slowly turning from her, she ascended the stairs, pausing, however, as she reached the landing, when, leaning over the railing, she said, with apparent calmness:

"It is you dat are right, madame. It must not indeed, dat you shall be blamed. But I would dat you remember whatever may happen dis night, dat I said, to *your* promise you have been faithful and true—always faithful and true—and good —oh, so very, very good to me!" she added, as she passed through the door leading to her own apartment.

Mrs. Kinahan hurried up the stairs after her, thinking that, in her present state of mind, she should not be left alone, but, on reaching the door, found that Estelle had bolted it after her, so she returned to the kitchen, sighing, as she murmured to herself:

" Ah, well ! poor lady ! Maybes she'd rather be her lone for awhile. Not that *I* think it's good for her or anny other wan to be shuttin' thimsilves up an' broodin' over their sorrows, wid no wan nigh to spake a cheerin' word."

Estelle, however, had no intention of shutting herself up, or of brooding over her troubles. She had bolted the door to prevent Mrs. Kinahan from following her, and, passing swiftly along the passage, through her own room, and from thence down a dark, narrow staircase, she found herself in the back garden of the inn ; and, creeping cautiously round the house under the shadow of the wall, she looked around in the hope of discovering some trace of the little party who had just started under the guidance of Sheymus Malloy ; but the sky was dark, with passing clouds ; it was bitterly cold ; and the snowflakes drifting into her eyes nearly blinded her. At the moment, however, when she stood gazing most hopelessly at the distant mountains, where the one she loved most dearly upon earth might, even then, be fighting for life or liberty, the moon shone forth from behind the leaden cloud which had o'ershadowed it, and revealed to her anxious eyes the little group, consisting of Sheymus Malloy and his companions, as they stood out in grand relief against the snow-clad mountains, having paused for a moment at a turning in the road, to consult together as to the best way to proceed.

Breathlessly Estelle watched, and waited, until she saw the party start once more on their road ; then, for some distance, she sped onward, always keeping them in sight, yet never following too closely, lest one of their number might turn, and see her pursuing them. But there was little chance of this, for, as they proceeded, the path became more difficult to traverse, and, in some parts, dangerous. All were, therefore, fully occupied in securing for themselves a sure footing, and reaching their destination with all possible haste.

Estelle's intense excitement and anxiety seemed, for the

time, to lend her a strange, fictitious strength—she felt neither cold, nor pain, nor weariness, for was she not going to the rescue of her beloved husband ? Soon—soon she would see him, she kept repeating to herself. Very soon he would know that his faithful Estelle had helped to save him, for surely Heaven would not be so cruel as to separate them, whether the issue of that night's conflict might be life or death, she would share it with him. So decided the devoted Estelle O'Neill—so she hurried onward to her doom.

Mrs. Kinahan allowed half-an-hour to elapse, and then growing uneasy about Estelle, and thinking she had been left alone quite long enough, once more tried the door at the head of the staircase, but finding it still bolted, and being a woman of determination when she had once made up her mind upon any point, she proceeded to Estelle's apartment by another entrance.

On reaching it, however, she paused, with a low cry of horror, for she not only found the room untenanted, but also discovered that a door, leading from the same passage to an old staircase which was seldom used, had been thrown open, and the breath of keen, frosty air which met her, and fanned her heated face as she looked down, told her that the door below must also be open. To descend the stairs was the work of a moment, and from the back garden she hurried round to the front of the house ; not creeping cautiously and stealthily as Estelle O'Neill had done, but wringing her hands in her despair, calling frantically to Estelle, begging, imploring, of her to return, in tones that were piteous to hear.

" *Och, wirrasthrue ! wirrasthrue !* it's hersilf must have been mad, sorra doubt av it. 'Tis out av sight she is now. Oh, Misther Morven ! Misther Morven darlin' ! what'll I say to yersilf whin we mate agin ? Sure I couldn't help it. I thried to kape her back, but the love in her heart made her too sthrong—too cunnin' for mesilf enthirely. She's gone afther the others to the mountains, but she'll niver overthake thim—niver get there alive. If I only knew the road they'd gone, sure I'd follow an' maybes find her. Oh! Heaven hould thim all in her kapin' this night, an' save thim that's in dhanger," cried the poor distracted woman, as she dropped on her knees at her open door. A pale moonbeam fell with a soft, tender light upon the kneeling figure, as with upraised hands and in tones of passionate entreaty Mrs. Kinahan prayed as she had never in her life prayed before, her very heart and soul in each word that fell from her pale, trembling lips, for with all her faults—and who among us is without them—this woman had proved faithful all her life—she would be faithful unto death to those she loved.

CHAPTER XX.

" Many a heart that now beats high,
  In slumber cold at night shall lie,
Nor waken even at victory's sound—
  But, oh ! how bless'd that hero's sleep,
  O'er whom a wondering world shall weep ! "

MOORE.

That particular spot on one of the Wicklow Mountains, which the peasantry had romantically named "The Rebels' Rest," was a large open space, formed, by a freak of Nature, into a sort of semi-circle.   It was surrounded hy wild rocks and jutting points of varied height, shape and size, between which were several crevices and cavities, all more or less hidden among the rugged lichen-covered masses of rock ; and forming excellent places for the purposes of concealment, or for escape on any sudden emergency, or surprise, several of these miniature caves having narrow outlets, through which a man of ordinary stature might contrive to creep, and, making his way to one of the other mountains, thus evade pursuers who knew nought of these passages.

The approaches to the " Rebels' Rest " were both difficult and dangerous ; but the worst of these was a narrow defile, flanked on either side by high rocks.   Admirers of pictur-esque scenery—lovers of nature in her grandest, most majestic form, would, however, have felt amply rewarded, even on that cold December night, when having safely reached the spot, they paused to look around upon the sight—so sublime in its wild beauty—which on every hand would meet their gaze.

The snow had ceased, a peaceful calm—a subtle silence reigned supreme, it was as though all Nature had fallen into a deep sleep, to waken never more to life and activity. All around, and in every direction rose, one above another, higher, and still higher, the snow-crowned mountain peaks—the everlasting hills—in all their solemn grandeur; while, stretching far as the eye could reach, appeared the sombre purple and grey outlines of distant mountains and hills of other counties in the fair Emerald Isle, many of these being densely wooded from the base to the summit. Here and there were exquisite glimpses of the restless, shimmering sea, and calm silver lake, and a far-away view of the wild heath-clad, gorse-covered stretch of country between Killakee and Glencree, now enveloped in a soft, white mantle of glistening snow. A glorious panorama of Nature—still unspoilt—still untouched by human hands ; and over which hung the jewelled canopy of Heaven, with its clear, brilliant moon, its myriads of bright stars, shining down upon the scene, as if in pitiless mocking anticipation of the sorrow and strife, despair and death, of which they were so soon to be silent witnesses.

The chief party of the Marines from Glencree Barracks had at last arrived upon the scene, having had the advantage of the guidance of Shilrick O'Toole, who, alas ! trusting too completely to Thaddeus Magin's advice and good faith, had, at the last moment, on receiving the Yankee's treacherous letter—as the reader will remember—consented to act as guide, and had carefully led his comrades by the safest and easiest route to the "Rebels' Rest," thinking that, according to Magin's false information, the "Bold Boys" would take care to keep far enough away in the opposite direction ; or else remain, for that night at least, within the safe concealment of their cave.

The Marines—who were in full dress uniform—being well armed, and wearing their canteens and haversacks— were now drawn up in two lines, and "standing at ease," within the circle of rocks. In the centre of each line stood a little drummer, with bugle and drum, two of Shilrick's favourite companions. Near the two principal entrances to the "Rebels' Rest," Sergeant Simpson and Corporal Hickson were stationed, partly concealed among the rocks, and watching for the approach of the Rebels; while Sergeant

Marks, who, with his party, had also reached the spot, having fallen in with the main body of his corps, and joined them, was concealed near the end of the narrow defile before mentioned, also intently listening and watching.

Not far away from him stood Shilrick O'Toole, leaning against the rocks, and looking dejectedly around him, his sad, earnest eyes, with their wonderful depths of mingled tenderness and fire, pathos and humour, were from time to time raised to the sky, scanning each bright star, as if in their light he might read the fate in store for him. The anxious expression on the pale, boyish face, the compressed lips, and the tightly-clasped hands were the only outward signs of the inward struggle—the fierce tension of heart and brain which this youthful hero—this child in years, but oh, so manly, so noble, in heart and mind ! had undergone within the last few hours of that fatal day.

He was guarded on either side by Privates Marlow and Clark, armed with muskets, with fixed bayonets. These soldiers were both friends of the little prisoner, and accordingly most heartily disliked the duty they had to perform.

They had been sent by Captain Ellis, to arrest Shilrick, immediately after that officer's unfortunate interview with the drummer, but just before the poor lad received Magin's letter ; and afterwards the discipline of the service prevented Captain Ellis from countermanding his orders until Shilrick had gone through at least the form of a trial.

Moreover, the cavalry officer, Lieutenant Rochfort, the young midshipman, Harry Nelson, and, worse still, Jeremiah Stalker, the patrol, had unfortunately appeared upon the scene at the very moment when the drummer had been brought on to the parade under a guard. By a few dexterous questions put to Lieutenant Geoghegan, Rochfort soon learnt even more than he wished to know, for the young Irish officer's flow of conversation, and his dangerous aptitude for mixing up in delightful confusion his own thoughts of what *might* have been, along with the real facts of the case, had on more than one occasion proved disastrous to himself and his brother officers. Not that Geoghegan was either ill-natured, or a mischief-maker, nor was he intentionally untruthful ; the mistakes in his life, the harm he sometimes unwittingly did to others was from pure thoughtlessness, not from want of heart. Rochfort, however, was not slow to take advantage of the young Irishman's failing. His bitter hatred and jealousy of his rival, Annesley, seemed to have changed this man's whole nature and made him ever watchful for the opportunity to annoy the Marine officer, and he knew that one way of doing this was through Annesley's little favourite, Shilrick O'Toole.

On hearing the circumstances of the drummer's arrest, therefore, Rochfort lost no time in expressing so much suspicion of the boy's conduct, and so many doubts as to the sincerity of "his last move," as he was pleased to style Shilrick's sudden consent to act as guide, that Colonel Corrie, and Captain Ellis—who was the officer in command of the chief party going to the mountains—could do nothing less than send a guard with the drummer, feeling, however, no fear in their own minds that their little favourite would prove treacherous. There had also been, at the very last moment before the party started, a somewhat stormy discussion, with regard to the necessity for searching the person of Shilrick O'Toole for papers or letters, Lieutenant Rochfort insisting that the boy might be the medium for sending secret despatches of a treasonable nature; and in this idea that officer found an eager supporter and seconder, in the person of Jeremiah Stalker, who was ready to swear that he had, on more than one occasion, seen the drummer receive mysterious and secret missives from Anty Kinahan.

Shilrick, however, here found an unexpected ally, in the person of the young midshipman, the Honourable Harry Nelson, who chanced to be on shore, on leave for the day, being a guest of one of the younger Marine officers, whom he had accompanied on parade, when the foregoing discussion was at its height; the sharp little sailor lad was about the same age as Shilrick, and his sympathy for the drummer was easily aroused. He had stood, for some moments, quiet and silent, listening anxiously to the conversation of those around him, an unwonted expression of grave thoughtfulness on his boyish face, and his hands thrust deep, and very determinedly, into his pockets, as he looked from one to the other of the speakers. At last, gradually, and with an air of well-assumed indifference, softly whistling " Hearts of Oak," he strolled up to where Shilrick was standing, and when close to the drummer, contrived, unseen by the officers, to whisper into his ear :

" Shilrick ! I am going to drop my cap—*by accident*—at your feet. You pick it up for me, and if you have any letter, or paper, you don't want them to find, if you are searched, try and slip it into my hand with the cap. Quick ! get it out of your pocket now—while they are not looking —do you understand ? I think they are going to search you ; but I mean to help you if I can."

For an instant these two brave lads stood looking earnestly at each other—then, in a voice trembling with emotion, the drummer whispered his reply :

" Heaven bless ye, Masther Nelson ! for yer kind thought, but I wouldn't be the manes av gettin' yer honour into throuble ; sure I—"

" Oh, rubbish ! " exclaimed the midshipman, impatiently. " Do you think I am such a mean coward as to see *you* in danger and not put out a hand to help you ? Do you think that I have forgotten that night when—"

Here the youthful conspirator was suddenly interrupted by Stalker, who had come creeping up softly behind the two boys, while they were speaking.

" Don't you be a-talking to that young vagabond of a drummer, young gentleman ! " he said to the midshipman, " or like henough he'll be a-drawing of *you* hinto some of them Rebel plots ; the which he's hunder harrest now, an' that's a mussey, as he can't do no more 'arm ; he's a-going for to be searched now, an' I makes no doubt as treas'nable dock'ments will be found on his person as'll himplicate more'n hisself, so it won't look well for a young naval gent like you to be found talking a'most ' 'ail-fellow-well-met,' and haidin' an' abettin' so to speak, it might hend in *your* bein' took hup likewise," concluded the patrol, in insolent, threatening tones, and with a malicious glance at both the boys.

The young midshipman, however, who, owing to his pluck and audacity, was known among his shipmates by the *sobriquet* of " The Game Cock," was quite equal to the occasion, and he now turned fiercely upon the astonished Jeremiah Stalker :

"Look here now !" he said, boldly, "if you think that *I*, a sailor in the King's Navy, am likely to be frightened of such a sneaking old spy as *you*, I can only say that you are very much mistaken. You go and look after the land-lubbers, that's what *you* were sent here for. The Army and Navy don't want *your* help. The last time you came on board our ship, telling false tales about some of the seamen, our Captain said he should like to give you a ducking, and, if he had only given the word, there's not a man of us but would have been delighted to carry out his orders ; British soldiers and sailors don't like *spies* and *informers*, Mr. Stalker."

How long this stormy altercation might have lasted, it is hard to say, but, at that moment, Colonel Corrie and Captain Ellis were seen coming towards the group, and Stalker, being well aware of the estimation in which he was held by the Marine officers, slunk away into the background, decidedly glad of the excuse for thus ending a discussion in which he was certain to get the worst of it, seeing that his opponent was the Honourable Harry Nelson, who would probably have spoken his mind, upon any subject, quite as freely and fearlessly to the Lord High Admiral himself, had the opportunity occurred.

Captain Ellis had intended, for mere form's sake, and his own satisfaction, to have searched the boy ; but he would have done so in private, or, at least, only in presence of Colonel Corrie, as, on Captain Annesley's account, he wished to spare his friend's young *protégé* as much as possible. In his own mind Ellis repudiated the idea of treachery on the part of Shilrick ; but he knew that many of the drummer's friends had joined the Rebels, and he thought it possible that the lad might have letters in his possession which would compromise, if not criminate, him with the suspicious Rochfort, and the vindictive patrol, and yet which might be perfectly innocent so far as treason was concerned.

The argument on the barrack parade lasted so long, and knowing that there was no time to lose, and that the men had been ready to start some time before, Colonel Corrie at last ordered the sergeant of Shilrick's company to search in

his coat pockets, trusting that if the drummer really had anything of importance, it would be concealed in some safe place.

He was startled, however, for a moment, when the
sergeant produced Magin's fatal letter, and when he saw the
despair so plainly written on Shilrick's expressive features
as he tried to seize the packet before it was handed to
Colonel Corrie.

Much to the chagrin and indignation of Rochfort and
Stalker, but to the evident delight of the midshipman, who
actually executed a short and lively hornpipe to show his
satisfaction, the Colonel deliberately pocketed the treacherous
missive, and walked off with it to his own quarters, saying
quietly to Ellis, "We will examine this at our leisure,
Ellis, when you return ; there is no time now. Good-even-
ing, Rochfort. I hope you are satisfied."

Little did Colonel Corrie dream what were the contents of
the letter he carried away with him ; or of the vital importance
it would prove as a silent, yet incontestable, witness against
as innocent, loyal-hearted a little soldier-lad as ever wore the
King's uniform.

It was the thought of this letter that was troubling
Shilrick O'Toole, as he stood among the watchers that night at
the "Rebels' Rest," and he almost regretted not having
accepted the young sailor's kindly offer of help. He felt that
to the Colonel, officers and men of his ever loyal and gallant
corps, that letter could have but one meaning—one interpre-
tation—and that was *treason*—treason, too, of the worst
description ; for it would speak for itself—that fatal missive
—it must show that he, a soldier in the King's service, was
actually in league with the Rebels to deceive his Colonel and
his trusting comrades.

No wonder, then, that the deep, despairing sighs, the hopeless expression on the boy's face, and the murmured words
of sorrow which, from time to time, fell from his lips, more
than once attracted the attention of the officers, who were
standing conversing together in the centre of that warlike
group ; or caused the other two little drummers—Shilrick's
youthful companions in arms—to gaze wistfully and wonderingly at him.

These were no less personages than the indomitable

Parker and Smith, before-mentioned, whose artistic propensities to draw grotesque figures on their drum-heads, and otherwise to display a powerful development of the bump of destruction, especially exercised upon His Most Gracious Majesty's properties, which had given Shilrick so much anxiety during the time he was absent from barracks, and had proved to the long-suffering sergeant of the drummers'-room a continual source of misery and vexation of spirit.

On this occasion, there were no traces of mirth or mischief on either of the roguish little faces, indeed, there were unmistakable signs of tears in the keen bright eyes which followed every look, every movement, of Shilrick O'Toole, with mute, but most sincere, sympathy.

"Well, Digby, this is pleasant, I must say!" at last remarked Captain Ellis to his friend, having watched him curiously for some time, and wondered at his unusual silence, " all the different parties of our men have now joined us, and they have seen nothing of these Rebels. I wonder how much longer we shall have to wait?"

" I do not know, Ellis; but it is certainly a most disagreeable, and—it seems to me—useless expedition altogether. Even if we do chance to come across these insurgents, the meeting cannot be very satisfactory, for it will only be, after all, a small body of them, and the encounter will not be as if we were on real, active service, and engaging with an army of regular disciplined troops," returned Lieutenant Digby, slowly, having been suddenly roused from a reverie in which he had been indulging, despite the excitement and the conversation going on around him; indeed the young officer's thoughts had wandered very far from the present scene, and at that moment were lingering with a strange mingling of pleasure, and pain, upon the memory of the few eventful hours before, when he had met, and parted from, Lady Mabel O'Hara. The joy that had filled the true hearts of both at their mutual confession of love, was sadly marred by anxious thoughts of when—if ever—they would meet again.

Although Lieutenant Digby was wont to despise the foe he was going forth to meet, as Englishmen are too often wont to despise, and depreciate everything that is not purely English, yet he was well aware that the expedition was not without its dangers ; while Lady Mabel —who had heard countless stories of the wild daring, and undaunted courage of the Mountain Bhoys—knew that the soldiers would have no mean antagonists to contend against.

"Ah, Digby !" said Ellis, smiling at his young friend's contempt for the enemy, "it is a pity you were not with us in our last campaign, you would have seen some real, genuine 'active service' *there*."

"The last campaign !" returned Digby. "Oh ! well, there *was* some honour and glory in fighting at that time ; but in this instance—why we may meet a few Rebels, and a fellow may possibly receive a knock on the head when his back is turned for a moment, with one of those wretched shillelaghs —as they call them—and get no credit for it afterwards ; never be able even to return the compliment."

" Do we *junior* officers *ever* get credit for anything we do ?" asked Ellis, bitterly, " I have not had much experience of it *personally;* but I have known a grateful country to bestow, most lavishly, praise and rewards on the *senior* officer in command, even if he only arrived on the field of action at the eleventh hour, after all the hard work and the fighting had been done for him before he appeared.   Ah, Digby, the most of us have to be content with the reflected glory !   But, there, do not let us harbour this spirit of discontent within our minds, and hearts, or we shall catch the infection of the disloyalty and treason that seem to hover around us, like evil spirits, in the very air we breathe.   Besides, it is my province to remind you, Lieutenant Charles Digby, that you should be thinking more, of honourably doing your duty as a soldier, than of the reward, and the credit you are to obtain for performing that duty.   Oh! my young comrade !" added the older officer, smilingly, " I expected better things of you, I did, indeed ! "

" You know well that it is not as you have said, Ellis ; but you know also how I have longed for fame, and *now*—now I am especially eager to win it, when—" here Digby hesitated, and with heightened colour came suddenly to a dead pause, as he caught sight of an amused smile on the face of his companion. " What is it ? " he demanded, indignantly, " what are you laughing at ?"

"Nothing! nothing!" returned the other, quietly, "I had only intended to complete your sentence for you. When the woman, who is the chief cause and motive in every case, whether for our weal or woe, has in this instance consented to share your life with you, eh! Digby? That is what you were going to tell me, is it not?"

"Why, how did you know, Ellis? Or, how did you guess?"

"My dear fellow," laughed Captain Ellis, good-naturedly, "let me advise you never to commit any serious crime, under the impression that you would get off easily; for that very expressive face and honest eyes of yours would betray your secret, and convict you any day—who is she, Digby?"

"Find out for yourself, since you can read my thoughts so easily," retorted the other, sharply. "But to continue our conversation, which you had the politeness to interrupt. As you know, I have always, from my earliest childhood, from the time when I could first think or act for myself—been imbued with an ardent desire to win fame and glory. I would use every effort," continued the young officer, enthusiasticlly, "make any sacrifice. Ay! and I would live or die to attain that desire. 'Death or glory,' shall ever be *my* motto, as it should be of every true soldier."

"A glorious and a noble ambition without doubt," said Ellis, kindly. "But, perhaps you may win both fame and glory to-night, who can tell? For let me remind you, Digby, that if there is any fighting at all, it will not be with shillelaghs only, as these honourable gentlemen-at-arms, who compose the Rebel brotherhood, do not go on their expeditions without being well armed; and having a perfect knowledge of the use of those arms."

"It may be as you have said, Ellis; still, I should imagine they could have but little idea of military tactics. It is well, however, for *you* to talk thus easily and jestingly of *my* chance of active service. You, who have been the hero of so many gallant engagements—and who have received the praises and thanks of the Parliament," said the young man, reproachfully.

"Well, you need not grudge me those *thanks*, Digby, they are all I ever received for *my* services," returned the other, quietly. " Any appearance yet, sergeant ? " he called to Sergeant Simpson, who was still keeping a look-out.

" None whatsomever, sir ! " replied the man, saluting Captain Ellis, and once more returning to his post.

" It seems useless to keep the men standing under arms all this time ; we shall have full warning if any of the Rebels are in sight," said Ellis, as going into the centre of the circle he gave the words of command to the soldiers.

" Attention ! Close on the centre ! Quick march ! Halt ! Pile arms ! Stand clear ! "

Rapidly the soldiers go through their several manœuvres, and pile arms in the very centre of the large open space around which they have been standing, while the two little drummers, Parker and Smith, approach and place their drums beside the arms, with the drumsticks crossed on the top of them. Parker taking particular care to conceal, from the watchful eyes of Captain Ellis, a long slit he had accidentally cut in his martial instrument previous to starting, when using it as a resting place for a stick of wood which he was amusing himself cutting into small pieces. The men then form in groups, and stand conversing together in low tones ; some of them now and again taking drinks from their canteens.

"I certainly hope that we may meet with this wonderful brotherhood, the 'Bold Boys of Wicklow,' as they are called," said Ellis, thoughtfully, as he returned to his old position beside Digby.

" It would be some consolation, after our long and weary waiting," returned the other.

" Sergeant Marks ! keep a sharp look-out there ! " called Ellis, anxiously.

" Yes, sir ! " replied that trusty soldier.

" I say, Ellis ! " said Digby, sarcastically. " If you had only been a little higher. in the service, you might have received the honour of knighthood for this grand expedition, or, at the very least, some substantial acknowledgment, particularly if you managed so that we retired without firing a single round, and so kept down the Army expenditure for powder and shot."

" Scarcely, Digby," replied Ellis, bitterly ; "for, doubtless, at the last moment, when I had done all the hard work, and had the full responsibility of the command, some *senior* officer would turn up to march the men quietly back to barracks. And then—well, you know what would follow," added the officer, sarcastically, " as *merit* always meets with its full reward in the service now, the *senior* officer would, in that case, be selected to receive *all* the honours a grateful government could bestow. But, there, we are growing discontented again."

" Are you ? Why, I was just thinking that you all seemed awfully jolly up here ! "

Captain Ellis started on hearing these words, spoken in a clear boyish voice, close beside him, and, on turning to reply to the speaker, was astonished indeed to see the midshipman, Harry Nelson, standing before him, a quiet smile on his audacious young face, his cap pushed far back off his forehead, and hands, as usual, thrust deep into his pockets.

" Harry ! " exclaimed Ellis, " how in the name of goodness did *you* come here ? "

" Followed you and the men, sir," replied the boy, complacently. " You don't think I could stay quietly in Glencree Barracks, when all this fun was going on up here ? Besides, I wanted to see what became of Shilrick O'Toole."

" Well, it was very wrong of you, Nelson, to come here without leave," returned Ellis, sternly, " very wrong indeed ; and now what on earth am I to do with you, and I suppose you are not even properly armed ? "

" Oh, yes ! I have my sword—and you *must* let me stay with you now, Captain Ellis," returned the midshipman, coolly. " You can't send me back alone, you know, because, if anything happened to me on the way, you would be held responsible."

" Well ! " said Ellis, resignedly, " since you have come, I suppose you must remain and take your chance with the rest of us, and all around seems quiet now. I do not think that the 'Bold Boys ' intend coming in this direction to-night. And, Digby," he continued, seriously, " I am beginning to fear that we, as well as the other troops, have been decoyed here to-night, merely to allow of the Rebel forces successfully attacking the barracks, when so many of us are absent and——"

"Ellis !" cried Digby, in horror, "you don't mean it ? Oh ! surely you do not fear that there is danger for those in barracks ?   Danger ! and *she*, my Mabel, is there to-night."

What Captain Ellis might have replied was never known, for a strange and unexpected interruption brought their discussion to a sudden close.

The sound was heard, apparently coming from a considerable distance, of some one whistling the old Irish air known as " *Crooghan Venee.*"

Sweet, clear, and distinct as the intonation of a flute, fell each note upon the ears of those anxious listeners, the echo being repeated again and again among the mountains, until the last tones dying away in the distance all was silent once more ; but before a word could be spoken, or Cptain Ellis had time to give a single command, the weird, pathetic air was again heard ; this time it appeared to come from an opposite direction from that whence the first sound was heard.

" A Rebel signal !" exclaimed Lieutenant Geoghegan, excitedly.   " Sure, then the rascals are on the march at last ! "

" Hush !" said another officer, laying his hand on Geoghegan's arm, as at that moment a woman's voice, far in the distance, had taken up the strain, and with exquisite pathos she sang, evidently in reply to the whistler, the following words, which the Irish bard had written for the air " *Crooghan Venee.*"

> " Avenging and bright falls the swift sword of Erin
> On him who the brave sons of Usna betray'd—
> For every fond eye he hath waken'd a tear in,
> A drop from his heart-wounds shall weep o'er her blade."

"There be some people a-comin' in this direction now, sir !" cried Sergeant Marks, suddenly, " but they be a goodish distance off yet, I reckon ; I can't quite make 'em out."

As Captan Ellis, Lieutenant Digby, and the other officers hastened to join the sergeant, and were standing beside him, eagerly looking out, the clear, sweet voice once more fell upon their ears.

"Tis Anty Kinahan!—sure 'tis Anty Kinahan!" cried Shilrick, forgetting for the moment, in his excitement, where he was, and that he was surrounded by officers and soldiers who were all looking curiously at him, and listening in astonishment to his wild, half-incoherent exclamation. "She must be lookin' for 'the Bhoys' to warn thim. Oh, Heaven grant she may mate thim, an' be in thime to kape thim from comin' here!"

"What is that you are saying, Shilrick O'Toole?" demanded Lieutenant Geoghegan, laying a heavy hand on the drummer's shoulder and turning him round so that he had him face to face. "Have *you* been deceiving us? Which side have you betrayed? We are of one country, you and I—oh! say that you have not disgraced that country, and the corps to which we both belong, by proving yourself one of the basest of traitors!"

"He's *not* a traitor! *I* say it is false and I don't care who accuses him of being one," said the midshipman, boldly. *I* wouldn't believe it of him."

"Oh, sir! what *can* I say?" cried the poor boy, despairingly. "What can I do but ax yer honour only to thrust me still? Oh! what can I do, at all, at all? How can I be thrue to wan parthy widout provin' thraitor to the other? *Och, wirra! wirra!* sure 'tis iverythin' in this world is goin' right agin mesilf enthirely, an' there's sorra friend near me this night."

As though in contradiction to Shilrick's words, he felt an icy cold touch upon his hand, as a little black nose was unceremoniously thrust into it; a soft tail was wagging as energetically as the exhausted condition of its owner would permit; and two tender, affectionate brown eyes were looking into his, full of silent sympathy. In another moment Shilrick had the panting, quivering form of poor tired Nap in his arms, and pressing the faithful little creature closer, and still closer to him, the boy buried his face among the long silky hair of his favourite, and gave vent to all the pent-up sorrow and anguish of that sad day of trial, in a burst of honest, boyish tears, sobbing out all his grief and trouble in a torrent of hopeless, despairing words, spoken in the soft, beautiful native Irish.

CHAPTER XXI.

" There are more things in Heaven and Earth than we
Can dream of, or than Nature understands ;
We learn not through our poor philosophy
What hidden chords are touched by unseen hands.''

ADELAIDE A. PROCTER.

Horses and dogs are said to be the especial friends of man ;
and never was there a truer saying, but more particularly is
it so with the latter.

Human love may wane, and grow cold, but the faithful
affection of a dog is unchangeable, it will cling to the loved
one through trouble, sorrow, and misfortune, whether that
loved one be a reigning monarch, or a travelling tinker ; it
matters not whether the home be a palace or a barn, the
couch a velvet cushion or a heap of straw.

This may possibly be read with a satirical, or incredulous,
smile by those who are no lovers of animals, but those who
do care for them—who can value and appreciate those
treasures sent into the world to cheer and to comfort all who
like to seek for, and to hold them, will understand, and remember the words of the poet Coleridge—

" He prayeth best, who loveth best
All things both great and small,
For the great God who made us,
He made and loves them all."

There is always something wanting in the man or woman
who dislikes animals—such an one is generally found to be
selfish and insincere, and decidedly not to be trusted. The

animals themselves know this, for they have a keener instinct than human beings in such matters, and they are not
slow in showing their mistrust. How often has some
treasured favourite, a horse, a dog, or it may be a cat or a
bird, proved a faithful friend and companion to a lonely man
or woman, or given pleasure to a little child ? How often
have hearts seared by continued disappointment in life, em-
bittered and hardened by the world's coldness and treachery,
or the inconstancy of some dear and trusted friend, been
softened and cheered by the faithful affection, the loving devotion, of one of those Heaven-sent messengers ?

A vast amount of cunning had been exercised by Nap to
enable him to effect his escape from Colonel Corrie's quarters,
and successful *sortie* through the barrack gate, when he
resolved to start off in search of his beloved mistress. He
had been long watching for his opportunity, with the most
laudable patience, and as, according to the old proverb
—" all things come to those who wait," Nap was rewarded
at last.

While Mrs. Corrie and the Colonel were both—as the
reader will remember—engaged with Lady Mabel O'Hara,
he managed to slip out of the room, and waited quietly in a
dark corner of the hall until Colonel Corrie went out, when
—quick as lightning—he sped past him, before that officer
had time to close the door, and indeed the Colonel's thoughts
were far away, and his mind so preoccupied that he never
noticed Nap, or his proceedings, at all.

The next difficulty which presented itself to the patient,
persevering, little animal was how to get out of barracks ;
but in this Nap was equal to the occasion, his sagacity
enabling him to surmount every obstacle. Cleverly evading
the sentry on duty, by running close to the wall, and keeping
well out of sight in the shadow, until the soldier's back was
turned, then making a bold dash for the barrack gate, he
darted silently, but swiftly, past a sergeant and corporal who
were conversing together at the guard-room door, and trotted
triumphantly out, unseen by anyone ; after which gallant
sortie he paused for a moment to take breath ; his next
move being to run round and round in a circle, with tail
down and black nose close to the ground, persevering

diligently until he scented the trail of Eveleen Corrie's footsteps.

On he went, the little pattering feet going over the rough ground in an incredibly short time, until he came to the old guard-house, where Eveleen and Thalia Coghlan had, but a short time before, held their important interview with the drummer, Shilrick O'Toole. Here Nap paused once more, and listened intently ; instinct, however, seemed to warn him not to go inside, lest he should be detained ; so round and round he ran once more, so rapidly that an onlooker might have imagined him to be an animated ball of wool, for by this time Nap was, so to speak, warming to his work, and had evidently determined that "Onward to Victory" should be his motto. Onward accordingly he went, following up the trail with that keen scent and instinct, and the marvellous intelligence and sagacity, for which the faithful Skye terrier has always been so famous, at last reaching the "Shamrock," at the door of which he scraped and whined until it was opened by Mrs. Kinahan. Her hands were trembling and her face white with terror, for the superstition that the howling of a dog outside the door was the forerunner of dire misfortune to the inmates, immediately took possession of her mind. Seeing, however, that the unexpected visitor was Nap, and knowing the distress that it would cause Eveleen Corrie, should her little favourite come to any harm, she tried to detain him, but, having run round the room several times, and looked into every corner, he suddenly darted past the astonished widow and out at the door, when again he started ; this time in the direction of the mountains ; but here commenced his greatest difficulties. In some parts the scent was almost obliterated by the snow which had blown over the path, or been swept aside by the tramp of the parties of soldiers who had passed that way. Back again the little creature went—round and round again, until his head must have been in a whirl—then onward once more, until at last the trail was entirely lost, and poor Nap sat down hopeless and helpless, whining piteously, wondering why the fond mistress— who was always ready to comfort and caress him whenever he was in pain or distress, did not hear him and come to him now. Poor unhappy little Nap, so lonely and forlorn—his was indeed a terrible plight—Nap who had been used all his days to a home of warmth, comfort and luxury, to the tenderest care and affection—-for he now found himself homeless and friendless, hopelessly lost among the cold, snowy mountains; his tender feet were bleeding, and his strength was well-nigh spent. One more effort he made, a little higher up the mountain-side he toiled, and would have fallen, fairly exhausted, but rallied suddenly, and with head uplifted, tail wagging, and a faint, but joyful bark, he scrambled on a little farther, for he had heard—not far off—the voice of a friend. In a few minutes more Nap had reached the "Rebels' Rest," and was clasped in the arms of Shilrick O'Toole.

Although the words spoken by the drummer in his excitement, and which were so eagerly listened to by both officers and men, were in the *Erse*, or native Irish—a language generally spoken among the peasantry of Wicklow, at that time —and no one near him could understand a single word, yet he had one true sympathiser in poor Nap, who, from time to time, contrived to raise his tired head so that he might be able to lick the kindly hand that caressed him, and look into his friend's face, as though pleading for praise for what he had done. The faithful creature was utterly worn out, and no wonder, considering the long, weary journey those little feet had wandered that night.

After all, he might have been lost, perhaps buried in the snow, and never more seen or heard of by the mistress to whom he was so dear, had he not at last—when strength was failing, and eyes growing dim—heard the well-known voice of his friend, Shilrick, and with one final effort, managed to reach the drummer's side.

Lieutenant Geoghegan was right in his supposition that the sound which had so startled and surprised the party of Marines lying in ambush at the "Rebels' Rest," falling so suddenly upon their ears, and coming to them in such sweet, clear tones through the still night air, the whistling of the weird but beautiful "*Crooghan Vence*," was indeed a Rebel signal; and Shilrick O'Toole was no less correct in his idea that the woman's voice they had heard singing—evidently in reply to this signal—was that of Anty Kinahan.

When the " Bold Boys " left their cave for the purposes of drill, or of meeting for consultation at some particular spot arranged beforehand, they generally divided their detachment into several small parties, so that, in the event of their falling in with pickets of soldiers, they could the more easily disperse and be lost to sight.   Although it was seldom that the military penetrated so far into the midst of the higher range of mountains.

The Rebels were always prepared, however, in case of a sudden surprise or attack ; and it was their custom, at such times, for the leader of one of their bands to whistle the air, " *Crooghan Venee*," which had been especially selected for this purpose—and then listen for the reply, which would be given by the leader of another party, and possibly repeated by a third.   Thus the Rebels were well able, with considerable accuracy to ascertain how many detachments were out on the mountains, and in what direction they were marching.

At times, when the " Bold Boys " dare not show themselves—and often, for days together, this might be the case, when they received warning that the military were likely to be out—then Anty Kinahan would bravely take up her basket, and alone set out, finding her way to one or other of " the Bhoys' " places of rendezvous ; and to discover their whereabouts, as well as to let them know that she was near, with sundry provisions, and mayhap important news, she would sing a verse of the song before mentioned, to which someone would reply by whistling the same air ; and thus it was that Anty Kinahan's voice was heard that night among Wicklow's wild mountains.

As the reader may remember, Anty had proceeded thither in company with Sheymus Malloy, Eveleen Corrie, and Thalia Coghlan.   They unfortunately more than once missed the right path, and were therefore obliged to retrace their steps for some distance, and try another pass, or defile, only to find themselves still farther from their destination— the " Rebels' Rest."

The snow upon the ground was not very deep, but the wreaths which had drifted over many of the paths, entirely concealing them, made it a most difficult task to find the right track when once it was lost, and their progress was fraught with danger on every hand.

As Sheymus Malloy and his brave-hearted companions anxiously paused for a moment to consider what was best to be done, and while Eveleen Corrie was looking somewhat hopelessly upon the wild, desolate scene around her, they too heard the Rebel signal, and on Anty Kinahan explaining the reasons for its being given, the others all agreed that it would be well for her to reply in the usual manner, and the insurgents, hearing her voice, would probably imagine that she had a message, or a warning for them, and would therefore be certain to advance in the direction from whence the voice had sounded, and so each party might, in this way, be able to discover the whereabouts of the others.

But alas ! while Anty Kinahan was singing, she was approaching nearer and nearer to the " Rebels' Rest "—surely, but unconsciously, luring Morven O'Neill and his brave followers into the very midst of their enemies.

Meanwhile, not one of Sheymus Malloy's devoted little party had noticed the silent form that followed them so stealthily, pausing when they paused, and keeping well in the shadow until they were ready to proceed once more ; for footsore, faint and weary—with heart full of tender, loving thoughts of the one who was so dear to her—with wildest fears for his safety—Estelle O'Neill went bravely onward.

CHAPTER XXII.

" A Mirage at times from the Causeway's wild shore
  An Islet of beauty at sunset is seen,
Where ivy-clad round towers, those temples of yore,
  Seem wreathed in rich foliage of emerald green,
But woe to the boatman who launches his bark,
  And bounds o'er the waves this fair isle to explore,
The phantom he follows grows distant and dark,
  The boat and her steersman are heard of no more.

And this oft, alas! is the Patriot's fate,
  Who, lured by a vision, entranced by a dream ;
Alone on the billows of discord and hate,
  Regardless of danger, pursues his fond scheme.
He sees but the laurels of valour achieved ;
  The bright star of Liberty beams through the gloom ;
But finds, tho' too late, when by false hopes deceived,
  The pathway to glory oft leads to the tomb."

T. C. S. CORRY, M.D., F.R.C.S.L.

Once more the sweet, flute-like notes of " *Crooghan Vence* " were heard by the anxious watchers at the " Rebels' Rest," and this time the whistler seemed to be very near.

"It's the Bhoys! it's the Bhoys!" cried Shilrick, despairingly. "*Och, wirrasthrue! wirrasthrue!* 'tis Magin has bethrayed thim all—he must have written that letther to make me bring the souldiers here. Oh! Kerry, Kerry, me own brother! An' poor, brave *Ua Néill!* Ochone! sure they'll be thinkin' 'tis *I* done it, that *I've* bethrayed thim. Oh, Heaven help me! what'll I do, at all, at all ? "

"What do you mean, boy?" demanded Captain Ellis, sternly, laying his hand on the drummer's shoulder. "Why do you hesitate ? Do you not hear me speaking to you ? " he added, seeing that Shilrick still remained silent. "Come, answer me at once ! "

"*Och, faraoir! faraoir!*" sobbed the boy, seeming in his grief as though he scarcely noticed who was beside him. "Sure it's the murther av the poor Bhoys that'll rest on *my* head now; but I didn't mane it—oh, I didn't mane it!"

"Ah! I see it all now," exclaimed Captain Ellis, indignantly, as he stood watching the agitated face of the drummer who was still clasping little Nap closely in his arms, as though in a panic of terror that this one true friend might be taken from him. "I see it all! You have been a traitor; and when you consented at the last moment to accompany us, and to be our guide, you imagined that you were bringing us all here on a fruitless march—no doubt laughing at our credulity. Truly you are young in years to have shown such clever cunning and deceit—to have proved such a consummate traitor. Fool that I was to trust to that innocent face of yours! It is well, however, that you have been found out in time."

There was keen regret mingled with the anger and evident disappointment in the tones of the officer's voice as he spoke, and he gave a long searching look at Shilrick, ere he turned away from him, and addressed the soldiers who were guarding him:

"Guard that boy more carefully," was his stern command. "See that he has no chance of escape; or of communicating in any way with the Rebels. Take him over to yonder corner out of the way."

The two soldiers approach closer to Shilrick, and march across, with the boy between them, to the spot indicated by Captain Ellis, which is a small cavity between two rocks; the men glance sorrowfully at their little prisoner from time to time, and their duties are evidently performed with the greatest reluctance. The officer had given no orders concerning Nap, so the drummer still carried him in his arms, and when he seemed tired of that position Shilrick laid him down carefully in a corner, among some bushes of bracken, which were growing out of the rocks; and Nap, being thoroughly worn out, was, for once, quite content to remain quiet, and still, beside his friend, after having been duly petted and caressed by most of the officers and men, who were all alike astonished at his unexpected appearance in their midst.

Again, all those assembled at the " Rebels' Rest " were startled by suddenly hearing the voices of a great number of men singing, or rather chanting in a low undertone— apparently quite close to them—the continuation of the song which Anty Kinahan had sung in reply to the Rebel signal, and there was a characteristic and vengeful tone in the sentiment of this Rebel song, and a sound of suppressed passion and vindictive feeling in the low voices, which added a strange, subtle import to the following words, and seemed to chill the brave, stout hearts of the listeners—

> " We swear to avenge them ! no joy shall be tasted,
>   The harp shall be silent, the maiden unwed,
> Our halls shall be mute, and our fields shall lie wasted,
>   Till vengeance is wreak'd on the murderer's head ! "

" Oh ! woorse luck to me that I should have thrusted to what Magin said in his letther," murmured Shilrick, hopelessly. " Was I *mad* whin I done it—whin I put anny faith in *his* words ? Oh, Kerry ! " he cried, burying his face in his hands, " what *will* become av yersilf, an poor *Ua Néill ?* "

After a moment's thought, and a hasty whispered conference with some of the other officers, Captain Ellis now came forward, and taking up a prominent position, gave a few words of command, in a low tone, to the men :

" Stand to your arms, my lads ! Unpile arms ! Open out ! Load kneeling, and conceal yourselves ! "

These commands were quickly obeyed, and with so much stealth and silence that, although there was a large body of men, yet each one seemed literally to glide noiselessly into his right position, and very near indeed must the approaching enemy have been to have heard even the slightest sound.

Nap, however, was very nearly betraying them ; his love for music was not of the keenest, and anything in the pathetic or solemn line was decidedly obnoxious to him. The song " *Crooghan Vence,*" therefore, was not to be endured with equanimity ; and in addition to this he had rolled himself into a ball in the comfortable nest Shilrick had made for him among the bracken, and was enjoying a calm sleep after all his exertions, so naturally felt indignant at being disturbed. His spirits, too, had rallied considerably, and he could not allow all the intense excitement going on around him, and the rapid movements of the soldiers, to pass without some remonstrance on his part. One of the Marines who stood near was only just in time in placing his hand over Nap's mouth before he could give vent to the first preparatory whine.

The party of soldiers, together with Sergeants Marks and Simpson, Corporal Hickson, and the drummers, Parker and Smith, soon divided, and concealed themselves in every direction around the circle, behind the rocks and crevices.

Captain Ellis, Lieutenants Digby and Geoghegan, and other officers stand together, keeping well under the shadow of the rocks.

In another moment the soldiers, who were on the look out as sentinels, saw the band of Rebels, with Morven O'Neill at their head, slowly enter the narrow defile leading into the space where the Marines had been so long lying in ambush waiting for them.

With this band of the "Bold Boys" came Silas Charlesston, Andy Rafferty, and the other Rebels from the cave. Charleston kept close to O'Neill, and from time to time glanced furtively around him, for he was apprehensive that a sudden attack might be made upon their young captain, knowing well the treachery of Thaddeus Magin, and always fearing that he, Morven, might be shot down suddenly by some one concealed among the rocks, and probably bribed by the Yankee. The Rebels carry with them the standard of the O'Neill, and several banners, which were described in a former chapter, and which they have brought with them from the cave, for a grand meeting of the Rebel forces had been arranged to take place that night ; consequently the insurgents were in uniform, fully armed, and carried all their paraphernalia with them.

As they entered the narrow defile they were still singing :

> " Yes, monarch ! though sweet are our home recollections,
>   Though sweet are the tears that from tenderness fall ;
> Though sweet are our friendships, our hopes, our affections,
>   Revenge on a tyrant is sweetest of all ! "

When Morven O'Neill appeared before the officers and soldiers, he was not recognised by any of them at first, for the shadow of a high, overhanging rock fell upon him, and he wore his hat well over his eyes. So well were the Marines concealed among the rocks, that O'Neill and his whole band had arrived at the spot called the "Rebels' Rest," and were actually within the circle before they noticed that it was literally lined with soldiers. Captain Ellis then went boldly forward to confront them, with drawn sword, and giving at the same time the word of command to his men :

"Up, my lads ! surround the Rebels !"

The soldiers rush out from their places of concealment and surround them, with their muskets at "the present," on every side. Lieutenants Digby and Geoghegan and the other officers draw their swords and stand ready for action.

"So, *Michael Cluny*!" said Captain Ellis, sternly, addressing Morven O'Neill, "we have met you at last. It is useless for you to resist ; for you will be overpowered. I call upon you in the King's name to surrender ; and it will be better for you, and your followers, if you do so quietly, and at once."

The soldiers meanwhile stand at the position of " ready," the Rebels do the same, turning so as to face their enemies on every hand ; both sides looking hard and steadily at each other.

"*Surrender*!" exclaimed O'Neill, proudly, " *I* surrender ! Never! while I have life within me to resist. See !" he continued, lifting his hat, and coming forward, so that the moonlight fell upon him. " Look you, Ellis, you see my men are scarcely so undisciplined as you imagine, neither is their leader inexperienced. My real name is not ' *Michael Cluny*,' I am your old comrade."

"Morven O'Neill !" cried Captain Ellis, in horror.

"Morven O'Neill ! !" echoed the astonished Digby. "Oh ! is it possible ? "

"Quite possible, Digby," returned Morven, quietly, "and now you know with whom you have to deal."

"Well !" said Ellis, firmly, but sadly, "you must surrender, O'Neill ! "

" Oh, do not make matters worse by useless resistance," entreated Digby, earnestly.

" I have not the slightest intention of yielding, but with my life," was O'Neill's determined reply. "Come, my lads !" he added, turning to the soldiers who had surrounded him, " I was in your corps once—some of you recognise me now, I can see. You would not, surely, harm your old officer ; give way there, and let us pass ! "

" Sure, Kerry is not with thim," murmured Shilrick to himself, as he looked around eagerly, while the discussion was going on between O'Neill and the officers. " Oh ! maybes he'll be saved yet—if he'd only kape clare av the ' Ribils' Rest ' this night ! "

The soldiers appeared undecided, on hearing O'Neill's words, and taking advantage of their hesitation and surprise, the Rebels commenced to fight their way through the line with their bayonets, after firing one or two shots ; those at the back trying to keep at bay the soldiers who had surrounded them on the opposite side.

Captain Ellis, indignant at the attack of the Rebels upon his men, immediately gave orders for action.

"Our King for ever !" he cried, fighting desperately with two of the Rebels. "Up, Marines, and at them! Quick, my lads ! do your duty ! Would you let these rascally Rebels get the better of you ? "

With loud counter-cheers, both parties now join in the fight.

"Fight well, Boys, and bravely !" commanded Morven, as he cleverly kept at bay several of the soldiers who had attacked him. " Oh ! remember our cause ! *Erin, our country and Liberty!*"

The battle now raged fast and furious, shouts and exclamations in many languages might be heard amid the clashing of swords and the din of firearms—" *Ua Neill abu ! Lamh dhearg, Eirin !* "

" *Vive O'Neill ! vive la Republique !* "

" *Plutot la mort que l'esclavage !* "

" Ireland for the Irish !" " Home Rule !" " A King av our own !" " Ould Ireland for iver !"

" *Alla vittoria !* "

" The stars an' the stripes for ever ! "

" Victory for the richt ! "

Then, above all, sounded Lieutenant Digby's clear, hearty voice :

" For your King and country, my lads ! For the honour of our corps !"

" Ay, ay, sir !" came the cheerful reply from Sergeant Marks and the soldiers. " Hurrah ! for the old corps ! King George for ever ! "

Ellis and Digby are now seen in the thickest of the conflict, while Morven O'Neill is fighting desperately with one after another of the soldiers; Sergeant Simpson and several others fall before him, all, more or less, dangerously wounded. Lieutenant Geoghegan is attacked by two or three of the Rebels at once, but manages to keep them off bravely, the young midshipman hastening to his assistance, and cutting right and left with his small sword.

And now Captain Annesley and Father Bernard appear upon the scene, they pause, and look horror-struck at the sight which meets their gaze.

The battle is still raging fiercely, and the dead and dying lie all around them.

" We have indeed come upon a scene of strife ! " exclaimed the priest, sadly.

" It is really fortunate that we lost our way after all," replied Captain Annesley, "as we may possibly be of some service here ; but O'Neill—where is he ?—I do not see him ! Oh, Father ! I fear that Kerry O'Toole and Owen Maguire have been too late to warn him."

Even as Annesley was speaking, he chanced to look in the direction of the narrow defile, before mentioned, and saw Owen Maguire and Kerry O'Toole hurrying towards them.

" Ah ! here they are, now ! " said Annesley.

" Oh ! masther darlin," cried Owen, in despair, as he hastened over to Morven's side, seeing that he was fighting with terrible odds against him ; but Owen had a hard task to reach O'Neill, for he was attacked on every side, he had no time to load his pistol, and could only force his way through the very midst of the combatants, by using the butt-end of his musket, as he would have wielded a shillelagh to parry the thrusts of the soldiers' bayonets. There had already been great loss of life, and many wounded among both soldiers and Rebels.

Kerry O'Toole was looking around anxiously, prepared either to attack, or to defend, wherever his assistance seemed most required, when he was startled by hearing a wild cry of horror from his brother Shilrick, who had discovered his presence.

"Oh! he's come—he's come!" cried the boy, despairingly. "Oh! Kerry, me brother, why are ye here? Sure, it's mesilf hoped an' prayed that ye were safe."

"Whist! be the whist, Shilrick *ma bouchaleen*!" said Kerry, in a whisper, holding up a warning finger as he paused beside the drummer for a moment. "Sure ye wouldn't have mesilf kapin' quiet an' aisy, an' hidin' away safe, while the other bhoys are fightin' for their lives? An' Misther O'Neill—*och, wirra! wirra!* Sure, 'tis Owen Maguire an' mesilf thried so hard to be here soon enough to warn him, an' if Magin hadn't roused up, an' come afther us, we'd have done it. There was a hape av thime lost in fightin' wid him—the blackguard—whin he overtook us, an' it's iverythin' went right agin' us enthirely, so it did. But, Shilrick!" continued Kerry, sternly, "I'd forgotten for the moment How is it that *you're* here, at all, at all? Sure it isn't *yersilf* that's been after bethrayin' poor *Ua Néill* an' 'the Bhoys?' It isn't *you* showed the souldiers the road to the ' Ribils' Rest ' ? "

"Ah, no, no!" cried Shilrick, indignantly. "I mane—sure I couldn't help it. Oh! how could ye think so ill av me? Listen now, Kerry wisha! an' I'll—"

"Ye couldn't help it!" exclaimed Kerry, furiously, recoiling from his brother in horror. "Then it's *yersilf* done it all, *ye've thurned informer*, an'—"

" Kerry, hear me! I"ll explain all to ye, enthirely."

As Shilrick was about to explain, however, Kerry, with a sudden exclamation, left him hurriedly, and joined Captain Annesley, whom he had just discovered.

"Is it yersilf, Misther Armoric? Och! how is it yer honour came here at all? Troth, I thought it's safe in barracks ye'd be by now. Ah!—see yondher!" he added,

excitedly, pointing to Morven O'Neill, who was evidently
being fast overpowered by the force of numbers, though his
resistance was brave and determined, his courage still undaunted.

"Look ! look, beyant there !   'Tis himself, *Ua Néill.* Oh,
save him, save him, Armoric machree ! See ! the souldiers
are surroundin' him an' Owen !   They'll be thaken !   Och,
begorrah ! they're overpowerin' O'Neill at last—I've no
weapon, but sure while I've two hands on me I'll thry an'
save him.   Armoric ! ye have yer sword.   Come wid me—
we'll maybes save him yet. Oh ! 'twill be worse than death to
our brave young captain, if he's thaken prisoner," added Kerry,
sorrowfully, as he hastened to the assistance of O'Neill, followed by Captain Annesley, who, in the excitement of the
moment, forgot the relative positions of himself and the young
Rebel Chief, and remembered only the days when they had
served together in the old corps, always true friends and
comrades. Many of the Rebels have by this time been taken
prisoners ; and now, at last, Thaddeus Magin puts in an appearance ; he creeps round the circle, behind the combatants, unseen by anyone save Silas Charleston, who, although
engaged in defending himself, is at the same time furtively
watching his treacherous compatriot.

At last Magin reaches the side of Ellis, and whispers
confidentially to him.

"Is *he* taken yet ? "

" Whom do you mean ? " asked Captain Ellis, sternly.

"Why ! I calc'late I mean the great prize—*Michael Cluny.*"

"No ! " returned Ellis, contemptuously.   " But, oh ! keep
back from me, wretched traitor that you are ! "

" Wa'al, mister," said Magin, now creeping fawningly up
to Digby, "p'raps *you'll* be more grateful, seeing the good
turn I've done yer this night.   I guess in another minute
' *Michael Cluny,*' alias Captain Morven O'Neill, will be fixed,
and safe in yer custody, dead or alive."

" Oh ! don't come near me ! " cried Digby, shuddering,
" you hateful. contemptible coward."

"Wa'al ! if *that* airn't gratitude ! But I calc'late yer'll
hev to shell out the reward, strangers, for all yer darned
starched-up manners."

" Gratitude ! and to *you ?* " exclaimed Ellis, scornfully.

" Why, certainly ! "

" If you looked for any such return from us, I fear you will be most wofully disappointed, double-dyed villain that you are," said Digby.

" All you have done, has been solely to benefit yourself," said Geoghegan, who happened to be passing the Yankee at the moment, as he was fighting his way through a group of insurgents.

"'That's so !" retorted Magin, insolently. " Did yer think I was such a cussed fool as to do it for anyone else ? I airn't too proud to own that I always hev an eye to the main chance. Ah ! " he exclaimed, suddenly, in a low tone, as he for the first time caught sight of Shilrick standing apart from the others with a sentry on either side of him, " I'd forgotten that darned boy. I guess he might prove awkward —betray my part in this affair to both sides. I must silence him ! "

With these significant words and with a sinister expression on his villainous face, he crept once more round the circle, until he stood very near the unconscious drummer. Shilrick's head was turned in the opposite direction, so that he did not notice Magin, who, with murderous intent, was gradually creeping closer, and closer to him, while both soldiers and Rebels were all too much engaged, either in attacking their enemies, or defending themselves, to see the boy's danger.

At last the Yankee raised the pistol he carried, and aimed it at the drummer's head, but, ere he could fire, or Silas Charleston had time to prevent it, Nap, who had been a witness of this little episode, and whose instinct taught him that Magin's position was antagonistic towards his friend Shilrick, dashed out upon him, barking furiously, and so startled and terrified the cowardly Yankee that, instead of shooting the drummer, the contents of the pistol struck against the rock just above his head, though unfortunately the bullet rebounded, and landing in poor little Nap's leg, lamed him severely ; in an instant, however, he was once more in Shilrick's arms, and was tenderly placed in his nest among the bracken, and destined from that time forth to be an honoured hero by both officers and men of the Marines, for he had, undoubtedly, saved the life of the pride and favourite of the corps.

Thaddeus Magin soon recovered himself. He had other and more important mischief in hand. and with a fierce imprecation against both Shilrick and Nap, he determined to make another attempt against the drummer's life later on, and vowed bitter vengeance against poor, faithful Nap, who had thwarted him for the time, for he could see that the men guarding Shilrick, as well as Silas Charleston and others among the Irish Rebels had witnessed his cowardly action, and would watch well whenever he went near the drummer. And after all, he decided that he was wasting time and losing opportunities of ridding himself of one whom he hated, and whom he chose to consider had stood in the way of his own advancement in the Rebel Forces. Once more, therefore, he retraced his steps, keeping as much out of the sight of those whom he suspected were watching him, as possible, until he came to one of the cavities in the rock ; here he took post, reloaded his pistol, and waited in readiness until his victim should pass within a good range of his shot.

It is a sad fact, but a true one, that fate seems often to favour the plots and plans of the murderer and evil doer, and, indeed, sometimes even to assist, by providing the opportunity and the means, and on this occasion Thaddeus Magin appeared no less favoured than others had been before him. Keeping well within the shadow of the rock, he watched and waited ; his patience being soon rewarded.

Captain Ellis, Lieutenant Digby, and Geoghegan, who was still followed bravely by Harry Nelson, each in their turn, passed by Magin's place of concealment, as they engaged in deadly conflict with members of the Rebel band. Then came Morven O'Neill, fighting desperately for life and liberty, successfully keeping at bay three powerful Marines, thinking and hoping that, if he could only hold them off until he reached the entrance of the narrow defile, he might escape through it, and if rapid in his movements, perhaps be able to make his way, by means of one of the numerous small caves or outlets, to the lower range of mountains, where he might find shelter until the military had dispersed.

Just as he passed Magin, however, the Yankee's murderous weapon was once more raised, and *this* time the bullet performed its work of destruction only too well, for brave Morven O'Neill, the noble, true-hearted patriot, fell mortally wounded at the feet of his bitterest enemy, treacherously shot down by one of his own band.

" Wa'al, mister ! thar you air ! " said Magin, triumphantly, but in a low voice, to Captain Ellis, who, with Digby, had hastened over to Morven's side on seeing him fall. " I guess yer'll fix him slick enough now, but remember the old sayin', ' Fast bind, fast find,' I cal'clate he has grit enough left in him yet to give yer the slip if yer don't look out."

By this time the greater number of the Rebels have been, after a brave, determined resistance, completely overpowered, and those men, together with the wounded, are now guarded by the soldiers, and from time to time glance sorrowfully and pityingly at the young chief, poor *Ua Néill*, to whom most of them were so devoted ; and now, for the first time Ellis and Digby notice the presence of Annesley and Father Bernard.

" Annesley ! " exclaimed Ellis, in astonishment, "*you here* !   Oh ! " he continued, with emotion, " this is indeed a sad night's work ; our poor old comrade ! See, Annesley ! it is O'Neill, our Colonel's nephew. What *can* we do for him ?   Alas ! he is to all intents and purposes a Rebel— Ay ! and an important one, too—against the Government."

" Would to Heaven that Ellis had never received that wretched traitor's letter this morning, to bring us all here tonight. But how did *you* come here, Annesley ? " asked Digby.

" Do not mind me at present," returned Annesley, hurriedly. " See ! yonder villain was the one who wounded poor O'Neill, before I could warn him of his danger. That arch-traitor, Thaddeus Magin, shot him down deliberately, from his place of concealment among the rocks. I saw it all, —but he shall not go free."

" Here, my lads ! " called the officer, pointing to Magin, who, as Annesley spoke, was trying to slink away unseen, " two of you go after that cowardly villain. He is a double traitor, on no account allow him to escape. Quickly ! or he will be gone."

Two of the soldiers obey Annesley's orders, and follow Magin with evident alacrity; they manage to overtake him, and, in triumph they return with him as prisoner.

As they are dragging him along, however—for he makes frantic efforts to break from their hold—one of the Rebels who had contrived to escape and to conceal himself not far off, having seen all that Magin had done, and overheard the officer's words, suddenly appeared, and taking aim from behind a rock shot the Yankee, who fell dead at the feet of his captors.

"So perish every traitor to the *great cause!*" cried the Rebel, passionately, "and I thank Heaven *I've* been able to avenge the murther of *Ua Néill*, an' rid my counthry av such a reptile!"

With these words the man once more disappeared, and so rapid were his movements that the soldiers could not overtake him, and he was nevermore seen, either by them or his old companions.

Kerry O'Toole, Owen Maguire, and Silas Charleston are still fighting with the soldiers, who are trying to make them prisoners; and Andy Rafferty, following always in the wake of the young American, his greatest friend, is defending himself with all the energy he can command.

Some of the soldiers have, according to the orders of Captain Ellis, surrounded the prostrate form of Morven O'Neill, while Annesley stands near him, and Father Bernard kneels beside his young friend, tenderly raising his head in his arms.

"Fall back, my lads!" called Annesley to the soldiers, who immediately obeyed his command, and stood in a group together near the entrance into the defile.

"Oh! masther darlin'! masther darlin'!" cried Owen Maguire, breaking through the lines of soldiers, and throwing himself down on his knees at Morven's feet. "If *I* could only have died for ye. *Och, wirra! wirra!* why didn't the cruel shot pierce *my* heart first?" he sobbed, burying his face in his hands. "Oh! if I could only have saved ye!"

"Father Bernard! do you think he is much hurt?" asked Annesley, anxiously. "O'Neill!" he continued, tenderly, as he bent over his old comrade, "do you know me?"

" Yes, Annesley ! " replied Morven, sorrowfully, as he tried to raise himself. "I know you; but oh ! surely *you* did not betray us ? "

" Ah no, my son ! it was that false-hearted traitor, Thaddeus Magin," said Father Bernard.

" And it was he who wounded you, O'Neill," added Annesley ; "but he has already paid the penalty of his double treachery."

" Oh, masther dear ! " cried Owen, rising, and pointing to the body of Magin, " see ! there he lies now ; 'twas wan av ' the Bhoys ' shot him—an' good luck to him who done it ! "

" Ah !—an' so *he* betrayed me into the hands of the soldiers after all ? " said Morven, sadly. " Well—*I never* trusted him."

Shilrick O'Toole, who is still standing at his old post, a prisoner, now tries to come forward, but Captain Ellis, who is near him at the time, gently but firmly puts him aside.

" You must stay where you are, my boy ! remember you are a prisoner. You must do your duty, my lads ! " he added, turning to the soldiers who guarded the drummer.

Captain Ellis next passes on, down the line of soldiers who are standing in the background, speaks to Sergeants Simpson and Marks, especially saying a few cheering words to the former, who has been wounded, and also to poor little Bill Parker, who is badly wounded about the head and face, and is now resting in Harry Nelson's arms. He gives various orders and directions as he passes ; he places two of the soldiers at the different outlets from the circle, a strong guard at the entrance to the defile, and a soldier at each intervening space round it, as sentinels.

" Oh, Kerry ! Kerry wisha ! where are ye now, at all, at all," murmured Shilrick, anxiously, as he looked around. " Och ! sure I hope he'll escape afther all ! "

At that moment Kerry was not in sight. He had contrived to escape outside the circle, and was now with Silas Charleston, fighting bravely for liberty, against two soldiers who had pursued them.

Ellis now returns to Digby and Geoghegan, who had been employed, with Dr. Conway, the young surgeon of Marines, who had accompanied the party to the mountains, in assisting their wounded comrades, and were now sorrowfully looking on, leaning on their swords, and conversing together in low tones.

Lieutenant Digby has himself been wounded, and severely too ; but has made light of it to the others, and Geoghegan has turned amateur surgeon, carefully binding up his friend's arm, and making a temporary sling with his handkerchief, and, though the pain is great, the brave-hearted young lieutenant tries to smile, and wonders what Lady Mabel O'Hara will say to see him return to barracks in such a fashion—and whether, if he eventually loses his arm, she will still be true to him.

Meanwhile, Sheil Casey, who has carried the Rebel standard, and protected it gallantly all through the fierce battle, now rushes into the circle from the outside, still fighting with a soldier who had pursued him, but yet bravely holding on to the standard with one hand, until at last he falls, severely wounded, and the banner he has so nobly defended, slips from his hand.

Shilrick O'Toole, seeing this, hastily stoops forward, and, in spite of the kindly remonstrances of the soldiers who are guarding him, picks up the flag, strips it off the long spear, and thrusts it into the breast of his coat, after carefully rolling it up.

" Sure, 'tis the O'Neill's standard, and it shall niver be throdden ondher foot when I'm near to prevint it," said the boy, triumphantly, and glancing, it must be owned, with considerable defiance, at his two guards. " It's mesilf that'll thake care av it. Maybes poor Misthress O'Neill might like to have it, or Miss Corrie, his honour's own cousin."

The soldiers did not again attempt to interfere with Shilrick. They looked at each other with a smile, and a good-natured wink ; for the feelings of both were decidedly lenient towards their little prisoner.

The midshipman had fortunately escaped unhurt, with the exception of a few bruises, and a slight cut on the left hand, although the brave little sailor lad had been one of the foremost in the conflict.

" Do you think that you are severely wounded, O'Neill ? "

asked Annesley, anxiously, again bending over his friend, and after having tried all the restoratives those present chanced to have with them. "Could you rise, with my help?" Then, hastily glancing round him, Annesley whispered, "If you could manage this—and I could get you away out of sight for a few minutes, until you have recovered yourself a little, I might perhaps be able to effect your escape unnoticed. Can you hear me? Do you understand me— dear old friend? Oh! try and listen if you can—I shall do all that is in my power for you; but I must not be precipitate—too great haste might ruin all."

"And yourself, Annesley!" replied Morven, faintly. "*You* would be—tried for treason—for aiding and abetting—in the escape of—of the notorious '*Michael Cluny*.' Ah, no, no!—don't mind me—things are better as they are,—it is my fate. Don't grieve for me, old comrade, and—and oh, I pray you, do not—oh! do not try to restore me!—do not let them take me—*alive*—for—to be made prisoner would be —to me—a thousand times worse than death—and Annesley!—remember—ah, remember!—*the traitor's* doom of which you warned me! Yes —*they* will call me *traitor*—but I care not. I have given my life for my country—to her I have been faithful and true."

"Ay! faithful and true *always*—to friends, or foes," murmured Annesley, softly.

CHAPTER XXIII.

" Night closed around the conqueror's way,
 And lightnings show'd the distant hill,
Where those who lost that dreadful day,
 Stood few and faint, but fearless still!
The soldier's hope, the patriot's zeal,
 For ever dimmed, for ever cross'd—
Oh! who shall say what heroes feel,
 When all but life and honour's lost."

MOORE.

With the greatest tenderness, Captain Annesley raised Morven O'Neill in his arms, and laid the once proud, beautiful head upon his breast.

"Can anyone bring me some water? And where is the surgeon?" he asked. "O'Neill has fainted again."

"Conway is attending to some of the men who are badly wounded," replied Ellis.

Shilrick O'Toole having heard Annesley's request for the water, was seen by Captain Ellis speaking eagerly to the soldiers who were guarding him, holding out his canteen and pointing to the prostrate form of Morven. Ellis was unable to resist the pathetic appeal and the anxious, earnest expression on the boy's face, he therefore gave orders to the soldiers to let him go to O'Neill for the time.

Shilrick was not long in availing himself of the desired permission, and hastened to the side of the young Rebel Chief.

"Thake a dhrop av wather, sir!" he implored, himself holding the canteen to Morven's lips, "it'll maybes make yer honour fale sthronger."

"Shilrick, my own little drummer!" exclaimed Annesley,

kindly. "I did not know you were here. It was kind of you to think of the water. See! how eagerly Mr. O'Neill is drinking it. I hope it may revive him."

"Moor like to poison him, comin' from such a base, ongrateful thraitor," cried the angry voice of Owen Maguire, as having come softly up behind Shilrick he now seized the boy by the shoulder, holding him in a passionate, determined grasp. "Then 'tis yersilf guided the souldiers up here, yersilf brought them afther my poor young masther, who niver done an' ill-turn to annywan in all his life, an' laste av all to *you*, that ye'd turn agin him that way, like a mane, decateful viper. Och! niver heed but ye'll get yer just reward—see," continued the man, wildly, not noticing in his intense excitement and grief that two soldiers had advanced to take him prisoner, and were only kept back by Lieutenant Digby, who pitied Owen, and wished the last moments of O'Neill to be peaceful. "See!" cried Owen again to Shilrick, as he pointed passionately, first to Morven, and then to the other Rebels who were standing around, prisoners in the hands of the soldiers, or lying wounded and dying, "D'ye like yer work, *ma bouchaleen?* Is it plasin' to ye, to see yer own countrymen, ay! an' faith many av yer own brave comrades too, lyin' dead an' dyin' foreninst ye this minute, an' to think that the blood av thim all is on *your* head. *Och! wirra! wirra!* —to think such a little bit av a gossoon should carry such a decateful heart wid him! But oh! couldn't ye have spared Misther O'Neill, me own brave-hearted masther?—Have ye forgotten the thime he saved yer life—how whin ye were wounded in the fight *he* carried ye to a place av safety ondher heavy fire av the enemy,?"

"Ah, no, no!" cried Shilrick, with passionate vehemence and stretching out his hands towards Owen, as though to ward off a blow, "I've niver, niver forgotten an' I haven't remimbered out av gratitude alone—but out av the love that's in me heart for *Ua Néill.* Oh! *Ua Néill! Ua Néill!*" sobbed the boy, "how *can* they think that *I'd* iver have harmed *yersilf,* or wan av yer faithful followers!"

"Och! it's aisy talkin' now ye've done all the harm that lay in yer power," said Owen, contemptuously, "an' the poor masther—"

"Stay, Owen!" interrupted Morven, in a low, faint voice, as he vainly endeavoured to raise himself. "Be not too quick in blaming the boy. Shilrick!—surely—surely *you* did not guide the soldiers to—to this place—after us?"

"Oh! Misther O'Neill, dear!" returned the drummer, sorrowfully. "Don't ax me—don't ax me. Sure 'twas me-silf done it all, but I didn't mane it. I didn't mane to harm annywan. Magin—oh, woorse luck to him, for the manest blackguard that iver set foot on Irish soil! *He* wrote an' tould me that yer honour an' the 'Bould Bhoys' would be far away from this place to-night; an' that some wan would tell us where to find Captain Annesley an' Father Bernard, if I brought the souldiers here. *Och, faraoir! faraoir!* I thought ye were all safe enthirely."

"Shilrick, my boy! *I* believe you!" said O'Neill, kindly, clasping the drummer's hot, trembling little hand in his. "There is truth in every line of that honest face of yours."

"Sure, I'd refused to go with the souldiers at first, sir," continued Shilrick, eagerly, "an' I'd have kept me word— I would indade, yer honour! but—but, d'ye see, sir, I re-caived that false letther from Thaddeus Magin. Ochone! bad luck to misilf for attendin' to what *he* said, the mane villain."

"Poor boy! poor boy! I see it all now," said Morven. "You have indeed been hedged round by a perfect network of treachery."

Shilrick, by this time quite overcome with grief, turned sorrowfully away, and again joined the soldiers who had been guarding him. O'Neill seemed to be every moment growing weaker, but making another effort, and clasping his hand around Captain Annesley's, as that officer still held him in his arms he spoke again, but now his voice was so faint, that his old comrade had to bend over him, before he could hear, or distinguish a single word. "Annesley! will you take one—last message for me—to my friends; to my uncle, Colonel Corrie —my aunt—and—my cousin Eveleen!"

"Most willingly, O'Neill, will I do anything for you," replied Annesley, earnestly.

"Tell—tell them,—" continued Morven, again trying to

raise himself, but falling back in the arms of Captain
Annesley and Father Bernard, who now supported him on
either side, "tell them—I died a soldier's death—fighting
for the country I loved so well—my own dear native
Ireland—and, Annesley—there is Owen Maguire! Ah! I
had forgotten!" he exclaimed, anxiously, "he must not
stay here—Owen!—my faithful Owen!—try to escape—
now—ere it is too late ;—you know many a turn—many
a safe hiding-place—among these mountains—unknown to
all others."

"Masther Morven!" cried Owen, reproachfully. "How
can ye ax me to do this ? What soort av a life will it be for
mesilf whin ye're gone from me ? Annyhow I've been seen
by the milithairy now, an' I'm well-known ; I daurn't show me
face in the light av dhay widout the chance av bein' thaken
prisoner, an' where would be the use av thryin' to escape
now ? Oh! *Ua Néill! Ua Néill!* sure I've followed ye manny
a thime through dhanger an' thrial, an misforthune—isn't it
mesilf went cheerfully into exile wid yer honour—don't—oh !
don't ax me to lave ye now, at the last."

"Oh, my true-hearted Owen!" said O'Neill, sadly, "well
do I know all this. Annesley, he has been faithful—more
faithful than words can tell! If—he should be taken,—will
you get a pardon for him ? He has taken no *active* part in—
in this Rebellion. He has—only been—alas !—too true to
me."

"I will do all you ask, O'Neill ! I promise—and while I
live Owen Maguire shall never want a friend."

"And—Annesley!" continued Morven, faintly, "there is
one favour—only one more—I would ask of you, dear friend.
Will you tell *her—my Estelle*—that the name last on my lips
—last in my heart, was *hers*—and that the thought of her
faithful love, and how she gave up all for me, makes me
happy now—in this—my last hour upon earth. Go to her !
promise me that you will go to her—and take her to my
uncle—my aunt—and cousin, Eveleen Corrie. Oh ! tell
them to love and care for her—for my sake, as in the old
days they loved and cared for me. *My wife !*—my beautiful
wife ! Oh ! would that she could come to me now. *You* saw
her, Annesley, you remember—she was with me that night

on the shore of the haunted lake—I told you in the cave—
Heaven protect and keep her now !—poor little Estelle ! "

Did Annesley remember ?   Ah ! could he ever forget that
night, when he felt that he had good cause to doubt
Morven's friendship, and the sincerity of Eveleen Corrie's
love for himself, when the demon of jealousy gained full
possession of that passionate, but warm, loving heart of his,
so that even now, when he found that O'Neill had never any
desire to be his rival, he still imagined that *Eveleen might*
have felt more than cousinly affection for the young Rebel
Chief, not knowing that he was married ; or again he would
torment himself with the thought that Lieutenant Rochfort,
or someone still more unlikely, was the successful rival, and
the cause of her late coldness to him, and so he would continue to indulge in his self-torture, for,

> "Trifles, light as air,
> Are, to the jealous, confirmations strong
> As proofs of Holy Writ."

Even now, the words of his dying comrade caused a pang
of regret when he thought of Eveleen, and the doubts and
suspicions which he could not cast out of his heart, but
Annesley's was not a selfish nature, and it was but for an
instant that his mind wandered from the friend beside him.
Once more he bent over O'Neill, who had fallen back in his
arms, his strength being well-nigh spent with the exertion
of speaking.

"I will remember all, O'Neill," he said, gently.   "The one
you love shall be tenderly cared for—you may trust to me.
I shall, to the best of my ability, fulfil all your wishes."

"Father Bernard knows her," continued Morven, slowly,
and evidently speaking with great pain.   "And Owen—he
will tell you all about her—all you may want to know. Oh,
Estelle ! my love ! my love !—jewel of my heart !—would
that I could have seen you once—only once more ! "

With a last effort, Morven raises himself slightly, and,
drawing from his finger the massive ring he has always
worn, on which is engraved the crest of the O'Neills, with the
motto, "*Lamh dhearg Eirin*," and which has been fully described in a previous chapter, he gives it to his friend.

" Wear it, Annesley ! " he says, faintly, " wear it—until you can give it to *her*—to my Estelle—she will understand. And—oh, tell them !—tell them all—I died for my country— for Erin—beloved Erin ! "

Before Annesley could comply with this request, and place upon his own finger the ring which had served as a sort of talisman to this brave descendant of the O'Neills, the young Rebel Chief had fallen back in Father Bernard's arms, and there breathed his last.

" Poor O'Neill !—brave, true heart ! " murmured the kindly old priest, laying Morven's head gently down. Then, turning to Annesley, " My son, we shall never hear the kind, cheerful voice again, we shall never more see the bright young face flushed with the hope of future glory. It is a sad end."

" Conway ! can nothing be done ? " asked Annesley, anxiously, of the young surgeon, who had just joined the group around Morven. " Surely, he is not really gone from us for ever ? "

Sorrowfully Dr. Conway shook his head in reply. " Alas, no ! Annesley," he said, " our old comrade has passed for ever beyond the reach of my skill. Perhaps it is better so, when we think of the fate that awaited him, had he lived even to see another dawn."

" Oh, yer riverence ! " cried Owen, turning, in his despair, to Father Bernard, "tell us that his honour has only fainted agin—let us carry him away from here—an', maybes, he'll revive, an'—an' thin," added the faithful man, in a whisper, " it's himsilf that'll be able to escape."

" Owen, my boy ! " said Father Bernard, " they cannot make him prisoner now. Your poor young master is dead. May his soul rest in peace. Noble, though mistaken; we will forget all his errors, while we remember only that he had a brave, true patriot's heart ; that he might have been as a precious ornament to our poor unhappy country, had his life been guided aright. Oh, Morven O'Neill ! hasty, impetuous as thou wert, I loved thee well."

" Owen ! " whispered Annesley, " lose no time ! try and save yourself, if you can, though I fear it is all but impossible, the men are watching us now. I was your

master's friend ; leave him with me, you can do no good
here. O'Neill! dear old friend and comrade ! " continued
the officer, sorrowfully, looking down upon the manly,
graceful form, the proud, beautiful face, now cold and still
for ever. " You were, indeed, one among a thousand, brave
as a lion in the hour of danger and trial ; gentle and sympathising in the time of trouble and sorrow. A good,
faithful heart, whose every instinct was noble, kindly and
courteous. A devoted spirit, so guided that no thought of
self was ever for one moment allowed to reign supreme.
Oh, Morven ! Morven ! noble young patriot ! *this* was the
secret of the love and devotion the people felt for thee,—in
truth a worthy descendant of the brave, proud race of
O'Neill."

"Annesley!" said Captain Ellis, now approaching the
group, "the night is far advanced, and, deeply as I sympa-
thise with this scene of sorrow, I think it is time to remember
our duty, stern and unfeeling as it may seem, yet it *must* be
done."

Finding that Annesley does not answer, Ellis seems to
consider that he has said sufficient to justify his next step,
which is to call forward the two soldiers who have been
standing at some distance from Owen, and, pointing to him,
he gives the following order :

"Take that man prisoner at once, and be careful that he
does not escape, he was one of our most determined
opponents."

The soldiers obey the order of Captain Ellis, with evident
reluctance, but Owen offers no resistance, he seems half-
dazed with grief, and scarcely conscious of what he is doing,
or of the fate that awaits him.

Once more Shilrick has been anxiously looking out, eagerly
scanning each outlet from the " Rebels' Rest," fearing that
his brother Kerry may reappear upon the scene, or that he
may be brought back a prisoner. "Och, sure ! " he murmured,
" I hope Kerry has escaped, an' that no harm has come to him.
I've seen nothin' av him this long while ; he'd aisily find
some hidin' place, wanst he'd got clare av our men."

Again the drummer's attention was diverted in watching
the movements of Captain Ellis, who, with Lieutenant Digby,

was now approaching the group gathered around Morven O'Neill.

"Now, my lads!" said Ellis, to the soldiers standing around, "here is the most important prisoner of all. There will be no chance of his escape, however, I fear that he has been too severely wounded for that ; but he must be gently and carefully removed with the rest of the wounded. Annesley, I am sorry it has come to this ; but I cannot help it. No one can be more grieved than I am at the fate of our old comrade, but,—as you know—*we* have our duty to perform, painful though it may be."

"Ellis," replied Annesley, speaking sorrowfully, yet eagerly, "O'Neill is dead. You are too late. No one can harm him now, and I for one can only thank Heaven that he has been spared the inevitable fate of a Rebel. Now, listen to me !—he was our friend—he was one of our own comrades ; his uncle, our Colonel, must never know of this. Oh, Ellis ! for *his* sake, for the honour of our corps, in which poor O'Neill once served, respected and beloved by officers and men, leave him here with me. And you, my lads," continued Annesley, addressing the soldiers, "you who are here this night, will remember that Lieutenant O'Neill was your officer once, and I believe was a favourite with you all ; will you guard this secret—that *he* was the patriot known by the name of '*Michael Cluny*'—and remember that, in so doing, you are guarding the honour of your Colonel, and the honour of the old corps."

"Ay, ay, sir!" replied the soldiers, heartily, their voices coming from every part, for Captain Annesley's earnest words, spoken in his clear, resonant voice had reached them all, and touched the hearts of these gallant Marines, so brave and true.

"Then, Ellis !" continued Annesley, "leave two or three of the men with me, and Shilrick O'Toole ; for I see that you have two other drummers with your party, so you can spare him."

"I scarcely know," replied Ellis, hesitating, "if I am doing right, Annesley, in yielding to your request ; but—"

"Pardon me, Ellis !" said Annesley, courteously. "It was not my wish to do so, but in this instance I am com-

pelled to remind you that I am the senior officer here,—and
I am willing to take all the responsibility."

"As you will then!" returned the other, coldly. "But,"
going closer to Morven, and looking searchingly down upon
him, "are you *quite sure* that poor O'Neill is not living
still?"

"Do you doubt my word, Captain Ellis?" demanded
Annesley, haughtily. "If so, there is Conway, you can ask
him."

"Oh, certainly not!" returned the other, quickly, "if you
are quite sure yourself; *you* are liable to make mistakes sometimes, I suppose, like all of us. However, you shall have
the men," he continued, calling to some of the soldiers in the
background. "Here—Shooter, Gibson, Thomson, and Jen-
nings, you will remain here, under Captain Annesley's
orders."

The four Marines then separate themselves from the rest
of the men, and coming forward to Captain Annesley,
they take up their position near him, awaiting his commands.

"There are four men for you, Annesley, do you want any
more?" asked Ellis.

"I want Shilrick O'Toole, the drummer, belonging to my
own company."

"I am sorry that I cannot grant that request," replied
Ellis, firmly. "Shilrick O'Toole is a prisoner, he must return
to barracks with us."

"A prisoner? Shilrick?" exclaimed Annesley, in astonishment.

"Yes!"

"And the charge against him?"

"Suspected treason—disobedience of orders—and general
insubordination. You shall hear the full account when you
return to barracks."

"But, Annesley," said Digby, "where have you been all
this time, and how did you and Father Bernard manage to
escape from the Rebels?"

"Oh, never mind that at present, Digby, I will tell you all
our adventures at another time," replied Annesley. "I want
to hear more about Shilrick—I do not understand—Ah!

who have we here ?" he exclaimed, anxiously, as at that moment Kerry O'Toole and Silas Charleston appeared, fighting desperately for life and liberty with two powerful-looking Marine soldiers.

"Oh, Kerry! Kerry, my brother!" cried Shilrick, wildly, and suddenly breaking through his guard, he hastened across to Kerry, who had now fallen, severely wounded, and apparently lifeless, at the feet of his foster brother, Captain Annesley. Silas Charleston, now being one among many, was soon overpowered and made prisoner, though he made a brave resistance, standing for some time with his back against the rocks, and keeping half-a-dozen determined men at bay.

"*Och, wirra! wirra!*" sobbed Shilrick, throwing himself down beside Kerry, "sure he was me own brother! an' ye've killed him!—ye've killed him!" he cried, turning fiercely upon the soldiers. "Oh, Kerry! Kerry! *asthore machree!* sure, it's yerself was all I had in the whole wide world!"

"Kerry!—my foster-brother!" said Annesley, gently, as he bent over the prostrate form. "Do you know who is speaking to you? Ah! Shilrick, I fear that poor Kerry is mortally wounded. Yet, no!—he breathes still, we may save him yet! Conway!" he cried, "can you come here for a moment?"

While the attention of Captain Annesley and Shilrick O'Toole, is occupied with Kerry, Captain Ellis, and Lieutenants Digby and Geoghegan, have hurried over to the entrance to the narrow defile, seeing that there is something going on there which is causing unwonted excitement among the men, both soldiers and Rebels. Great is their surprise and wonder, when they are confronted by the tall, stalwart form of the young farmer, Sheymus Malloy, who is manfully clearing the road before him, forcing his way through the soldiers, followed by Eveleen Corrie, Thalia Coghlan, and Anty Kinahan.

Eveleen Corrie, whose face is partly concealed beneath the large, broad-brimmed hat, and her form enveloped in a long cloak, is not at first recognized by the young officers, for the light of the moon is fitful, and uncertain, and from time to time it is hidden behind dark clouds ; and

Eveleen, though she seems to glance at them, does not really notice them, or indeed any of those present; she passes each one with sorrowful, unseeing eyes, and hastily approaching her cousin, Morven O'Neill, falls on her knees beside him, burying her face in her hands, and weeping bitterly. "Too late!—too late! Oh, Morven! cousin Morven!" she cries. Annesley, immediately recognizing Eveleen, was about to approach her, and to offer his sympathy, but it unfortunately chanced to strike his jealous fancy at the moment that her grief for Morven O'Neill, was the grief of a lover, rather than that of a cousin; so he hesitated, and during that pause —though it was but for an instant—all his old suspicions were aroused, and seemed to him to be fully justified by the fact of her presence there that night, in such a place and at such an hour. He turned from her, with a dark cloud on his brow, and a cold, cynical smile on his lips.

Another comforter for Eveleen, was, however, not far off. Poor wounded Nap had heard her voice, and scrambling out of the nest Shilrick had made for him, this ever faithful friend managed to make his way to the side of his mistress; and great was Eveleen's surprise when she felt two damp little paws upon her shoulder, and the touch of Nap's cold, black nose upon her cheek.

Lieutenant Digby, who chanced to be near at the time, was touched at the sight, and the little dumb creature's loving devotion, and in a few words explained to Eveleen how Nap had appeared among them, how he had saved Shilrick's life and been wounded in his defence, and Eveleen, who was too sad-hearted to speak, looked up gratefully at the young officer for his sympathy, and drew her little favourite closer to her, as he sat beside her, whining piteously, for his wound, which the drummer had bound up so carefully, was now paining him sadly, the effort he had made to reach his mistress having made it worse.

"Oh, Morven! Morven!" cried Eveleen, as she again bent over her cousin. "Oh, why did you leave us? Why were you thus lured onward to destruction and death, by that fatal phantom—the false hope of the patriot? Yet those who have loved you—can thank Heaven now that your patriotism was true and genuine—*your* motives were pure, noble, and unselfish—for the liberty, the welfare of your country—our own loved Erin !—you have even given your life !"

Anty Kinahan, who had paused for a moment beside Eveleen Corrie, looking sorrowfully down at Morven, now turns away, murmuring sadly, as she slowly wipes the fast-falling tears from her eyes :

"Poor Misther Morven ! an' oh, poor unhappy Misthress O'Neill !—an' hersilf so onable to bear this heavy sorrow ! An' mother ! Oh, sure, what'll mother say? It's Misther O'Neill was just the pride av her heart !"

As Anty turns, she suddenly discovers her lover, Owen Maguire, a prisoner among the soldiers, and hurries over to him.

Owen covers his eyes with his hand, as though to shut out the sight of the misery he knows that he will see in the face of his loved one ; but Anty bravely determines to keep a stout heart when in his presence, so that he may not be distressed with her hopeless sorrow ; but not yet being able to trust herself to speak, she takes his hand in hers and presses it tenderly, in silent sympathy, and even contrives to summon up a faint smile when she hears the voice of the good-natured American, Silas Charleston, whisper in her ear, "Why, certainly, Owen Maguire and myself are prisoners *now* ;—that's so—but you keep up your heart, my gal, things airn't always going to be so tarnation dark as they look. I calc'late we shan't come to any harm— these kind militairey gentlemen will take good care of us, so don't you fret. I guess I can't *act* much just at present," he added, significantly, "but I'm *thinking* a deal, my gal, I'm thinking a deal ! "

Meanwhile, Thalia Coghlan's eyes are wandering distractedly from one group to another in the tragic scene around her, and Sheymus Malloy, seeing the hopeless despair in her face, kindly takes her hand in his, and tries to whisper what comfort he can.

"*Och, wirrasthrue ! wirrasthrue !* " he says, sadly. "I'm feared we're too late, enthirely, darlin' ; but sure, I don't see Kerry O'Toole here, so maybes he's safe afther all. There's his riverince, Father Bernard, yondher, *cora machree*, he'll be able to tell us about—"

"Ah, there he is! there he is!" cried Thalia, suddenly wrenching her hand out of Sheymus Malloy's clasp. "There he is, lyin' yondher, my Kerry! Sure they've killed him. Oh, Kerry! Kerry! me own dear love!" she sobbed, despairingly, as she fell on her knees beside him, "oh! spake to me, darlin', spake to me, *asthore machree!* an' let me know ye're not dead enthirely."

"Thalia Coghlan! how did *you* come here?" exclaimed Annesley, starting back in astonishment at the girl's sudden appearance, and unable to suppress the tone of stern indignation, that would always, in spite of every effort on his part, creep into his voice when he addressed—as he thought—the *false* love of his foster brother. And there was another who bitterly resented the presence of Thalia Coghlan at the side of his brother, and immediately on her approach, Shilrick O'Toole had started up hastily, and reaching across Kerry, had tried to push her aside, with words of passionate sorrow and indignation on his lips.

"Go away! go away from him, ye false, deceatful colleen! sure ye're too late now wid yer love, enthirely! · An'—an' there's Sheymus Malloy, himsilf, sthandin' waitin' for ye beyant there!" cried the boy, with a shriek of wild, derisive laughter, that sounded, at such a moment, a thousand times more mournful to his hearers than the bitterest words of anger, or sorrow.

"Let her alone, my boy!" said Annesley, gently laying his hand on the drummer's shoulder, "we *may* have been mistaken; indeed I think now, when I see how she suffers, that she must really have loved poor Kerry, after all."

What more Annesley might have said to calm the anger of Shilrick, or how Thalia Coghlan might have replied in her own justification, was never known, for all present were alike held spell-bound by the sudden appearance of Estelle O'Neill. A few minutes before, her cloak had been caught by a rugged piece of rock, and heedless of cold, or any other discomfort, she had not waited to recover it, being intent solely, heart and mind, on finding Morven, with as little delay as possible, and with her long white robe, and her golden hair falling like a veil around her, she was indeed a strange apparition in the midst of that wild scene, as she hurried, or rather seemed to glide up the narrow defile, the steep rocks on either side of her, the moonlight from above falling on her pallid but beautiful face.

She passed the group of soldiers, unheeding their wondering gaze, and then paused for a moment, with her hand pressed to her forehead, while she looked eagerly around, and at last discovered the one she sought.

"Morven!" she wailed, as hastening to him she threw herself down beside him, in the wildest abandonment of grief. "Morven!—*mon ami!*—my husband! Oh! surely it is not, it cannot be dat he is dead! Speak to me! Oh! say to me one little word, dear love of my heart. It is Estelle! See!" she sobbed, as she tenderly lifted Morven's head in her arms. "It is your own Estelle who does now entreat of you to speak to her. Oh, my darling! say to me one word—only one word. Ah!—*mon mari!*" she cried, wildly, throwing up her arms above her head, "he is gone! gone for ever!—and I am left in dis cold world alone—all alone. Morven! Morven! now indeed it is dat I am desolate—quite, quite desolate! I cannot live widout de light of your love!"

Estelle tried to raise herself a little, but with a sudden cry of pain, followed by a deep, mournful sigh, she fell lifeless on Morven O'Neill's breast.

Eveleen Corrie, who had risen to her feet when Estelle first appeared beside Morven, now stands looking in silent wonder at her, and turns to Annesley, who has just approached, with sad, questioning eyes. That young officer, however, seems determined not to be the first to speak ; he is still carefully fostering the bitter feeling of jealousy in his heart, and thus he and Eveleen Corrie are daily drifting farther and farther apart.

Annesley speaks to one of the soldiers near him, and gives orders for Owen Maguire to come forward for a few minutes.

"Oh, the poor young misthress!" cries O'Neill's faithful follower, as he sorrowfully bends over the lifeless form of Estelle. "Sure she was his honour's wife," he added, turning to Eveleen, "an' 'tis Captain Annesley knows all about it, me lady."

"Oh! and he did not tell *me*, that I might have cared for

her, and been as a sister to her, for *his* sake," murmured Eveleen, regretfully.

"But sure, maybes her ladyship has only fainted," said Owen.

"Ah, no, Owen, my boy!" said Father Bernard, sadly, taking hold of Estelle's hand, and looking long and earnestly at her, " you can do nothing more, now, for your poor young mistress, she will nevermore need the care and love of any-one in this world."

"Oh, yer riverince! is it gone from us for iver she is, the beautiful, bright lady, that was so dear to poor masther's heart ; sure there's no wan in the whole world who could iver have comforted *her* for the loss of him she loved. May-bes it's betther that those whose hearts were wan from the first hour they met, should enther the long, dhark, unknown valley, hand in hand together. Who can tell what is for the best ? "

"Ah! who can tell ? " cried Thalia Coghlan, who had been a sorrowful listener to Owen's solemn words—raising her clasped hands above her head—"but, oh! Heaven hilp thim that's left behind, to mourn for the love they'll niver know agin in this world."

Eveleen Corrie's tears were falling fast, as she stooped and lifted in her arms her faithful little friend, Nap ; and as she bowed her grief-stricken face upon the soft, silken head, the tempest of sorrow in her heart was calmed, she was soothed, as Shilrick O'Toole had been, but a short time before, by the same little comforter, and felt that though human friends might change and grow cold, yet as long as he lived, the faith-ful affection of poor Nap would never fail her ; and, truly, this devoted little creature had done *his* duty that night. He had wandered a long, weary way in search of the mistress he loved so well, heedless of the bitter cold, or of tired, bleeding feet ; he had saved the life of his friend, Shilrick O'Toole ; and, ah! who can say that Nap, in bringing peaceful, soothing thoughts, even for a few moments, to two sad, troubled hearts, was not well performing *his* mission upon earth ? Ay! better, perhaps, than many of we, poor human beings, ever perform ours.

No one present on that fatal night need have grieved or

wept for the fate of Estelle O'Neill. It was the *living*, not
the dead, who must, in the dark, unknown future, claim their
sympathy.   Estelle's earnest wish had been fulfilled, she
would nevermore be parted from the one she loved ; there
would be no long waiting at Heaven's golden gates for *her*.
Together those true, noble hearts had entered the valley of
the shadow of death, on their journey to the silent shore—
that better land, where all is peace and love—" where the
wicked cease from troubling, and the weary are at rest."

CHAPTER XXIV.

"If you your lips would keep from slips,
Five things observe with care—
Of whom you speak, to whom you speak,
And how, and when, and where."

ANON.

Long and earnestly did the officers of the Marines, at Glencree, confer together upon the case of Shilrick O'Toole. His youth, his previous good conduct, his keen liking for the Service, and the loyal sentiments he had been always heard to express, together with the fact that he was a favourite, alike with officers and men ; all these points were brought forward to bear upon the subject, with an eagerness which plainly showed the respect and even affection, in which the boy had hitherto been held by all his comrades ; but, although there was not one in the corps who would not willingly have tried to hush up the affair, and given his veto against the Court Martial, had he been in a position to do so, yet each felt that it was impossible for their Colonel, or those in authority, to overlook such breaches of discipline as those of which the drummer had been guilty. There was, moreover, no doubt of his being on friendly terms with many of the Rebels, and this unfortunately, even those who were most favourably disposed towards him, could not deny ; nor could they refute the charge that he had been willing to shield his compatriots from the consequences of their disloyalty, whenever it was in his power to do so, and he was thus " aiding and abetting " the insurgent forces, a crime which, in those days—and especially in a soldier—was punishable with death, as was also that of mutiny and disobedience of orders, while on active service.

Again and again the officers went over these particulars, but, even with all the extenuating circumstances, there seemed no loophole—no possible excuse for them to avoid a Court Martial.

Unfortunately there were two individuals, unconnected with the corps, who were cognisant of more than one of Shilrick's misdemeanours, especially of the last, and those were two of the very worst men who could have known of them, Lieutenant Rochfort, the young cavalry officer, and Jeremiah Stalker, the English patrol. Both were officious—anxious to display their own zeal—and both were cruelly prejudiced against the Irish people ; and with the former there was also the feeling of jealousy against Captain Annesley, and a wish to annoy him, and Rochfort knew well that he could have no better opportunity of doing this than through his *protégé*, Shilrick O'Toole, in whom also Eveleen Corrie felt great interest, on her lover's account.

Then, in addition to this, there was Rochfort's desire that *his* regiment should be the chief means of quelling the rebellion in Wicklow, in which idea he very naturally met with the unanimous support of his brother officers, and it was with considerable triumph that he learned of the supposed disloyalty on the part of a drummer of the Marines, more especially as that drummer was the particular favourite of Captain Annesley, whom he knew well was a formidable rival.

Think as they would, therefore, the Marine officers found that there was no other course left, than for Colonel Corrie to call a Court Martial ; they, however, arranged that the charge should be only that of mutiny and disobedience of orders ; and decided to keep in the background—as much as possible—all suspicions of disloyalty on the part of Shilrick, and especially to suppress any information concerning the letter which had been found in the drummer's possession when he had been searched, previous to his departure for the mountains, the contents of which neither Lieutenant Rochfort, nor Jeremiah Stalker had yet seen, although, unfortunately, they, as well as the midshipman had been witnesses to its having been taken from the boy, and handed to Colonel Corrie ; and Rochfort had particularly noticed Shilrick's agitation at the time.

Harry Nelson had also seen and heard all that had happened, or had been said, at the Rebels' Rest, on the night of the encounter between the Marines and the Rebels, and, although the boy was friendly towards Shilrick, yet he might, without thought, have mentioned the facts to the other naval officers on board his ship.

So it happened that a week after the sad events recorded in the last chapter, the officers forming the Court Martial for the trial of Shilrick O'Toole, were assembled in a spacious oak-panelled hall in Glencree Barracks ; a long, heavy carved oak table occupied the centre of the room, and this, with massive chairs of the same description, formed the sole furniture of the apartment.

At one end of the table sat Major Ricardo, of the 30th Regiment of Cavalry, the President of the Court Martial ; a pile of papers and documents were before him. On either side the twelve officers forming the Court Martial were seated in the following order. On the right hand of Major Ricardo were Captain Norton, of the Marines, Captain Drelincourt of the 30th Regiment of Cavalry, Captain Leslie, of the Marines ; Lieutenant Saunders of the 30th Regiment ; Lieutenant Beaumont of the Marines, and Lieutenant Rochfort, 30th Regiment, who has papers, pens and ink before him, and during the trial is employed in writing down the charge, and all the evidence for the prosecution and the defence, word for word as it is spoken.

On the other side are Captain Durnford, of the Marines, Captain Harrison, 30th Regiment of Cavalry ; Lieutenant Howard, of the Marines ; Lieutenant Morley, 30th Regiment ; Lieutenant Despard, of the Marines ; and Lieutenant Renison, 30th Regiment ; these names having been called over by the President when the officers were all fairly assembled in the room.

At the opposite end of the table to that at which the President is seated, stands the drummer, Shilrick O'Toole, with two Marine soldiers, with drawn bayonets, behind him.

In a large, carved wooden chair, near the wide open hearth, is seated Lieutenant McIvor, the Adjutant of the Marines, who is present especially to watch the case.

At the door of the room stands Sergeant Marks, ready to

call and to admit the witnesses, each of whom, in his turn, is duly sworn before giving his evidence. Shilrick was very pale, and there was a hopeless, wistful expression on his face, and in the clear, earnest eyes, which was sad to see ; but beyond this there was no outward sign of the long, sleepless nights, and the days of fearful anxiety, and suspense, that the boy had endured. He entered, and took his place quietly, standing up bravely, and manfully, before the room full of officers, by whom he was about to be tried for his life. Only once did his heart fail him, and that was when he chanced to meet the cold, searching gaze of Lieutenant Rochfort ; but be soon rallied, and listened intently while Major Ricardo, who as President of the Court, now commenced proceedings by asking him :

" Prisoner, Shilrick O'Toole ! have you any objections to make, to any of the members of this Court, sitting on your Court Martial ? "

" No, sir ! " replied the drummer ; but there was the slightest possible hesitation, and an involuntary glance in the direction of Rochfort, which more than one officer noticed.

The President, and each member of the Court, having been duly sworn, and the usual formula observed by all, Major Ricardo then, slowly, and in a clear, distinct voice, read the following charge :

" The prisoner, Drummer and Fifer Shilrick O'Toole, is hereby arraigned upon the following charge, namely :—For mutiny and insubordination, in that he, the prisoner, Drummer and Fifer Shilrick O'Toole, on the afternoon of the twenty-eighth day of December, 1798, did positively disobey the lawful commands of his commanding officer, Colonel Clinton Corrie, of the Marines, by refusing, when ordered by Captain Ellis, to proceed with a party of the Marines as guide, in pursuit of a certain body of Rebels, known as the ' Bold Boys of Wicklow,' who were in arms against His Majesty's Government. He, the aforesaid prisoner, well knowing the various *routes* throughout the district, and the *rendezvous* of the said Rebels."

" Prisoner, Shilrick O'Toole, are you guilty or not guilty of the crime laid to your charge ? "

There was a moment's dead silence in the Court ; but at

last came the drummer's reply, in a sorrowful, but proud, firm voice :

"Guilty, sir."

"Then, Sergeant Marks," said Major Ricardo, "call in the first witness for the prosecution, Captain Edward Ellis, of the Marines."

The Sergeant opens the door, looks into the ante-room, and saluting, calls upon Captain Ellis. That officer enters, and takes up his position as witness behind Captain Norton ; his face wears a troubled expression, and his brother officers notice that, for the first time since they have known him, he appears nervous, and glances regretfully at Shilrick.

"Captain Ellis," continued Major Ricardo, "you are hereby called upon, as first witness for the prosecution, to state all you know regarding the case now before the Court."

"I have but little more to say, than to corroborate what has been already stated in the charge against the prisoner, which has just been read in presence of the Court. I am truly grieved that duty compelled me to make that charge at all, as the prisoner's general conduct has always been most praiseworthy during the time he has served in our corps. However, on the occasion now in question, he was so persistent in his refusal to obey the orders of Colonel Corrie, given through me, that there was no other course left open to me, than to arrest him, at once, on the aforesaid charge of mutiny and disobedience of orders. Shilrick O'Toole was on guard, on the afternoon in question, a short distance from the barracks, at an old ruin which is situated at the entrance to one of the mountain passes. I went *myself* to the prisoner, at Colonel Corrie's urgent request, to inform him that another drummer would be sent to take his place at the old guard-house, as we rather suspected that Shilrick O'Toole would not like the duty, and, indeed, that he would naturally have a horror of it, as he would be called upon to turn '*informer.*' Moreover he is a native of Wicklow, and the Rebels were his own countrymen ; but there was no help for it, there being no one in the whole neighbourhood who knows the mountain passes as he knows them, and, accordingly, Colonel Corrie found it necessary for the prisoner to

accompany the party of Marines, under my command, as
guide. I thought, by giving him the orders myself, that
I might possibly, by reasoning with him, manage to overcome his dislike to the duty ; I certainly was not prepared
for such determined insubordination. I have no other com-
plaint to make against the boy ; he has been guilty of but
one *very slight* offence since he entered the service, and has
always been a favourite with me, as well as with every
officer and man in the corps, ever since the day when Captain
Annesley first brought him amongst us ; but we are on
active service at present, and it is therefore the more necessary for us to be very strict in putting down the least act of
mutiny on the part of any of the men."

The Marine officers began to breathe more freely when
the evidence of Captain Ellis, so kindly given, was, as they
thought, concluded, but they were doomed to suffer still
farther anxiety on behalf of their little favourite, for, after a
slight pause, and an ominous pucker of the brows, the President again addressed the witness.

"But, Captain Ellis ! I heard a report that Captain
Annesley, the officer you have just mentioned, and to whom
I understand the drummer had hitherto professed the greatest
attachment, was a prisoner in the hands of the Rebels, and
that he, Shilrick O'Toole, knew this. Was that the case ?"

" It was, sir," replied Ellis, reluctantly.

" Then, pardon me ! why did you omit that fact in your
evidence ? "

"I considered it of no importance."

" No importance ! why it was of the gravest ! Was not
the rescue of Captain Annesley one of the principal reasons
for the despatch of the party of Marines to the mountains ?"

" I believe so, sir."

" Then do you mean to say that you felt no surprise that
the prisoner, knowing this, should refuse to do *anything in
his power* to assist in the rescue of an officer for whom he
cared—and to whom he owed so much ? "

" Well, I did certainly feel astonished ;" still more reluctantly.

"And you never thought to question him upon the
subject ? "

" Yes, sir! I *did* question him."

" And his answer ? "

" He refused to reply."

" Then he still continued rebellious ? "

" No—scarcely that—I had a right to ask the boy as many questions as I pleased, but I had no right to *insist* that he should reply. The greatest criminal has the privilege of remaining silent, if words are likely to criminate himself."

" You think, then, that had the prisoner spoken, his words would probably have had that result ? "

" I did not say so, sir."

" But you *thought* so ? "

" Pardon me, Major Ricardo ! The rules of the Court do not compel a witness to give utterance to his *thoughts*."

" Ah ! Have you any further evidence to give, then, Captain Ellis ? "

" No, sir ! "

" Prisoner ! have you any questions you would like to ask this witness ? "

" No, sir," replied Shilrick, listlessly.

" Has any member of the Court any questions they wish to ask ? " again inquired Major Ricardo.

" Yes, sir ! " said Captain Norton of the Marines ; then turning to Ellis, " was the prisoner's manner rude, or disrespectful, when he refused to obey your orders, Captain Ellis ? "

" No ! I have very much pleasure in stating that the conduct of Shilrick O'Toole was exceedingly gentle, and his demeanour most respectful, as became a soldier. He was rude neither in word nor look."

And now it was that poor Shilrick and those interested in him had cause to tremble, for Lieutenant Rochfort, availing himself of his privilege as one of the members of the Court, commenced a most determined course of cross-questioning, and it was evident to all present that he meant mischief, as he bent forward and asked Captain Ellis, " Was there any witness present when the prisoner refused to guide your party of men to the mountains ? "

" Not actually present, but 10th Company, Private Henry Pike, was sentry at the old guard-house, and was passing to and fro during the time I was speaking to Shilrick O'Toole."

" You mentioned in your evidence, Captain Ellis, that the prisoner had been guilty of one previous offence since he entered the service. Have you any objection to state to the Court the nature of that offence ? "

" I scarcely see that it bears upon the present case ; however, I may mention that it was a very simple matter ; the prisoner was found by me, one evening, outside the barracks after tattoo, and without leave."

" Well, Captain Ellis," said Major Ricardo, " you will please state the circumstances under which the prisoner was on that occasion discovered by you."

" There is but little to tell, sir. There is a small gate, or rather a door in the wall, at the back of our barracks, which is not much used ; there is no sentry placed near it, but it is barred up every night, on the inside, immediately after tattoo. I happened to be ' captain of the day ' on that occasion, and on going my rounds about half-an-hour after tattoo, I saw that the gate was ajar. On looking out I perceived the prisoner ; there was no one near him at the time, and all around was silent. The moon was shining brightly, and I could see that the boy looked very anxious and that he was gazing long and earnestly towards the road. There was certainly neither Rebel nor friend near him, nor even in sight, and I had no reason to suspect him of disloyalty. I was compelled to order him to the guard-room for being out of barracks at that hour, but he was released the next morning, and the offence was soon forgotten."

" Rather lenient for such an offence, was it not ? " said Rochfort, sneeringly. "*I* should have thought the circumstance *a very suspicious one*, considering the nationality of the prisoner, and that he is actually a native of this nest of rebellion and treason, half of his friends, I doubt not, being at this moment rebels against His Majesty's Government. I should have imagined that *any officer* would have given the case *his most serious attention*, and investigated it *most thoroughly*."

" Sir," exclaimed Captain Ellis, indignantly, as he glanced scornfully at Rochfort. "I must beg to remind you that, as one who has been very much longer in the service than yourself,

I am perfectly acquainted with my duties as a British officer —and," significantly, " *a gentleman.*"

"And may *I* also remind you, Lieutenant Rochfort," said Captain Norton, haughtily, " that Captain Ellis is not on *his* trial just now ; and I object to all such remarks as you have made, as quite irrelevant to the subject in hand."

"Certainly !—certainly !—Captain Norton, you are quite right," mildly interposed Major Ricardo. "But, Captain Ellis, did you not inquire what the prisoner was doing outside that gate, at such an hour ? "

" Yes, sir ! "

"And what was his reply ? "

" He would tell nothing, nor would he give any particular reason for being there."

" Was he rude, or defiant, in the manner of his refusal ? "

" No, sir—I have already stated that Shilrick O'Toole is *always* respectful."

"Have you anything more to state, Captain Ellis ? ".

" No, sir ! "

"Then I think—"

" One moment, sir ! " interrupted Rochfort, hastily, fearing that this witness was about to be dismissed before he (Rochfort) had had the opportunity of playing his trump card. Then leaning across the table, and with the blandest of smiles upon his countenance, he again addressed the witness :

" I think, Captain Ellis, that you must have forgotten to give an account, in your evidence, of the important letter, addressed to the prisoner, and found in his possession, when he was searched at Glencree Barracks, previous to his departure for the mountains."

" Searched !– yes, and at *your* instigation ; I remember the circumstance perfectly."

"Then, Captain Ellis ! " said the President, "what was your reason for omitting such important information in your evidence ? You read the said letter, I suppose ? "

" No, sir, I did *not* read it ! "

" But you heard it read, I presume ? "

"No—I did not hear it read ! "

" Ah !—well, at all events, you know the contents ? They were fully explained to you ? "

"Yes, sir, I *do* know the contents, but *explanation* was scarcely necessary, as the letter was such that any one, of the most ordinary intellect, could have understood."

"I consider it very strange that you should have kept silence concerning this letter until now."

"And I should not have mentioned it now, sir, but for Lieutenant Rochfort's interference."

"But it was most certainly your duty to have done so at the very first."

"I did not imagine that there was any necessity for me to do so; as the prisoner was arrested for *mutiny* and *disobedience of orders*, and the letter which was found after his arrest, had nothing to do with his *refusal to act as guide to the mountains*, which is the sole crime upon which the present charge against him is based."

"A regular law quibble!" muttered Rochfort, sneeringly.

"Have you the letter with you, Captain Ellis?" asked Captain Drelincourt, another of the cavalry officers present.

"No, sir, I have not—nor has it ever been in my possession."

"Then, who has it now?" demanded Major Ricardo, determinedly. "Come, Captain Ellis! I cannot see why you should thus detain the Court, with useless evasion. You must at least know who has possession of that letter."

"*I* have, sir!" said the Adjutant, Lieutenant McIvor, as he rose from his seat near the hearth, and faced Major Ricardo, "but I do not see that it has anything to do with the present charge."

"You must pardon me if I differ from you there, Lieutenant McIvor. I consider that every paper or document found in the prisoner's possession should have been submitted to the Court, and I must, therefore, request that you will immediately hand over the letter in question to me, together with any other papers which may have been taken from him."

Colonel Corrie had given the fatal letter from the treacherous Yankee, Thaddeus Magin, into the hands of McIvor, with express instructions only to produce it if absolutely necessary, and if he should be compelled to do so. Slowly, and most reluctantly, therefore, did the Adjutant draw it out of the breast pocket of his coat, glancing with kindness, and pity at the drummer as he did so. Shilrick now looked hopeless indeed, for he well knew the effect that letter would have upon the members of the Court ; he felt, that even those who were most favourably disposed towards him, dare not, in justice, shirk their duty by holding back from agreeing in the sentence which the strange officers must inevitably pronounce upon him, and his fears were confirmed as he anxiously watched Major Ricardo reading the unfortunate missive, and saw the frown on his brow as he refolded it, and laid it on the table beside him.

" I regret very much to have to state that this letter shows only too plainly, that the prisoner was in close league with the band of Rebels known as 'The Bold Boys of Wicklow;' it speaks for itself, and condemns him without a shadow of a doubt. His heart must indeed be disloyal to the core when he could hold such intercourse with these notorious insurgents. I also understand now, from this very letter—though I grant you, Lieutenant McIvor, the fact is not mentioned therein—all the prisoner's reasons for his refusal to act as guide. It must be passed round and read by every member of the Court, at the close of the day's proceedings. And now, Captain Ellis, if you have no further evidence to give, you may withdraw. Sergeant! call in the next witness. Lieutenant Patrick Geoghegan, of the Royal Marines."

There was considerable consternation among the Marine officers when this witness was called. They looked gravely at each other, wondering anxiously what jumble the young Irishman might make of his evidence ; or what confusion and misunderstanding he might unwittingly cause before he was allowed to leave the Court.

Various surreptitious signals were therefore made to him, from all parts, by his brother officers, who were seated at the long table, heads were shaken, eyebrows raised significantly, fingers pressed to the lips ; nods, and contortions of the human countenance, innumerable, all intended to warn, encourage, admonish, or threaten ; but Lieutenant Patrick Geoghegan heeded none of them, indeed, a heightened colour, and flashing eyes, together with an almost imperceptible smile which lurked about the corners of his mobile mouth, were the only signs that he noticed the above well-meant signals at all. Indeed, he felt quite equal to the occasion, and there was an unusually determined, self-reliant air about this bright young son of the Emerald Isle, as he took his place behind Captain Norton, quite prepared, either to answer, or to parry questions, as might be most agreeable to himself.

" Lieutenant Geoghegan ! " said Major Ricardo, " you will now be good enough to state all you know concerning the case before the Court."

" I, sir !—well, really I have nothing whatever to state ; I said so at the time I was told that I should be required as witness."

" Oh, indeed ! " remarked the astonished President, "then may I enquire why you are here before me now—why, indeed, you have been called upon as witness at all ? "

" Certainly, sir !—but sure I can't tell myself. I received orders to put in an appearance at this Court to-day, and I have obeyed those orders. Why I should have been called upon as witness for the *prosecution* I can't understand, as all I know, or have ever heard, about the drummer, Shilrick O'Toole, is in his favour entirely."

" Lieutenant Geoghegan, let me warn you that, whatever may be your private feelings upon this matter, here, in the presence of the Court, you are expected to answer all questions put to you, to the best of your ability, and remember that it is a serious case for the prisoner, if not for yourself."

" Serious enough for me, too, sir. I should never forgive myself if, through any evidence of mine, the poor little chap was condemned."

" That is rather a strange speech for a witness for the prosecution, certainly ; but now be good enough to let the Court hear your evidence."

" Upon my honour, sir ! I have no evidence to give."

" Can you deny, then, that one day, just a week ago, you made several statements to an officer belonging to my own regiment—Lieutenant Rochfort—about the prisoner ? The conversation, I understand, took place on the parade, at Glencree Barracks."

" Sure, I don't remember a single word of it, sir."

" Ah! then, in that case, your presence here is useless, and only occupying the time of the Court to no purpose. Prisoner, are there any questions you would like to ask this witness ? "

" No, sir," returned Shilrick, dejectedly.

" Has any member of the Court a desire to question this most extraordinary witness ? "

" Yes, sir, I have !" said Rochfort, with alacrity. " Lieutenant Geoghegan, may I be allowed to refresh your memory ? It was *you*—if you will try to call the matter to your remembrance, who distinctly told me how the prisoner had first refused to go as guide to the mountains, and then suddenly consented, and appeared most eager to go—you thought it looked very suspicious."

" Faith, then, Lieutenant Rochfort ! *You* were the one who remarked that the ' *whole affair was confoundedly suspicious.*' Yes—those, I think, were your exact words."

" Ah! then you *do* remember the circumstances ? "

" I remember *your words*, or I could not have repeated them."

" And you were present when the Colonel gave orders for the prisoner to be searched, and the letter was found in his pocket ? "

" I was."

" You also remarked that the prisoner seemed much disturbed, and put about, or words to that effect ? "

" Sure and wouldn't anyone be put about at having his pockets searched ? "

" Well, if you will not own to have expressed your opinion upon *this* point, there is another about which I would remind you. You may possibly be able to call to your recollection a conversation we had, at your own mess-table. When the *very mysterious* disappearance of Captain Annesley was mentioned, there was some suspicion cast upon the fact that the drummer, Shilrick O'Toole, had also disappeared at the same time."

" I am aware that *you* tried your best to arouse the suspicions of both officers and men at that time. You also generously remarked, if I remember right, that we *Irish* 'were all tarred with the same brush of disloyalty and treason—all Rebels at heart.'"

" Ah well ! I cannot call to mind the exact words I used ; but my reason for mentioning the circumstance was, that Captain Annesley, being so greatly interested in the prisoner, and both having disappeared together, you—that is *we*, thought that the Captain might have influenced the boy, and both possibly joined the Rebel forces."

" *Your own* suppositions, Lieutenant Rochfort, entirely. *I* expressed no such opinion."

" You also told me, which you cannot deny, that Captain Annesley had been indignant at some treatment he had received from the Government, and that he, with another Irish officer called O'Neill, had intended to leave the corps. The former, however, remained in the service, but the latter, your Colonel's nephew—I think you said he was—disappeared altogether. And you also mentioned that this O'Neill's father had died in exile, having had some connection with the revolutionary party, in Ireland. All this *I* consider as very important, when taken in conjunction with the strange and simultaneous disappearance of Captain Annesley and the drummer, a short time ago."

" But, sure, they have both returned now, what more do you want ? " demanded Geoghegan, defiantly.

" I do not consider that this conversation has anything to do with the case now before the Court," interrupted Captain Leslie, of the Marines.

" I must beg to differ from you there, Captain Leslie," said Captain Harrison, of the cavalry regiment ; " it may prove of the utmost importance in showing that the prisoner was mixed up in the intrigues of the Rebels, and was probably with the Insurgents' forces at the very time he was missing from barracks."

" I agree with you on that point, Captain Harrison," said the President, " but still, we have no right to *suppose* anything against the prisoner, we must stand to *facts* and *prove* those facts, he shall have every justice at our hands. And now, Lieutenant Geoghegan, I should like to hear a little more of your conversation with my brother officer on the night in question."

"I remember nothing more of what passed between us on that night, sir, than that which I have already told the Court."

"You cannot, surely, have forgotten!" continued Rochfort, maliciously. "I am alluding to the night when you sung so effectively that wonderful song—'Boyne Water'!"

"Hang, 'Boyne Water'!" exclaimed Geoghegan, passionately, forgetful of where he was—forgetful of everything, save his anger at being reminded of his unfortunate mistake that night at the mess-table; indeed, it had been a bye-word and standing joke among his brother officers ever since, whenever they wished to caution, or to warn, the excitable young Irishman, they would whisper in his ear, the magic words:

"*Remember 'Boyne Water'!*"

"Oh!" said Rochfort, smiling, and in such an exasperating manner that—as Geoghegan afterwards confided to his comrades "he longed to punch that young cavalry fellow's head for him."— "Shall I put that last expression of yours down in the report, Lieutenant Geoghegan?"

"Go to the devil!—impudent jackanapes that you are!" muttered the Adjutant to himself, his Highland blood now fairly roused.

"I beg your pardon, sir," said Rochfort, turning quickly and smiling blandly upon the fiery McIvor, "I did not hear quite distinctly what you said."

"The Adjutant was only relieving his mind by indulging in the same remark that *I* have been wishing to make for the last half-hour," said Major Ricardo, quietly, "only my position as President of this Court, and the senior officer present, has compelled *me* to restrain my feelings."

"You may well feel impatient, sir," returned Rochfort, coolly, never dreaming in his innate vanity that the President could possibly be alluding to himself. "It is enough to try the patience of a saint, having to question an *Irish* witness. But it must be quite apparent to the Court that Lieutenant Geoghegan, is evidently determined to give no more information, so it is useless to prolong the examination. I may be excused for saying that this officer seems strangely to have mistaken his position here to-day, for most assuredly he should have been called as witness for the *defence*, so very determined is he to divert all suspicion from the prisoner."

"I do not see that we are called upon to try and fix suspicions upon the prisoner, but simply to hear, and if possible to prove the truth of the evidence laid before us, I am sure there is not one present who will not rejoice if this trial ends in the honourable acquittal of the young prisoner," said Captain Drelincourt of the Dragoons.

"And *I* supposed that *my* duty here to-day was to *give evidence*—if I had any to give—honestly and truly," said Geoghegan, indignantly, "not to try and rake up—and actually tax my memory to find out, or call to my recollection, all I could against the poor boy yonder, who I believe is no more guilty of treason, in word or deed, than *you* or *I*. Sure, you need not sit and scowl at me like that, Rochfort—you cannot, and you *shall* not, prevent *myself* or any other witness at this trial, whatever evidence we may be compelled in honour to give, from earnestly hoping that there may be found extenuating circumstances which will lead to the acquittal of Shilrick O'Toole ; and faith I think it's *yourself*, Lieutenant Rochfort, who are in your wrong position to-day, entirely, instead of being a member of the Court, you should have been *chief witness for the prosecution*, so anxious are you to *convict* the prisoner."

"Sir ! do you dare," commenced Rochfort, angrily starting to his feet ; but being quickly pushed back into his seat by one of the officers near him.

"Order ! order !" cried Major Ricardo, at last, "this bickering is undignified and unseemly, besides being most irregular. Pray remember, young gentlemen, that you are not in your own barrack-room, where you can say what you please to each other, but on the very serious duty of Court Martial."

There was a dark, sullen expression on the face of the young cavalry officer, as he hastily took up his pen and once more applied himself with apparent diligence to the writing of his report of the day's proceedings. Geoghegan, however, was triumphant, especially as he met the approving glances of one and all of his brother officers, and noticed a grateful gleam in the eyes of the drummer.

"Lieutenant Geoghegan!" continued the President, "as you have no further evidence to give, you may as well withdraw. Sergeant! call in the third witness for the prosecution, —Midshipman, the Honourable Henry Plantagenet Nelson, of the Royal Navy."

There was an amused smile on the faces of several of the officers present, when this youthful witness entered, and having been duly sworn, and taken up his position as the others had done, stood boldly and fearlessly opposite to the President, evidently, as usual, quite prepared to hold his own in any situation in which he might find himself.

"My boy!" said Major Ricardo, "I suppose I need scarcely remind you of the serious duty you are called upon to perform to-day; that of giving evidence concerning the charge against the prisoner, Shilrick O'Toole. You understand that you must speak to the point only, and nothing but the plain truth?"

"Ay, ay, sir!" replied the midshipman. "Do you wish me to say just what I think, sir?" asked the boy, innocently.

"Certainly," returned the President, gravely. "That is, of course, with certain reservations."

"Then, sir, it's not a bit of use having called *me* as witness for the *prosecution*, for, even if I knew anything against Shilrick O'Toole, I should not tell it. I'd sooner be tried by Court Martial and shot myself, first; but *I haven't* anything to say against him. If they were determined to call me as witness at all, it should have been for the *defence*; but as they *would* call me for the prosecution, I thought I could say all I had to say, as well one time as another, and so here I am, sir."

"So I see," said Major Ricardo, who found it a hard task to maintain a proper amount of stern gravity, as he listened to the young sailor's quaint style of address, and noticed the expression on the bright, boyish face, in which roguish fun and seriousness were so strangely blended. "Well, Master Harry Nelson," he continued, "you were, I understand, with the party of Marines when they were sent to the mountains in search of the Rebels, on the occasion when the prisoner was forced to accompany them as guide?"

"Yes, sir !" replied the midshipman.

"You were not on duty—how came you there ? "

" I went of my own accord, sir ; I followed the party of Marines."

" Ah ! and did you see, or hear anything that would lead you to suppose that the drummer was in league with the Rebels, and likely to prove a traitor to his King, and the English Government ? "

" No, sir," returned the boy, indignantly, "and if you ask *my* opinion on the matter, why then I say this trial is a *horrid shame*, for I am sure *Shilrick O'Toole* would never be a traitor, and *I* call him a regular brick, for acting as he has done, and I only wish he was in the Royal Navy instead of the Marines, because when I became Admiral I should have had him for my cox'ain."

"Well, my lad ! I only wish we could all see matters in as favourable a light as you appear to see them ; but, unfortunately, we have to take a more stern and practical view of the case, and as you do not seem to have any evidence to give, that would aid us in any way, it is useless to take up the time of the Court any farther. Prisoner ! have you any questions you would wish to ask this witness ? "

" No, sir," replied Shilrick, hopelessly ; " sure I thank the young gintleman for spakin' the way he has av mesilf, but I can't think av anny quistions to ax at all."

" Have any members of the Court any questions they wish to put to this witness ? " asked the President.

" Yes, sir ! I have," said Rochfort. " Master Henry Nelson, you were on the parade at Glencree Barracks, at the time when the Marines were about to start for the mountains, when the prisoner was searched, and a letter taken from him ; do you remember the circumstance ? "

" Remember it ? I should just think I did," replied the midshipman, laughing merrily, in spite of the grave faces around him. " We had such jolly fun when I went on board afterwards, and told them all how disappointed you, and that sneaking old spy, Jeremiah Stalker, looked, when Colonel Corrie pocketed the letter and marched off with it. Oh ! Captain Collingwood and our Lieutenant *did* have such a laugh over it, and so did all the others ; even that sneering cavalry fellow, Saunders, who had come on board to see the Captain, said it was 'a deuced good story,' and the best thing he had ever heard for ever so long—oh ! I see he is here ! " added the midshipman, with evident delight, as he suddenly became aware of the presence of "that sneering cavalry fellow, Saunders," among the members of the Court, the officer in question being at that moment engaged in glaring fiercely at the midshipman, his face even more ruddy and coarse-looking than usual.

Captain Drelincourt here interposed, in the hope of lessening the awkwardness of the situation for his two brother officers, and hastily turned to the witness with another question :

"When the prisoner was about to be searched, did he show any great anxiety, or dread of the discovery of any letters or papers he might have about him ? "

"Oh, no ! " returned the young sailor, glibly, "he was not in the least afraid, sir."

" How did you know this—did you speak to him ? " again inquired Drelincourt.

"Why, of course I did, Captain Drelincourt, and when I heard he was going to be searched, I went straight over to warn him, and I said I would drop my cap, and if he had anything he did not want to be found on him, he was to pass it into my hand when he picked up the cap."

"And what did the prisoner say ? " asked Rochfort. "I suppose there was not time for him to carry out your excellent directions ? "

"Oh, yes, there was, but he would not do it, and that quite proved that *he* did not think there was anything treasonable in the letter," concluded the midshipman, triumphantly.

" My boy ! do you know what you have been saying ? " demanded the President, gravely ; " do you not know that you have actually confessed to having offered to shield the prisoner from the consequences of his treasonable intercourse with a notorious band of Rebels ? "

"You had better be more guarded, Harry Nelson," said Rochfort, warningly ; "all that you say at this Court Martial will be reported, with the evidence of the other witnesses."

"And if it is, and if anything I can say will help Shilrick
O'Toole, I shall say it, at whatever cost to myself," returned
the midshipman, bravely.

"Stay, foolish lad!" admonished the President, "you are
mad to speak in such a manner; think of your father, Lord
Thornbury, and your mother, too; what a trial it would be to
them to hear that the boy they thought was a loyal sailor,
and in whom they felt so much pride, had disgraced the uniform he wears and was arrested on such a charge as aiding
and abetting *a traitor.*"

"It has not been proved yet that Shilrick O'Toole is a
traitor, sir," said the boy, quietly. "He tried to prevent the
Marines and the Rebels from meeting, and that showed he
wanted to save the lives of the King's loyal soldiers and
subjects."

"Have you any special interest in the prisoner, Master
Harry?" asked Drelincourt, curiously, and looking, with a
kindly interest, at the anxious, flushed face of the "plucky"
young sailor.

"I should rather think so, Captain Drelincourt. Why, but
for the bravery of Shilrick O'Toole, I should not be standing
here before you to-day. One time when he was on board
our ship, there was a heavy storm. I fell from the rigging,
and, in a moment, without staying to think of the danger to
himself, Shilrick jumped overboard, and fished me out of the
water. And, as to my father and mother—well! I think
they would have good cause to be ashamed of me, if I was
such a mean coward as to see the boy who saved my life, in
trouble and danger, and not say one word to help him, or
make an effort to save *him*. You may arrest me, and have
me tried, and punished as a traitor, if you think it is your
duty to do so, sir," added the boy, proudly, to Major
Ricardo, "but I shall suffer in good company, when with
one so loyal and true as Shilrick O'Toole."

For some moments the President remained silent; he
could see that there was no satisfactory evidence to be
obtained from this witness, and he also feared that farther
cross-examination might only end in the arrest of the midshipman.

After all, however, Harry Nelson had done some good for

Shilrick, by his frank statement that the drummer had shown no anxiety to dispose of the letter in his possession before he was searched, which was accepted by some of the members of the Court as evidence that the prisoner did not consider it of a treasonable nature.

"Well, Midshipman Henry Nelson, as you have evidently no farther information to give us, you may withdraw. Sergeant! call the fourth witness for the prosecution—10th Company, Private Henry Pike, of the Marines."

In passing Shilrick, on his way to the door, the young sailor paused for a moment, to say, encouragingly:

"Cheer up, my hearty!—there's a heavy gale on now, and the waves of trouble are tossing you about a bit, but never fear! that brave, true heart of yours will weather the storm yet. It can't *always* be rough weather old chap!—it can't always be rough weather—so cheer up!" he repeated, with a friendly slap on Shilrick's shoulder, and before the astonished President, or any member of the Court had time to express his disapproval of such an outrageously irregular proceeding, the youthful officer had made a triumphal exit, and the next witness had taken his place.

Very slowly and unwillingly the next witness—Private Henry Pike—the kindly sentry at the old guard-house —entered and took his place behind Captain Norton, fully determined to say as little as he possibly could, and dreading lest the episode of that fatal night, in which he had taken part, namely, the strange visit of Eveleen Corrie and Thalia Coghlan to the guard-room, might have come to the ears of the President, or any member of the Court, and that his evidence might harm his little comrade; indeed, he was thinking so deeply upon the subject that he actually started on hearing Major Ricardo's voice.

"Private Henry Pike! come forward, and give your evidence; and remember that this is a most serious trial, to which you have been called. You must speak the whole truth, and nothing but the truth; you must be unbiassed by any friendship you may feel for the young prisoner."

"Well! it ain't so much as *I've* got for to say, sir—but they tell me as I must come here to tell all as I knows 'pon the subjeck. I see Cap'en Ellis on that there afternoon, when our men went up them mountains after the Rebels, a-talkin' to the drummer, Shilrick O'Toole, most partickelary, sir. I were the sentry on dooty at the old guard-house that afternoon, an' as I kep—as in dooty bound—a-marchin' up an down, to an' fro, an' up an' down again, sir, I thinks to myself, thinks I, as I heard the Cap'en orderin' of the little chap to do somethin', the which didn't seem agreeable to he. Then I says to myself, says I, 'Henry Pike! you ain't no manner o' right to be a-listenin' to talk as weren't meant for you,' so I continood on the line o' march again, sir. Then, next time I see Shilrick O'Toole—he was a-standin' by hisself for some time ; I were goin' t'other way then, but when I were returnin', I see'd Cap'en Ellis come back with a guard to take 'n away. I were on dooty, so 'twouldn't ha' bin proper for to ask no questuns o' the pris'ner. That's all, sir, as *I* knows with regard to he ; an'—an' we're all main sorry for the little chap, sir."

"Prisoner, have you any questions to ask of this witness? " inquired the President.

"No, sir," replied Shilrick, sorrowfully.

"Has the Court any wish to question him ? "

"Yes, sir," said Captain Norton. "Private Henry Pike! when you saw the prisoner standing alone, after Captain Ellis left him, did you speak to him ? "

"Yes, sir ! I just went for to say a word, in passin' like, but he didn't seem to hear me, an' 'tweren't according to reg'lation for me to stop an' talk with 'im ; he looked sorrowful a bit, sir, an' were a-talkin' to hisself."

"Ah !—did you hear what he said ? " asked Rochfort, eagerly.

"No, sir ! "

"When the prisoner was arrested, did he make any resistance ? "

"No, sir, he appeared, as far as *I* could see, to go quite willin'."

"Oh !—and did you hear his reason for this sudden docility and willingness to go, when he had so determinedly refused to obey orders at the first ? " demanded Lieutenant Saunders, cunningly.

"I know nothin' about his refusin' to obey orders, sir, an'

didn't hear then as he had got any. I on'y said, he appeared willin'—I might a-been mistook, more'n likely, as I couldn't quite ketch all as passed." Private Pike here looked from one to another of the officers of his own corps, hoping to gain from them fresh inspiration; he began to fear that he had done wrong in telling that Shilrick had seemed to go quite willingly at the last; but he had done it for the best, thinking it might be in the boy's favour. Great was his relief then, when he heard Major Ricardo say, that if he had no farther evidence he might withdraw, and accordingly he withdrew, and with such haste that he came into violent collision with the next witness, whom the President had desired the Sergeant to call—Private Robert Marlow, of the Marines, and thereby incurring a stern rebuke from one of the officers.

"Now, Private Robert Marlow!" said Major Ricardo, "come forward and state your evidence, as plainly and as briefly as possible, and recollect we want the *real truth only*."

"On the harfternon of the twenty-heighth of December, I were hordered, sir, in comp'ny with Private Samuel Clark, by Capting Hellis, to go along of 'im for to harrest the pris'ner, who were on guard at the hold guard-'ouse. When we came alongside of the guard-room, the pris'ner were hout-side, an' seemed a goodish deal hexcited; 'e 'adn't took no notice of us a-comin' at fust, an' were lookin' hout t'other road. I think as 'ow that's hall I've got to state, sir."

"Prisoner! have you any questions to ask this witness?" said the President.

"Yes, sir!" replied Shilrick, hesitatingly, "I—sure I'd like to—to ax him to be afther tellin' the Coort—that—that when his honour, Captain Ellis, arrived, wid the guard, I said I'd go wid the party as guide to the mountains."

"Private Marlow! is this the case?"

"Yes, sir, the pris'ner seemed most hanxious an' willin' for to go when we come hup; but Capting Hellis he refused, an' hordered me an' Clark for take un in charge."

"Has the Court any questions to put to this witness?"

"Yes, sir. Private Marlow, did you hear the prisoner's reason for being willing to act as guide to the 'Rebels' Rest' *then*, when he had refused at first?" asked Rochfort.

"Can't say as I did, sir ; leastways I didn't take no particklar notice."

" Ah ! well you seem all to have been singularly unobser-
vant, and utterly devoid of curiosity."

" Well, Private Marlow," said Major Ricardo, " since you
have no farther evidence to give, you may withdraw.   Sergeant, call in the next witness, Private Samuel Clark."

If the other two soldiers had seemed to be unwilling witnesses, Clark was apparently still more so, and he looked
nervously and anxiously around him, as he took his place
behind Captain Norton.

" Now, Private Samuel Clark ! let us hear _your_ evidence,"
said Major Ricardo.

" I were ordered a few arternoons agone, sir, along of
Private Robert Marlow—same comp'ny—to 'rest the prisoner.
When the two on us comed near to the guard-room, at that
'ere old 'ouse by the pass, we seen the pris'ner a-standin' on
the outmost side ; there were no un nigh 'im, 'an he 'peared
eager-like, an were a-lookin' the opp'zit way to what we was
a-comin' ; he were a-talkin' to 'isself. _I_ didn't know nothink
'bout what the pris'ner were 'rested for, till arterwards.   I
ain't got nothink more to say on the subjeck, sir, as I can
think on at present."

" You have none of you given any evidence at all, as far
as I can see ; we appear to be going round in a circle.   How
long the Court Martial will last at this rate I cannot tell,"
said Major Ricardo, irritably.

" Very sorry, I'm sure, sir, as I can't do nothink to 'luci-
date matters," commenced Clark, anxiously, " but—"

" I was not blaming _you_ in particular, my lad, but the
whole of the proceedings to-day have had about them a
certain irregularity, and a tone that would imply a suppression of evidence upon certain points.   Prisoner ! have you
any questions to ask of this witness ? "

" Yes, sir ! Sure I'd be likin' if he'd let the Coort know
that I tould Captain Ellis I'd go wid the men to the ' Ribils'
Rest,' whin his honour came back to the guard-house."

"Private Clark I state what you know of this," said the
President.

" Yes, sir ; certainly sir !" replied the soldier, briskly.

" The pris'ner were very pressin' for to be allowed to go with the party to the mountings, and begged very 'ard, sir, over and over agin, for that Capting Ellis might let him go, which he' ad 'tended at first, but the Capting he up an' he said, says he, as 'ow he must go under a guard now ; an' ordered us—-that was me an' Marlow, sir—for to take 'im in charge."

"Can you not remember anything else that Captain Ellis said to the prisoner ? "

" I —I don't think," said Clark, hesitating, " as I've any-think more for to say—not as would bear upon this 'ere case, sir."

"Come, my man, speak out !—there is something you know that you have not told the Court. What did Captain Ellis say to the prisoner ? Never mind whether *you* think it may bear upon the case or not ; the Court must judge of that."

"Well, sir, it weren't much," commenced the man, most reluctantly, " on'y Capting Ellis said as 'ow the pris'ner were too late in sayin' as 'e'd go, an' that rules was rules, an' very strick 'bout soldiers dis'beyin' of orders, an' that officers couldn't allow theirselves to be made fools of in that there way, which it would never do, bein' a bad 'xample to the others ; an' he said, says he, as the pris'ner 'ad refused for to go, he must bide by what he 'ad chose, as he were warned of the consekences afore-hand—them was Capting Ellis's words, so far as *I* can think on."

" Has the Court any questions to put to this witness ? " asked the Major, hopelessly.

" Yes, sir," said Captain Harrison. " Private Clark, did you not hear in the conversation between Captain Ellis and the drummer—any mention of the reason for the prisoner being so willing and anxious to go with the party at the last moment ? "

"No, sir ! "

" Have you never, at any time, heard the prisoner speak of any friends he might have among the Rebel forces ? " asked Rochfort.

" Sir ! I object to that question, most decidedly," said Captain Norton.

"And so do I, sir!" said Captain Durnford. "We want only fair, straightforward evidence in this case; not to set a trap for a witness in such a manner."

" Besides this, the prisoner has been charged with *mutiny* and *disobedience of orders*, not *disloyalty*," added Captain Norton.

" Pardon me, Captain Norton," remarked the President, "but I fear this letter, now in my possession, and which I shall lay before each officer of the Court, at the close of to-day's proceedings, shows only too plainly that the reason for the prisoner's disobedience of orders was most assuredly disloyalty—and that of the worst description. However, for the present, we will continue the examination of the witnesses for the prosecution. Ah! I see there is only one more on the list. Private Clark, you can now withdraw. Sergeant, call in the next witness, Jeremiah Stalker, the patrol."

Shilrick, and those who were kindly disposed towards him, now felt anxious indeed; they had known that whatever the previous witnesses might say that would tell against the drummer, would be said inadvertently, or on compulsion, and without animosity, but here was one whom they knew, only too well, had for some reason of his own taken a private spleen against the boy; and one, moreover who was unscrupulous, and whose face, with its expression of low cunning and cruel triumph, told them plainly that they need expect no mercy at his hands; he would tell unreservedly everything that he knew, or had ever heard, against Shilrick, and a great deal more besides, the invention of his own fertile brain, if he could only find the opportunity. They were all well aware that Stalker was a spy, and a general informer, both of which characters are exceeding obnoxious to every brave, true-hearted soldier.

Even the President, Major Ricardo, who had no personal interest in the little prisoner, felt, on glancing at the patrol as he entered the room, full of pomposity and self-satisfaction, a certain sense of repulsion and mistrust, which betrayed itself in the sharp, stern tones of his voice, as he addressed Stalker, and pointed to the place where he was to stand, behind Captain Norton.

" Stand there!—Now let us hear your evidence!—and

remember you are on your oath! Your name is?"

"Stalker, sir!—Jeremiah Stalker!" said the patrol, pompously, "yours to command, sir, I were born in Lun'un town an' comes of honest hand respeck'ble parents; my hage is—"

"Stop!—stop!—this has nothing to do with the case now before the Court; please state your evidence concerning the prisoner, as *clearly* and briefly as possible."

"Beg parding, sir! but I halways makes it *my* custom for to do heverythink in a reg'lar hofficial way—'owsomdever, it's hall the same to me, an' if so be as my way ain't the ways used in millingtairy Courts Martials I shall be 'appy for to be made sensible of it, the which—"

"The case! Mr. Stalker, the case!" interrupted the President, "if you will be good enough to oblige us by stating only what you have to say with regard to the case before us, and let us hear *the truth* only."

"Certingly, sir, certingly! Well, sir! I've knowed the pris'ner hever since I comed to this 'ere neighb'r'ood as partrol, which I can't say *I* thinks much on it—the people's a good-for-nothin', lawless set, hand—"

"The point, Mr. Stalker—if you please, keep to the point!"

"I'm a-comin' to it, sir, which I don't know as 'ow I've hanythink werry particklar to hobserve along of this 'ere case halone, for the which the pris'ner is now bein' tried—"

"Then, what did you come here for at all?"

"Well, sir! I come for to see as justice was done; that there boy didn't hought to go free—I al'ays said as 'e'd come to a bad hend, like that brother of his'n, for I've a-watched the pris'ner pretty frekent, 'avin' 'ad a sort of a kind of hunaccountable suspicion of 'im."

"What cause had you for this?"

"Couldn't 'xackly say, sir! Leastways, unless 'e bein' Hirish. I never could abide them Hirish, an' never goes for to put much faith in hany of them furrin people, but as I were a-sayin', sir, I kep a heye on the pris'ner, for he were halways a-lurkin' about the roads, he 'ad a many secret meetin's and a carryin' of myster'ous letters an' a parlar-verin' with a young 'ooman, as I heerd arterwards were

called Hanty Kinahan, an' he were meetin' continual with
hall sorts of men an' skittish-lookin' young gals, an'
a-talkin' to 'em—not but I b'lieve as Miss Kinahan's a respeck'ble enough young 'ooman, though she do be Hirish an'
a furriner, so to speak, an' her mother she do keep a decent
'ouse for 'freshments an' heverythink of the best."

"If you have nothing more than this to state, I do not
think you need detain the Court farther," said Major Ricardo,
sharply.

"I am a-comin' to the grist of it, sir," continued the patrol,
his eyes now blinking rapidly in his excitement ; "the pris'ner
he were halways a meetin' with one as I heerd tell arterwards
was his hown brother, a finish-lookin' dare-devil gipsy sort of
a chap, huncommon wild an' fiery, an' halways a-lookin'
hout for squalls so to speak."

"Oh ! it is useless to keep the Court waiting to hear all
this preamble.   Have you, or have you not, anything to say
against the prisoner ? " demanded the President, sternly.

"Comin' to it d'reckly, sir !   One fine hevenin', as I were
a-goin' for to say, I see the pris'ner a-talkin' *werry myster'ous*
to the young 'ooman, Hanty Kinahan, an' she give 'im a letter
the which he put in 'is pocket himmediate, then she went 'er
way an' he went his'n, so I thinks, thinks I, 'ere's summat as re-
quires for to be looked hinto, so I goes hup to 'im an' hasks
'im questions, the which he didn't seem for to like, then I made
bold to tell of the hadvantages he 'ad, a-knowin' hall the
'idin' places of them Rebels if he'd on'y tell, an' then he would
get a good reward, but lor' bless you, sir ! he hup an' said as
he wouldn't betray one on 'em for hall the gold that could be
hoffered to him, he said as 'ow he would rather see the reward
a-meltin' an' a-smoulderin' in the nearest fire, so that no
'onest 'ands should hever touch the gold as went for to buy
the life of a fellow-creetur.   Now, hof course, sir, I leaves
you an' these gentlemen 'ere present for to judge if them
wasn't hout an' hout Rebel sentlements, sir ! "

Rebel sentiments !   Oh, why had it fallen to his duty to
be President of the Court Martial at the trial of this noble
boy ? thought Major Ricardo, as he sat silent and stern for
a moment, covering his eyes with his hand to hide the
emotion he knew could be seen only too plainly. Even the

hard, cynical Rochfort's heart was touched. Meanwhile, the patrol was exulting in the idea that he had at last fairly impressed the President and other members of the Court with the importance of his evidence against the drummer, little thinking that his last speech had exactly the opposite effect to that which he had intended, for it had turned the tide in favour of poor Shilrick, and had roused all the humanity and chivalry in the heart of every officer present.

"Go on !" commanded Major Ricardo, shortly.

"There ain't werry much more to tell, sir, and I s'pose as it's halready been laid afore these 'ere gen'lemen 'ow the pris'ner was houtside the back gate at the barracks hafter the last drums 'ad gone for the night, which was a cur'ous carcumstance, more particklar as I ketched 'im a-lookin' for some paper as he were a talkin' to 'isself habout, an I' ear 'im say it were to 'ave been 'id somewheres in a 'ole in the wall, an' was to 'ave the words, *hall's well*, writ on it ?"

"What became of that paper—did *you* get possession of it?"

"Lor, no, sir ! prisoner didn't find none there hafter all, an' if so be as he '*ad* I s'pose as Capting Hellis would 'ave took it, and got hall the credit of the find," concluded Stalker, viciously.

"Then Captain Ellis knew all about this paper ?" asked the President, sharply.

"Hin course 'e did, sir, 'twere 'im 'as 'ad the pris'ner took to the guard-room, but, lor, sir 'e blamed *me* a deal more'n 'e did the young chap, an' if you'll believe me, gen'lemen, you might a-knocked me down with a feather when Capting Hellis hup an' charged me with a sneakin' habout, pryin' an' watchin' in hall the safe places, an' negleckin' of my dooty helsewhere, 'e said as 'ow there was soldiers enough to look hafter their hown barracks theirselves."

"Ay—and Captain Ellis was quite right. Now, will you be so good as to proceed with your evidence, and bring it to a conclusion as speedily as possible."

"Certainly, sir ; well there's one more hincident as hought to be mentioned. You know, sir, as pris'ner fust refused to go as guide to the mountings an' then was quite willin' an' hanxious for to go."

"Yes—well ?"

" Well, sir, *I* can tell the reason.   While Captain Hellis was away—gone to fetch the soldiers, I reckon, to have pris'ner took in charge—the same young 'ooman I've spoke habout before happeared, an' give pris'ner a letter, then hafter that she went hoff hagain, myster'ous as she'd a-come ; he read the letter, and then seemed huncommon lively, an' was quite ready by the time Capting Hellis turned up hagain for to go *hanywhere.*"

" Who told you all this ? "

"Seen it myself, sir,"

" Did you hear what the prisoner said to the girl who gave him the letter, and to Captain Ellis afterwards ? "

" Lor' bless you, no, sir.   I had to keep well hout of sight.   If hany of the men in the guard-'ouse 'ad a-seen me, they'd a-been hasking questions, an' my dooty is to see heverythink an' say nothink.   No doubt, sir, that was the same letter as was took from pris'ner on the barrack parade just afore he started for the mountings.   Perhaps you knows habout *that*, sir ? "

" Yes.   Is that all you have to state ? "

" Well, sir, there's a many little diff'rences come an' gone atween me an' the pris'ner, not as I bears hany malice, only I thought as 'ow it were my dooty, when I 'eard of this 'ere trial, for to come an' tell hall as I knowed, an' to say as *I* halways thought the pris'ner a most suspicious charackter."

"That is enough, we do not wish to hear the opinions, or personal experiences of the witnesses, only their *direct* and *truthful* evidence given *without animus.*—Now, prisoner I have you any questions to ask of this witness *?* "

" No, sir ! " replied Shilrick, sorrowfully.

" Prisoner ! " said Rochfort, turning to Shilrick, " from whom was the letter that the girl Anty Kinahan gave to you, on the afternoon mentioned by the witness ? "

" I object," said Captain Norton, " to any question being asked of the prisoner, that might cause him to criminate himself."

" Has the Court any questions to put to this witness ? "

"Yes, sir !" said Captain Norton, " why have you never mentioned about the paper for which you say the prisoner was searching the hole in the wall, when you found him ? "

" I made no doubt that Captain Hellis would 'ave done it."

" And did you not keep a watch afterwards to see if any-one placed a paper there after the prisoner was taken to the guard-room ? "

"No, sir—I did not ! "

" Oh !—well I should have imagined that would have been a duty after your own heart, especially if the delinquent had been a young girl, or a little child," remarked Rochfort, sarcastically.

Unfortunately satire was quite lost upon Jeremiah Stalker, and he was about to reply in suave tones, when Major Ricardo interrupted farther conversation, by saying, sharply :

" Jeremiah Stalker, you can withdraw. Sergeant ! recall Captain Ellis."

The patrol's withdrawal occupied some time ; he retired backwards, as if in presence of Royalty, with a succession of pompous and elaborate bows to right and left, even the gallant Sergeant at the door coming in for his share.

Captain Ellis was both surprised and annoyed at his recall, and still more so when he heard the reason, for he had found some difficulty in parrying the questions at his examination as witness, and was anxious lest at this second inquiry, cir-cumstances might be revealed which he had thought it best to suppress in his evidence.

" Captain Ellis ! " said Major Ricardo, " two of the witnesses, namely, Privates Marlow and Clark, having stated that the prisoner, Shilrick O'Toole, was willing to proceed to the mountains with the party of Marines, and that he so informed you, when you returned with the guard to arrest him. We now wish you to state your reasons for not mentioning this fact when you gave your evidence here this morning."

Captain Ellis paused for a moment ere he replied. It was from the kindest of motives, he had not, at first, told of Shilrick having so suddenly changed his mind, as he feared that the Court might demand to know the boy's reasons for so doing, and in the cross-questioning which he well knew would ensue, the fact of the drummer's intercourse with the Rebels would be brought to light. The unfortunate letter, however, which Major Ricardo had forced Ellis to produce during the

latter part of his evidence, had betrayed that fact, but the
officer dare not, then, have explained why he had not
mentioned Shilrick's wish to go with the men at the last, as
he would himself have been suspected of complicity with the
drummer, and a wish to shield him from justice.

Indeed, Ellis now felt himself in a serious dilemma, for he
did not know how much, or how little, the other witnesses
had revealed. He decided, however, that there was nothing
for it now but to tell everything in a straightforward manner,
or at least, to answer all questions put to him without
evasion, mentally resolving never again to allow sentiment
to gain the upper hand of duty, or to be led into such
a maze of difficulty ; the straight, narrow path had always
been *his* choice hitherto, and, in the future he would never
swerve from it ; but he had now to think of the present
trouble, and must get out of it the best way he could.

On looking up suddenly, and finding Major Ricardo's eyes
bent searchingly upon him, he replied, with all the coolness
he could assume :

" I never intended, nor did I consider it necessary, to mention the circumstance at all, sir, had it not been brought forward during the prosecution, as it does not, in any way,
alter the facts of the case, namely, the prisoner's disobedience
of orders in the first instance."

" But, Captain Ellis, it was of the utmost importance, as
the letter, now in my possession, will prove, for it shows
that the prisoner was acting under the direction of one of
the Rebel band, known as the ' Bold Boys of Wicklow,' and,
therefore, clearly points to disloyalty on his part as a reason
for his sudden change of determination."

" Sir ! I am not here as witness for a prosecution for *disloyalty*, but simply *disobedience of orders.*"

" I am afraid you will find that in this case, the one is so
inseparably mixed up with the other, that the charge must
comprehend both."

In that case, thought Ellis, sadly—and his thoughts were
shared by the prisoner himself, as well as every officer present—there was not a shadow of a chance for the drummer
—nothing could save him from being convicted for
treason.

Again Major Ricardo addressed Captain Ellis.

"When you found that the prisoner was willing to go as guide to the mountains, and actually asked to be allowed to do so, why did you refuse his request ?"

"It was too late, sir, when he informed me that he was willing to go. I gave the prisoner every chance before he was arrested. I even tried to persuade him, and warned him of the consequences of his refusal, if he persisted in it, but the boy was resolute : he said that he was under a promise not to betray the Rebels, they had put their trust in him, and he would not be dishonourable and break his word. He even said," added Ellis, with emotion, "'that *a true soldier would rather meet death than dishonour.*' Had he only consented, a few minutes before, as I entreated him to do, all would have been well ; but he only expressed his readiness to accompany the party, when I returned with the guard for his arrest."

"Which was, unfortunately, just after the girl Anty Kinahan had given him a letter, doubtless the one now in my possession," said the President, gravely. "Prisoner ! have you any farther questions to put to the witness ?"

"No, sir ! onless maybes his honour would let the Coort know, 'twas bekase I couldn't be the wan to thurn *informer*, and bethray me own counthrymen, that I was unwillin' to go. Oh, sir ! sure it wasn't traison, at all : indade, indade it wasn't," cried the boy, with a low, half-stifled sob.

"Hush, hush, my lad !" said the President, kindly, "you shall have your say soon, you shall tell us what you like then, but not now. Captain Ellis, did the prisoner give that as his reason for disobeying orders ?"

"He did, sir : he repeated it several times ; and a most natural and noble excuse it was !" added the officer, boldly.

"Has the Court any farther questions to put to the witness ?"

"Yes, sir !" said Captain Harrison. "Captain Ellis ! the last witness told us something about a paper for which the prisoner was searching in a hole in the wall, when you found him one night outside the barracks after tattoo ; do you know from whom he expected to receive such a paper ? You did not mention this fact in your evidence."

" For the very good reason that there was no paper to be found, and I had forgotten the circumstance. I may mention, however, that on questioning the prisoner at the time, he admitted that it was a *colleen* for whom he was watching, and that the paper was simply to contain a message from her."

" Prisoner, was that *colleen* Anty Kinahan ? " asked Rochfort, quickly.

" I object to that question ! " interposed Captain Norton.

" Had the girl a message for anyone else, which you had been asked to deliver, prisoner—*Your Captain* for instance," queried Saunders, in a sneering tone, and with an insolent self-sufficient smirk upon his countenance that was extremely annoying to those of the officers present who were especially friendly with Annesley.

" I object to that question," said Captain Leslie.

" And so do I," said Captain Drelincourt, indignantly.

"Have you any farther evidence to give—anything more that you may have *forgotten*, Captain Ellis?" asked Major Ricardo, with the slightest possible shade of sarcasm in his tones.

" No, sir ! " replied Captain Ellis, with some hauteur.

" Then I think you may withdraw."

As Captain Ellis left the Court, the President produced the fatal letter, which was to prove so disastrous to the little drummer, and handed it to the officer who was seated nearest to him, saying, shortly and sternly :

" Read that carefully—then pass it on. I wish each member of the Court to peruse it thoroughly, so that he may remember its contents when called upon to pronounce a verdict upon the case now before us."

Silently, each officer read Thaddeus Magin's letter, while Shilrick watched their faces, in a fever of anxiety, and saw, with dread and despair, the clouds of doubt, suspicion, and stern displeasure, slowly gathering on every brow. At last the cruel, treacherous missive—written by the hand of the base traitor, who was now silent and still for ever, but whose bitter venom and evil passions were, in their sad, fatal consequences, destined to live after him, and to extend beyond the grave—the missive, so innocent-looking in itself, and yet on which hung the life of a human being, was returned to

Major Ricardo, who, receiving it in silence, folded it, and replaced it among his other papers, thinking, as he did so, that of all the Courts Martial at which he had been present during his military career, this was the most painful. Whenever he had been called upon hitherto, to agree in pronouncing an unfavourable verdict, even against a man of well-known bad character, and of whose guilt there was no doubt, he had felt miserable for weeks—nay, months afterwards—but now, in this case, he knew that, should the drummer be convicted, the boy's noble face, so full of beauty and innocent pathos, would haunt him to his dying day.

The last evidence of Captain Ellis, and his kindly mention of the drummer, together with that of the young midshipman, had again influenced the members of the Court in Shilrick's favour; but alas! the letter they had afterwards read had been terribly compromising, and yet, despite all, the same impression was left upon the heart of each officer, that the boy was one of Nature's gentlemen! Slowly, Major Ricardo rose from his seat, and gathering up his papers prepared to depart, but it was some moments before he could steady his voice sufficiently to pronounce the formal dismissal of the Court, for that day ; at last, however, he spoke :

"The case for the prosecution being now closed, the Court will adjourn until to-morrow at ten o'clock, to give the prisoner time to prepare his defence."

CHAPTER XXV.

" Shame knew him not, he dreaded no disgrace,
Truth, simple truth, was written in his face."

CRABBE.

Once more the officers were assembled in the Court Martial room, for the second hearing of the trial of Shilrick
O'Toole. The case for the prosecution had been closed the
day before, and now, the usual forms having again been
observed, the President addressed the drummer. "Prisoner
Shilrick O'Toole, the case for the prosecution being closed,
you are now called upon to state all that you can in your own
defence."

" I—I—oh sure, sir !—I don't know what to say, at all, at
all !" cried the poor boy, hopelessly.

"Speak up like a man, now !" said Major Ricardo, kindly,
" you have no enemies here, and you shall have every justice
from myself and the other members of the Court."

" Thank ye kindly, sir.   Sure it's mesilf knows that,"
replied Shilrick, falteringly, and with another doubtful glance
at Rochfort and Saunders, " but I can't say annythin' to excuse mesilf, sir ; bekase—bekase I *did* refuse to go as guide
to the mountains when his honour, Captain Ellis, ordhered me."

" Take time—and think well, my boy, there is no hurry.
We are anxious to hear all you have to say, and to find out
everything we can in your favour. Try to collect your
thoughts. Had you any *very particular* reason for refusing
to obey orders ? "

" The Rebels were me own counthrymen, sir. Oh, sure I
couldn't be the wan to bethray thim."

" Well, do not be afraid to answer the questions which

may be put to you, there is no one here who will take advantage of anything you may say. Tell me—had you any other reason that you can state before the Court?"

"Yes, sir."

"What was it? Come! tell us, my boy; remember that your very life may depend upon the issue of this trial; try and think if there is *anything* that you can say in your defence; or that may at least be brought forward as some excuse for the crime with which you have been charged. There *was* some other reason, besides that of the Rebels being your own countrymen, of that I am convinced. Do not keep anything from us that might make your offence seem less, not only in our opinion, but in that of the authorities in whose power will be the confirmation of your sentence. What was it that caused you—for the first time since you entered the service—to disobey orders?"

At last the despairing words fell from the boy's pale, trembling lips:

"Oh, sir! sure it's me own brother was wid the Ribils—an'—an' there was wan there, too, the Captain av the 'Bould Bhoys,' had been very, very kind to me wanst, sir, a long thime ago, but if it had been a lifethime I'd niver have forgotten. Oh! yer honour, sure it's mesilf would rather have died than bethray thim—I wouldn't have done it for all the wealth av the whole wide world—but *och, wirra, wirra!* it's been a sad thime for *me* enthirely."

"Had your brother been long with the Rebels?"

"No, sir; an' troth 'tis mighty little *he* thought av thim, annyhow."

"Then why did he join the insurgent forces?"

"Sure an' it's crassed in love he was, yer honour, an' jist joined 'the Bhoys' out av revinge."

"Ah! a curious revenge, truly," remarked the President, dryly.

"An' wanst he was wid thim, he was over-persuaded and mulvathered to sthay, an' thake the oaths av the band, sir."

"But what became of your brother at the time of the fight?" asked Rochfort. "Was he killed, or was he made prisoner?"

"I object to that question, sir," interposed Captain Norton,

" it has nothing to do with the case before the Court; we are not here to inquire into the fate of Kerry O'Toole."

"There have been few questions to which you have *not* objected, Captain Norton," remarked Saunders, insolently.

"Prisoner!" continued the President, "we have heard in the evidence, the circumstance of your being found outside the small gate, or door, at the back of your barracks after tattoo; will you tell us for whom you were waiting on that occasion?"

"No, sir! sure I can't tell that," replied the drummer, firmly.

"But why? I have only asked you the question, because I know that it will be much in your favour if you can explain this matter to the Court, and so free yourself from the suspicion that it was someone connected with the Rebels for whom you were waiting, or whom you expected would leave the paper, for which you were searching, in the crevice in the wall."

"Sure, sir, the sacrit isn't me own, an' I *promised* I wouldn't tell annythin' about it," returned Shilrick, determinedly. "I've niver in all me life broke me word yet, yer honour, an' I'll not do it now."

"Then, my boy, I fear this determined obstinacy will tell very much against you when your case is considered by the Court, and represented to the authorities, as it must be, and remember that with them will rest the final decision."

"I know it, sir. Oh! sure I know it, but I can't help it. For no power livin' will I break me word."

"So be it then!" said Major Ricardo, regretfully, "I can do no more."

"There is another circumstance, prisoner, upon which you may be able to throw some light, and to your own advantage," observed Captain Harrison. "We have all heard of your long and mysterious absence from barracks, when it was said that you had been first detained by the Rebels, and had afterwards met with an accident, which had delayed your return. "Will you inform the Court why you went to the mountains at all, and where you spent your time while you were absent from barracks?"

"Captain Harrison!" exclaimed Captain Leslie, indignantly, " I object to that question, most decidedly. The incident you have mentioned has formed no part in the charge, nor in the evidence for the prosecution."

" Allow me also to assure you," said Captain Norton, "that the fact of Shilrick O'Toole's absence from barracks was fully explained, to the complete satisfaction of Colonel Corrie, his commanding officer."

" Ah ! " returned the discomfited Captain Harrison; but although the word uttered was short, yet both tone and expression were full of significance.

This proved extremely irritating to Captain Norton, who was about to make some sharp retort, but a look from the Adjutant stopped him; the shrewd young Highlander, Lieutenant Donald McIvor, feared lest the constant dissension among the officers might, when they came to sum up the evidence, and pronounce the verdict, prove detrimental to the drummer.

" Prisoner! have you any excuse to offer for the letter which was found in your possession, and which has been laid before the Court ? " asked the President. " Was the writer a particular friend of yours ? "

" A friend av mine, is it ? " exclaimed the drummer, passionately. " *Thaddeus Magin!* a friend av *mine*, sir ? Oh ! yer honour, sure ye may think ill enough av me, but not that—niver that—an' he, the manest blackguard—the worst thraitor that iver set foot on Irish soil, an troth wasn't it mesilf he thried to murther first—an' he'd have done it too, if it hadn't been for Nap—good lock to the innocent dumb craythur—before he shot the poor young Captain av the ' Bould Boys '—but he paid for it. Ay! paid for it wid his own life."

" But why did you hold any communication with such a man ? How came you to receive that letter from him ? A letter which will, I fear, prove of such vital import to you."

" Sure, sir, 'tis the decateful villain had first thurned *informer*, an' sint woord to Glencree Barracks, where the Ribils were to be found," explained the boy, eagerly; "he wanted the reward d'ye see, sir ! but sure it's himself knew that sorra wan av the souldiers could find their way to the place he'd mintioned widout a guide, he knew well too that *I'd* niver bethray 'the Bhoys,' an faith he was right, there.   I wouldn't *inform*, sir, if it were to save me own life.   So he wrote that letther thinkin' I'd go willin' if I knew the Bhoys would be far away at the thime.   Oh ! the *bocaun* I was to put anny faith in what *he* said.   Oh ! the horror and the misery av it all ! " sobbed Shilrick, as he covered his face with his hands, " whin I'd sane the thrap he'd laid for thim all, an' they walkin' sthraight into it—whin I'd sane those who were dearest to me in all the world—my friends—my brave comrades, fallin' wounded, an' dyin', and dead around me, an mesilf done it all—for if *I* hadn't guided the souldiers up the mountains they'd niver have found the 'Ribils' Rest.'   Both sides blamed me,   yer   honour—both   sides   called   me   thraitor.   *Och*, *wirrasthruc ! wirrasthruc !* I should niver—if I were to live for a hundhred years—be able to shut out the sight av it all from me eyes—niver beable to forget that dreadful night."

With a deep, kindly interest the officers present listened to the drummer's sad words—their hearts were touched, and Shilrick was fast winning the liking and respect, even of those who had neither seen nor heard of him before the first day of his trial, and who had, indeed, looked upon him, at first, with grave suspicion.   Yet each felt that the letter could not be explained away, and that, in spite of all he could plead, the fatal missive would still stand against him, a silent,   but, alas ! indisputable, witness.   The poor boy knew and felt this himself, and had but little hope.

" My boy ! " said Major Ricardo, kindly, " why did you not take that letter to your Colonel at once, when you received it ?   Can you not see how it would have altered matters altogether ?   The Marines would, probably, never have been sent to the mountains, and by your action in giving information immediately you would have clearly proved that *you* had no wish to be in league with the insurgents.   But now," the President here paused, and shook his head, sorrowfully, "we cannot tell how it may all end."

" Sure, sir, I hadn't thime, aven if I'd wished, to thake the letter to his honour, Colonel Corrie.   I was arristed at wanst, jist afther I received it ; an' I belave the Colonel didn't raad it onthil afther we'd stharted."

" Poor lad! poor lad! there has indeed been a strong tide of adverse circumstances against you. But now—can you not think of *anything* more to say in your defence ? "

" No, sir !—onless—onless that mesilf bein' willin' to go aftherwards, even though it was too late, would maybes sthand in me favour."

" That does not alter the fact that you refused to obey orders in the first instance, and that you were in direct communication with the Rebels ; also that your very refusal was caused by your wish to assist the insurgents in evading the consequences of their treason."

" Oh, sir ! " cried Shilrick, hopelessly, " thin sure I've nothin' moor to say ; only, maybes, 'tis Captain Annesley would spake a word for me. It's his honour that's the Captain av me company."

" Captain Annesley intends to speak for you, my boy," said Major Ricardo, kindly ; " he is one of the witnesses for the defence ; but meanwhile we will hear the evidence of the two naval officers, Captain Collingwood and Lieutenant Gray, as they have to be on board again at an early hour this evening."

These two officers had kindly volunteered to attend at the Court Martial, and to say all they could as to the high character for steadiness and good conduct which Shilrick O'Toole had always borne when on board their ship with the party of Marines. Their evidence was soon given, and at last Major Ricardo, turning to the drummer, said, " It is your Captain's turn now, my boy. Serjeant Marks," he added, " call in Captain Armoric Annesley, of the Marines,—third witness for the defence."

Sergeant Marks was not long in obeying this command, and indeed he seemed to move with much more alacrity when summoning the witnesses for the defence, than he had those for the prosecution. Each of the former were duly sworn, as the latter had been, when taking their places behind Captain Norton.

Anxious indeed was the drummer when Captain Annesley appeared ; he felt as though, in that officer, rested his last hope; and the fearful intensity with which he watched him, and listened to every word that fell from the lips of this tried

friend, so good and true, was plainly visible in the brave
boy's face, from which every vestige of colour had fled, in
the burning, fever-bright eyes, and the tightly-clasped hands
pressed so closely to the wildly-throbbing heart. For the
first time since the commencement of his trial, Shilrick
almost broke down, on meeting the kindly glance of his
beloved Captain.

"Another *Irish* witness," said Rochfort, but no one
present seemed to think it worth while to take any notice of
his remark. Annesley merely glanced contemptuously at him.

" Captain Armoric Annesley," said Major Ricardo, " you
are aware of the charge against the prisoner, Drummer and
Fifer Shilrick O'Toole, and you are, I believe, thoroughly con-
versant with the case now before the Court, and being Captain
of his company you are, therefore, called upon, as witness
for the defence, to state all that you possibly can in favour of
the prisoner."

"I was absent at the time of the drummer's arrest, sir,"
replied Annesley, " but I know the charge to which he has
pleaded guilty. I can only now say, that if any words of
mine can avail to turn the scale of evidence in favour of the
young prisoner, I shall be truly happy. I can plead his
youth, the exceptional circumstances in which he has been
placed throughout a most trying time—his good conduct
ever since he entered the service. I can plead his respectful,
soldierly demeanour at all times, which, together with the
faithful discharge of his duties, his bravery during the time
of action, frequently won for him the praise of his officers,
and non-commissioned officers. I can also speak of the gentle, kindly disposition which has long ere this won the hearts
of his comrades. Never before has any doubt been cast upon
his loyalty; indeed, all his deeds in the corps would show the
utter absurdity of charging this boy with such a crime. Possibly, it may not be known to the Court all that Shilrick
O'Toole has done for our corps, whose badges he has hitherto
worn so bravely ; and how—in our last campaign—he was
then, as now, in my company, he saved my life at the risk
of his own, by placing himself before me, and, ere I could
perceive his intention, the brave little fellow's hat was pierced
by the bullet he had seen coming, and which, but for him,

would have struck my heart. The attack was sudden and unexpected, mine was the first company, had I fallen and my men become confused, those in our rear might have been thrown out of order, and the glory we won on that memorable day been lost to us. Many other acts of undaunted courage could be told of Shilrick the Drummer; and there is more than one mother could testify to the life of a drowning child being saved by him; while I can only again say, that there is not one of us who would not be deeply grieved if we knew that any evil had befallen him. You may possibly consider, sir, that all I have pleaded in defence of the drummer has but little to do with the case now before the Court; but I hold and maintain that its connection with the said case is of the utmost importance, inasmuch, as that it would seem utterly inconsistent, and incompatible with the candid, truthful nature of Shilrick O'Toole, and the character which he has hitherto borne, both in and out of the service, that he should suddenly turn traitor, and be guilty of such base conduct, and so grave a charge as that which I have heard imputed to him—treason of the worst, the meanest description. You may think that my opinion of the young prisoner is prejudiced—perhaps exaggerated; but I may tell you, sir, that there is not an officer, nor private, in our corps, who would not willingly corroborate every word I have said in my evidence; and I only wish it had been in my power to have brought forward the positive proofs to lay before the Court, in order that every member might be as perfectly assured as I am, of this boy's innocence of all disloyalty, in thought, word, or deed; and I would ask you to consider, Major Ricardo, that, if sentence is passed *against* the drummer, then will the Service have lost a brave soldier, and the King a loyal subject."

Shilrick here buried his face in his hands, being overcome with emotion, and there was dead silence for some moments, after Captain Annesley had spoken; it was evident that his eloquent words, and graceful manner, had deeply impressed every member of the Court, not excepting Lieutenant Rochfort, although that young officer's handsome features were still disfigured by the hard, cynical expression they generally wore, in the presence of his rival. In Annesley's evidence there was praise—unqualified praise of the prisoner—supposition of innocence—assertion of brave and noble deeds, but alas ! not one word of proof—absolute proof that Shilrick was guiltless of treason.

Moreover, Major Ricardo, as President of the Court, felt that he could not, in justice, pass over the fact that Annesley had, in his evidence, carefully avoided all mention of the first charge against the drummer ; that of disobedience of orders.

" But, pardon me, Captain Annesley ! " he said at last. " If the prisoner was so devoted to you, as to save your life at the risk of his own, why did he then refuse to obey the orders of Captain Ellis, to act as guide to the party of Marines who were going to your rescue, when you were a prisoner in the hands of the Rebels ? "

" I object to that question as too personal, sir," said Captain Norton, firmly, "and not bearing upon the case now before the Court."

Major Ricardo hesitated for a second, then once more turned to Shilrick with the usual form of inquiry :

" Prisoner ! have you any questions to ask this witness ? "

" No, sir ! " replied the boy shaking his head, sorrowfully, " it doesn't same to do anny good axin' questions, at all, at all ; only—only I'd like to tell his honour, Captain Annesley, how I do be thankin' him for all the good words he's said in favour av mesilf, an' sure 'tis Heaven's best blissin's that'll be wid him now an' iver for all the kindness he done me."

" Has the Court any questions to ask this witness ? " said the President, hurrying over the words to hide the emotion in his voice.

" Yes, sir ! " replied Rochfort, glibly.   " We understand, Captain Annesley, that you are Captain of the prisoner's company ; and it has been already stated by Captain Ellis that there was one previous offence against the drummer, Shilrick O'Toole, which appeared to *me*—and I think I may say to others also—to bear a somewhat suspicious character, as taken in connection with the present grave case now before the Court, and more especially when combined with the evidence of Jeremiah Stalker, the English patrol.   Do *you* know anything more of the circumstance to which I allude ?

Perhaps, however, *you also* have forgotten all about it, or thought it '*too simple*' to mention."

Shilrick raised his head once more, and hastily passing his arm over his eyes, to hide the glistening tears, he stood looking anxiously at Annesley, wondering how he would reply to Rochfort's sarcastic tones. The answer was not long in coming, and was calm and dignified; in look and manner only, did the Marine officer rebuke his insolent questioner.

"No, Lieutenant Rochfort, I did *not* forget ; but I certainly considered the offence to which you allude, *a very slight one.* Shilrick O'Toole had been found—*as I believe you already know*—after tattoo, one night, outside a small door in the wall at the back of the barracks ; the door is little used, and is always fastened—every night—just after nine o'clock. Captain Ellis saw the prisoner there, questioned him thoroughly, and sent him to the guard-room, from whence he was released the next morning. Have I now thrown enough light upon this subject to satisfy you ? " asked Annesley, haughtily.

"I rather differ from you, Captain Annesley, about the offence being *slight*," returned Rochfort, persistently, "particularly at such a time as this, when we are living upon a perfect volcano of treason. *I* should have imagined that an officer in *your loyal corps* would have considered the case one of the gravest importance. The circumstance certainly pointed to mystery and intrigue of some sort, most probably in connection with the Rebels, with whom I have no doubt the prisoner has had frequent communication."

"Stay, Lieutenant Rochfort," cried Captain Norton, " we have no right to advance our own ideas and mere suppositions to the detriment of the prisoner."

"And I had no occasion at that time to doubt the loyalty of the drummer, nor do I doubt it now, Lieutenant Rochfort," said Annesley, proudly, "and you must pardon me for saying that I understood that the case for the *prosecution* was closed."

"Certainly, Captain Annesley," interposed Major Ricardo, mildly, "but a few inquiries, especially those which I am about to put to you are—I consider—absolutely necessary."

Annesley bowed courteously, and prepared to listen atten-
tively to all that the President might have to say to him,
but was more determined, even than before, that the whole
Court should not extract one whit of information from him
about any subject upon which he had decided to keep silence;
and Annesley, being clever, sharp-witted, and an *Irishman*,
the Court might expect a lively time of it.

" Did the prisoner state nothing in his defence, at the time
he was found outside the barracks after tattoo, as you mentioned in your evidence ? " asked the President.

" Pardon me, sir ! that circumstance was not in *my* evidence
at all.   It came out in *Lieutenant Rochfort's* inquisitorial
course of cross-examination."

"Well, well ! that matters but little ! "

" Excuse me, sir ! it is of the *greatest importance* to
me, seeing that I have been called as witness for the *defence* ;
it would appear rather strange in after-reports of the proceedings of this Court Martial, if it were found that I had
deliberately brought forward one of the charges *against* the
prisoner in my evidence."

"Then you refuse to reply to my questions, Captain
Annesley ? " said the President, angrily.   " If you continue
in this determination I must remind you that you can be
charged with contempt of Court."

" I never objected to answer any inquiries you might make,
sir."

" I object to the questions which have been asked this witness," said Captain Leslie, "they are useless, and most
certainly pertain more to the *prosecution* than the *defence*."

"I do not agree with you there, Captain Leslie," replied
Major Ricardo, "and must, therefore, continue the course
which I have decided to pursue.   And now, Captain Annesley ! you must answer me, if you please.   Did the
prisoner give no reason for being out of barracks after
tattoo ? "

" I never *asked* him, sir ! "

" That was curious ; as the Captain of the prisoner's company, and having a very special interest in him.   I should
have thought that you would have felt *some* anxiety in the
case ; for the circumstance assuredly *does* add considerably

to the suspicions entertained of disloyalty on the part of the drummer, and I cannot altogether hold you blameless, Captain Annesley, that you should have passed the matter over so lightly."

" It was by the orders of Captain Ellis that the prisoner was sent to the guard-room, not by mine, sir."

" Captain Annesley!" said the President, impatiently, " your manner would lead me to infer that you could, if you were so disposed, tell the Court more of this case. Do *you* know for what purpose the prisoner was at that spot, on the night in question ? "

" I do, sir."

" Then be good enough to explain the whole facts of the case to the members of this Court."

" I cannot do that, sir !"

" Ah! Well, perhaps you can at least inform us whom the prisoner expected to meet there ? "

" It was no Rebel for whom he was watching, nor was it anyone connected with the Rebels ; farther than that I have neither the intention, nor am I at liberty to state, for the secret is not my own."

" Ah ! some girl in the case, no doubt," said Saunders, cunningly, in an aside to Drelincourt; but that officer only gave him a contemptuous glance, and with a significant shrug of the shoulders replied : " you judge others by yourself, Saunders."

For a moment Major Ricardo had remained silent with astonishment at the determination—not to say defiance— expressed in Annesley's words, and when at last he once more addressed the Marine officer there was a tone of grave displeasure in his voice : " Then if you will not give me a direct answer to my questions, Captain Annesley, I am sorry to say that the Court is left to infer anything but what is favourable to the prisoner."

" Or to himself either," murmured Rochfort, but although the tone was low, yet he evidently intended that all present should hear his remark.

" Many thanks, Lieutenant Rochfort ! " retorted Annesley, with a low, mocking· bow. " Believe me, for those generous words I shall for ever remain your debtor. May I remind

you, however, that I am not on *my* trial at present, but
should I ever have the misfortune to be in that position, I
shall certainly object to *you* sitting as one of the officers on
my Court Martial."

"Stay, gentlemen," interrupted Major Ricardo, hastily,
"the Court cannot be detained by arguments and disputes
such as these.   Captain Annesley, if you have no further
evidence to give, you may withdraw."

"One moment, sir," said Annesley, hesitating, "I think
if you will give me permission to leave the Court for a few
minutes that I *might* be able to bring a witness who could—
in a great measure—clear the prisoner from all suspicion
with regard to the subject under discussion."

"Do so then, Captain Annesley," replied Major Ricardo,
kindly, "we shall only be too glad to hear *anything* in his
favour, and which may help to mitigate the sentence against
him.   In the meantime we will hear the next witness for
the defence.   Sergeant, call in Lieutenant Charles Digby, of
the Marines.

Digby cast a keen, inquiring glance at Annesley, whom he
passed in the corridor outside the Court-room.

He could see that his friend looked pale and troubled, and
that there was an expression of quiet, but set, determination
in his face, which boded ill for anyone who might cross his
will, or oppose his wishes at that moment ; indeed, the stern
demeanour of his Captain somewhat unnerved the young
subaltern, who was himself very far from well, and who was
even then, disobeying the strict injunctions of the doctor in
being out of his room at all, let alone undergoing the intense
excitement of this Court Martial, for the wound in his arm
had turned out much more serious than was at first expected,
and had caused the surgeon to feel more anxiety than he
would as yet express to Digby himself, as to the probability
of his eventually losing his arm.   The young officer
was feeling very weak and ill, as he entered the Court-
room, and took his place as witness ; his arm was
causing him great pain, but his kindliness of heart,
and invariable good nature and sympathy, precluded the
idea of his staying in peace and quiet in his barrack-room, if
he imagined that he could be of the smallest use in turning

the tide in favour of the drummer, Shilrick O'Toole. He wore his arm in a sling, and this, together with the extreme delicacy of his appearance, now won the sympathy of the President and the Court.

"Lieutenant Charles Digby ! you have been called upon as witness for the *defence* to state all that you can in favour of the drummer, Shilrick O'Toole—but I see that you are very ill, and certainly not in a fit state of health to stand there and give evidence."

"Thanks, sir ! " replied Digby, manfully. "I am all right —I can manage quite well."

"Then let the Court hear what you have to say ; we will not detain you longer than is absolutely necessary."

Only Captain Norton, who could feel his chair vibrate and creak beneath the nervous clasp of the young officer, as he leant against it for support, knew the brave effort made by Digby that day in the cause of friendship and justice. He had somewhat indignantly repudiated all offers of a seat while he gave his evidence, which was spoken in a low, though steady, voice.

"I'm very glad to be called upon to state what I know regarding the prisoner, as all that I have to say is most favourable to him. I have been for some time the subaltern of Captain Annesley's company, and I have invariably found Shilrick O'Toole's conduct most satisfactory. I have never had the least fault to find with him on any occasion, and he was always most attentive in the faithful discharge of his duties. On muster mornings, at the inspection of our superior officers, Captain Annesley and myself have frequently been complimented upon the tidy, soldierly appearance of our drummer ; his manner was at all times most respectful, and here, sir, is a letter from the Drum-Major of the Portsmouth division of Marines, testifying to the good conduct of Shilrick O'Toole while serving there, and he states how steady the boy was at all times, and how, in his leisure hours, he would amuse his young comrades by relating to them tales of war, and chivalry ; he also mentions how every boyish remark of the prisoner, and all his thoughts and hopes, so innocently and candidly expressed to his young companions, were thoroughly loyal, and that this charge against him has therefore caused the greatest astonishment at Portsmouth, amongst those who knew him best, and had long ago learnt to like and respect him, boy though he is. But perhaps you will kindly look over the Drum-Major's letter yourself, sir ? I have it with me now."

"Ah, yes !—let me read it," said Major Ricardo, eagerly, " and then I shall pass it round, so that every member of the Court may know the contents, and I sincerely trust that they may give this, along with every iota of evidence we can gather in favour of the prisoner, their most earnest consideration. Lieutenant Digby ! have you anything more to say with regard to the case now before the Court ?"

" No, sir !—I have nothing more to state. I sincerely wish that I could give the proof of his innocence, of which I feel so certain myself, I can only add that we have all been very proud of the drummer, Shilrick O'Toole, since he enlisted in the Marines ; for, though so young, the noble deeds done by this brave boy, have, on more than one occasion, added a lustre to the laurels of our corps."

" Prisoner, have you any questions to ask of this witness?" inquired the President, kindly. " My boy, this officer is the last witness for the defence on my list. Can you not think of anything that you would like to ask, that might be to your advantage for the Court to know ? I fear that this will be the last opportunity you will have of speaking a word for yourself."

" Sure, sir, I thank yer honour, but there's nothin' I could say would be anny good at all. I—I only want to thank Lieutenant Digby for what he has said for me ; an' oh ! Heaven bliss him for his kindness comin' here this dhay, an' himsilf so ill he's scarce able to sthand ! " cried the boy, earnestly.

" Has the Court any questions to put to this witness ? "

There being no reply this time to the President's inquiry, after a pause of a few seconds, he turned to Digby, saying :

"Then, Lieutenant Digby, you may withdraw ; not, however, before I have expressed my admiration at your conduct in attending the Court at a time when—as the little prisoner himself has remarked—it is quite evident that you can scarcely stand, and, indeed, as your surgeon, Conway, said, you are too ill to be out at all. You will have your reward, however, in the thought that you have done all you could for the poor lad who is in such sore need to-day of help and comfort."

"I thank you, Major Ricardo, for your kind expressions towards myself; I only hope my words, together with the other evidence for the defence, may be of some benefit to Shilrick O'Toole," said Digby, as he bowed to the President, and with sorrowful face, and slow, faltering step, left the Court-room.

As soon as he had disappeared, Major Ricardo produced the Drum-Major's letter, and after having read it carefully himself, handed it to the officer who was seated next to him, requesting that it might be passed round the table, until each member of the Court had perused the contents. This was the work of some time. Education was not in those days, as in the present time of school-boards, compulsory learning—or rather cramming—Cambridge examinations, etc., etc. That letter had been a laborious task to the honest Drum-Major; but it had been a labour of love, and so every misspelt word, each incorrectly turned sentence, had due weight with the officers who now read them, for there was about them the unmistakable evidence of genuine truth and honour.

When this letter was once more returned to the President he was truly gratified to see—by the faces of the other members of the Court—that it had certainly impressed them all favourably.

"Sergeant," he asked, then, "has Captain Annesley returned yet?"

"Yes, sir."

"Then recall him."

Intense curiosity had been felt in the Court as to whom Annesley intended to bring forward as witness—thus, at the eleventh hour—in defence of the drummer; but in their wildest flights of imagination not one had come near the truth.

Great was the astonishment, therefore, of every member present, when Captain Annesley entered, with Eveleen Corrie leaning on his arm.

Eveleen appeared very much agitated, and was looking pale and sorrowful. Annesley's bearing was stern and haughty, and there was a certain calm, proud defiance as he glanced from one to the other of his brother officers and the different members of the Court, which seemed to challenge criticism as to his present actions, or those of his fair companion.

"*Miss Corrie !*" exclaimed the President, starting from his seat in his surprise, and regarding Eveleen with wondering eyes.

" Yes, Major Ricardo, it is I ; you will be astonished, I know ; I come as a witness for the defence, to take away a cruel suspicion that rests on this poor boy, Shilrick O'Toole."

" But, Miss Corrie ! this is madness, what can *you* know of this case ? "

" Perhaps more than you think, Major Ricardo," was the quiet reply.

" Well ! I suppose, Miss Corrie, you must take your place, and be duly sworn, as the other witnesses have been."

Each officer had risen to his feet as Eveleen entered the room, and many chairs had been offered to her; with a courteous bow, however, she declined them all, and Captain Annesley led her up to the place appointed for the witnesses, behind Captain Norton's chair, when, after having gone through the usual formula, she stood calmly waiting until the President again addressed her, Annesley meanwhile retiring into the background, and taking up his position beside the Adjutant, Lieutenant McIvor, where he stood, with his elbow resting on the high carved-oak mantel-shelf, and his face partly concealed with his hand ; his heightened colour, however, and flashing eyes, betrayed only too plainly, to those who knew him best, the displeasure and annoyance he felt at the position in which Eveleen Corrie, by her own rash act, was now placed.

Shilrick glanced from one to the other in the greatest anxiety and perplexity. He had, hitherto, shielded Eveleen's name so well, and so bravely, and would have continued to do so, at any cost to himself. This noble boy, with his sympathetic nature, could see, and even feel, the pain Eveleen's presence at the Court Martial was causing Annesley, to whom he was so devoted ; and he was grieved to think that she should have come there on his account ; for after all, the incident which occurred outside the barrack gate, was only one of the charges against him. He was somewhat reassured, however, on meeting a kindly glance from Eveleen herself, and with a deep sigh of resignation, he once more set his mind to listen to the following proceedings :

" Miss Corrie ! " said the President, politely, "Captain Annesley informed us in his evidence that he might possibly be able to bring forward a witness, who would throw some light on one of the charges against the prisoner, namely, his very suspicious appearance outside the barracks on a certain evening after tattoo. Are *you* that witness ? "

" I am, Major Ricardo ! "

" Then please state all you know."

" All that I have to tell, can be said in very few words. Shilrick O'Toole was waiting at the small door in the wall, at the back of the barracks, after tattoo, on the night to which you allude—for *me !* "

" For *you*, Miss Corrie ? "

" For *you ?* " exclaimed the other officers of the Court, incredulously.

" Yes ! He had promised that if I were detained by any chance on the mission on which I had gone forth, and which circumstances compelled me to undertake alone, until after the time the gate is always locked, that he would find some way of admitting me. That little gate, or door in the wall is the entrance nearest to our quarters."

" It was a strange act, Miss Corrie, and a daring one," said Major Ricardo, somewhat sternly. " If you had no fear or scruples on your own account, I think—pardon me for speaking thus plainly—that you might at least have hesitated before implicating a young lad like the prisoner, in your plot, or plan, whichever it might be. You—an officer's daughter—must have known the penalty *he* would incur if discovered in such a breach of discipline, more especially at a time like the present."

" It was thoughtless—oh, so thoughtless of me," owned Eveleen, sadly, " to forget for a moment the consequences to

Shilrick O'Toole if he were found outside the barracks after tattoo ; but I have been justly punished, for I have never since ceased to reproach myself."

" Why did you not explain all this before, Miss Corrie, instead of keeping silence, at the time, and allowing the boy to be sent to the guard-room, and to have the first and only offence lodged against his name in the service?" asked the President, gravely.

" Major Ricardo !" replied Eveleen, with dignity, " I did not know of this at the time.   I only heard afterwards that Captain Ellis had sent Shilrick to the guard-room, and—and then I heard, too—how bravely he had borne his punishment, and how my name had never once passed his lips, for he had promised most faithfully to keep my secret.   How nobly he fulfilled that promise you know well.   It seemed too late then for me to speak; and it would have made his generous sacrifice of no avail."

" Where were *you*, Miss Corrie, on the night in question ? Did you go to pay an evening visit, or to meet any particular friend ? "

" I did, Major Ricardo ! "

" May I ask *whom* you met, Miss Corrie ? "

" I must decline to answer that question, sir !" returned Eveleen, haughtily.

" Miss Corrie *met me*, sir !" said Annesley, as he stepped boldly forward and stood beside Eveleen.

" *You* ! Captain Annesley—why, bless my soul ! she could see you any day of her life in her own home," exclaimed Major Ricardo.

" Pardon me, sir ! but I have yet to learn that there is any reason why either Miss Corrie, or myself, should consult others as to the hour, and place, of our meetings," returned Annesley haughtily.

" No—ah, no, no ! of course not !" acquiesced the now bewildered President.   " But there is one thing more I have to ask you, Miss Corrie—was it *you* whom the prisoner expected would leave some paper in a crevice in the wall, outside the barrack gate ?"

" It was, sir.   Had my expedition proved successful, and had I been able to return to barracks before the tattoo was ended, I had told Shilrick that I would place a paper, on which would be written the words, 'all's well,' in the aperture in the wall, which you have just mentioned, and he would then understand that I had reached home safely, and that he need watch no longer."

"Ah! an easy arrangement for *you*, Miss Corrie, but a most disastrous one for the prisoner. Well, have you any farther evidence to give?"

"No, sir; I have *not*."

"Prisoner, have you any questions to ask this witness?"

"No, sir; only from me heart I thank her, for comin' here this dhay," said Shilrick, fervently.

"Has the Court any questions to ask the witness?"

"Yes, sir," said Rochfort, eagerly; then turning, with a significant smile, to Eveleen, he asked:

"Had you any *special reason*, Miss Corrie, for wishing to meet Captain Annesley in a *clandestine manner* on that particular evening?"

"I object to such a question," interrupted Captain Norton, sternly, "it is altogether irrelevant to the subject."

"And I shall answer no more questions of the kind, sir," said Eveleen, proudly; "I have explained all that was necessary for the defence of the prisoner. I have nothing more to state."

"Then, in that case, Miss Corrie, you may withdraw," said Major Ricardo.

The fair witness, however, did not wait to hear the President pronounce the formal words of dismissal, she had already taken Annesley's arm, and after a sweeping bow, intended to include all the officers present, was proceeding with him towards the doorway, when their steps were suddenly arrested, and there was silence in the room, for at that moment all present were startled by the sound of "The Retreat" just outside the Court Martial room, followed by the sweet strains of an old Irish melody, as the little band of drummers and fifers—Shilrick's young comrades—passed on their march round the barrack parade. The sorrow-laden, pathetic tones of "*Savourneen Dheelish!*" seemed to find an echo in the hearts of most of those officers assembled in the Court; all paused to listen, and many of the more sympathetic amongst them felt that never again could they hear "*Savourneen Dheelish*," without the old air bringing to their memory, the deep anxiety, the weight of awful responsibility, and all the sadness of the duty that still lay before them on that day—ay! and for many a weary day after.

Shilrick, who had all through his trial borne up so bravely, was now quite overcome, and, burying his face in his hands, he gave way to a burst of uncontrollable grief and despair.

"There they go! there they go!" he sobbed. "Sure, that's 'The Retrait'—they'll all be there now, happy an' free—happy an' free, but *I'll* niver be wid thim annymoor—niver again—oh, niver again!"

Captain Annesley now hastened to the boy's side, and kindly placing his arm over his shoulders, whispered some soothing words into his ear, at which Shilrick rallied, and, hastily passing his arm over his eyes, he then looked up into the face, so full of sympathy, which was bending over him.

"Thank ye kindly, sir!" he said, with a smile which seemed for all the world like a bright sunbeam after an April shower. "Sure, it's yer honour always does ivery wan a hape av good. Troth, 'tis mesilf that's a coward this dhay, annyhow. But I'll be brave now, sir—I'll be brave enthirely. Livin' or dead, I'll niver be a disgrace to the ould corps!"

"Ah! *you* could never be that, my boy—never that," said Annesley, softly, and with a world of tenderness in his voice.

Once more Major Ricardo spoke:

"The evidence for the defence of the prisoner, Drummer and Fifer Shilrick O'Toole, being now closed, all those present, with the exception of the members of the Court Martial will please withdraw, while the Court closes for deliberation."

The trial is over—the sentence alone now remains to be considered—the sentence upon which depends the future fate—nay the very life or death of a human being—and that human being, only a little fatherless, motherless lad, drifting onward upon the world's stormy ocean, with all the wonderful possibilities of life before him, its joys, and its sorrows, its hopes, failures, and disappointments. Yet one who would be sadly missed, for, young as he was, Shilrick O'Toole seemed to be able to win and to hold the hearts of all who knew him.

Within that Court Martial room were now gathered together a group of serious, anxious men, among whom were hearts brave, honourable, and true ; but whether good, or bad, as the world might judge them, there was not one who did not bitterly regret that he had been called upon to give his verdict in this case.

Without, the regular routine of military life was going on as usual—the little band of drummers and fifers were marching on their way, as if no young comrade was absent from their ranks, and, but a few yards from them, well-nigh breaking his heart—a prisoner, just tried by Court Martial for one of the most serious crimes of which a soldier could be guilty— but, alas, such is life ! and so thought many of those grave-faeed officers, as sadly they listened to the sound—now dying away in the distance—the mournful strains of " *Savourneen Dheelish.*"

END OF VOLUME. II.